Passion Fish

A NOVEL BY

ALISON OBURIA
AND
JESSICA MCQUINN

OMNIFIC PUBLISHING
DALLAS

Omnific Publishing
P.O. Box 793871, Dallas, TX 75379
www.omnificpublishing.com

First Omnific ebook edition, February 2010
First Omnific trade paperback edition, February 2010

Library of Congress Cataloguing-in-Publication Data

Obruia, Alison; McQuinn, Jessica
Passion Fish/Alison Oburia and Jessica McQuinn – 1st ed.
ISBN 978-1-936305-12-4
1. Romance—Fiction. 2. Museum—Fiction.
3. Santa Barbara—Fiction. I. Title

10 9 8 7 6 5 4 3 2 1

Book Design by Barbara Hallworth

Printed in the United States of America

For E, who brought two strangers together to create this story and so much more. ~Jessica and Alison

For Diane, the most gifted writer I know. ~Alison

Prologue - The Son

"What the hell kind of shit is this? Marjorie! Marjorie, get out here."

Arnold Merchant stood, one hand on his hip, the other holding open the trunk of the beaten-up Ford in the graveled driveway.

"Marjorie!"

"I'm coming, Arnie." The plump woman waddled down the cement front steps of her home and ambled as quickly as she could over to her husband. "What's all the ruckus?"

"What's all this?" he said, gesturing to the contents of the trunk.

Marjorie began to wring her hands. "Well, that's Justin's. He must have forgotten to put it in the barn." Her voice was meek, and she winced as she spoke.

"Goddamn it, I told you that boy had better stop this homo painting shit and get a job. He's sixteen. It's about time that lazy bastard started contributin' around here."

"He said he put in an application over at Thurgood's Market the other day and—"

"Well, I talked to Gene Thurgood and he said he ain't seen him in there at all, and he ain't got no goddamn application on file."

"But he said he—"

"He lied, Marjorie." Arnold slammed the trunk, and his wife jumped at the sudden noise. "Where the hell is he right now?"

She glanced toward the shed at the side of the house and quickly returned her gaze to her husband. She knew how he felt about their son and his pastimes, and she knew that someone would be punished. Today she didn't want it to be her.

"Shit," Arnold spewed as he made his way over to the shed, Marjorie trailing behind him. This wasn't how she had thought her life would be, but at this point she was just trying to stay alive. Justin was big enough to look after himself.

Arnold pulled the shed's door open so fiercely it nearly came off its hinges. Inside, a pale, thin boy sat on a stool next to a table covered in tubes of paint. He jerked his head up as he saw his father fill the entire doorframe.

"Justin! Justin, you jackass. Why the hell didn't you go see Mr. Thurgood like I told you to?"

"Arnie," Marjorie uttered from behind her husband. This time he might kill the boy. And then what would she do?

"Shut up, Marjorie!" He returned his stare to the boy. "I told you to stop this goddamn painting shit." He stepped inside the shed, and the boy stood up, backing away from him.

"You remember what I told you would happen if I caught you again? Hmm?" Arnold swept his arm across the table, sending the paints flying.

Justin sat totally still; he had given up fighting back long ago. He knew what was coming.

"You like what I do to you, boy?" Arnold sneered. "You're a goddamn homo, painting all this shit. You think anyone is going to have anything to do with you when they find out you're a fag? The only thing anyone is going to want to do is beat the shit out of you. Time to start learning what your life's gonna be like."

Arnold Merchant closed the shed's door behind him, locked it from the inside, and showed his son exactly what he meant.

Julian's strokes with the black paint became more forceful with the memory. *Black covers up the pain. Black covers up the past.*

As he put the final touches on his painting, he was beside himself at how it had turned out. The way the moon shone down on the meadow that had been his safe haven; he had truly brought the scene to life under his hand. It was where he went to escape his father's wrath. It was the place where he was transformed, where he finally left Justin Merchant behind and became Julian Meadows.

Yes, Julian sighed, *this one shall be titled* Redemption.

Chapter 1

"Ugh! I forgot to do one more edit for the presentation piece for the Boston Museum of Art." Eve groaned loudly enough for her colleague to hear. "Josie?"

From her office across the hall, Josie responded lightly, "Gotcha covered, Eve. Just leave the rough draft, and Skye will take care of it tomorrow and email it to you before you even board the plane. Are you ready to call it a day?"

"Absolutely. I've left everything with sticky notes for Skye to figure out while I'm away. I know it will only be for a week, but..."

"You worry too much, we know. And we love you for it. We wouldn't even be in the running for this grant if it weren't for all the work you've done."

Eve Carwyn smiled as she closed up the files on her desk, everything now in neat piles with colored tabs jutting out from papers that would need attention while she was gone. She leaned down for her briefcase, clasping it shut as she lifted it. Swinging her purse onto her shoulder, Eve stood and grabbed the briefcase in one hand, her laptop bag in the other, and walked out of her office. If she'd forgotten anything at this point, she'd just have to wing it when she got to Boston. As the Santa Barbara Museum of Art's curator, Eve was used to giving presentations; this time, however, was for big money—possibly a three million dollar grant—so she was feeling a bit nervous.

"I'm ready as I'll ever be!" she said with a sigh as she stood just outside Josie's door. "How about you?"

"Just shutting down," Josie responded absently as she focused her gaze on her monitor and continued to click her computer's mouse. "I hope we don't have to work another ten-hour Saturday for a long time." She peered up at Eve with a grin. "You get us this grant and maybe we can even take a few days off, huh? Go check on Skye. See if she's ready to go, too."

Josephine McInnis and Skylar Montgomery, lead accountant and director of public relations, respectively, were the other two key people at the SBMA, as well as co-authors of the grant application. They were two totally different women, but Eve respected and trusted them equally.

Josie was a bundle of energy captured in a body on the heavier side of thin for her five-foot frame, with sparkling green eyes and bright red hair that ran down her back in long ringlets. She was the number-cruncher, the one who made sure the museum made enough money to keep its doors open, and she was brilliant. When she signed off on the grant application, she'd created the cost estimates with the perspective of the people who would be reading it in mind: Would they see her numbers as too high, meaning unnecessary fluff was added, or too low, a sure sign they'd end up asking for more money or not finishing the project? When she'd handed Eve the final budget, she had full confidence that the grant committee would see a realistic set of numbers.

Skye was equal parts beauty and beast. Her silky skin, straight auburn hair, and tanned legs that went on for a mile caused a stir wherever she went. While she could have made a career modeling on Parisian runways, she was the master of public relations for the museum. With a degree from Columbia University, Skye was a savvy sharpshooter who, in a year's time, had turned the SBMA from a boring school field trip destination to a place businesses recommended to tourists and where local artists lined up to display their work. The museum wasn't quite "on the map" yet, but she was determined to make that happen.

Skye was also witty and sharp-tongued. She was smart like Josie and Eve; but with street-smarts, not bookish intelligence.

Museum meetings with the directors always went smoothly and quickly when Skye was there. Cut to the chase, leave the BS and the whining at the door, and get down to business. Men longed for her, but she wasn't tying herself down to anyone just now. Instead, she was waiting for the right guy to come along. No need to waste too much time with any man who couldn't keep up with her.

Josie, Skye, and Eve worked seamlessly together, each recognizing the strengths that made them the perfect team. They were also the best of friends. And although their backgrounds and personalities were quite different, they had many common threads. They loved their work, loved to meet people—OK, *men*—who could and would challenge them intellectually, and they loved to have fun together.

Eve was always amazed that the three of them were such great friends. If, on the first day she'd met Skylar, someone had told her that would happen, she would have laughed at them. While Eve and Josie had hit it off from the very moment they'd started working for the SBMA nearly six years ago, the first time Eve had to sit in on a meeting with Skye, she'd wanted to hide under her desk. The thought of having to work alongside the ball-buster she had seen was terrifying. At the end of that day, though, Josie—without telling Eve—had asked Skye if she wanted to meet them for a drink, and she'd instantly agreed.

Eve always enjoyed being out with Josie; the girl was so vivacious that within minutes of walking into a place, total strangers—including some attractive men—were talking to them like they'd known the two women for years. Eve decided there was no way anyone *couldn't* like Josie. Coming from a big Irish Catholic family, Josie learned at a young age that she needed to stand out in a crowd, and she did it well. Even with four sisters and two brothers, everyone knew exactly who she was, and that was just the way she wanted it.

On that night nearly six years ago, Josie and Eve walked to the corner pub and fell into their easy banter about life and work. It wasn't until Eve was well into her second Sex On The Beach that Skye's voice broke in behind her, interrupting their conversation. Eve immediately stiffened.

"Don't worry, I don't bite...hard," Skye said with a smile. In that split second, Eve saw a completely different woman standing before her. And she kind of liked her.

While Eve and Josie had become best friends quickly, her friendship with Skye took longer to develop. But now, Eve wouldn't trade Josie's vibrant, loving personality or Skylar's protective, overbearing, but incredibly loyal one for anything in the world.

Eventually Eve introduced Skye to the rest of the group she considered her family: her best friend from childhood, Noelle, and her roommate from college, Dana. Now the five of them were as close as sisters. Eve considered herself lucky to have such a wonderful group of friends.

Tonight, after they'd worked all day, long past the museum's normal Saturday hours, they were going to enjoy a night at Stratus, the hottest club in town and their favorite place to meet up. Eve would be heading to Boston in the morning to hopefully convince Townsend Industries to fund the development of a partnership between Santa Barbara's lackluster museum and Boston's world-renowned Museum of Art. Tonight would celebrate the months of work that led to tomorrow's trip.

It was also a night of good-byes for Eve. She was making one last trip to her ex-boyfriend Julian's apartment. She had made him promise not to be there; that was the only reason she was even going. Their last encounter hadn't been pleasant. He had become not only verbally abusive but had threatened her physically about leaving him. After that, in her haste to leave, Eve had left a few of her belongings there. It had taken her a couple of weeks to get up the nerve to retrieve them.

Knowing that after tonight she'd have a week away from Santa Barbara was thrilling, as well as comforting. Eve was ready to move on, or at least find a new distraction. Maybe a week in Boston, hopefully with many opportunities to discover the city's night life, would help her heal. Maybe she would meet somebody who knew how to treat a woman the way she knew she deserved to be treated. *OK, enough of that dream,* Eve thought. Tonight's focus would be on the festivities at Stratus.

As the three of them walked to their cars, Eve noticed Josie and Skye eyeing each other suspiciously, a secret held between them.

"OK. What's up? Or better, what do you know that I obviously don't?"

Skye hesitated. "Well, we all decided that you need to go fishing tonight."

"Oh no. How many of you are in on this?" Eve stopped dead in her tracks and closed her eyes.

"Well, there's the two of us—and you *know* you can trust us! Noelle will be there, and Dana said she'd be late but to include her, too. And Noelle is going to keep you company while we get things arranged. Please don't be mad at us. You need this. You know you do!"

Eve groaned. *Ugh! Can I catch that plane now instead of in the morning?*

Eve knew exactly what was in store for her. She was going to be the bait in their Passion Fish game. The girls had started playing the game a few months ago after another miserable night of fending off their dates' unwanted advances. They had come up with a way to find the one thing they were all looking for: that perfect passionate kiss.

The rules of Passion Fish were simple: Any of the group who were not the "bait" for the night would scour the club for a man they thought could knock a girl's socks off with just one kiss. Whoever was lucky enough to be on the receiving end of those kisses wouldn't arrive at the club until 11:30, after all the players had been chosen. Once the "bait" arrived, she was led straight to their booth where she was blindfolded and her hands restrained behind her back. No cheating by trying to feel the fish.

The big twist—and one of the hardest things for the men—was that they had to agree to just walk away after delivering the kiss, so that neither the "fish" nor the "bait" would feel any sense of obligation when it was over.

The purpose of the game was to remind the "bait" that there *are* men out there who are passionate, at least in their kissing. And if a man could be properly passionate in one kiss, there had to be a damn good reason for it. That passion should carry over into other aspects of their lives, too.

So far, they had only had the nerve to play a handful of times. Josie, of course, was the first to volunteer. That was the night they realized the need for the "walk away" rule, after one of the worst kissers they'd ever seen followed Josie around the bar the rest of the night, and Skye eventually had to threaten the guy's life. After that little incident, the women sat down and solidified the rules.

Eve had been the bait one other time. Sort of. She had agreed to do it, and had made sure she had enough liquid courage for the evening, but when they put the blindfold on, she panicked and backed out. Dana had also gone a couple of times, but was having about as much success in the romance department as Eve, so she decided to take a break. The only ones who wouldn't do it were Noelle, who had been happily married for three years to a successful commercial real estate broker, and Skye, who said she didn't need the game—yet. Spoken like the true drop-dead-gorgeous bitch she was.

Eve was chosen for tonight for an obvious reason: Her most recent boyfriend had turned out to be an arrogant, possessive jerk. Her friends didn't want her to think all men were as bad as he was. Maybe that was why she wasn't totally unwilling to participate, despite the potential embarrassment or, worse, the possibility of being mauled by a bad kisser. Eve needed to get over *him*. Many regular patrons, as well as the bartenders at Stratus, had watched their game before, so they would be in on the whole thing. *And I'm sure they'll be laughing hysterically when I officially become the evening's bait,* Eve thought.

"I'm not agreeing to this enthusiastically, you know."

Josie and Skye both squealed in delight. Josie quickly got Noelle on the phone and made the arrangements for her to meet Eve at nine o'clock at Scales, the restaurant next to Stratus. Then they all set off in different directions from the parking lot: Josie and Skye to get ready for the evening and Eve to her ex's apartment.

Just breathe, Eve said to herself. *It'll be over with by midnight. And, who knows, maybe you'll actually catch a Passion Fish worth keeping.*

Without the knowledge of the Santa Barbara Museum of Art's grant writers, William Prentiss had boarded his private jet from Boston yesterday. As founder and president of Townsend Industries, he wanted to see what his money would be used for before he wrote any check. Santa Barbara was a decent city, certainly not as dynamic as Boston, but with the celebrity invasion that had occurred in recent years, it had potential, as did the museum he spent a day and a half exploring in detail.

As he'd toured the facility this morning, in addition to the impressive Local Artists Gallery, he had noticed several very attractive women who, judging by the suits they were wearing, worked for the museum. *A bonus! I'm single, I'm in another city, why not enjoy* all *of the scenery?* he mused.

He kept spotting one of the women speaking to employees of the museum and determined she must be the curator, or in some similar position. *Striking* was the first word that came to his mind. *Breathtaking* came second. Her long, ash-blond hair, held back in a low ponytail, was styled simply yet sophisticatedly. She carried herself with authority and confidence. *Intelligent...she was definitely intelligent*, he thought.

Will caught a glimpse of her brown eyes as she smiled at something one of the security guards said. She threw her head back in a laugh that just lit up the room. *Why can't I find someone like this back in Boston*? he wondered. It wasn't like he hadn't been searching, that's for sure. But he kept encountering women who, once they discovered he owned a successful business, felt the need to try to impress him. And while they were beautiful, they were also vapid and shallow. No genuineness to them at all. This woman was real—not putting on airs because she was attractive and smart. Judging by her interactions with the other staff members, it was clear she was liked, as well as respected.

Will was pleased with how the grant proposal had accurately presented the Santa Barbara Museum of Art's current state, as well as its potential. He felt more confident about approving this request for so much money, confident that this woman and her colleagues would take good care of it and use it appropriately to reach their goals. Having accomplished his investigation, he headed back to his hotel room. Tonight, he wanted to go out and just people-watch.

When Eve let herself in to Julian's apartment, she was more than shocked to find him there. He greeted her with open arms, like she was home, like they were still together, like she still *wanted* to be together.

"You said you wouldn't be here."

"Eve, honey, why would I leave and miss my chance to see you? Come on...enough is enough...we belong together. You know that." Julian got closer and began to stroke her cheek with the back of his hand. Eve backed up, her eyes intent on his.

"I just want my things. I'm done with you. I don't need your lies or your threats. Just let me—"

With that he grabbed her around her waist and pulled her to him. Placing his hand roughly on her breast, he pushed his face against her neck, kissing her.

"No! Didn't you hear me? Let me go—just let me get my stuff and leave!"

"I don't think you understand *me*, Eve." His arms became more forceful and his kisses harder on her shoulder. She tried to push him away and fell back against the sofa, him on top of her, and he held her there. Panic began to rise in Eve. *He's not going to let me go.* She tried to stamp down the fear and think clearly.

"What did I tell you if you tried to leave me, huh?" His eyes were burning her as he moved his hands to fiercely grip her face. "You're my muse, my inspiration. You're why I breathe, Eve. You're mine."

Terror quickly enveloped her as Julian moved his hands around her neck. He pressed each finger slowly against her skin, and she could feel her throat constrict. Her thoughts began to race. *He's going to choke me to death—I can see it in his empty eyes. All I've ever been is something for him to own. To possess.* Eve hated that this was how it was going to end for her.

Julian shifted slightly to get in a better position and, in that moment, Eve's fight-or-flight reflex kicked in, and she quickly jerked her knee upward with every bit of force she could muster. Meeting her mark with a sickening thud, Eve watched as Julian immediately released his grip and fell to the floor, doubled over in pain. She jumped from the sofa, grabbed her purse, and ran out the door as Julian screamed her name and his promise to kill her.

Eve got into her car and quickly locked the doors. Her hands were shaking so violently that starting the car and getting it out of the parking lot took great effort. The twenty-minute drive to her apartment allowed her to calm a little, and a sense of relief settled over her. By the time she arrived home, her panic had subsided considerably.

As she climbed the steps to the second floor of her building, Eve could hear loud, bass-laden music coming from her neighbor's apartment. She felt immediate comfort in knowing that Gage was home.

When she'd first moved into the building, she'd been wary of having a neighbor that looked like The Incredible Hulk. In the end, however, Gage Vandenberg turned out to be wonderfully protective of Eve, treating her as he did his own younger sister back in Cleveland. The fact that the man was a six-foot-four personal trainer and body builder always made Eve feel safe. Knowing that Gage was only seconds away let her sleep more soundly at night.

She rapped on his door and quickly wiped under her eyes with her fingertips, trying to compose herself before he opened the door.

"Hey, Eve...whoa, what's wrong?" Gage immediately stepped forward, leaning down to look directly at her.

"I'm OK. But will you do me a favor and be on the lookout for Julian? He's really gone crazy since we broke up, and I wouldn't put it past him to try to break into my place while I'm gone for a week or something else equally insane."

"You got it. Mind if I beat the shit out of him if he comes by? I'd love the workout." Gage smiled his big goofy smile at her in hopes of changing the sad look on her face. "Are you OK, though? You look pretty shaken up."

"Yeah, I'll be fine. I'm 'going fishing' tonight," she said with a half-hearted smirk. Gage also worked as a bouncer at Stratus and had been there when the game was played. He had mentioned on more than one occasion that he wanted Skye to be the bait and Eve to pick him as her Passion Fish. So far, Skye had been unwilling to play that part. Her excuse was always that she was much better at finding guys for her friends. Eve figured Skye just didn't trust that her friends could come up with anyone she would find worthy. *Gage...hmm.* Eve contemplated that. She'd make a point of talking to Josie about trying to get him and Skye together. They just might be a match made in Heaven, or at least at Stratus.

Gage let Eve know he would be there tonight as a bouncer, and she felt comforted. There was no way he would let anything happen to her, and he knew what Julian looked like, just in case. Reaching up to wrap her arms around Gage's huge body, she hugged him and gave him a small peck on the cheek before entering her apartment next door.

She changed quickly. She only had a half hour before she was supposed to meet Noelle. Knowing that she was going to be the "star attraction" for many eyes at Stratus tonight—and wanting to forget the incident at Julian's—she picked out her favorite club outfit: skin-tight little black skirt paired with a low-cut black camisole and topped with a sheer ivory blouse, with just a hint of bling in the rhinestone buttons, tucked at the waist. She finished off with her highest stilettos.

When Eve finally got to the mirror to look at her face, reality stared back at her. She still looked pale and distraught. Lifting her chin up and to the side, Eve could clearly see finger-shaped bruises beginning to form on either side of her neck. *Lovely!* Makeup would be of no use, and she didn't want to wear anything high-necked since the bar tended to get warmer as the night progressed. Eve pulled up the collar of her blouse and shrugged her shoulders. Noelle would see the marks immediately at dinner. While the low lighting in the club would hide the ugly reminders of Julian later on, there was no way she could hide them in the brighter lights of the restaurant.

Heading back to her closet, she shifted through other shirt options, but they were all either too stuffy and more for work, or offered no more concealment than the one she wore. Out of the corner of her eye, she saw a strip of red fabric. It was the silk scarf Skye had given her for her last birthday. Normally it wasn't something she would wear to Stratus, but it seemed to be her only option. Realizing she might look a little like Hugh Heffner with his silly ascot, Eve quickly changed to a sleeveless silk tank. The pop of color, she decided, was actually quite nice with all the black she was wearing.

Draping the scarf around her neck, Eve resolved at that moment not to say anything to anyone about what had happened. Loving Josie would want her to call the police, thus jeopardizing the trip to Boston and the grant, and Skye would spend the evening plotting revenge for while Eve was out of town. She didn't want either to happen, and since she was through with Julian forever, it really didn't matter. Taking a deep breath and one last look in the mirror, Eve thought it would have to do.

Ready or not, mystery Passion Fish, here I come!

Gage had stayed in his doorway and watched Eve go inside her apartment. He was definitely going to make sure he kept an eye out for that loser. No one was going to touch Eve unless she said it was OK. He was going to make damn sure of that.

Eve had clearly been crying, and that alone made Gage want to hunt down that prick and make *him* cry. Eve was like a baby sister to him, and he vowed right then that if Julian were to hurt her, he would castrate him, preferably with a dull butter knife.

Closing his door, he went back to turn up his music, his thoughts on Skye. He felt like such a wuss that he hadn't had the nerve to actually ask her out. They were friends and hung out together, but he wanted more than that. There were many nights that he'd spent his entire shift at Stratus just watching her from across the room. He wished he could get Eve to talk her into playing that game and letting him kiss her. Her knees would buckle like a belt.

Being a bouncer at the hottest club in Santa Barbara, Gage had seen a lot of crazy things, but what those girls did with that game of theirs had to be one of the strangest attractions around. He knew the rules, and he made sure no one ever touched his girls inappropriately. If they did, their asses would be out on the sidewalk before they knew what was happening. In a college town like Santa Barbara, if they were going to play that game, Stratus was probably the safest place to do it. They knew Gage would always watch out for them, and the clientele tended to be a little bit classier than most bars where the frat boys hung out.

Gage was also in charge of making sure that once each "fish" had delivered his kiss, he got the hell out of the club. It was a rule that the guys agreed to before they even started the game, and if any of them decided to change their minds, it was Gage's job to explain to them, by whatever means necessary, the error of that choice. He actually really liked his job some nights.

It was a little bit of a shock when Eve told him that they planned on playing tonight, though. Normally the girls wouldn't even attempt to play on a Saturday night. Saturday was busy, and often the university crowd would venture out of their normal comfort zone into his territory. Yeah, there was definitely a chance that some drunken frat boy would get out of hand. Gage knew he had to be extra cautious tonight.

As Will Prentiss drove to his hotel, he tried to get a feel for the city and its night life. Most of the places he saw looked like trendy college bars, not really his crowd. He wanted to go somewhere that he could get a drink without getting the attitude of a drunken twenty-two-year-old college kid.

Soon he was walking through the hotel lobby, still wondering what he was going to do for the evening besides sit in his room and work. There were no messages on his phone, so he was sure any work that awaited him was of the mind-numbing variety. He hesitated in the lobby. Then he saw the concierge desk and decided to ask for suggestions. *Tonight I just want to be Will, a tourist looking for a nice night out.*

"Stratus is really the only decent place to go," the man explained. "Honestly, the other places are either full of drunken college kids or so boring you'll fall asleep. There's a decent DJ at Stratus, and the bartenders are good folks—they'll take care of you. Tell them I sent you over." Will pocketed the man's business card and headed up to his room to change for his night out.

Chapter 2

Arriving at the club for his shift around ten, Gage saw Josie, Skye, and Dana working the room looking for their fish. He couldn't help but watch Skye as she approached the guys, as well as their reactions when they realized she was going to talk to them. *I'm glad I can't read minds, because by the looks on their faces, I would have to hurt a few of them for what they are thinking about her,* Gage thought as his body tensed from the urge to lay claim to Skye. Of course he was thinking a few of those things himself, but that was different. She would be his one day, and these guys didn't have a chance in hell with her. That was what he liked to tell himself, anyway.

Just as he was starting to enjoy some of those thoughts he'd been having (*again*), he looked down to see Josie waving her hands. As he came back to the here-and-now, he heard her complaining that Eve was going to be arriving soon, and she still didn't have a fish for her.

"All these guys are such losers, Gage. I swear every single one of them made some stupid perverted comment when I tried to explain the rules of the game. What is the matter with you men?"

"Hey, don't group me with them." Gage held his hands up in front of him as defense.

He stood with Josie for a few minutes surveying the club. *She's right, most of the guys here tonight look like they would break a lot of the rules.* Gage caught sight of Preston Langley coming toward them. Preston had been chasing Eve for longer than Gage had known them. Preston was a rich kid who never grew up, and unfortunately, he had set his sights firmly on Eve. Always too compassionate, Eve never had the heart to tell him the whole truth. So years later, the poor guy still thought he would someday work his way into her life.

Preston had a big smile on his face, and his dark hair was slicked back with so much gel, Gage was thankful, for his own safety, that there was no smoking in Stratus. Otherwise, one spark and the dude's hair was going up in a puff of smoke. He was headed straight for them, his gaze focused on Josie.

Josie ducked behind Gage when she saw him, but it was too late.

"Hey there, Josie! I hear you're looking for someone to kiss Eve tonight. You haven't asked me," Preston said, adding a spastic dance move and contorted eyebrow wiggle as he spoke. *Do I sound this pathetic when I grill Eve about Skye?* he wondered.

Josie let out an exasperated huff. Because Preston was actually a pretty good-looking guy, he had been chosen as a fish the first time they had played the game. Josie had firsthand experience of the slobbering and grabbing he thought equated to passion. There was no way she would subject Eve to that.

"Preston, the whole point of this is so Eve can experience some *passion*!" The whole club seemed to have stopped to listen. "Sorry to tell you this, pal, but I have unfortunately been on the other end of that tongue, and it wasn't even pleasant, let alone passionate. I truly don't think you are capable of doing anything for Eve besides making her change teams and start looking at women!"

Poor guy looked like he was going to cry, which, truth be told, Gage thought was pretty funny. But he was surprised Josie could talk to him like that. Talk about humiliation.

Preston tried to look cool, but he was pretty much running for the door when Josie finally finished.

Following Preston's hasty departure, Josie stood with her hands on her hips, surveying the crowd once again.

"Ahh! I can't believe that on a Saturday night I can't find a decent guy for Eve. She finally agrees to play, and now there are only going to be two guys to kiss her. Do something," she demanded, swatting Gage on his massive chest.

Gage looked out to the dance floor and his eyes landed on Skye's ass. It was hypnotic watching her. Lost in the undulating motion of her hips, Gage allowed himself a moment of fantasy, where she was moving just for him. That was when he made a risky decision.

"Josie, I have an idea," Gage whispered. He quickly told her his plan.

"Ohhhhhhh, I like it!" she squealed and ran off to tell the other girls.

By the time Eve and Noelle arrived at Stratus, the place was packed. Eve caught Gage's eye at the door and winked a hello to him. The ladies waved to their favorite bartenders as they headed to their usual booth, and Eve couldn't help but notice a sly "I know what you're in for" look in their eyes. *Ugh. Why did I ever agree to this?* Eve thought.

Since this was Eve's night in the spotlight, Noelle took it upon herself to buy her a drink. Eve immediately began looking around, trying to figure out whose lips would soon be on hers. She was pleased. There were an exceptional number of attractive, intelligent-looking men, many of whom did not appear to be attached to similarly attractive and intelligent-looking women. None seemed to be looking her way, though; they'd clearly been warned not to give anything away.

Where is that drink? Eve tapped out a rhythm on the table top, working off her nervous energy. All her friends would say was, "It's all good—we *promise*!"

An hour or so before, Will Prentiss had found an empty stool at the bar that provided a decent view of the dance floor. He was in a beautiful city, with beautiful people all around him, but all he could think about was catching up on work. He was about to call it a night when his attention—along with the attention of several other men—was drawn to the door as Eve and Noelle entered the club. The ladies acknowledged the big bouncer, then headed through the crowd to a table with three more very attractive women. *Maybe I could stay for one more drink*, Will thought.

When Eve turned toward the bar and gave a small wave to the bartender, Will knew immediately that she was the woman from the museum. He was instantly glad she hadn't noticed him there; he wouldn't have wanted her thinking he was a stalker. His night of people-watching suddenly took on new life, and work seemed much less pressing.

The bartender closest to Will saw his head crane as the women walked by. Leaning in, he said, "You want in on something interesting that's about to happen?" The bartender glanced at the table where "museum girl" was sitting as he spoke, so Will was instantly curious.

"You see that woman that just passed us?"

Oh, most definitely! Will nodded nonchalantly, trying not to appear eager.

"She and her friends play this game once in a while." The bartender explained the rules and reason for their quest for a Passion Fish, including the fact that the fish all remained anonymous after the kiss. The men would be on their own if they wanted to pursue the lady they'd kissed on another night, but she was off-limits after the game this evening.

As Will sipped his drink, the woman who had arrived with his new crush came up to the bar and perched at the open spot next to him. "Hey, guys, how about a margarita for me and a Sex On The Beach for Eve. Were the others able to secure some good fish for her?"

Eve, Will mused. *She must be Eve Carwyn, the curator. She* does *hold some authority at the museum.*

"Yeah, I think she'll have fun." The bartender patted two napkins on the bar in front of the woman. "Of course, not as much fun as the rest of us will in watching! And I'll tell ya, that creep Preston that's always hanging around and asking her out? He kept begging Josie to pick him. She all but spit in his face to get him to back off. He left an hour ago, rejected by every woman in here once again."

As the bartender mixed the requested drinks, Will swiveled his stool to face the woman. "I couldn't help overhearing this devious plan of yours," he said. "Sounds interesting. Did *you* have a chance to pick out a Passion Fish for her yet?"

"No. I was keeping her company elsewhere while the others made the, um, arrangements." Noelle looked at his deep blue eyes and was mesmerized for a moment. Then she silently reminded herself that she was happily married to a wonderful man, even if he did work a lot. "I haven't seen you here before. I'm guessing this will be your first time observing our little game?" She smiled at him. Will liked her instantly.

"Actually, I wanted to know if I might possibly participate in the game."

Noelle's eyes lit up. "You know the rules? No contact with her other than the kiss, which means no groping or anything. The guys behind the bar will back us up on this! And do you see that gorilla-sized guy by the door? He's like a big brother to Eve. If you hurt her, he hurts you. After the kiss, you leave the bar for the night. Got it?"

"Absolutely. Not a problem. I'm from out of town and have an early flight in the morning. I promise to leave the bar as soon as this is over."

"I'm Noelle. It's nice to meet you, if only for tonight. Wait here, and don't look our way at all—that may make Eve suspicious. The guys will let you know when it's time to come over."

Will smiled devilishly to himself as he sipped his drink once again. *I am enjoying Santa Barbara more and more every second I'm here!*

As it got closer to midnight, people gathered at the edge of the dance floor, waiting for the show, and the excitement began to build. Gage worried he was actually going to have to work as a few of the drunker guys started to get *too* excited.

One of them crashed into Skye and almost knocked her over. It looked like his friend had "pushed" him in a lame attempt to help him feel her up as he caught himself by grabbing Skye's breast. Gage's vision went red, and he started across the room, but he stopped when he realized she was already in the guy's face screaming.

"Hey, asshole! If you think you are going to touch me like that without buying dinner and a diamond first, you are stupider than you look." She punctuated her statement with a quick right hook square in his nose. He was more embarrassed at having been hit by a girl than physically hurt, but he quickly made his way out of the club. Once Gage stared down his idiot friend, that guy made a quick exit as well.

Man, I love a girl who can take of herself. Gage's whole body went on high alert at Skye's actions. There was a lot about that woman he wanted to learn.

Noelle rejoined her friends, handing Eve her drink with the biggest cat-that-swallowed-the-canary look on her face. Eve was about to ask her what was going on when she was interrupted by a bouncing Josie.

"It's time! It's time! Oh, you are going to be so pleased with your Passion Fish!" Josie danced in front of Eve with the blindfold. "Come on, it's getting close to midnight, and you know the rules. If they haven't kissed you by midnight, they don't get a turn. We don't want you to miss out on any good kissing!"

"Ugh. I can't believe I'm going to go through with this."

"Hey, look what good came out of *my* bait experience!"

Josie was right. One of the men who had kissed her—the one she said made her toes curl when he did—had shown up again the next night and made a bee-line toward her. She and Beau now spent every moment they could together. *A perfect couple,* Eve lamented, *if only I could be that lucky.* The only reason Beau wasn't out with the group tonight was because he was in New York City on business. As a rare coin dealer, he traveled constantly. While Josie didn't care for all the traveling, his experience did come in handy. He was very familiar with Boston and had provided Eve a list of restaurants and night clubs to check out while she was there.

Eve drained her glass, throwing the liquid down her throat and hoping it would work quickly to help her relax.

"Okay, Skye, I need the ribbon for her hands," Josie called over her shoulder.

Unfortunately Skye wasn't there. She had gone to the bar to get some ice for her knuckles. Putting an asshole in his place wasn't an issue, but her hand was already swelling a little, and she wanted to nip that in the bud.

"Where the hell is Skye?" asked Josie.

"It's alright, Josie." Noelle stepped in to try to calm the situation. "I don't think Skye will mind if we start without her."

"She has the ribbon for Eve's hands, and I don't trust Eve not to touch without it," said Josie. "She's very tactile."

"Okay, we can improvise." Noelle looked around, trying to find something suitable to bind Eve's hands.

"What about her scarf?" Dana asked.

"Oh, great idea. Eve, take off that scarf. We'll have to use it to keep you in check."

Eve's eyes opened a little wider. It was humiliating that she had allowed Julian to do this to her, and she really didn't want it to ruin the night—or the trip to Boston. She fingered the silk of the scarf, trying to work up an excuse to keep it on.

"Come on, Eve. Time is ticking away." Josie walked over and undid the scarf herself. Eve sucked in a breath as she pulled her hair up over her shoulders, making sure it would cover the worst bruises. When Josie didn't comment, Eve let out a sigh of relief.

Finally, Josie was satisfied, if not still a little pissed off that Skye had disappeared, and went to work preparing Eve for the game. Once the blindfold was in place and her hands firmly tied behind her back, Eve's mind began to race. *Back out now! Back out now! This is the stupidest game! It's only fun for those watching. Being the bait is* not *what it's cracked up to be!*

But there was no escape, and Eve soon found that the first two fish were just that—all wet! While she was sure they were good looking—she knew her friends made sure of that much—their kissing skills left much to be desired. The first licked her cheek from chin to eyelashes, wrongly assuming that this was sensual or desired. The second forced his tongue into Eve's mouth as soon as he started kissing her. He was taking the fish idea too seriously; Eve felt like he had inserted a flopping goldfish into her mouth that was desperately trying to find water. She was glad she couldn't see Skye or Dana as she put on a sour face. They could tell right away that their choices had bombed.

Josie's choice fared better. He *did* seem to understand the basic goal—to kiss her as passionately as possible. He was gentle, Eve noticed immediately. He placed his hands on her shoulders as he slowly took her lips in his. He politely waited for her positive reaction before increasing his intensity. She gladly opened her mouth to him and could feel the sincerity—the passion—in his kiss. The crowd was cheering him on, but he didn't act rudely at their urging. He finished with one more gentle kiss to her lips. *This guy I'd want to meet again,* Eve thought and smiled, knowing that Josie would see she was pleased. The people around Eve and Fish #3 gave them a round of applause. Eve blushed profusely but was relieved to have received a decent kiss. Between that last kiss and downing her drink so quickly, she finally relaxed, the terrifying memory of Julian's apartment now fading.

"OK. How about undoing the ribbon now, eh?" Eve called out over the noise of the music and collection of people still standing nearby. "And I could use another drink, too!"

"Ah, but you've got one more Passion Fish, Eve!" The sing-song voice was Noelle's.

But she was with me at the restaurant. How could she... Even with the blindfold on, the others could see Eve's nose wrinkle and eyebrows pull together in confusion.

Suddenly the crowd roared again. And then Eve felt him. He stood in front of her and touched his hands to her shoulders, caressing them gently, letting his hands run down her arms slowly and back again. Eve could actually feel his eyes caressing her body as they followed the path of his fingers. *Oh. My. Word. Now* this *guy knows that passion doesn't necessarily start with the mouth!* Eve could feel her heart race as her blood rushed through her.

His touch ghosted over her and goose bumps sprang up instantly on Eve's skin. The space between them seemed to disappear. With his new proximity, Eve could get a better sense of his body, and judging by the erratic breathing near her forehead, she guessed he was probably about six feet tall.

Moving his hands back to her shoulders, he gently placed them on her neck. Eve winced, feeling the bruises she knew would be noticeable in the morning. Her quick jolt almost made Will break contact, thinking he had hurt her, but after a slight hesitation, his hands slid back to her shoulders. He leaned down, and Eve was breathless in anticipation of his kiss. But then he moved his head lower, and Eve realized he was trying to see what had caused her to jerk away. He hesitated, then ever so lightly kissed her throat. His breath was delicate and intoxicating against her neck as his kiss lingered. *Oh my Lord, please don't stop.*

With his hands still on her shoulders, Will raised his mouth to her ear. "I want to hurt whoever did this to you," he whispered. "Are you all right?"

Eve nodded, and she could feel tears welling up in her eyes. She could no longer feel his breath against her cheek, and she knew he had pulled back to evaluate her reaction.

Once more, he moved his lips to her ear and said, "I would *never* hurt you. If you were with me, I'd be doing *this* to you every chance I had." With that, he moved his mouth to her jaw and placed kiss after kiss as he worked his way to her mouth. Eve couldn't wait for his lips and opened hers, inviting him to her. She arched her body into his and his arms wrapped around her, one hand on her lower back and the other under her hair at the nape of her neck. Eve wished her hands had been free—she had an overwhelming need to embrace this man thoroughly. They continued their kiss, neither wanting it to end.

"Ahem!" It was Josie. The entire bar was whistling and cat-calling, clapping, challenging them to keep going. Eve tried to ignore her friend's interruption.

"AHEM!" Josie put her hands on both of their shoulders, separating their bodies and breaking their kiss.

"Thank you, sir. Your work is done here. *Well* done, I'd say."

No! thought Eve, remembering the game's rules in agony.

Before heeding the little redhead's instructions to leave, Will leaned in quickly and whispered to Eve, "You are *amazing*." Then he hesitated, worried about incurring the wrath of the bouncer, but decided to go with his gut. He cupped her face with his hand once more and said, "Keep yourself safe, OK?"

Then he was gone. Josie and the others kept Eve restrained and blindfolded until all the men who had kissed her had left the club. Once her hands had been freed, she tore off the blindfold and quickly searched the room for anyone six feet tall, hoping against hope that he was still there.

"Was his kiss as good as it looked? You two had this place going wild! What did he whisper to you, Eve?" They all wanted to know. If this were a contest with a proclaimed winner, Fish #4 would have been it.

"He was... Oh my..." Eve closed her eyes again, trying to relive the tenderness of his kisses, his words, him. She didn't say another word but the smile on her face let them know tonight had been a great success.

Chapter 3

When the club finally started to clear out, Gage walked the women to their cars, making sure none of the creeps from the game thought they could push their luck. Once they were all on their way home, Gage went back to close up for the night.

As he wiped down tables, his thoughts returned to the evening's game. He wasn't quite sure why he'd suggested being Josie's pick for Eve; it just seemed like the right thing to do at the time. Eve was special, and after seeing how the first two guys had failed her miserably, he felt even better about offering to be her third fish. And, of course, he hoped it had gotten Skye's attention.

According to the plan, Josie had made sure Skye was standing nearby, and Gage watched her face as he quietly approached Eve. When she raised her eyebrows in surprise, he winked at her and shrugged. As he moved closer to Eve, Skye's look changed to a smirk of disbelief—or perhaps jealousy, Gage hoped. He wanted Skye to see he was a gentleman under all that brawn and bravado. Skye's eyes opened wide when Eve leaned into the kiss a little bit, and Gage smiled, imagining it was Skye he was kissing instead.

Then Eve had gotten that fourth kiss and, man, he about knocked her off her feet. Gage shook his head, remembering. He'd been a gentleman, though, that's for sure. Once Josie was able to pull the two of them apart, the guy had smiled and bowed slightly to Noelle with a whispered "thank you." Then he turned toward the door, waved and nodded to the bartenders, and left.

As soon as Eve's hands were freed, the other girls started nailing her with questions. Gage had ignored them until he'd heard Skye's voice.

"Oh, Eve!! That guy was *gorgeous*! Noelle, where did you find him?" Skye was in awe, and Gage was pissed. Had she not noticed him at all?

Will Prentiss couldn't believe Eve's friend practically had to pull him off of her. That had been decidedly the most intense few minutes of his life. He could have kissed Eve for hours, days…*forever*. But he'd had to walk away from this woman who—unlike so many others—stirred feelings in him he'd never experienced before.

Will had left Stratus as instructed, though his body was screaming, "Screw the rules! Go back! Go back!" He hadn't wanted to incur the wrath of the gorilla-sized guy Noelle had pointed out to him.

Will wondered again about how close he and Eve were. He'd watched the guy give Eve her third kiss—and she'd seemed to enjoy it—but just before and right after, he'd seemed to have eyes only for Eve's long-legged friend. And as much as Eve seemed to enjoy being kissed by the bouncer, Will knew she'd responded to *him* even more. She'd not wanted to stop any more than he did.

But now it was all over. He was a stranger who gave her a kiss. He felt lost thinking that would be all they'd ever share.

After an eternity of standing in the parking lot, Will decided to call it a night and head back to his hotel. Alone. He was dedicated to his company and the charity work he did, and he'd never been willing to break away from either long enough to build a relationship with anyone, let alone start something with someone who lived on the other side of the country.

As he drove back to the hotel, he talked himself out of what he was feeling for this mystery girl, Eve. By the time he left his rental car with the valet, he was convinced it would be best to just stick to the rules and walk away, back to his life in Boston.

Once back in his room, Will realized he hadn't checked his phone for hours and wondered if he might have messages from his assistant, Megan. She didn't call him often, but when she did, it was important.

Will reached into his pocket for his cell phone.

"Damn it. Where is it?" Frantically, he looked through all of his pockets. He needed his phone—his whole life was programmed into it.

He picked up the phone in his suite and dialed his own cell number. On the third ring, a male voice answered.

"Hello?"

"Hello, who is this?"

"This is Steve. Who is this?"

Will was quickly getting annoyed. "Well, *Steve*, this is the owner of the phone you just answered. Can you explain why that would be?"

"Well, I found it on the bar where I work, and I picked it up thinking someone would come back for it."

"Steve...Stratus, right?" Will felt instantly calmer. "You're the guy who let me in on the game tonight. I guess I should thank you for that."

"Oh, Eve's fourth fish!" The man laughed into the phone.

Will's head began to swim at just the mention of Eve's name. The memory of her lips came flooding back.

"So, Steve, can I come down and grab my phone?" He glanced at his watch and knew they would be closed soon.

"Yeah, man. I'll hold on to it for you. I should be here for about another forty-five minutes closing up."

Will quickly ran down the stairs, forgoing the slow elevator. It was going to take at least twenty minutes to get back to the club, even at this time of the morning. Factor in the wait for the valet to bring his car, and he knew he needed to get gone fast.

He entertained a glimmer of hope that the beautiful, intriguing, intelligent Eve would still be there. But he reminded himself that when he'd walked out of the club earlier, he was walking out on anything the future might hold with her. *And that's the way it needs to be.*

It seemed years later when the valet pulled his car around, and Will let out an irritated sigh as he slid into the driver's seat and pushed the gas pedal almost to the floor. Unfortunately, twenty minutes was a long time to be alone with his thoughts, and by the time Will turned into the club's parking lot, his commitment to forget about Eve had wavered.

Damn! He once again chastised himself for not having ignored the idiotic rules and gone back to her, or waited outside, no matter how long it took.

When he finished cursing himself for getting into this impossible situation, he pushed the car door open and got out. He could smell the ocean on the air, and wondered why he hadn't noticed that earlier. Probably because he had been so caught up in Eve's sweet scent and the taste of her lips. *Damn it. Get your mind back in order.*

Will had a whole company to run and couldn't worry about his personal life anymore. He had Jeanette in Boston to go with him to any of the formal events he was required to attend, and that's about all he could handle at the moment. *Keep telling yourself that, pal.*

The club's doors were locked, so he knocked lightly at first, then more forcefully when no one answered. When the door did finally open, he was startled and stepped back quickly as the opening was eclipsed by the massive man he had seen during the game.

"Dude, we're closed. We open again at nine tomorrow night."

"Yeah, um, Steve's expecting me," Will said, more as a question than a statement. "I need to pick up something from him."

"Hey, Steve!" the big man yelled back into the club. "Some guy here says you're expecting him."

"It's all right, Gage, he's Eve's fourth fish," a distant voice called out. Steve's reply didn't seem to have helped his situation, though, because the Gage guy now looked at Will like he was thinking of all the ways he could remove his head from his body. Gage's eyes squinted as he tilted his head to the side to better see him. Will stiffened, bracing for whatever might come next.

Steve must have sensed Gage's unease, because a few moments later he appeared in person to let Gage know everything was all right. Will wasn't sure if he'd taken a breath in the past few seconds, and when he exhaled loudly, both Steve and the linebacker burst out laughing, easing the tension.

Suddenly the big guy was clapping him on the back and apologizing. "Hey man, I'm sorry about the whole 'I'm gonna kill you' look, but I take Eve's safety—well, all those girls' safety—very seriously."

"It's all right. I understand. If I were around Eve, her welfare would be the most important thing in my world." *Did I just say that out loud?* Will tried not to let his horror show. *I sound like a total stalker. This guy is going to kill me now.*

When he glanced back at Gage, though, the man had a big smile on his face. Will was surprised when he stuck his hand out.

"I'm Gage Vandenberg. Eve's my next door neighbor and a good friend." Gage could see Will's relief and chuckled.

"Will Prentiss. Nice to meet you, Gage."

Steve handed over the cell phone, and Will thanked him. As he turned to leave, Gage stopped him.

"You wanna have a beer?"

"Uh, sure," Will said, not sure it was wise to refuse, and headed back to the bar with him.

"So, you really kind of rocked Eve's world tonight, you know? I have never seen any of the girls react like that, and I've watched them play plenty of times." Gage slipped behind the bar and grabbed two beers, handing one to Will and popping the top on his own.

"Well, I was as surprised as anyone." Will wasn't sure how he was supposed to respond. This huge bouncer was Eve's self-proclaimed protector—and one of the men who had kissed her.

"I'm gonna tell you something, 'cause I kind of like you," Gage said as he sat next to Will. "Eve is just coming out of a really crappy relationship with a total ass who treated her really bad. I think she needs some fun in her life right now."

"And so you joined in on kissing her?" Will kept his eye on Gage as the two of them took a swig of their beers.

"Aw, hell, that didn't mean a thing to me. Eve's a great girl, and I was just helping out. One of the girls couldn't find any other suitable fish so I volunteered." Before Will could question his motives, Gage leaned on his elbows, his beer cradled between his hands. He looked over at Will and continued. "Didja see that hot brunette in the shortest skirt ever standing right next to Eve?" He paused as Will nodded. "That's the woman for me. Man, I want her so bad it hurts. And since she'll never *be* the bait, I was trying to impress her."

Will nodded as he took a sip of his beer. He was more than pleased to have that mystery solved. But he just couldn't help himself as the next question tumbled out.

"Tell me about Eve's ex," Will said. "Is there a chance they'll reconcile?"

"Hell, I hope not. That guy's a total freak. Creeped us all out the few times we met him. She even came to my apartment earlier tonight to tell me he's freaking out about her dumping him. I'm afraid he might have tried to hurt her. She was pretty shaken up when I saw her. She said she was OK, though, so I let it go."

"That explains the marks on her neck," Will whispered to himself.

But Gage heard and immediately began to ball up his fists, a look of fire in his eyes. "I'll kill the little prick! I will totally kill him!!"

"Calm down. Going to jail isn't going to help Eve at all right now. This guy who hurt her will get his punishment, but you may have to be patient. Eve will have to go through legal channels if he's a real threat to her." Will couldn't help wanting to plot revenge himself, though he didn't even know this woman.

Gage calmed down slightly but his fists remained clenched as he returned to leaning on the counter.

"Gage, I have to go back home tomorrow. I have potential business here in California, but I'm not sure if or when I'll be back. Can you give me your number so I can contact you and make sure Eve is OK?" Will really wanted to ask for Eve's number, too, but he pushed that thought to the back of his mind.

Gage looked at Will for a minute, trying to decide if this man was worthy of Eve.

"Yeah, I think you might be good for Eve, when she is ready," Gage finally said. "Here's my card."

Taking the card, Will flipped it over to read it. It was a simple white card with black block lettering: Gage Vandenberg, personal trainer, and it included a phone number.

"That's my cell. You can reach me anytime," Gage said.

"Thanks." Will felt better knowing Gage was there to look out for Eve since he couldn't. He had to walk away from her. For now.

Chapter Four

The phone in Will's hotel suite rang at 5:15 a.m. He groaned as he reached over to answer and heard a computerized voice announce the wakeup call he had requested. Unfortunately, he had gotten in only about an hour earlier, and really didn't want to get up and fly back to Boston.

Rolling over and pulling the pillow over his head, he made the decision to sleep longer. *Hell, I own the jet. I can leave whenever I want.*

Then his cell phone started beeping. Even with his head firmly buried under the pillow, Will was unable to ignore the incessant sound of his damn phone. He felt around on the nightstand for the maddening device. *Why was I so concerned with getting the damn thing back last night?* he wondered as his hand finally wrapped around the phone.

"Yeah?" His voice was raspy and harsh. He and Gage had talked for nearly two hours.

"Late night, *boss*?" Will knew instantly that Megan Stepanski was not happy with his greeting. She had worked for him for three years and had absolutely no problem calling him an ass when he needed it, something most people wouldn't dare do. In the way she had just said *boss*, she'd done just that.

"Sorry, Megan. I just woke up."

"Did you get lucky?" The laughter on the other end of the phone rang in Will's head. All he wanted to do was close his eyes so he could see Eve's face. "Hello? Will?" Megan brought him back to the present.

"Sorry again, Megan. I didn't sleep well or," he looked again at the clock, "actually, at all."

"Uh-huh?" Will could hear the smile in his assistant's voice.

He knew he needed to get Megan off this mental track: the one where he finds the right girl and settles down. She was like his mother the way she worried about his love life. "Is there a reason you've called me at the crack of dawn, Megan?" he asked in a teasing voice.

"Well, first of all, it isn't the crack of dawn here. It's after eight, and the office is already busy, so get your lazy butt up and get back here. Second, I wanted to make sure you were on your plane before seven your time. You have dinner tonight with Jeanette,"—the name was like a curse when she said it—"and I thought you might like to freshen up before it. Plus you're supposed to pick up Josie McInnis from the Santa Barbara Museum."

"Ahhh, okay." Even though he had already done this for the other two museums vying for the grant, he'd momentarily forgotten he would be the contact for the SBMA's representative during the week. He chose to do this for the same reason he'd anonymously visited each museum: He wanted to know where and who his money was going to.

"Go get in the shower, and I'll call the pilot and make sure he's ready when you get there." The line went dead, and once again Will was thankful he had Megan. If not for her, he would have crawled his ass back in bed and slept for hours, not only missing the rep from Santa Barbara, but also missing dinner and risking angering Jeanette even more than he already had.

Tossing his phone on the bed, he followed Megan's directions and jumped into the shower, hoping it would wake him up. The flight back to Boston was about five hours, but since he'd neglected his work while in Santa Barbara, he wouldn't be able to sleep during the trip.

When Will finally got to the private airport, the sun was just starting to make an appearance, and his plane was already on the runway. Glancing at his watch, he was actually proud of himself for making it to the airport before seven. Sure it was 6:58, but considering he spent the entire night out, that was pretty damn good.

Will's pilot, Eric, greeted him with a big smile and a warm "good morning." His knowing look made Will think Megan had been talking to him, but unlike Megan, Eric would never say a word to him about why he had been out all night and looked like absolute shit, so he just shook the man's hand and proceeded onto the plane.

Once he was seated, Eric let him know they were cleared for takeoff, and Will pulled out his laptop.

Eve had distracted him so much in just a couple of hours that he couldn't imagine trying to maintain a relationship. He told himself this so he could move past her and get back to his real life. Except that even with this convincing argument, he still couldn't concentrate. The flight was smooth enough but his brain was full of turbulence.

Which one is Josie? Was she possibly one of the other women at Stratus last night? The more he thought about it, Will really wasn't sure he wanted to recognize the person he'd be working with so closely for fear that...what? What was he afraid of? *That this Josie will remember me from last night and tell Eve? Why wouldn't I want Eve to know who I was?*

Some of his concerns centered on the grant: He didn't want Josie to know he was both the representative of Townsend Industries *and* her colleague's Passion Fish from a silly (*wonderful*) game at a Santa Barbara bar.

By the time he landed at the private airfield just outside the city, Will had convinced himself that the rep from SBMA had to be a nerdy type who crunched numbers all day. She would never be caught dead at a club like Stratus, let alone playing a kissing game. With a name like Josie, he was sure she was a fifty-something spinster who probably wore orthopedic shoes. Neither of the representatives from the other two museums had been anything but stuffy and boring, so why would he expect anything different?

Will's phone was already at his ear when the plane came to a stop and he was able to exit. He wanted to be sure all the meetings were arranged to his specifications and that Jeanette, the Boston

Museum of Art's curator, was prepared for their third and final candidate for the grant.

That situation in itself was a problem, and he should have known better than to get even socially involved with someone that he had to work so closely with. Megan assured him that everything was ready and that, despite a very evident "snip" in Jeanette's voice when they spoke, the BMA was also set up for the week's events.

Jeanette had a temper, and Will could only hope she could put her anger with him aside while their guest was here. His including her in the dinner tonight was to try and soothe her hurt feelings over her most recent attempt to seduce him. She had a hard time understanding or accepting that he simply failed to return the romantic—and sexual—interest she had in him.

Will knew he didn't have enough time to go home before he had to pick up the SBMA rep, so he headed straight to Logan after picking up his car. For a Sunday afternoon, the traffic was pretty heavy, and stuck in the Ted Williams Tunnel, Will had lots of time to think. His thoughts inevitably returned to the previous night.

How can it be that a woman I don't even know could capture me so immediately and so completely? He thought for a moment about his parents. They'd been married nearly four decades before death took his father, and then his mother two years later. His parents had claimed it was love at first sight for them—something Will had always scoffed at. He'd never believed that a man could simply look at a woman and instantly *know* that she was the one, but it seemed a little more possible now.

Despite her night of tossing and turning, reliving probably the best kiss she had ever received in her life, Eve made it to the airport on time. After clearing security and putting her shoes back on, she had a few minutes to grab a coffee before boarding started.

She tried to relax on the plane but it was useless. Last night kept swirling in her head. Amazingly, Julian's attempt to choke her to death was *not* foremost in her thoughts. She absentmindedly brought her hand to her neck, checking to be sure her turtleneck was covering the bruises. The horror of what he'd done would sink in eventually, but for now, Eve focused on how she'd been the lucky recipient of back-to-back great kisses.

Trying to break the hold that final kiss seemed to have on her, Eve thought about how proud her dad would have been to see her making a pitch for millions of dollars to help build a museum. She let out a small sigh as she thought of how much she missed him.

Her relationship with her mom hadn't been much since she moved to New Mexico while Eve was in college. They talked every couple of weeks, but it had been more than three years since they'd seen each other. Things were never the same after they lost her dad.

Jonah Carwyn and Gretchen Hamilton were what many would call "hippies." But not because they wore clothes woven out of hemp, or didn't have steady jobs, because they did. Gretchen taught in the English department at Pepperdine University, while Eve's father taught art at the University of California, Los Angeles. Her parents had never married, claiming they didn't need the approval of the government to be in love and share their lives. They also probably could have afforded to live somewhere other than the small cottage in Venice Beach, but they had never wanted to.

They had always treated Eve as more grown up than her friends' parents treated them. Weekends were spent walking the boardwalk at the beach and talking with the eclectic group of people who called it their home. Or her parents would take her to the abundant galleries and museums around Los Angeles. Those were some of her favorite days. To listen to her father explain the contrast in one painting, or the hidden meaning in one tiny figure of another, never ceased to enthrall her.

While Eve loved art, she was even more drawn to books. She worshipped her mother, and found that she was so proud of her when she read. By the time she was eight, Eve was reading at a college level, and having discussions about what she was reading with her mother. Gretchen loved that she could spend an hour just talking with her daughter about Hemingway or Fitzgerald.

Eve's life couldn't have been better if she had written the story herself until her first day of sixth grade.

She could remember the feeling of dread when Principal Palmer had come to get her from the front steps of the school. She had been waiting for her father to pick her up, and as she followed the principal into his office, Eve had known something was terribly wrong.

As she sat in the too-big chair in the principal's office, the fabric was itchy on her bare legs. She had tried to focus on anything other than the man sitting across from her. He had tried to make small talk, but Eve could do nothing but nod and stare at the small stain on the carpet in front of his desk.

Eve remembered her shock when Mr. Palmer called her mother Mrs. Carwyn and she hadn't corrected him. That had never happened before. And when Eve looked up to see her mom standing there, her face was all wrong. Everything was all wrong.

"Where's Dad?" Eve had finally asked—but then immediately willed her mother not to answer. Now the scene played clearly in her head. She could remember the exact words and every expression on her mother's face.

She had stopped to take a deep breath before looking Eve in the eye. "Dad was in an accident today, baby. H-h-he's..." she had stumbled over her words as Eve stared at her. "Dad's gone, Eve."

It was after her father's death that Eve shifted her interest to art and art history. It was a way to keep a part of him with her. Fortunately, her mother had encouraged Eve's passion, and had continued to take her to galleries and museums.

"Miss? Did you want something to drink?" The flight attendant's voice brought Eve out of her memories and into the reality that she was soon landing in a strange city for the most important meeting of her career.

"Just water, please," she answered.

Eve pulled out the itinerary the Boston Museum of Art had sent. Everything was addressed to Josie. Since hers was the top signature on the grant proposal, the Boston staff had assumed Josie would be giving the presentation. However, the SBMA board of directors felt that as the curator, Eve should represent the museum. They had arranged everything for her trip but were working with a small museum's budget. Her accommodations were not going to be as fancy—or as close to where her meetings would be—as she would have liked.

Nevertheless, this trip was a major deal. The Santa Barbara Museum of Art was just a little place with grand ideas; Eve was thrilled to be given the opportunity to travel, rub elbows with Boston bigwigs, and hopefully head back home on Friday with news they'd won the grant. She thought about how far she'd come personally and professionally over the six years she'd worked at the museum—was it that many already? It had been the only job she'd ever held, really, having been hired the summer she turned twenty.

When she began as a college student, she hadn't been given too much responsibility by the directors. Soon, though, they learned of her knack for knowing the right people to contact if the SBMA wanted to become a presence in the art world. When she'd been able to procure a Manet and two Van Goghs for a six-month stay at their tiny museum during her second summer with them, the directors began to take notice. When she graduated from the University of California at Santa Barbara with a degree in art history, they didn't hesitate to hire her—and pile on even more responsibilities. A year ago, they'd promoted her to curator, passing over other employees who had worked there longer.

Lowering her tray to hold the water the flight attendant presented her, Eve turned her attention once again to the itinerary. There would be a formal luncheon the next day that would include a representative from Townsend Industries, the largest donor to the BMA. According to the paperwork they'd sent, Townsend Industries would also be graciously providing Eve's transportation throughout her stay, so she would not have to worry about taxis or the T. As part of the grant-application process, Eve would have meetings with the Townsend rep, as well as talking extensively with various program directors at the museum. The Santa Barbara proposal was one of three they were considering, and Eve was the last to meet with the decision-makers in Boston.

Her presentation would take place in two days, and she was glad to have at least some time before then to visit the museum and enjoy it from a tourist's perspective. This also gave her time to check (and recheck) the slides they had prepared. Then on Thursday evening, Eve would be attending a black-tie affair where the grant winner would be announced. Butterflies fluttered as Eve considered what lay in store over the next four days. She tucked the itinerary back in her purse and readied herself for her arrival at Logan International Airport.

The weather in Boston looked far different from the sunny skies she'd just left in Santa Barbara. It was dreary, bordering on a rainstorm, as Eve watched out the window during landing. *I miss my sunny California already*, she thought as she waited to retrieve her laptop and exit the plane.

She walked to the baggage claim area and, after retrieving her single suitcase, began to search for someone carrying a sign that said "Boston Museum of Art" or "Townsend Industries." It was an assumption based solely on what always happened in the movies and television shows she had seen where someone other than family or friends picked someone up at the airport.

Laughing to herself at the thought of a driver dressed in a black suit with a little black hat, she scanned the area. Her eyes stopped at a man across the crowded room who was, in a word, stunning: sandy blond hair that curled deliciously at the nape of his neck, chiseled jaw line, and the most beautiful deep-blue eyes she had ever seen. *Earth to Eve! You're looking for your ride, not a date!*

She forced her eyes past him, but when she began her search again, she noticed he was holding a sign and obviously looking for someone as well. The large white card he held read: JOSIE MCINNIS.

He's looking for Josie. Or me. Or the rep for the SBMA, and that would be me. Take a deep breath, Eve. Jeez.

On the other side of the chaotic baggage claim, Will thanked the gods once again for Megan, because she was smart enough to have slipped a little sign into his car before he left. She really did know him too well. With the sign held at chest level, Will began to scan the area. Then saw *her–Eve.* He gasped as he realized she was walking very deliberately toward him.

How did she recognize me? She was blindfolded. But...how could she know it was me*? What do I say? "Hi, yeah, that was me who kissed you last night, and now I'm standing in front of you at an airport 3,000 miles away. What a coincidence, eh?"*

"Um, are you looking for Josie McInnis from the Santa Barbara Museum of Art?" Eve asked, a bit timidly. Will froze when they made eye contact. He didn't speak, but Eve thought she saw his face turn a dark shade of pink. *Wow! Is he blushing? Is he blushing because of* me?

Will felt the heat burn in his cheeks—the blaze a combination of remembering last night's kiss and sheer relief at realizing she didn't seem to know who he was.

Having clearly caught him off guard, Eve wanted to apologize, but she was afraid of embarrassing him further. And as he still hadn't taken his eyes off her, she was beginning to rethink the whole "stunning" thought—perhaps "stunned" was the more appropriate word.

"If you're here for Josie McInnis of Santa Barbara, you're really here for me," she said. "I'm Eve Carwyn." She extended her hand in greeting.

Speak, you idiot, speak! And shake her hand already! Will heard his own voice screaming in his head. This never happened to him. He ran a multi-billion dollar company, regularly stood up to the stodgy board of directors, and faced down Jeanette on almost a daily basis, yet this petite blonde woman with eyes so intelligent and caring left him speechless.

"Yes, I was expecting a Ms. McInnis. Are you the museum's grant representative then?" Will was finally able to compose himself. Eve nodded yes as he grasped her hand in return. "I'm William Prentiss from Townsend Industries. I'll be your contact throughout your stay in Boston."

It was Eve's turn to be stunned.

So he's not *just my driver?* Realizing she would get to spend a week with this man, she made a mental note to send a hearty thank you to the SBMA directors.

"Ms. Carwyn?" his velvet-soft voice brought her back to the conversation. "Is this all of your luggage?"

"Yes. Um, yes." Eve stuttered as she reminded herself to breathe and quit staring at him. "Just the suitcase, my carry-on bag, and my laptop."

Will quickly took hold of her bag. His thoughts were racing as he considered the bland itinerary the selection committee had laid out. That definitely wasn't going to do. He had Eve in his town, and she had no idea who he was. After the effect that one kiss had on him, he wasn't going to let her get away without getting to know her much better. He needed to call Megan immediately and make some additional plans for the week.

"Come this way. I've got a car waiting outside."

Things were politely awkward as the two walked out of baggage claim and Will led Eve to his car. As he stowed her luggage, she stood hesitantly between the front and back passenger doors of the car, clearly not knowing which seat she should select. After placing her belongings in the trunk, Will opened the front door for her.

"Is this OK? It's just the two of us. I'd feel like a cab driver if you were sitting in the back."

She smiled in relief. *Beautiful.* The word slipped into Will's head as he watched her slide into the front seat and glance back up at him. "Thank you, Mr. Prentiss. And, by the way, please call me Eve."

"You're quite welcome, *Eve*. And, by the way," he said, repeating her phrasing, "I'm Will."

Will went around and climbed into the driver's seat, pulling out his cell phone before starting the car. He turned on the CD player, selected a disc he thought she might like as background music, and adjusted the volume accordingly.

"I have to make a call. You don't mind do you?" Will asked Eve, trying not to stare at her.

"Oh, no. Go right ahead. I've never been to Boston, so I'm just going to take in the city as you drive. Don't mind me." He could hear the weariness in her voice, and wondered if she'd been up all night thinking about her little bar game. With a smile playing on his lips, he pressed "2" on his cell phone to call his office. As he did so, it struck him how sad it was that work was the first number in his contacts. But before he could delve too deeply into that thought, Megan answered the phone.

Will had to figure out how to get done what he needed with Eve sitting next to him—and without Megan jumping to the conclusions he knew she would. He closed his eyes and prayed that just this one time, his assistant would be professional, and quiet.

"Megan, can you contact Javier, please, and have arrangements made? ...Yes ...Same as what I had at Christmas two years ago if possible—just tell Javier. He'll take care of it."

He glanced over at Eve. Her head was turned to look out the window at the city as it passed. Even in profile she was stunning. He hated ignoring his lovely passenger, but this was something that couldn't wait.

"And I'm rethinking tonight's dinner...Yes, just two. I thought you'd be pleased to hear that. You'll call Jeanette for me? I know, but you are so good at dealing with her ...Yes, Apex at eight sounds about right. ...Good, yes. Arlene knows where my favorite table is...Megan, you're indispensable. Thanks."

Glancing over (*again*) at Eve, Will smiled, his mission accomplished. Megan must have sensed his need for secrecy, but he knew she would corner him later and demand every last detail.

When Eve turned to look at him, he offered her a small smile and said, "I'm so sorry. That was very rude of me but it truly was necessary."

She smiled in return and the interior of the car suddenly felt very warm, despite the wet grayness outside. Traffic around The Commons was always busy on a Sunday afternoon, and the pedestrians didn't make things any better, but Will was adept at maneuvering around the city. Soon they were heading to her hotel; her *new* hotel. Will would have to tell her he'd changed her reservations.

"About your hotel arrangements…?" Eve turned her head toward Will as he spoke. "Townsend Industries has taken the liberty of changing your accommodations to be closer to the museum. I hope you don't mind. We'll be picking up the tab, of course, since we did this without checking with you first."

He watched as her face showed a mixture of curiosity and relief, confirming his hunch that she hadn't been the one to select the low-budget place along the highway, fifteen miles outside the city.

"I've got reservations—"

"I know. I've had my assistant Megan cancel them for you. The Santa Barbara Museum won't be charged."

Unsure exactly how to respond, Eve instead gestured toward the CD player and said, "This is nice. Who is it?"

"Lila Marin. Her *Inside Out* CD."

It had started to rain lightly, and the drizzly drops on the windshield were constant enough that Will had the wipers going, creating a "thup-thup-thup-thup" sound that often seemed to be in time with the music.

"So this is your first trip to Boston?" Will decided he needed to keep up the talk or he would just gaze at her and be distracted from the road.

"I've only been east of the Rockies twice in my life. Once to visit New York City and the other as a child on a family trip to Disney World."

"So are you planning a little sightseeing while you're here?" As soon as he said the words, Will worried whether she'd perceive his question as invasive, but her demeanor remained relaxed.

She reached into her purse and pulled out a folded piece of paper, holding it up but not opening it. "Well, a friend of a friend gave me some suggestions of places to see. I *do* want to visit the Boston Museum extensively, of course. Virtual tours on the Web just don't cut it, you know?" She returned the paper to her purse and gazed out toward the highway in front of them.

Smiling in agreement, he looked over at her again, lingering on her profile, and quickly taking in her outfit as well. It fit her nicely. Growing up with his mother, Will was a pretty good judge of style, and he could tell Eve definitely had it. Her hair was swept into a casual ponytail with wisps softly framing her temples and cheekbones.

Will's eyes stopped briefly at her neck just when she turned toward him. *Shit!*

Eve noticed he was looking at her neck, and while she knew her turtleneck sufficiently covered the bruises there, a blush crossed her cheeks, and she brought her hand to the collar of her sweater, adjusting it upward.

Will quickly refocused on the road, worried that he had scared her. He knew what was underneath that cream material, and he tightened his hands on the steering wheel at the thought of it. *Shit! Shit! Shit!*

"So, how about you?" She seemed to want the conversation to continue, and Will relaxed his posture.

"Hmm?"

"Have you ever been to Santa Barbara?"

Answer carefully, he thought. "Yes. Once."

Fortunately, Eve didn't push the issue. Instead she changed the subject.

"Can you tell me about Townsend Industries? I mean, as we were applying for this grant, we did a lot of research and found their website to be a bit cryptic about its background."

That was intentional, Will thought as he tried to figure out a way to answer her question without telling outright lies.

"Well, it's a fairly new company but has grown quickly. The medical field has found our product to be extremely effective in surgical procedures."

She nodded, turning her head toward him, her eyes showing genuine interest.

"It was named for Camille Townsend, the owner's mother."

"You mean Camille Townsend the designer? I was wondering if the two were connected."

"You've heard of her?"

"I love her stuff. I can't always afford it, but the few pieces I have always receive compliments. My dress for Thursday night is a Townsend."

Will couldn't help but wonder if his late mother somehow had her hand in this whole situation.

"Camille Townsend died of heart failure—ironically just before the approval of the device her son had designed that could have saved her. He named the company as a tribute to her. He got the AMA's approval about a month after burying her."

"Wow."

This time the silence was reverent, and it was good. Will's mother had been an amazing woman, a patron of the arts, a giving soul. He could feel her smiling down on him. On them. It felt comfortable sharing this story with Eve, he realized, even if he wasn't revealing *all* of the details.

Before she heads back to Seattle, she'll know, he vowed silently.

As they pulled up to the front of the Fairhaven Hotel, Eve's face was a mix of concern and awe.

"Um, is *this* where you've booked a room for me? Oh, my..."

"Yes, this will be your home while you're in Boston." Will was pleased that Eve was impressed, if not embarrassed. "Like I said, it's important that you be available for a number of meetings, and the museum is just two blocks away. The BMA often uses conference rooms here, and Thursday night's awards presentation will be held here as well, in the grand ballroom. This really is for the sake of convenience." He didn't mention that Townsend Industries had not been this accommodating to the other two grant applicants.

Will pulled into a parking space rather than allow the valet to approach the car. He had decided he wasn't going to linger, as much as he wanted to, but he also didn't want to leave her to the valet when he was so willing and able to assist her himself. He'd get her checked in, that's all, he told himself. Eve needed some time to get settled into her room. *My favorite room.* Will smiled. *It has the best view in the entire hotel.*

"Hello, Mr. Prentiss. It's nice to see you again, sir," said Javier as they approached the front desk. "I understand this will be put on the Townsend account?" Will nodded and passed Eve her room key.

As Eve walked to the elevator with Will, she looked coyly at him. "Well, *Mr. Prentiss*, I want to thank you for making my arrival in Boston so pleasant. I am looking forward to my stay."

"I'm glad you're enjoying Boston so far. It really is an amazing and friendly city."

Looking up at the labeled circles above the elevator door, Will noted how quickly the light was moving toward 'L' for Lobby. As the numbers got smaller and smaller *…6...5...4...* the voice in his head kept telling him, *Ask her before she gets in the elevator!*

"I don't know how tired you are from your flight, but I wanted to know if you'd be interested in joining me for dinner tonight," he finally stammered out. *3...2...*

"Umm, yeah." Eve gazed at him as though quickly looking for some hidden agenda, and perhaps a reason to say no. Then she straightened her shoulders, a sense of self-assuredness seeming to have overtaken her concern. "Yes, Will, that would be very nice. Thank you." *1...DING!*

The elevator opened silently behind her. Will stepped forward to hold the door with his foot, and Eve turned and entered the elevator, taking her things from him. She shrugged her shoulders in a gesture of confidence and smiled brightly at him. *Oh, you are melting me!* Will thought.

"I'll be back at 7:45 and call you from the lobby, if that's all right."

"Yes, that sounds fine. May I ask about appropriate attire?" She blushed a little, feeling unsure about what type of restaurant Will had in mind.

"Well, I'll be wearing a jacket and tie. Does that help?" Will suddenly remembered that she had been right next to him in the car when he'd told Megan to make reservations at Apex. Had she heard that? He hoped tonight would be a surprise for her. He so enjoyed seeing her eyes light up in amazement.

"Yes, I think so. Other than my dress for Thursday, I have mostly business suit-types of clothing with me. Would something like that be OK?"

"Perfect." *I'm sure you'll look amazing in whatever you wear,* he thought. "I'll see you in a few hours then."

Will backed away from the elevator and, as the doors closed, Eve flashed him a radiant smile that melted him once more.

Chapter 5

Gage cursed as bright sunlight streamed into his room and across his face. He wondered for the hundredth time why he'd chosen an apartment where his bedroom faced east. Even with an overcast sky, the glint of the sun kept sneaking in and waking him up. He kept meaning to buy some heavy-duty curtains for that window; he just never got around to actually doing it.

"Oh, screw it. I'll just get up. I need to talk to Eve anyway," he mumbled to himself.

He knew Eve would be excited when he told her that her fourth fish had come back to the club last night. For a minute, he wondered if the guy really meant it when he said he wanted to know if Eve was safe. The last thing he wanted to do was to get Eve involved with another asshole. But Will had seemed like a pretty genuine guy.

After what he had learned from Will the previous night, well earlier that morning, he also wanted to see for himself if that asshole ex of Eve's really did hurt her. Taking a minute to breathe deeply, he tried to control the thoughts he was having about that subject.

He also needed to let Eve know he'd been her third fish—and that he only did it to help Josie and attract Skye's attention and they should both forget it ever happened. Eve knew how to kiss, that was for sure, but it was Skye who made him hard.

He rolled out of bed, the dream he'd been having about the leggy brunette still apparent, and headed to the shower. Looking in the mirror he wondered what more he could do to get her attention. This had never been an issue for him; between working at Stratus and being a personal trainer, he constantly had hot women throwing themselves at him. And he'd been known to take advantage of this. *So why can't I get with the one woman I really want?*

Thinking about Skye was not helping Gage's current state. He knew he needed to stop mooning over Skye as he stepped into the shower. The warm water was soothing enough, but there was only one way to relieve the pressure the very vivid dream about Skye and her long legs had caused. Just the thought of her legs, and more accurately, her legs wrapped around him, had his blood boiling again.

Once he was able to think with his brain instead of other parts of his anatomy, Gage spent some time deciding what he should and shouldn't tell Eve. He decided that first he needed to find out what the ex had done to her, because if what Will said was true, he might not be calm enough to talk to her about anything else.

After drying off and dressing, Gage decided he should bring a peace offering, in case Eve was mad when he told her about his part in last night's fishing.

He ran down to the corner store to grab some doughnuts and coffee, making sure to get Eve one of those girlie, mochachino-latte-carmel-swirly ones, thinking maybe it would soften her up a little bit and she'd let her guard down so he could catch a look at her neck. He perused the racks behind the counter, his eyes lighting up as he picked out a variety of doughnuts, including several of his favorite ones with the vanilla frosting and sprinkles. There was a juvenile aspect to Gage that most people mistook for being a meathead gym rat, but in reality, he had a master's degree from USC in kinesiology. His work as a personal trainer was so he could get experience in a gym as he prepared to one day open his own.

It only took a few minutes for Gage to get back to the apartment building. He loved that he could hear the sounds of the ocean as he walked and thought again about Skye. He made a promise to stop being such a nancy boy and ask her out. What was the worst that could happen?

She could turn you down in front of the whole world and dismiss you just like Josie did Preston last night.

He let out a long sigh as he knocked on Eve's door. After a pause he gave it a good pounding, and there was still no answer. There was no way she could still be asleep. The girls had left the club hours before he had, and his ass was out of bed already. Gage's forehead wrinkled with worry as he remembered what Eve had looked like when she'd asked him to watch out for her ex while she was gone for the week. *Uh, gone for the week.* It finally dawned on him why he wasn't answering the door. Gage took his doughnuts and headed back to his damn sunny bedroom.

For nearly three years now, the girls had met for their usual Sunday brunch at their favorite diner, Marlowe's. It had started as an initial "getting to know you" meeting of the three museum employees when Skye had joined Eve and Josie on the staff. Soon it became a regular habit for them, and Dana and Noelle joined them most Sundays.

Today, of course, they were missing Dana, who had a shift at the hospital, and Eve, who had left for Boston a few hours earlier. In a way, Skye thought, this was better. She'd wanted to talk more about the last two kisses Eve had gotten and didn't know if Eve was ready to hear that Gage had been one of her fish.

Skye glanced to the side, catching her reflection in the diner's front window, and tucked a loose strand of hair behind her ear. When she turned to Josie and Noelle, they were both quietly laughing at her.

"Skye, have you ever passed a reflective surface and not looked at yourself in it?" Josie asked with a smartass smirk on her face.

She thought for a moment and then, in a very dignified manner, extended her middle finger in her friend's direction.

"Very nice, Skylar," Josie shot back.

"Girls." Noelle scolded the both of them.

Noelle was the mother of their group. Eve had known her since they were little girls in school, and she was the only one of the group of women who had found "Mr. Right." Well, in Thomas' case, Mr. *Perfect*.

They all were extremely jealous of Noelle and Thomas' relationship and often wondered how lucky one girl could be. The man was gorgeous, smart, caring, rich, and he adored Noelle like nothing else! They had met about eight years earlier in their junior year of college when Noelle had been visiting Eve for Halloween weekend. Normally, neither girl was much into parties, and in fact Noelle attended a Lutheran college where partying was greatly frowned upon.

But Eve had been invited to the party by Dana, and she had dragged Noelle with her for moral support. Thomas later claimed he knew as soon as he saw Noelle that she was the one for him.

Unfortunately, Thomas had been on a date that evening, and being a gentleman, he never did anything more than introduce himself and make small talk with Noelle. The next day, however, he tracked her down, and the rest, as they say, is history. Even though Noelle went to school about an hour away from Santa Barbara, they dated for the rest of their college careers, and Thomas proposed the day after they both graduated.

Some days Skye thought she wanted to be like Noelle—have the wonderful husband and build a future with a family and a little house with a garden. However, Skye's last few dates had been with a gorgeous baseball player who, for some reason, never seemed to remember his wallet. The third time that happened, she reminded him that her rules for dating were the same as for baseball: He'd struck out.

She left the restaurant as soon as she saw the bill and his shocked "I can't believe I forgot again" look. Somehow he'd found a way to pay, but she was long gone.

She glanced again quickly at her reflection in the window. There was no need to settle for—or settle down with—a less than the perfect guy. She looked damn hot!

After the trio ordered coffee and food, the conversation moved to the night before. "Good Lord, Josie. I can't believe the kiss Eve got," said Skye.

"I know! That kiss was H-O-T!" Josie shrieked, looking across the table at Noelle. "Where in heaven did you find that last fish?"

"I wasn't talking about him, Josie. Although Eve did look like she was pretty happy with him. I'm talking about that giant hunk of a man, Gage."

Josie's eyes grew wide and a sly little grin spread across her face. Skye could see the evil wheels turning in that curl-covered head of hers. Josie was the matchmaker, whether she was building friendships like the one between Eve and Skye or—now that she had Beau—finding the perfect match for the rest of them. Poor Dana had already been fixed up with four of Beau's friends, none of which turned out to be "the perfect match" Josie had declared each one to be.

"Why, Skylar Montgomery! Do you have a little crush on one very handsome bouncer we all know and love?"

"Well, judging by the dream I had about him that involved a blindfold, a nice red ribbon, and *nothing* else, I would have to say it is a definite possibility." Skye was trying to hide the lust she was feeling, but from the look on Josie's face, she hadn't done a very good job.

Her mind wandered back to the very steamy dream she'd had last night. She remembered every muscle that rippled on Gage's incredible body. She only hoped that when she got to see and *touch* him in real life it would be just as–what was the word? *Perfect.*

"Yoo-hoo, Skye!" Josie waved her hand in front of Skye's face.

"Where did you just go?" Noelle asked.

"Oh, sorry, ladies. I just had a moment with Gage in my head."

"Wow! I have never seen you like this before." Josie still had that silly grin on her face, and Skye didn't trust her in the least. "You know, like Noelle's fish, Gage actually *asked* to be my fish for Eve."

Skye was stunned—like she'd just taken a size-11 boot to the stomach. *Why on God's green earth would he* ask *to kiss Eve and then stare at me like he wanted to take me right then and there? Ugh!* Skye groaned internally. *Idiot men!*

When Josie saw the expression on Skye's face change so quickly, she started talking—fast. "Skye, don't let that crazy imagination of yours get going. Gage told me he wanted to kiss Eve to save her from all the other losers in the club last night. Right before he offered, that vile Preston Langley had begged me to include him."

As Skye calmed herself down, she noticed that the booth behind Noelle was now occupied. The man was sitting alone with his back to them, and he seemed to be leaning a little too far back, trying to overhear their conversation. Skye decided to test her theory.

"Josie, did I tell you how many different positions Gage and I tried last night?" She winked at them and nodded her head toward the pervert behind Noelle.

The three women stifled their laughter as they heard the guy spit out whatever he'd been drinking. Skye had her proof and hoped that would teach him a lesson about eavesdropping.

As Josie and Noelle continued to giggle, Skye's thoughts returned to her dream. A more accurate comment would have been "Josie, did I tell you how many positions I *imagined* Gage and I tried last night?" *Wow! Even in my imagination, that boy was creative. Damn! Why can't I get him and his amazingly beautiful body out of my head?*

"So, go ahead, Josie. You were explaining about Gage *volunteering* to be a fish," Skye prompted, almost growling the word "volunteer."

"Oh, yeah. So I had just completely destroyed Preston. As if he even has a concept of what passion is," Josie sneered. "And Gage says he wants to kiss Eve, but he says to make sure you are standing directly behind her. Skye, honey, that was a show for *you*."

Skye liked that explanation better than some of the alternatives she'd conjured up, as she wasn't a second-choice kind of girl. She also wasn't sure she could go much longer with only her *mental* image of a completely naked and oh-so-ready Gage.

The next half hour passed with the three laughing about the other two losers they'd inadvertently picked for Eve. Skye remained glad she never played that game. If *she* could be such a poor judge of strangers' kissing abilities, she didn't even want to think about who her friends might pick for her.

They were in a deep discussion about the fourth fish, trying to pull as much detail from Noelle as they could, when their eavesdropping neighbor got up to leave. As he walked past their booth, Skye suddenly recognized him: Eve's ex.

Gage looked at the clock for the hundredth time in the last hour. He couldn't wait to be rid of this chick for another week. Suzanne was one of those girls who practically threw herself at Gage. Most days it didn't bother him, but he was restless today, and her leaning way over so that he could get a good look at the boobs she'd paid a fortune for was not amusing—or tempting—to him.

Most of Gage's clients were like Suzanne. He made a lot of money off these chicks who had nothing better to spend their money on than bigger boobs, tighter asses, and the clothes to show them off. Gage was just a perk for them. None of them really worked out hard, and most of them spent their time leaning forward or bending over to give him a better look at their "cosmetic enhancements."

The vision of Skylar watching him kiss Eve at the club last night ran through his head. Unfortunately that caused a big grin to cross his face and the skank in front of him thought he was flirting. Suzanne still had fifteen minutes left in her hour-long training session. Gage had to think fast before she asked him to help her in the shower. Again.

"OK. So, Suzanne, what I want you to do for this last part of your session is walk at a brisk pace on the treadmill. That'll get you some good cardio in this week. I think you need to start adding that to your workout anyway. Here, let me get you set up."

Hot damn! That worked out nicely, Gage realized as he started the treadmill running. He could even slip out a few minutes early. *Gage, you are a freakin' genius! I'll have to incorporate fifteen minutes of cardio into all the bouncing bimbos' workouts.*

He grabbed his bag quickly, glancing back at Suzanne on the treadmill. She was not happy to actually be doing some exercise instead of just letting him look down her shirt for the whole hour. He didn't really care. Gage waved to the girl at the front desk.

"I'm outta here, Heather. My last appointment is on the treadmill. Just make sure she doesn't fall off for me, will ya?"

"Sure, Gage, no problem."

He was out the door before anyone could say anything else. He would be working at the club tonight and hoped Skye might pay a visit. Gage headed home for another shower, feeling the need to get the stink of skank and sweat off before his shift started.

He parked in the garage of the apartment building and decided to take the elevator, rather than his usual stairs, to get himself into the shower as quickly as possible. As he stepped off the elevator onto his floor, he noticed a guy at Eve's door. Shit. The ex was back.

"Hey, buddy! You lookin' for Eve?" Gage walked toward Eve's apartment. *What the hell was his name again?*

"Umm...hey. Gage, right?" The ex looked uncomfortable. Gage considered that a good thing. "Yeah, do you know when she'll be home?"

Just then, Gage heard the tapping of high heels on cement. He turned slightly as Skylar sauntered down the hall toward them. Gage eyed the long, gorgeous legs he'd been dreaming about all day. Her skirt was so short and her legs so incredible, it was almost impossible to drag his eyes away.

"Hey, Gage. Hey, Julian," Skye called out to both of them.

Julian! That was it! What the hell is she doing here, though? She knows Eve is out of town.

Skye read the look on Gage's face, immediately producing her keys and starting toward Eve's door.

"Eve wanted me to check on something for her," she said, quickly winking at Gage. "She just called me from Boston."

She stared directly at Julian. His expression changed, seeming to relax slightly. Skye's arrival had kind of ruined the whole "scare the shit out of the guy" vibe Gage thought he'd had going. Julian probably thought Gage wouldn't hurt him with a lady present.

Obviously he didn't know Skye very well. She was much more lethal than Gage was.

Damn! She is so hot. Stop. Focus on the asshole ex. Gage had to bring himself back to the situation at hand. What exactly was going on? He wasn't quite sure.

"Julian, I'm pretty sure Eve gave you all your stuff back. If there's something you *think* you need, just tell me and I'll ask her about it."

Man, you had to love a chick who could cut a guy off at the knees without even sounding like a bitch.

Even Julian knew better than to linger too much longer and let Skye have another chance at him. Gage had to give the prick at least that much; he was a quick learner.

"No, I just wanted to talk to her. I guess I forgot that she was out of town."

Was his voice actually trembling? Gage was impressed all over again. *I think I'm in love!*

"You don't have to tell her, though," Julian continued. "I'll just wait until she gets back and talk to her then. It was nothing important." He turned and, trying not to look like he had just been caught, walked back to the elevators.

When he was gone, Gage turned to look at Skye. She had a huge smile on her face.

"Uh, what just happened here?"

"Well, I was at lunch with Josie and Noelle at Marlowe's, and that asshole sat at the table next to us. I don't trust this prick at all. I mean, come on, anyone who knows us knows we can be found there every single Sunday. To top it off, he sat so we couldn't see him. *And* he was trying to listen to our conversation." Skye stopped and thought for a minute.

Gage wasn't sure what she was thinking about, but the way she looked at him made him want to push her up against the wall and do all the things he'd dreamt about last night. He was suddenly very aware that he was still in gym shorts, which were thin and had no pockets to allow him a quick adjustment.

Baseball. Suzanne. My grandma. Baseball. Suzanne. My grandma.

His excitement back in check, he looked at Skye. Fortunately, she didn't seem aware of Gage's Herculean calming effort. She had started her story again.

"...noticed that it was Julian. Josie was leaving to go pick up Beau at the airport, and Noelle had to get home to Thomas, so I decided to follow the creep. And sure enough, he came here."

"Skye! You can't just go following every moron out there. What if I hadn't come home? You would have been alone in the empty hallway with that guy." Gage wasn't sure how Skye would take his outburst. To his surprise, she lowered her eyes and stared at the floor for a moment.

"I knew that if I needed any help, you and all those *big* muscles of yours were right next door," she said as she looked back up at him from under her long eyelashes.

Is she flirting with me?

"I stayed in the stairwell until I saw you get off the elevator." She pushed her hand gently against Gage's chest and let it rest there. Just her touch had his mind wandering back to all those really naughty things.

"What do you think he was doing? Do you think he was just trying to talk to her?" Gage asked, trying to control his voice.

"No. He knew she wasn't here. She would have been at lunch with us. I just don't trust that asshole. It's a good thing Eve has you here to watch out for her." She started moving her hand up his chest, stepping closer to him as she did.

"You know, Gage, I was impressed with your performance last night," she continued. "I was wondering..."

Suddenly Skye's phone rang out, cutting off what she was about to say.

Are you kidding me?

Skye glanced down to see who was calling. She looked a little pissed that the phone had interrupted their moment, too.

"It's Eve. I have to get it." The phone was still ringing.

"Are you going to tell her about Julian being here?" he asked, just as she flipped her phone open.

"Hey, Eve! What's up?" she said, and shook her head at Gage.

Sensing this was the end of his time with Skye, Gage turned to go to his apartment. When he looked back to wave to her, Skye put the tips of her fingers to her lips, kissed them, and blew the kiss at him. He unlocked his door and slipped in before his damn flimsy gym shorts gave anything more away. He could hear her beautiful giggle as she talked to Eve and the clicking of her shoes in the hall as she made her way to the elevator.

All Gage could think about was her legs and where they ended just under that very short skirt. He immediately felt the effect of his imagination.

That's enough, Gage. Get your ass in gear or you'll be late for the club. Cold shower. Cold shower.

Chapter Six

Eve couldn't get into her hotel room fast enough. Once she did, she closed the door, dropped her things, and jumped on the king-size bed, cell phone in hand.

"Hey, you've reached Josie! Sorry I can't take your ca—"

Eve snapped the phone shut, then re-opened it to call Skylar instead. She had to talk to one of them before she exploded with excitement. Eve tapped out the rhythm of the wonderful song Will had played in the car while she waited for her friend to answer the phone.

"Skye!" *Yay!*

"Hey, Eve. What's up?" Skye sounded a little distracted, but Eve didn't care. This was too good not to share!

"I am *so* glad you're there! Oh, have I got things to tell you and Josie. I wish you were here right now so I could show you my room and tell you about everything!"

"Eve. *Eve*! Damn, girl, slow down. What'd you do, hook up to a caffeine IV or something? Just breathe for a second, will ya?"

Yes, good idea, Eve thought, stopping to take a deep breath before continuing. "Oh, Skye. I have just spent the last hour with *the most gorgeous guy* that I have *ever* seen in my *life*! Oh, I wish you could have been here to see him. No, wait, scratch that. If *you* had seen him, you would have already had your way with him in an airport broom closet. Oh my *word*, Skye. He is incredible!"

"OK, Eve, you're going to have to back up a little because I'm not quite getting the connection between you going to Boston to present our proposal to a bunch of old stuffed shirts and some gorgeous guy you just spent the last hour with." Skye was trying her best to be patient. "Wait a minute! Did *you* just spend the last hour in an airport broom closet with this guy? Because if you did, I am *very* impre—"

"No, Skylar. As much as I wanted to, I totally behaved myself the entire time we were together."

"You were with some hot guy in a city where nobody knows who you are and you chose to *behave*?" Skye was unimpressed. She sneered the last word as if Eve had done something so sinful she needed to go to confession. "Have I taught you *nothing* about seizing opportunities like this? Damn!"

"Skye. He's my escort for the week!" Eve wasn't sure why she was feeling guilty about being a perfect lady with Will. Only Skye could make her feel that way. She heard Skye giggling and realized her word choice had been a mistake.

"Before you get your mind heading down *that* path, he's the rep from Townsend Industries," Eve explained. "He's going to be the one making sure I get to the various meetings while I'm here. He met me at the airport and drove me to the hotel."

The hotel! Eve got up from the bed and walked around the spacious two-room suite that would be hers for the next four days.

"And the hotel, Skye! Townsend Industries upgraded me to the Fairhaven in downtown Boston! It's got to be, like, $500 a night here—and *they're* paying for it. No roach motel for me! Isn't that amazing? My room is huge, with a living room *and* a bedroom and..." She moved to the window and opened the drapes. "Skye, this view..."

"Yeah, yeah, the view is amazing, right?" Whenever Skye spent time at a hotel, her views were generally limited to her reflection in the bathroom mirror or the ceiling over the bed. "Get back to the hot guy, will you?"

"Oh...Will." Eve immediately felt warmth creep into her cheeks. "Skye, he is beautiful! Can I *say* that about a guy? I mean, I have no other way to describe him. And he's *nice,* too. Really sweet."

"Forget 'sweet.' Are you gonna get a chance to *do it* with him while you're there?"

Ah, dear Skye, Eve thought. *Always cutting to the chase.* "This is a *business* trip. He is completely professional, and I plan to be the same with him and everyone else I meet."

"Yeah. But you wouldn't be opposed to mixing business with pleasure with this guy, would you?"

Eve's hesitation told Skye all she needed to know.

"Well, I *will* have the 'pleasure' of his company this evening," said Eve. "He asked me to go to dinner with him."

"Oh, are you shitting me? He's known you for, what, an hour and he's already hitting on you?"

"I don't know. He really took me by surprise when he asked me." Eve knew she must have looked stunned at the elevator. She couldn't read him but she also couldn't resist him. *Those eyes...that smile...*"He probably did this with the other two applicants," she rationalized. "It must have been listed on the agenda and I just didn't see it."

Eve quickly accessed the stapled packet from her purse and looked at Day One's activities: Arrival at Logan International Airport, car service to motel in Framingham, dinner/evening at the discretion of the grant applicant.

"Hmmm. The itinerary doesn't indicate dinner with anyone from the BMA or Townsend. Hmm..."

"Oh, Eve! You've got yourself an opportunity to have some *fun* tonight with this guy! Was he flirting with you at all?"

"No. Like I said, he's been totally professional." Eve ran through the afternoon with Will in her mind. Yes, he'd smiled and looked at her a lot, but she didn't know him—that could just be how he was. Like one of those people who has to hug everyone all the time.

He must have offered dinner since he knew she'd never been to Boston before. Maybe he took the other applicants out, too, or at least offered to. This would be business. Strictly business. *And I have never looked forward to a business dinner so much in my life!* Eve thought, a huge grin plastered on her face.

"What are you going to wear?" Skye's tone was a little terse. Eve wondered how many times her friend had asked the question while she was off inventing scenarios to explain her dinner invitation.

"I have no idea," Eve confessed.

The two spent the last five minutes of their phone call with Eve describing what she'd brought and Skye critiquing—and criticizing—the options. Eve had packed all the high-necked tops she could, not knowing how long it would take for the bruises on her neck to fade. She was still not certain she'd be able to wear the off-the-shoulder cocktail dress she'd brought for Thursday night's affair.

In the end, Skye was no help at all, and Eve made the decision herself. By the time she settled on a longer black skirt and lavender ribbed turtleneck, it was already 6:15. Looking around at the entire contents of her suitcase strewn around the room, Eve took a few minutes to actually unpack. When she was done, she inspected the room once again, stopping at the window to take in the amazing view. Whatever Eve had imagined this trip to be, everything was now completely different. So much better. She laid out what she'd need for tonight and headed to the bathroom for a shower.

When she was finally dressed and willing to look in the full-length mirror, she couldn't help but smile. Her ensemble outlined her body nicely but discretely. *I look good,* Eve thought. And then she reconsidered. *No, you look* hot, *and you know it!*

At precisely 7:45, the telephone rang.

"Hello. It's Will Prentiss from Townsend Industries." He sounded so formal, and like he actually thought Eve could have possibly forgotten him. This made her smile. "Would you still like to go out to dinner?"

Eve's smile faltered a little. Did he regret having asked her?

"I only ask because I failed to provide you with any way to contact me if you changed your mind, and I was concerned that perhaps you were tired from your flight or preferred a quiet evening in your room."

Eve let out a small breath. "Oh, no. I mean, yes, I'd still like to have dinner. If you're still asking me?" She felt her face turn hot. She was making a fool of herself.

"Yes, I'm still asking."

"Then I'll be down in just a minute." Eve was sure he could hear the excitement in her voice and was a little embarrassed as she hung up. She quickly went back to the bathroom mirror for one last check of her hair, which she had decided to wear straight down, just in case the turtleneck wasn't enough to hide the bruises. After putting on a little lip gloss, she tossed the tube into her purse along with her cell phone and room key. Grabbing her black wool coat, Eve stuffed her beret into one of its pockets and headed out the door.

Eve's heart raced as the elevator descended to the lobby, but when the doors opened and she saw Will leaning against the wall about twenty feet away, she was pretty sure her heart actually stopped for a moment. He had been dressed nicely at the airport, but standing in front of her now was a man who was turning her into mush. *Pull yourself together! He's just being a polite Boston business rep taking a client out to dinner—that's all. Don't you* dare *think of this as a* date*!*

Will smiled as she approached. "Are you ready for our date?" he asked.

Eve's eyes went wide. Could he read her thoughts? Was he teasing her?

The shocked look on Eve's face had Will trying to backtrack, and quickly. He hadn't meant to use the word "date." She just looked so perfect, and it slipped out before he could think to stop himself.

"I mean our *dinner*," Will corrected.

I think I just caught him blushing again! Eve thought. She nodded as Will directed her toward the door.

They walked through the lobby, neither of them daring to look at the other. Just as they were about to step outside, he paused.

"You may want to put your coat on. The place we're going is about four blocks away so I thought we'd walk, but the wind can be a bit harsh in the evenings."

Will graciously helped Eve into her coat and stepped back as she adjusted the sleeves. He swept his arm outward, indicating the direction of their path, and they began to walk. The sidewalk was busy, but not crowded. Most of the people they passed were dressed in "after work" attire, and there were lots of couples, many huddling close to minimize the chill of the wind. *Huddling with Will would be* very *nice, with or without the excuse of a cold wind*, Eve thought.

"I really do apologize for my faux pas back there," Will said, breaking the silence. "You just took me by surprise. In all honesty I really haven't been on an actual date in, well, longer than I care to admit. And well, you do look very nice tonight."

"Thank you." She glanced quickly up at his face and smiled. She was grateful for the cold at that moment, hoping she could use it as an excuse for the pink she knew was coloring her cheeks. He held her gaze for a moment, and then they both turned their eyes ahead again. *He seems so sincere,* Eve thought. He wasn't trying to be funny or inappropriate with her. *But if this is his way of flirting, he can just keep on doing it. Stop it! This is a* business *dinner, Eve, a* business *dinner!*

Within ten minutes they had arrived at their destination. Sort of. They were at the entrance to a glass-front professional building, and Apex, the restaurant, was located on the 52nd floor. As they began their ascent, Eve was thankful to be sharing the elevator with six other people; their lack of conversation did not seem awkward or out of place.

When the elevator doors slid open, Eve couldn't help but gasp as the restaurant came into view; its earth-tone colors and crisp lines were simple yet sophisticated. Without a doubt, it was the nicest—and most expensive—restaurant Eve had ever been to. The Santa Barbara Museum of Art had provided Eve with a credit card for use during her trip, but she immediately worried that when the directors saw what she had spent the first night they'd regret ever sending her.

"Mr. Prentiss! So good to see you again!" Eve's trepidation only increased when the hostess greeted Will by name.

"Thank you, Arlene." A stout woman wearing a black sequined pantsuit approached Will with the open arms of an aunt greeting her favorite nephew. They leaned in to give each other a quick kiss on the cheek. *Like in an old movie*, Eve thought. "Arlene, this is Ms. Eve Carwyn of California, and she is visiting our lovely city for the first time."

"Ahh… Say no more, Mr. Prentiss." She turned her exuberant smile from Will to Eve and, grasping Eve's right hand in both of hers, added, "We shall be sure to make a wonderful and lasting impression on you, Ms. Carwyn. Welcome to Apex."

Eve could tell the table Arlene showed them to was reserved for the restaurant's preferred guests: It was away from the common pathways used by the wait staff and located along the ceiling-to-floor windows that overlooked the sparkling city below. Their table, like every one they'd passed, was adorned with a small sculpture. Will explained that these, and the paintings displayed throughout the large room, were a way for the restaurant to showcase local and international artists' work.

Eve was overwhelmed as she quickly scanned the room and then leaned in to examine the clay-colored sculpture of a woman in front of her; the place was absolutely breathtaking. *I should use my* own *credit card for this one,* she quickly decided. *I'm not sure the SBMA put enough on the corporate card.*

"Good evening, I'm Michael and I'll be your server." The man had a delightful smile and a hint of a Boston accent. "Here are your menus. We have a few specials, if you would care to hear what they are." Will and Eve both nodded, and Michael explained in fully memorized detail the additional entrees the chef was offering this evening. He then bowed politely and let them know he'd be back with water in a moment.

As Eve began to look over the menu, which didn't include any prices (*not a good sign, Eve!*), Will reviewed the wine list.

When Michael returned, Will looked across the small table. "Would you like a glass of wine?"

"Oh, yes, please. Do you have any suggestions for someone who likes Pinot Grigio?"

Michael pointed out a few options to Will. "A bottle of this, please," Will said, placing a finger on his selection for them.

Once Will had ordered the wine, they ordered their dinner as well. Eve insisted that she wanted to eat light, so Michael suggested the fish. Will ordered the braised lamb shank. Once Michael collected the menus and left, Will leaned forward, his forearms against the edge of the table and his hands clasped in front of him.

"Now," he began, "since this is not a *date*, we'll need to keep our conversation strictly business-centered. Deal?"

Laughing, Eve nodded. *Strictly business*. She knew she shouldn't be disappointed, but she felt a small twinge tug at her heart.

"OK, I'll start. What is your role in applying for this grant? What do you do for the Santa Barbara Museum of Art that has resulted in you being in Boston this week?"

Eve explained that she was the museum's curator and, when Will's eyebrows went up in a "but you look so young" look, she added that this was a new position for her, having been an assistant for the previous four years.

Will watched her face light up as she talked about her work. He wanted to see that look in her eye again, so he asked her everything he could under the cover of "business conversation" until their meals arrived. He wanted to ask her why she was letting strange men kiss her at Stratus, and who had hurt her, and what she wanted out of life. But he knew he couldn't.

The way he looked at her, soaking in what she was telling him, had Eve mesmerized. *I don't care what anyone wants to call this. It* feels *like a date—a* fantastic *date!*

After sampling their delicious dinners, the conversation turned to Will's background. Eve was eager to find out as much as she could about him. The hard part was keeping everything professional. She decided to start with simple things.

"Educational background?"

"Harvard," Will said. "Graduated with a degree in mechanical and biomedical engineering."

"Wow. Impressive," Eve said. She found herself even more amazed by this man sitting across from her. "Hometown?"

"You're looking at it."

"And what is it that you do for Townsend Industries?"

With this question, Will swallowed hard and quickly took a sip of wine. He chose his words carefully. "Well, it's a small company so I, along with everyone else, am responsible for a little bit of everything."

"Like?" Eve continued to probe.

"Well, I have two passions." He looked up at her through his eyelashes as he said this.

Would you like a third? Eve thought.

"First, I love to design—you know, invent new things. Our company motto is 'Innovations for Life,' and we are very dedicated to making a positive impact on the medical community. Our first big break was the development of the Townsend defibrillator. That invention has made us a lot of money, but more importantly, it is credited with saving more than 2000 lives worldwide in the past five years."

"Wow. That is quite impressive. Did you design this device?"

"Well," Will hesitated, taking another sip of wine. "I had a hand in it anyway."

He seemed nonchalant, but Eve wondered if Will Prentiss was due more credit than he was willing to admit. She decided not to press him further.

"And your second passion?" This time Eve was the one to look up demurely.

"The arts." Eve could not contain her smile at this simple answer. "My mo—my *family* has always believed it is important to learn about the art of every culture." Will leaned in toward Eve again like he had when they'd first been seated.

"When I was growing up, we would visit museum after museum, art show after art show, and see every theater production and symphony concert. It was crazy, really, but *that's* what we did for fun on the weekends. I played a little baseball and hockey as a kid, but I often missed games because of some new exhibit or show." Will looked off at the city lights below. "But it was all good. When I got into a little rebellious trouble when I was around fifteen, my 'punishment' was that I had to go to Dorchester twice a week and teach art classes. At the time, I hated it. But now I understand the importance of art and *teaching kids* about art. In fact, Townsend has backed the program I worked with all those years ago, and I still go and work with the kids when I can. At Townsend Industries, I take sole responsibility for determining and maintaining the charitable work we do with various art programs and museums."

Eve was amazed by the similarities in their childhoods. "In Santa Barbara, not a week went by that I wasn't dragged off to some art or music festival," she said. "But I remember, when I complained pretty loudly once when I was about twelve, my mother simply said to me, 'Eve, when archeologists dig up ancient ruins, what do they find?' I didn't follow her line of thinking and told her in a smart-aleck way that they find pots and jewelry and tombs full of treasure."

Will could already see where she was going with this, a hint of a smile playing on his lips.

"And then she said, 'Eve, the last time you were at the museum, how many math tests did you see displayed behind glass? How many spelling lists? And when someone writes a will, do you think they include those items?' And then, I 'got' it." Eve relaxed her shoulders, only then realizing she had been keeping them tense. She sat back in her chair and took a sip of wine. "It wasn't that my mom thought math and spelling weren't important—they were vital! But that wasn't *all* we needed to learn. It is the *art* and the *music* and the *literature* that are worth passing on, and are even 'worshipped,' in a way, through museums and concert halls and libraries and festivals."

Will's eyes just sparkled, never blinking and never breaking from hers.

He understands, Eve realized. More than that, he knew that *she* understood and shared his passion for the arts. *Wow. If Skye were here, she would describe this as a simultaneous intellectual climax!*

At that moment, Michael approached hesitantly, clearing his throat to get Will's attention. As he slipped him the burgundy leather folder containing the bill, Eve immediately reached for her purse, but Will raised his palm slightly toward her to stop.

"Please, let me," he said. "I was the one who asked you to join me this evening, and I wouldn't be playing a very good host if I let you even *touch* the bill!" He gave her that smile that made everything else disappear. "Now remember, this was not a *date* or anything just because I'm paying." He winked. "This was a *business dinner*. Remember that! Otherwise I won't feel right when I write this off on my taxes." *Again with the smile!* The mixed signals were driving Eve crazy.

As they walked past the host's podium, Arlene stopped them to ask if everything had been to their satisfaction. Will and Eve both agreed that the meals and service were perfect. Arlene embraced Will again, thanking him for coming, and then surprised Eve by also pulling her into a warm hug. As they turned to leave, Eve noticed that Will's and Arlene's eyes met, and Will smiled and winked.

When they reached the ground-floor lobby of the building, Eve once again put on her coat and this time donned her beret, certain that the temperature had dropped in the past few hours.

"Nice look." Will smiled his pulse-racing smile as he glanced from her hat to her face. Once again, Eve didn't know how to take his comments. With a small sigh, she pushed through the door back out into the cold Boston night.

Eve immediately closed her coat tighter around her with one hand and placed her other on her beret to keep it from flying off. The wind had really picked up, and her cheeks burned. They headed quickly down the sidewalk toward the Fairhaven Hotel, both of them eager to be indoors again. As they crossed an alleyway, a strong gust knocked Eve off balance, sending her falling toward Will. He was quick to put one hand under her forearm and the other gently across the small of her back. *Mmmm...we're huddling a little,* she thought, suddenly not minding the cold. He continued to guide her, and protect her from the wind, for the remaining half-block to the entrance of the hotel.

Safely back in the lobby, Eve removed her coat and beret and quickly swung her hair to get it back to "pre-hat" condition. Thawing out, they stood awkwardly for a few moments. Then over Will's shoulder, Eve noticed the entrance to a cocktail lounge, and hoped their evening didn't have to be over yet.

"After you've treated me to such a lovely meal, may I at least buy *you* a drink before we say goodnight?" Eve was being bold, but she didn't care. She didn't want him to leave.

"Absolutely." Will's smile became radiant. "But on one condition. We must allow ourselves to learn at least one thing about the other that is *not* business-related. Are you game?" His look became mischievous, and Eve threw all her calculations about the business or pleasure nature of their evening out the window again.

"Are there any other rules to this game?" she asked.

"Hmm, no. I don't think so. We'll just have to play and see."

They entered the lounge and selected the two seats at the bar that were farthest from the television.

Eve ordered one more glass of wine but Will decided on tonic water. "I've got to drive home," he explained.

"All right." He turned toward her, leaning his hand against his temple and his elbow on the edge of the bar. He sounded like he was scheming, his face becoming almost devilish. "What do I want to know about you that *isn't* business-related? Hmm."

Eve began to sense that she had just stepped into a snake pit.

"OK," he continued. "Now I'll certainly understand if you don't want to answer. Just tell me if you want a different question."

Eve was getting nervous now.

"Are you currently in a relationship with someone?"

Simple question, loaded answer, Eve thought. Before answering, she reflexively brought her hand to the collar of her turtleneck, making sure it was where it should be. *Good. Bruises are still hidden.*

"No."

"Is that all you're going to tell me?" He frowned.

"The phrasing of your question called for a yes-or-no answer, not an explanation."

"Can I ask the question over then?"

Eve considered telling him he could ask her anything he wanted to, but instead she adopted a saucy tone. "I'll think about it. In the meantime, it's my turn to ask *you* a question." This time Eve was the one to adopt a devilish look. "What is one significant detail you are willing to share about a current or previous relationship, prefaced by which it is—current or previous?"

He dropped his shoulders, clearly beaten at his own game. Then his dimpled smile returned. "You're good. You sure you didn't study law in college?"

"I'm waiting for your answer." Eve grinned triumphantly.

"OK. My *previous* relationship ended fairly recently, once I came to my senses that all she was looking for was status and recognition. Mine was a name she could throw around the social circles here in Boston, and frankly, I just got tired of it."

Eve quickly processed what he had told her. It seemed like he was probably single now—unless he was talking about his *last* girlfriend and had a better one now that he didn't want to talk about. Eve realized she might not have learned anything at all.

"My turn again? I mean, can I ask you another question?"

Eve nodded yes and took a gulp of wine.

"It's a double question—just in case you decide to end the game before I can ask the second one." He studied Eve's face to be sure she was still a willing participant. "What was a reason your last relationship *started* as well as a reason it *ended*?"

"Who's the lawyer now with the tricky, multi-faceted questioning technique, eh?" She smiled coyly at him.

He brought his hands together in his lap and shrugged his shoulders sheepishly.

"OK. Well, we *started* dating because of our common interest in art. He fascinated me with his intelligence and worldliness, and his paintings were full of emotion—he could convey tremendous passion or terrifying rage on a canvas. I was mesmerized by him—there's just no other way to describe it. But, then there were times he'd be gone for days. He'd tell me he was a guest lecturer at a university somewhere but would never call or return my calls while he was gone. Once, when I checked on him, the university where he said he was going didn't even know who he was. When I asked him about it, he avoided answering and turned it around so I was the bad guy for not trusting him. He was moody—and my friends felt he was too controlling. And...I could see their point. So, I finally ended it."

Will was quiet, soaking in what Eve had told him. He continued to just look at her, studying her.

What are you trying to figure out about me, Will Prentiss? "Um, I think I'd better head up to my room now, you know? Busy day tomorrow." Eve finally broke the silence hanging between the two of them.

Taking out some cash, enough for their drinks and a tip, Eve left it next to their empty glasses. Will stood up and offered his hand to her. She gladly took it, carefully slipping off the raised barstool.

As they walked to the elevator, both stole small glances at the other, each trying not to get caught. Eventually they both stared at the numbers over the doors, as the elevator gradually approached the lobby.

"Thank you for a wonderful evening." This came out of Eve's mouth, but her mind was actually screaming, "*Don't leave! Come up to my room, spend more time with me even if it's just to talk.*"

"Thank *you* for a wonderful non-date business-dinner evening." Will said with a laugh—hitting the evening's running joke one more time. "I truly enjoyed your company and look forward to seeing you at our meeting tomorrow."

The elevator dinged, and the doors opened. Eve entered and immediately spun around to get one last glimpse of Will. He seemed to do the same, locking his eyes on hers until the metal doors separated them.

As the elevator took Eve to her floor, she couldn't help but compare Julian and Will—two men so passionate about art, two men who fascinated her so thoroughly, two men who could not have been more different.

Tonight, I will dream about Will, she told herself.

Will couldn't move. He couldn't take his eyes off the elevator doors. When they closed, he felt a sudden and overwhelming ache, like he'd just lost part of himself. He willed them to open again so Eve could come rushing into his arms and he could hold her tightly and bury his face in her hair and never let her go. It had been a perfect evening until the moment she said goodnight and left him to stand here without her. *What are you doing to yourself, Prentiss?*

He was in love with her. Right then, right there, he knew it, and he wanted so badly to go up to her room—professionalism be damned—and tell her. He didn't want to have to wait until tomorrow to see her again.

Minutes passed as he just stood there. Finally, he willed himself to put on his coat and head to his car. He didn't have far to drive, but as he started the car, the CD that had been playing earlier began again. Lila Marin's sweet voice sang "the memory of every moment...don't let it go...the love will wash over you...don't let go...stay with me...don't go..."

Will had found Eve intriguing from the first time he saw her at the museum in Santa Barbara. That night at Stratus had only added to his interest. And tonight, he had found her intelligent, passionate, sexy, wonderful. He had *found her.*

Chapter Seven

"I'd like *une avocate salade avec le fromage du cheval*, please." Jeannette Sheldon, the Boston Museum of Art's curator, attempted to ask for an avocado salad with goat cheese in French. Eve's head shot up at the horrible mispronunciation and quickly scanned the table to see if others had noticed. Both Will and Martin Calloway, Townsend Industries' financial advisor, were still perusing their menus.

The waiter was clearly insulted at the way this woman had butchered his native tongue, but Eve caught his eye and smiled in a "please forgive her" way. Eve had already ordered her meal in perfectly accented French, and it seemed Jeannette was hoping to one-up her. Will glanced curiously at Eve as she ordered, and noticing the rise of his eyebrow, Eve mouthed, "minored in French." Her admission earned her a knowing nod and one of Will's heart-stopping smiles.

Unfortunately, Will's reaction also earned her a death stare from Jeannette.

Eve sighed, glad the informational meeting portion of the day was already over and hoping Jeannette didn't wield too much influence over who would receive the grant. However, despite Jeannette's current hostility, Eve was pretty sure the morning meeting had gone well. Jeannette spent much of the time explaining other projects the BMA-Townsend Charitable Foundation had taken on in the past and their current status, including how much and the manner in which each grant had been spent. Eve had been a bit surprised to note that previous grants had most often involved traveling exhibits.

She realized how different her museum's proposal would be. The SBMA would use the grant from Townsend to build a whole new permanent wing on their museum. She hoped this new approach to using the grant was what had earned their proposal a place in the final three.

After the meeting, the four of them had decided to go to lunch. And given the fact that there were two men and two women, it probably looked like two couples dining together, except that neither Jeannette nor Eve would have wanted to be considered Martin's date. However, Eve didn't think he minded the lack of female attention, as Martin's one true love was numbers. He typified the term "nerd" right down to his horn-rimmed glasses, white socks, and penny loafers. He was money-smart, though, that much was very evident. Throughout the meeting, Martin had leaned over to whisper to Will every time Jeannette showed slides about how the grant money was being spent, seemingly to point out particular line items and expenditures. There were a few times Eve saw Will purse his lips in frustration.

The host had seated the group at a round table, with Jeannette and Eve sitting on either side of Will. Jeannette had immediately moved her chair to be noticeably closer to him. To say she was beautiful was an understatement: a leggy blonde with light-blue eyes, well-defined cheekbones, and collagen-filled lips, she could have given Skylar a run for her money. Eve suddenly felt a little...less.

Not helping the situation was the fact that from the moment they had arrived, Jeannette had been very obviously flirting with Will. She found every opportunity to touch his arm, laugh at something he said, and even wink at him as she made comments with some kind of double meaning. In response, Will was simply polite, involving everyone in the conversation and refusing her any special attention.

Eve knew this because she couldn't help but watch the two of them keenly. And she was jealous as hell. She wanted to be the one to bat her eyes at Will and drag her finger over his arm. But, as that would be grossly inappropriate, Eve simply sat and watched things play out in front of her—gritting her teeth every time Jeannette touched Will.

When lunch was over, Jeannette nodded politely to Martin but pulled Will into a close embrace. Eve's hands curled into fists at her side. *She may as well be lifting her leg and peeing on him*, Eve thought. It didn't escape her attention, however, that while Will hugged her back, he broke away from her quickly. Jeannette pouted and placed her well-manicured hands on either side of his face. Then she stroked his cheek with her thumb as if to wipe off lipstick she had left there.

Once everyone else said their cursory goodbyes and Eve and Will were walking in the opposite direction of Jeannette and Martin, Will let out a slight laugh.

"I am *so* sorry for that!" He looked down at the sidewalk in front of them. "She can get a bit out of hand sometimes."

Eve didn't know what to say, so she chose to remain silent.

When she did not respond, Will turned to sneak a look at her. She didn't appear upset, just...accepting, so he decided not to say any more. If she was going to let it go, who was he to keep going?

"So, you're in a new city, and you've got a list of suggestions for sight-seeing," he said instead. "Would you like to do that on your own or would you like a tour guide for the afternoon?" Will flashed the smile he knew women swooned over.

"Uh, but don't you have to work?"

"Remember, I'm the grant rep this week," he said. "My job is to take care of our guest. Besides, everything is under control. Megan keeps me posted when things come up, and I don't anticipate any emergencies on the horizon. I'm available if you want me."

Oh, the thoughts that statement was conjuring. "That would be wonderful, thank you." Eve was able to control the tone of her voice and kept it smooth and even, though inside she was screaming. Will's face broke into that grin again, and Eve knew he was pleased she had agreed to his suggestion. She couldn't help but wonder if the other candidates for this grant had received such star treatment from Will. She hoped *not.*

"Then, how about this for a plan: I'll walk you back to the hotel so you can change, then I'll go to my apartment and do the same, and we can meet back in the lobby at, say, 2:30? That would allow for two hours at the museum anyway." He looked at Eve, trying to read her thoughts. Her face lit up with a radiant smile. That gave him courage to continue, "And I'd like to show you the town this evening, too—introduce you to some places only true Bostonians know about."

Eve smiled and nodded. The idea of spending another evening with this man had her almost giddy. She was feeling like a teenager again, asked out by the captain of the football team.

It was already close to two by the time Eve got back to her room. Quickly changing into her khakis and a t-shirt, she examined her neck in the mirror. The bruises, while lighter, were definitely still there. All the wishing in the world wasn't making them disappear any faster.

With a small sigh, Eve applied some makeup to cover the worst of them, then arranged her hair to try and hide the rest. There really wasn't much more she could do. The weather was too warm for a turtleneck, and her outfit too casual for a scarf. She cursed Julian under her breath as she turned from the mirror.

It had only taken twenty minutes for Eve to change, but she was too excited to sit around her room and wait until 2:30. Grabbing her sweater and tying it around her waist, she headed out.

On the elevator down to the lobby all Eve could think about was Will. *Business, business, business,* she chanted in her head. Then the doors opened and there he was, leaning against the same wall as the previous night, dressed in jeans and a button-down shirt, with his fingers tucked slightly into his pockets. His smile temporarily stopped her heart.

As they headed out into the afternoon, Will longed to walk arm in arm to the museum, nuzzling Eve's hair and brushing kisses across her temple. In reality, they traveled side by side with a business-appropriate distance between them, chatting casually as Will doled out a few pieces of historical trivia. The museum was only three blocks south of the hotel, but the sidewalks were crowded so there were plenty of times the pair had to move in closer, or Will would gently place his hand on Eve's back to move her in front of him as they passed people. She didn't seem to mind these casual touches he was able to sneak in. Will tried to convince himself that he was simply being a gentleman.

As they toured the museum's Renaissance wing, admiring the paintings and tapestries that hung in the dim light, each took turns commenting on the pieces they liked or knew something about. Stopping in front of a battle scene during one of the Crusades, Eve said she remembered studying it in college. She pointed out a soldier who had two ears on the same side of his face and explained that the artist had originally placed the ear too far forward and had painted over it. During the restoration process, the second, more forward-placed ear had reappeared.

She amazes me more and more every moment I'm in her presence, Will thought.

It seemed as if mere minutes had passed when suddenly the museum's employees began to usher people toward the lobby. Glancing at his watch, Will was shocked to see it was already five o'clock—his time with Eve ticking away far too quickly.

As they exited the museum they were greeted by a cool blast of wind. In the few hours they had been inside the sky had become heavy and dark, and the wind had increased. It was still warm, which was welcome, but rain seemed imminent.

Hoping to avoid being caught in a downpour, they quickened their pace. Will steered them toward his favorite local diner, Mulligan Stew. Its quirky name fit its eclectic ambiance. The place was just two blocks from Will's apartment and offered decent sandwiches and simple dishes. He dined there with friends on occasion, and would often stop in on his own for a cup of coffee.

The bell that hung over the door jingled as Will pulled it open, announcing their entrance. He waved a hello to those who knew him, which, sadly, because he was a bachelor who worked way too much, was most of the staff.

Will led Eve to an open booth along the windowed front wall, waiting for her to sit before sliding in across from her. He pulled two menus out from behind the napkin holder and handed one to Eve.

"Is anyone here going to call you Mr. Prentiss?" Eve had a sly smile on her face and a sparkle in her eyes as she leaned in from across the table.

"No. Here I'm just a local guy who justifies their need for fresh coffee throughout the day." Will was embarrassed. "Because of

Townsend Industries and my work with the museum, I end up playing host to a lot of out-of-towners. The people at the hotel and some of the local restaurants have gotten to know who I am, that's all."

"You sound like you don't like it when they refer to you so formally." Will wasn't sure he liked that Eve could see right through him.

"It comes with the territory, I guess. I like to think that hotel and restaurant workers remember who I am because I treat them with as much respect as I do the clients I'm hosting, not because they're trying to impress me or earn a bigger tip. I work hard, so do they."

As they looked over the menu, Will suggested a few dishes and Eve elected to have a half-salad and a pressed Cuban sandwich. Will ordered a grilled chicken sandwich with a side of fresh fruit. When their meals arrived, he noticed that Eve eyeing his sandwich and made a move.

"How about we cut our sandwiches in half and share?"

Eve seemed delighted at the suggestion and quickly took a knife to her Cuban. Will loved watching the way the littlest things made her whole face light up.

As the night moved forward, the conversation became more casual. When Will asked Eve about her minor in French, she started to giggle. She put her hand across her mouth as she attempted to swallow mid-laugh. This reminded him that he wanted to ask her a question.

"What did Jeannette try to order, anyway?"

Eve broke out into a full laugh. "A lawyer salad with horse cheese!" Will joined her in her laughter, both nearly in tears over not only Jeannette's error, but the look on the waiter's face when she said it. They finally calmed down, but were still smiling when Eve added, "And Jeannette, poor thing, was so sure of herself and was trying so hard to impress you!"

Will bristled slightly. "Jeannette makes my life...interesting at times." He suddenly wanted—no, needed—to make it clear to Eve that he did *not* return Jeannette's feelings and had no desire to pursue her whatsoever. *Next to you, Jeannette is a shadow, a mere wisp of nothing,* he longed to say. But he knew he could never say that—at least not as long as her museum was in competition for the grant from Townsend.

"What do you mean?" Eve looked directly at him, and for a moment Will was lost.

He hesitated. *We're already into this conversation. What's the harm in setting the record straight?* "When I answered your question last night about my most recent relationship..." he let the statement trail off as he looked intently at Eve. Her eyes were bright with...what? Worry? Anticipation? Lust? Love? "We went out a few times, mostly to museum functions and fundraisers—black-tie affairs where who you were with was more important than the honesty of a relationship. Jeannette's a social climber and deserves to be with someone who doesn't mind being stepped on for her advancement."

He knew it sounded harsh, but he had to be sure Eve understood that Jeannette had been a brief fling and that was all. The waitress broke the tension as she laid the bill on the table. Will slipped cash directly to the waitress before Eve could react. She looked at him with a furrowed brow, but her eyes were sparkling. Giving her a "Sorry, I beat you to it" look—even though they both knew he wasn't sorry at all—Will slipped out of the booth and waited for Eve to do the same.

As they stepped out into the cool evening, Eve felt a sense of relief settle over her. She had no right to even care about Will's relationship with Jeannette, but knowing he wasn't currently involved with her—or anyone from what Eve could gather—made her feel better.

They turned east now, traveling another few blocks, and Will regaled Eve with the history of some of the buildings along the street. He told her he had lived in this area of Boston his whole life, and he was the third generation of Prentisses to live in his apartment, his grandparents having bought it years ago. But with his parents both now gone, he was the only remaining member of his family in Boston. His other relatives—cousins mostly—had relocated over the years to various cities around the country.

Eve felt a small pang in her chest at how lonely an existence Will seemed to lead. He didn't seem to have any close friends, at least he hadn't mentioned any, and no family to speak of. It made her appreciate her mother, and of course her "family" of friends in Santa Barbara.

As they walked, the weather turned stormier, and the sky looked like it was about to open up—and then it did. What started as a sprinkle soon became heavy drops of rain. Before they could find cover, the clouds let loose, and they were stuck in an all-out downpour.

People everywhere were scrambling for open doorways or their cars, seeking shelter from the deluge. The rain was loud as it banged into auto roofs and splattered against the street and sidewalks. A flash of lightning erupted in the distance, and the boom of the thunder soon followed. This was going to be a bad storm.

Will crouched closely and all but yelled in Eve's ear, "Will you trust me about where I'm going to take you?"

"Why?" she called out to him.

"Because I want to take you to my apartment. It's just one block further."

"Yes—but hurry! I don't like how close the lightning is!" Eve peered up into his face through the rain. The way he looked at that moment...

My word, this man overwhelms me even when he's soaking wet.

Will grabbed Eve's hand and began to sprint along the sidewalk, not even trying to avoid the puddles and streams of water gushing from the gutters.

By the time they reached the small entrance to the brownstone, they were drenched from head to toe—and laughing heartily. They sloshed over to the elevator, leaving a trail of footprint-shaped puddles behind on the ancient carpet.

His apartment—*his apartment!* Eve thought somewhat nervously—was at the top of the nine-story building. On the ride up he explained that his apartment was actually half of the top floor of the building, and there was only one other apartment he shared the space with. He told her that originally there had been six separate small apartments, but after he bought the other two on his side of the hallway and renovated it to one large loft, the building's owner decided to convert the other three as well. What he didn't tell her was that he was the owner.

They left the floor of the elevator a slippery hazard, but Will knew there was a yellow caution cone in the super's closet. He had

Eve hold the elevator door open while he grabbed the cone and placed it in the middle of the elevator.

As they stepped into the empty hallway, Eve felt a chill and crossed her arms, hoping to hide any evidence. Will was pulling his keys from his pocket when his gaze fell on Eve's clingy wet t-shirt. When Eve caught him glancing at her chest, his eyes darted quickly to hers and he knew he'd been caught in the act. Coughing uncomfortably, he refocused his efforts on unlocking the door.

Will let Eve enter his apartment ahead of him. He then closed and locked the door and placed his keys on the entryway table. She immediately removed her shoes and shivered. She was freezing but trying to take in the apartment at the same time. It was spacious, with high ceilings bordered in dark crown moldings, and it was beautifully decorated with rich mahoganies, tasteful artwork, and classic lines and color schemes. Definitely masculine, but from a by-gone era. *Humphrey Bogart would feel at home here.*

Will interrupted Eve's inspection of his place. "There's a bathroom just down that hallway. I'm thinking I need to get you some dry clothes. I've got a dryer to put our wet things in. I'm pleased to say that I don't keep any women's clothing here, but that means I'll have to loan you something of mine, if that's all right." He hesitated. "I mean, I guess the alternative would be for you sit around in a towel until your clothing is dry."

They both blushed at that.

"Right. Something of mine then."

Eve watched as Will started toward what must have been his bedroom, but he turned back before entering. "I'm sorry, this is awkward. But I'm guessing, based on how soaked I am, that your underclothing may also need to go in the dryer? Would you, um, want to wear a pair of my boxers under the sweatpants I'm going to bring you?" He winced in embarrassment as he spoke. "I'll find a shirt for you, too, but I'm sorry I can't help with *that* undergarment," he said sheepishly as he nervously glanced again at her chest.

Eve had to bite at the inside of her cheek to keep from giggling. Will's face was precious, so flushed and childlike. Eve loved that despite how uncomfortable he was, he still wanted to accommodate her as much as possible.

She nodded and told him the shirt and sweatpants would be fine. "Thanks for the offer of the boxers, but I think I'll go without anything for a little while." At this point, Eve was having way too much fun watching him blush. She winked at him, entered the bathroom, and closed the door behind her. The room was elegant, with gold fixtures and marble throughout. Even the ceiling was ornate.

Will stood frozen at the bathroom door, his emotions running amok. He was thrilled that Eve was here, but mindful that this could be a potentially compromising situation. There was no way he could ever let anyone on the grant committee know he'd had the third prospect in his apartment—even if the circumstances that led to it were surely justified.

It had never been his intention that they would end up at his place—that was all on Mother Nature. But now that she *was* there, what opportunities lay ahead for this evening? Could he tell her about his visit to Santa Barbara, that night at Stratus? *The kiss?* No. Someday, but not tonight.

Along the wall next to the claw-footed tub were two thick bath towels. Eve quickly undressed and wrapped herself in one of them, securing it as best she could across her chest. Then she flipped her head down toward her knees and used the other towel to rub briskly, trying to hasten the drying of her still very wet hair.

The idea to call Skye, just to tell her that she was standing, practically naked, in Will's bathroom, crossed her mind. Skye would certainly have some helpful tips about what to do. Eve giggled, and her rambling thoughts were interrupted by a gentle knock at the door.

Will called out, "Um, I have some clothes for you." Eve opened the door just wide enough for him to pass things through to her, but the mirror allowed him to catch a glimpse of her standing behind the door. She was breathtaking. "I looked for a sweatshirt for you but they were all huge, so what you've got instead is one of my old baseball shirts. I hope that's OK."

Eve closed the door, and Will returned to his room to change. He turned on the shower, originally wanting to warm himself. But when he realized just how quickly his body had reacted to that one enticing glimpse of Eve, he decided to let the water run a little cooler than normal.

When he was clean, dry, and his body calmed, Will padded barefoot down the hallway, wearing a fresh pair of jeans and a t-shirt. Carrying his wet clothing, he stopped by the bathroom where he had left Eve. The small room was now empty, but the towels and her clothing lay in a neat pile in the tub. He put his things on top of hers and gathered them back into his arms.

On his way through the living room, Will spotted Eve. Her back was to him as she studied the many shelves of books that lined one of the walls. Letting her be, he continued on to the laundry room. Once there, he began sorting the clothing and towels—his things into the washer, hers directly into the dryer. He couldn't help but pause, allowing his fingers glide gently over her clothing. Will knew from Jeannette's many failed attempts at seducing him that she wore a thong; something that for one reason or another he associated with drunk college girls on spring break. He was infinitely grateful that Eve's items were satin and lace—modest, yet sexy.

"Um…do you want some help there?" Eve's question startled him, and his heart pounded at being caught red handed, or black-lace handed, actually. Thankfully, with his back to her, Eve couldn't see that he had been worshiping her delicates.

Recovering quickly, he turned to her and asked, "I...uh...um...are these OK to go in the dryer on regular heat?"

"Yes," she smiled coyly. "You can put all of my clothing in the dryer on the same setting, unless you feel the need to examine those further."

Will let his shoulders drop, his chin hitting his collarbone in defeat. Then he tilted his head and looked up at her sideways for forgiveness.

"Oh, quit with the sad puppy eyes," she said. "I guess it's only fair that you've seen my underwear—you *did* offer to let me see yours." Will was surprised to realize Eve was flirting with him. Not that he minded.

"My apologies—and my compliments to you on your previous attire. *All* of it." He decided if she could flirt, so could he. "And may I say you look lovely in your *new* attire as well."

She beamed and turned a full circle to show off his clothing. He had never seen anything sexier than Eve in his clothes. The only thing better would be his clothes in a pile and her on his bed.

"Why thank you. It's a Townsend original!"

Will was stunned. She was just kidding, he realized. She was referring to their conversation about Camille Townsend in the car yesterday. She didn't know any more than that. Yet.

"Oh, really?" he finally countered. "Well, she does design the most exquisite clothing line. The fine diagonal lines of a baseball shirt paired with drab gray sweatpants are the latest fashion for women caught in rainstorms, you know."

They both laughed, the embarrassment over the underwear evidently gone. Will closed and started the dryer, watching as Eve turned and headed back through the kitchen to the large sofa in the middle of the living room and plopped down comfortably. Will closed the laundry room door and stopped at the kitchen counter that separated the two of them.

"Are you still chilled?" Some distant thunder could be heard, but the rain had finally stopped.

"A little—but your sweats are helping to warm me up. Thanks again for your quick thinking when the rain started, and for providing me a change of clothing."

Will took a mental picture of her sitting there—something to keep for when she returned to Santa Barbara. After she was gone, Will would imagine her in that spot until he could get her to return.

"A glass of wine, perhaps?"

"Sure, what have you got?"

"Well, that's not an easy question to answer." Will looked at her and smiled. "Come here and select something you'd like."

Eve unfolded her legs and bounded into the kitchen, curiosity in her eyes. He led her to a large glass door along the back wall of the kitchen and opened it.

"You have a *wine cellar* in your *kitchen*?" Her mouth was agape as she glanced over row after row of bottles in the chilled little room. "I'm sorry for being so shocked, but this is a first for me. I'm quite impressed, *Mr. Prentiss*."

Once again, Will felt embarrassed. He never wanted to come across as high-brow, and he feared he was showing off to her.

"My grandfather had this room built in 1942. Being that he and my grandmother hosted many dinner parties for city officials and visiting celebrities, it made sense for him to have his own personal stash of favorite wines. Some of the bottles in here date back to the turn of the last century."

"So, *this* is the place you were talking about earlier? Your grandparents were the original owners, then?"

"Yes. When Boston was beginning to recover from the Depression, my grandfather was wise enough to invest all he could in land and construction. He helped the developers of this building because he wanted to buy the apartment on the top floor. He knew that when it was complete, he would have the grandest view of the city available at that time. And it's still not so shabby a view. Here, take a look for yourself."

Will splayed open the central panel in the row of French doors opposite the kitchen. Eve padded, on bare feet, to the balcony's brick ledge and leaned over, taking in the view. A breeze caught her hair, and she swung her head from side to side to clear her face. Will went and stood beside her, enjoying a different view: her. He loved how she soaked it all in. She closed her eyes and inhaled deeply, letting her head fall back and the gentle wind continue to toss her hair. *Oh, to kiss you right now . . .*

This time, he behaved. Or at least he tried, but his gaze lingered longer than it should have. Reaching back inside the doorway, he grabbed the small blanket that was lying across a wing chair. He opened it up and draped it across her back, letting his hands rest for a moment on her shoulders. Everything felt perfect: the night, the lights of the city, the woman who was almost in his arms.

Eve was startled by the blanket and looked back hesitantly at Will. Quickly stepping back, he moved his arms to his sides. "I'm sorry. I was worried about the cold, with your wet hair and all." Even to his own ears he sounded ridiculous.

Not wanting to ruin the moment, Eve simply smiled, pulling the blanket down over her shoulders more securely. "Thank you," she replied softly, then returned her gaze to the horizon.

"This view...I can see why your grandfather wanted this apartment so much. It's...wow."

"Well, my intention this evening was to show you the town from a true Bostonian's perspective. I guess I accomplished my mission after all, eh?" Will swept his arm out toward the open air. "Ms. Carwyn, *this* is Boston."

She once again leaned out, closing her eyes and enjoying the breeze. Will stood beside her, mimicking her stance. He closed his eyes as well, and then...

Her left hand was on his left hand, her fingers begging entrance between his, her thumb caressing his. He turned to her. She was looking for permission to continue, and he gave her no reason to stop. She gazed at him, holding his eyes to hers, and gently lifted his hand to her face. She opened his fingers and placed her mouth on his palm, kissing it slowly and tenderly. Then, closing her eyes, she placed his warm palm on her cheek, holding it there while she breathed a deep sigh.

Will stepped toward her, moving his hand from her cheek to the nape of her neck, letting his fingers get lost in her hair. As he slid his other hand around to the small of her back, the blanket slipped from her shoulders and silently fell to the floor. She lifted her hands to caress his face and pressed her body to his. Will began with lingering kisses on her forehead, but she brought her head upward, her mouth seeking his. Her lips were soft and inviting, and they were soon entwined in each other's arms, holding each other as closely as they could, their mouths full of want and desire.

He turned with her so that her back was to the city beyond them and lifted her up onto the brick ledge. Instantly she wrapped her legs around his waist, pulling him to her and locking her ankles behind him. Their kisses were deep, meaningful, honest, pure—so much more than the kiss they had shared in Santa Barbara.

Will finally broke from her lips and moved his mouth to her neck. He desperately wanted to replace her memory of the fiend who had hurt her with the tenderness—the love—he had to offer. This time she didn't wince at his touch as he kissed her over and over. Instead, she simply spoke his name: Will... *Will...*

"Will?"

Will opened his eyes, and the dream ended. Eve stood beside him, still wrapped tightly in the blanket he had given her.

"The dryer just stopped. I think I'd better be getting back to the hotel—presentation tomorrow, remember?"

Glancing down, Will prayed for no evidence of the thoughts he'd been having. Thankfully, Eve had already turned to go back inside.

"Yes, of course." Will adjusted himself and made sure his shirt sufficiently covered anything embarrassing before following Eve. "Would you like a bag to put your other clothes in and just keep mine on for the night? I've got a light jacket you can use as well."

Eve agreed, and Will quickly found a Saks bag for her clothing and a plastic grocery bag for her still-soaked shoes. He also brought his slippers for her bare feet. After slipping on a dry pair of shoes himself, he led her out of the apartment and down to his car.

Will caught her looking at him a few times during the short drive. It was nice. *It was amazing!*

As was becoming their habit, Will parked and walked her to the elevator where they said their goodnights.

"Thank you. I had the most wonderful time, Will. I appreciate you 'showing me the town.' You're a fantastic host and tour guide." Eve gave him another of her beautiful smiles and turned to enter the elevator.

As the doors closed, Will smiled as well. "It was truly my pleasure." He let out a breath as the doors closed, and Eve was gone.

Chapter Eight

Julian sat on the bench facing the largest piece in the Santa Barbara Museum of Art's Local Artist Gallery. *His* painting. He loved that from where he sat he could see and hear almost everyone in the gallery. A familiar sensation began flowing through his body at the thought of all these people admiring his work. The feeling was better than any drug or even sex. This is what he had been struggling and suffering for his entire life. And now, because of Eve, that could end.

Eve just didn't understand that all his success was because of her. She didn't understand that he could never let her go. Never let *this* go. Not only had she been the one to convince the museum to show his work; she was the inspiration behind it. If she were gone, Julian knew all this would be gone too.

That isn't going to happen. I will make her stay with me. He knew he could do it, too.

The incident the other day at her apartment flickered in his mind. Things had not gone the way he planned. He'd just wanted to talk to Eve. After going to that awful place where she met her friends every week to find she hadn't showed up, he had decided to check her apartment. All he wanted to do was explain what happened when she came to pick up her stuff. It was never his intention to hurt her. He just couldn't allow her to leave him. If she only knew, then she would understand and stay. And then *they* showed up. That bitch Skylar and the steroid freak neighbor.

Julian glanced over at another of his paintings hanging in the gallery. It was one of his more recent pieces. *Sins of Man* showed a bedroom floor with fancy-lace women's underthings, a pair of red high heels, and in the background, just out of focus, two entwined hands hanging off a bed. The piece was an homage to whores like Skylar. Whores like the ones his father took him to trying to "cure" him all those years ago.

Julian had told Eve over and over that Skylar wasn't the kind of friend she should have. His sweet, beautiful Eve being around a whore like that just made him even angrier every time he thought about it. Her revealing clothes, her foul mouth, and her overt sexual behavior... Eve was better than that.

They'd had several arguments over the few months they'd been together about Eve's friends. In the end, Julian had won, and Eve spent less time with Skylar and Josie. He had still *allowed* her to see her friend Noelle, though. Noelle was a nice girl. She was married and quiet. Just the type of friend Julian felt his Eve should have.

In the end, though, he knew they must have gotten to her. They must have told her lies to convince her to leave him. He would show her, though. She wasn't going to take away all he had now.

Looking around at the people in the gallery again, Julian saw several stopped in front of his favorite painting, *Hell*. It was simply the old house where he had spent his childhood. There was nothing in it but the house, with one light on in what had been his bedroom. In the shadow of the house was the shed. It was hidden, buried, so unless you looked really closely, you would never even see it. But Julian knew it was there.

He could hear people wondering what the artist must have been trying to convey.

"This is so moving."

"It's haunting."

"I've never seen anything so...just...there are no words."

Better than sex, Julian thought with a smile of extreme satisfaction on his face.

But while he was basking in the glow of his own success, he heard something that made his mind rage: the click, click, click of a whore's high heels echoing on the tile. Skylar.

Bitch.

"No, Josie. I don't like that little creep just hanging out in the museum." Skye had caught Josie outside her office and informed her that she'd seen Julian slink in about ten minutes earlier. He acted like he owned the whole place as he cozied up to the security staff. Skylar knew he was trying to find out when Eve would be back. She didn't trust that sneaky prick one little bit.

"Skye, he's an artist with pieces hanging in our museum. It's not like we can tell him he can't come here."

Skye sighed. All she wanted was for Josie to agree with her and have this *asshole* thrown out. "Josie, he was at lunch on Sunday, and then I followed him to Eve's apartment. He's up to something. And I don't like it."

Josie just shook her head and left Skylar to watch as she walked away. Since there was nothing Skye could do about Julian Meadows being in the museum, she'd just have to make him *want* to leave.

It wasn't hard to find him. Skye knew he would be perched on that bench in the Local Artists Gallery, staring narcissistically at his own work. He was such an ego-centric dork. It never made any sense to her why Eve had even been with him. He was small and the way he wore his hair slicked back made his nose even more prominent and gave him a rodent-like appearance. Then again, even if he had been fantastically hot, the tortured, brooding artist thing had never done anything for Skye. As director of public relations for the museum, she spent a lot of time with artists, and while most of them were normal human beings, every now and then, she'd had to babysit one of the whiney, self-centered morons. The ones who thought their work was created on a higher plane. *Ugh.* She shuddered just thinking about it.

"Hey, Julian. Nice to see you again so soon." Skye made sure she was in public relations mode. She didn't want to give him anything to complain about.

"Hello, Skylar. I was just checking on my exhibit." Even his voice was slimy.

"I know, it's hard to believe it's been almost two months already. Just a few more and the new exhibits come in." Skylar watched Julian's face to see what he thought about his *fabulous* work being pushed aside for the next local artist. She wasn't disappointed.

"Wh-What do you mean? New exhibits?" He looked panicked.

She had to fight the urge to laugh, still wondering what the hell Eve had ever seen in this guy.

"Oh, I'm sorry, Julian. Did you not realize? The whole point of this part of the museum is to allow many different local artists to show their work. We rotate the work out every four to six months." She tried to hide the sarcasm in her voice. Fortunately, the news had caught Julian so off guard that he no longer seemed to be paying attention.

"No, actually, I didn't know that,." he managed.

"Well, you can always submit more of your work to be displayed again, but unfortunately, the selections for the next few groups have already been made. I'm so sorry that no one told you about that." Skye was really trying to sound as if she gave a shit about him and his work. It must have worked because he quickly composed himself, thanked her, and walked out of the gallery.

My work here is done, Skylar thought as she clicked back to her office.

With Julian gone from the museum, Skye turned her thoughts to something, actually someone, much more pleasant. Most of those thoughts involved a naked, hot, very buff guy she knew. "Josie, I want to go to Stratus tonight," she informed her friend as she walked back into her office. "Call that man of yours and tell him he is taking us out."

Josie looked up at Skye to see her eyes sparkling. "And just why would you want to go to Stratus tonight, Ms. Montgomery?" A knowing smile played on her face.

"Well, you see, there is this bouncer there who, for some strange reason, has been starring in all of my *really* good dreams lately, and I want to see if I can make a few of those come true."

"How do you know that Gage will even be working tonight? I thought that he hardly worked during the week."

"Because, I called Blaine, the normal bouncer for tonight, and offered him his night's pay to call in sick." Skye's face lit up with a devious smile Josie recognized. If Skye was going after what she wanted, Josie was definitely going to be ringside for the show.

Josie picked up the phone and called Beau, who immediately agreed to whatever Josie wanted to do. Skye had noticed how Josie had started to change since meeting Beau. She just seemed calmer, more content. Skye really did envy her. A little.

Gage hated working on Tuesday nights. It was the slowest night of the week—worse than Sunday even. All he'd be doing is standing around watching drunk guys try to find a chick drunk enough to take them up on whatever ridiculous pick up lines they used. Not that this didn't happen every night, but when it was really slow, it was much more horrifying because the bouncers and bartenders could actually see and hear almost everything.

He wasn't even supposed to work tonight. But Steve had called a few hours earlier to let him know the normal guy for weeknights had called in sick, so Gage said he'd work. The thought that he might see Skye flicked through his mind, but there was no way she would go to Stratus on a Tuesday night.

"Oh, and dude, tonight is '80s Night, so the boss says you have to come dressed in '80s clothes. Sorry," Steve informed Gage after he had already agreed to work.

"Are you shitting me? What the hell does that even mean?"

"Just put on some Levi's with a golf shirt and pull the collar up, man. That's what I'm doing."

"Alright. I'll be there at nine."

Gage hung up the phone and went on the hunt through his closet. Recently, the club had started these "event nights" to drum up business. So far they had tried karaoke, Beach Party, and some other bullshit that never worked. Now not only did he have to deal with drunk guys groping women all night, he had to listen to crappy music, too!

When he was finally dressed in what he hoped passed for the '80s–jeans and a blue golf shirt (he'd even found a Lacoste in his closet)—he headed for the club. It was actually pretty busy when he got there, which surprised him. Waving to Steve behind the bar, Gage went to his post near the doors.

Instinctively, Gage glanced over to the girls' normal table just off the dance floor. Shock. Complete and utter shock. He saw Skylar there with Josie and Beau.

Josie had gone all-out, dressing like Cindy Lauper. Her hair was straightened with streaks of bright pink in it. Beau had apparently been attacked and forced into some horrible "costume." Gage had to stop himself from laughing. He was wearing black parachute pants with a Member's Only jacket and had his hair pulled back into...Gage could only guess that Josie had tried to do some sort of MC Hammer cornrows in the poor guy's hair. It looked ridiculous.

That right there is a man in love, Gage thought. *Because that would be the only reason to allow someone to do that to you.*

Then, there was Skye. Gage couldn't help the low curse that escaped when he took the time to really look at her. She was dressed like Madonna. Not the older, fake-British-accent Madonna either. The young hot one from the '80s. He couldn't really tell, but it looked like she was only wearing a bra. Gage could feel his already tight jeans getting just a little tighter as he scanned her entire ensemble. With the white lace bra, she had on some sort of white puffy skirt thing, fishnet stockings, and white high heels. Her hair was pulled off her face with some kind of bow, and she'd finished off the look with classic black Rayban sunglasses.

OK, Gage pondered, *maybe the '80s weren't so bad after all.*

Tonight, Gage told himself, he was going to ask her out. The game they'd been playing was getting to be too much. He was determined to make her his, and tonight he would set that in motion.

Then *Like a Virgin* started to play. Skye had asked the DJ to play it when he saw Gage come into the club.

Gage looked out onto the dance floor, and sure enough, Skye was right in the center, staring at him. As she moved, Gage noticed that the entire place was watching her. He didn't like that. As the music blared, Skye danced, and her eyes never left his. Again, the damn jeans he was wearing strained as his excitement grew.

The song finally ended, and Gage so turned on, he wanted to take her right there. Then, she crossed the room and sidled up to him. Letting her gaze roam over his perfect body, she giggled a little at his outfit. It wasn't that he looked bad. On the contrary, he looked absolutely fabulous. What made her giggle was imagining that it took him forever to pick out the outfit.

"Hey, Gage." Skye saw him shift once again and knew she was winning this battle.

"Hey, Skye. You look, um, yeah." He was stammering. "Okay, look, I've been wanting to tell you for a while that..." Gage started again, still struggling to find the right words, and even though Skye was thoroughly enjoying watching him squirm, she decided to put him out of his misery.

Stepping toward him, she pressed her entire body into his. One thing Skylar had never been accused of was subtlety. Her hands snaked around Gage's neck and pulled his face down to her. The sheer size of him up close like that was overwhelming. Even in her highest heels, the boy still towered over her.

Following Skye's lead, Gage wrapped his arms around her small waist and pulled her close so she could tell the little dance she had done had had its intended impact. When his lips found hers, Skye's knees went weak.

She couldn't remember ever being kissed the way Gage kissed her. Most men acted as if they were trying to trade tongues, but Gage's kiss was gentle and sweet.

And she wanted more.

All of a sudden, Gage pulled Skye's body away from his and looked into her eyes. Immediately she was pissed. She had made the decision to be done with the teasing, and then he pulls shit like that. Skye was about to tell him what an ass he was when she noticed how he was looking at her. Never had any man looked at her with as much passion and desire in his eyes. With a blast of heat, Skye's body responded to Gage. She wanted him in that instant more than she had ever wanted any other man.

"Skye, as much as I would love to continue this, uh, activity, unfortunately I am working. And if I get started with you in that bra thing, I won't be able to stop, and that kind of show could get the club shut down." Gage smiled down at her, and she knew this wasn't part of the game they'd been playing. "Besides, I'm supposed to be the one making sure these guys don't take advantage of all you innocent girls."

Innocent? What the hell? A look crossed Skye's face.

"I mean, you *are* all in white, and even though you just about killed every red-blooded man in here with that little dance, the song was *Like a Virgin*." His eyes raked over her again, and she noticed him shift yet again. She wondered if his tight jeans were helping or hurting the situation. She laughed, and he looked at her with so much lust, she thought she would actually faint.

She wanted him to touch her. She wanted him to kiss her. She wanted him to...

"Skye, we *will* finish this." His voice was pure desire, and her skin tingled as his breath brushed her cheek. His hands slid down her sides, and his touch left a heated trail on her exposed skin until his hands finally stopped on her hips, pulling her into his own obvious excitement. "But, not right now."

He kissed her lightly, his surprisingly soft lips grazing her own and causing that weak-kneed thing to happen once again. She could only imagine how her body would respond when he kissed her with as much passion as she could sense in his touch and see in his eyes.

Suddenly he let go of her. With her legs like jelly, Skye stumbled slightly before finding her balance again. She turned to see Gage, a head taller than most of the crowd, making his way across the dance floor to a spot where a fight was about to break out between a couple of drunks.

Her whole body was still tingling.

Sometimes Gage was actually embarrassed that he was a guy. What was it about alcohol and testosterone that made these morons fight? He couldn't remember the last time he'd worked that he didn't have to break up a potential fight. This time he was particularly pissed off because the drunk assholes had interrupted his moment with Skye. A moment that was a thousand times better than what he'd been thinking it would be.

With the idiots separated, he turned to make his way back to Skylar, but she was gone. Gage quickly turned around again to look at their table, but it was empty too. *Shit!* Now he really wanted to kill those assholes.

The rest of the night, Gage was pissed off—first at the drunks and then also at Skye. How could she just leave without telling him? Fortunately, he was kept busy with a room full of idiots who thought they were God's gift to women. By the end of the night, Gage had thrown out more people than usually showed up on a Tuesday night. At midnight, he started ushering the poor, lonely drunks out into the night. He was finally able to lock the doors at around 12:30.

Just as he turned to finally get a drink at the bar, there was a knock on the locked front doors. Gage instantly thought of Eve's fourth fish and wondered briefly why he hadn't called. He'd been sure that he would. Suddenly he was very glad he hadn't been able to tell her about the guy.

"Hey, Steve! Did you have another visitor coming tonight?" Gage called out on his way to get rid of the straggler.

"No, man. Not tonight."

He unlocked the door and opened it just enough to stick his head out.

"All right, bud—" His usual speech was cut short when the most exquisite pair of lips met his.

Ahh. My Skye.

"Hi," she said as she pulled away slightly. She looked up at him through her long eyelashes and again his body betrayed him. He'd be throwing out this pair of jeans when he got home.

While his mind was telling Skye she was the most beautiful, sexy, ballsy woman he'd ever met, his voice came up with something else. "Skye. Well, this is a surprise." *Damn it! Why does my brain just stop working when I look at her?*

"So, are you going to let me in there, or leave me out in the cold?"

"Sorry. Come in." Gage realized he had to get his act together fast. All he had to do was talk to her, plain and simple.

He stepped back to let her pass by, and her body brushed against his as she squeezed past, trailing her hand across his chest. Gage took a deep breath and watched as Skye headed to the bar where Steve was finishing up his closing duties. Gage liked Steve, but if the guy didn't stop looking at Skye that way, he was going to have to hurt him.

When Steve caught sight of Gage's face, he quickly averted his eyes. "Hey, Gage, I'm done here. If you want to hang for a few that's cool. I can walk the girls to their cars. Just be sure to lock up."

Gage nodded and even may have said "Thanks," but his eyes never left Skye. *Good God! How can this incredible woman want me?*

"Wow, stud, I thought you were a little smoother than this. Are you going to offer me a drink or what?"

"Skye, I am totally smooth. Usually. I don't know what it is you do, but I think you have some secret powers that make me act like a moron around you."

She laughed, and it was the most beautiful sound he'd ever heard. She didn't have one of those prissy girl laughs. Skye's chuckle was hearty and true, and it filled the room.

"Just get me a glass of wine, before I use my powers for evil instead of good."

"Your wish is my command. Chardonnay OK?"

Skye nodded as Gage stepped behind the bar, poured the glass of wine, and grabbed a bottle of beer for himself. When he glanced over at her, Skye had a grin like the Cheshire Cat.

"What are you smiling about?"

"Just thinking about that last statement you made. I have a lot of wishes, Gage. Want to hear a few?"

He swallowed hard as he walked back around to where Skye was sitting. Gage wasn't one for flirting and being witty; he figured Skye was doing enough of that for the two of them. Instead he stepped into the space between her legs, and she gladly accepted his new position, wrapping her legs around his hips. He slid his hands under her ass and pulled her up to him, his mouth finding her lips quickly and attacking them.

She let out a small moan and his arousal deepened, a fact Gage was sure didn't go unnoticed by her, given their current position. Her hands gripped his shoulders as he held all of her weight in his arms. Her head fell back, exposing her long, pale neck to him, and he immediately moved his mouth down to the skin there. She tasted like no other woman he had ever known. It was indescribable. He felt a sudden urge to run his tongue over every inch of her exquisite body.

He set her on top of the bar, never breaking contact with her. She leaned back on her elbows, elongating her already sexy body. This time it was Gage's turn to moan.

"Skye, you are the most incredible woman I have ever seen." Gage could barely breathe and was amazed that he got the words out.

"Gage, I need you to touch me *now*."

He almost lost it right then and there. As she sat up, moving her body closer to his yet again, she reached out and pulled his shirt out of his jeans, her fingers running over his abs. Her touch made him shudder. *No woman has ever made me shudder before. I think I'm in love.*

That's when it happened. Gage's heart betrayed the rest of his body.

"Skye, wait." Gage couldn't believe the words had come out of his mouth. He glanced around to see if there was anyone else in the bar, because otherwise surely he wouldn't be stopping the oncoming train that was a glorious night in bed with Skylar Montgomery.

The look on Skye's face was as shocked as Gage's. Then he saw something else flash in her eyes. She was pissed, and Gage knew he was going to take the full brunt of her anger. He braced himself and tried to form a coherent argument.

"Damn it, Gage! What the hell? Here I am practically throwing myself at you—for the second time tonight I might add—and you...what? What exactly are you doing?"

Gage could hear the hurt in her voice. She thought he was rejecting her. He had to make her understand why he was stopping before he lost everything he had been working for.

"Skylar, please, wait." She looked at him and Gage thought he saw a tear escape the corner of her eye. He knew this was not something that had ever happened to her. Really, what man in his right mind would turn down Skylar Montgomery? Gage Vandenberg apparently. "Skye, I have wanted this to happen for a long time now. Trust me, watching you on that dance floor night after night has made for many, many dreams just like this. But, I want more than just this from you."

Gage couldn't help but cringe at the words he had just spoken. It was definitely the most girly thing he had ever said.

"What does that mean, Gage?" Her bottom lip pushed out in an irresistible pout. Gage couldn't help himself, and he leaned down to gently pull it into his mouth. She moaned his name this time, and he almost lost all his willpower.

"Ahhh! This is har–uhh...difficult for me, Skye. I want you. Oh, God, how I want you. But, not here, not on a bar. I don't want this to be something either of us regrets. I mean what kind of story will we tell our kids about how we got together?"

He mentally corrected himself, because *that* was now the most girly thing he had ever said.

Gage looked at her to gauge the effect of his words. The fact that they hadn't even been on a date and he had just mentioned having kids with her was a complete surprise to him. Judging by the look on her face, it had surprised her as well.

"Kids? What will we tell *our* kids, Gage?"

Gage still couldn't tell what she was feeling about the prospect of a future with him. Then a small smile touched her lips.

Reaching over to her, cupping her cheek in his hand, Gage leaned in to place a light kiss on her beautiful lips. Skye closed her eyes and sighed. With a great effort, Gage stepped away. He knew he had to do it or all his efforts would have been for nothing, and he really wanted this. He wanted Skye to want it too.

"Skye, believe me, I had every intention of having my way with you tonight. But, I want you more than just in my bed. I want you in my life. I want dates and all that other crap that goes with it."

"Oh, Gage, you sure do know how to charm a girl." Skye let out a small giggle that instantly made Gage wonder again why he was not just taking her right then.

"I get it. Now that you explain it that way, I can accept it. I don't know if I like it." Skye poked her bottom lip out, just to torture

Gage a little for getting her all worked up and not delivering. "If you want to take it slower, I guess we can try things your way. But, we better get back to *this*," Skye waved her finger between the two of them, "pretty quick, or I'll explode."

"Deal. How about Thursday? Can we go on an actual date?"

Skye agreed and accepted Gage's help as she hopped off the bar. When his hand gently brushed against the lace of the white bra she was still wearing, Skye shuddered.

Gage smiled at the thought of what he could do to make her not only shudder, but quiver and moan his name. And he cursed his damn tight jeans again.

After a few moments of catching their breath and making needed adjustments, Gage turned out the lights and walked with Skye to the doors. Holding hands, he walked her to her car. Once there, Gage grabbed her one last time, pulling her close to feel her whole body against him, and kissed her. He liked that he could feel her losing her balance just a little, and he smiled against her lips.

"Don't be too proud of yourself there, stud boy! I'm already thinking of ways to make *your* knees go weak."

Gage gave Skye a devilish grin, kissed her once more, and sent her on her way. Then he took himself home for yet another cold shower.

Chapter Nine

On Tuesday, Will and Eve were again together for the presentation. Unfortunately, they were in a room full of Boston Museum of Art board members and the grant committee, including Jeannette.

The presentation itself had gone more smoothly than Eve had expected, and she was tremendously relieved. Skye and Josie had both spruced up the slides on Monday before resending them to her with the presentation's final edit—and they were dynamic. Eve loved talking about the museum, and she soon found a groove.

Will had had to be professional—in other words, distant—with her in front of the committee, and Eve's heart was heavy even though she knew this. She had hoped he would give her some sort of signal, but he had been all business. Not one little sign that what they had together was anything more than a professional relationship.

Eve took some comfort in the fact that the committee seemed impressed with the ideas from the Santa Barbara Museum of Art, and they indicated by silent nods that their budget was well-researched and not overestimated. In the end, she felt confident that, if nothing else, they were still a strong candidate to win the grant.

As she cleaned up her presentation, Eve was surprised to find Will standing in the open doorway when she turned around.

"Hi," he said as his eyes met hers.

Eve wasn't sure how to react to him at that point. After looking around to see if there was anyone else left from the meeting, Eve finally allowed herself to respond. "Hi."

"I thought maybe it would be OK if I walked you to the elevator? I mean it is kind of our thing now. And you have your hands full." Will nodded to the handful of charts and handouts Eve was wrestling with.

"Uh, yeah, that would be great." Eve smiled. His professional façade had been for the benefit of the committee.

Will graciously took some of the bulkier items as he steered her down the hall to the bank of elevators. On their walk from the meeting room, Will informed her that until the gala they wouldn't be able to see or talk to each other. He seemed apologetic, even sad, about that—as was Eve.

Just before the elevator doors slid closed, after handing Eve all of her materials and ensuring that she could make it back to her room without dropping them all, Will told Eve he looked forward to talking with her again after the grant was awarded, and, regardless of who won, he hoped she would want to spend much of the evening with him.

Eve's heart leapt, but too afraid of what she might say, she just nodded her head in agreement as he disappeared from view and she was left staring at her own reflection in the metal doors.

Now Eve had to occupy her thoughts and hours with anything that would keep her from daydreaming about Will Prentiss. When she had changed into her khakis and t-shirt (which had gotten soaked in the rain with Will last night), she plopped down on the bed with a pad of paper and a pen. Propping herself up against the pillows, she began to list things she could do to pass the time until the gala in two days: get caught up on email *(tell Josie and Skye about Will)*, go walking and check out the boutiques and shops *(and look for another pair of comfortable shoes as my other ones are still damp from the rain with Will)*, visit some of the other smaller museums *(it would be best to stay away from the BMA)*, go to the hotel's gym and run a few miles on the treadmill *(and bring my iPod—I need music to keep my mind from wandering!)*, maybe go find that diner they'd gone to and have a cup of coffee.

As Eve looked over her list and tried to keep from tying each item to Will, the phone next to the bed rang. *Did he change his mind about the no talking thing, maybe?* "Hello?"

"Hi!" The effervescent voice was certainly not Will's. It wasn't even male. "This is Megan Stepanski. I'm Will Prentiss' assistant." She paused for a moment and then continued. "I'm calling because, as you know, Mr. Prentiss is going to be in meetings for the next few days. He's asked that I take over as the Townsend Industries rep. You know, take you places you want to go?"

Eve's day suddenly looked more promising. "Oh. Hmm, what a coincidence. Actually I was just sitting here making a list of things to do *(to keep my mind off your boss)*, and I would love some advice at least. Then I guess I'll know whether I need a ride anywhere."

"OK. Shoot!" Eve liked this woman already.

"Well, if I were to prioritize, I guess I need to put shoe shopping on the top of my list. Just casual shoes, though. The pair I was wearing yesterday got soaked in last night's rain, and I'm afraid they're pretty much goners. I can wear them today just long enough to replace them. Any ideas?"

"Yeah, sure." Megan rattled off the names of a few shops that were reasonably priced and within walking distance of the hotel. "What else?"

Eve was excited at the prospect of getting out of the hotel. "Hmm, I guess once I get the shoes, then I may just want to keep on walking—explore some of the shops and enjoy the afternoon's nice weather. Would you be available to join me on my adventure?"

"Me? And shopping?" Megan started to giggle. "Twist my arm!" They arranged to meet in the lobby at 2:00.

When Eve exited the elevator after her room-service lunch, she couldn't help but realize this was the first time she hadn't been immediately greeted by Will's smile *(and the gorgeous face and body that was attached to it).* Instead, Megan came bounding over and introduced herself. They immediately fell into easy conversation as they left the hotel.

Eve was fortunate that the first place they went to had a cute pair of flats that were reasonably priced, for Boston anyway. After paying for the new pair, Eve tossed her old ones into the new shoes' box and threw them into the first trash can she found.

"OK. Main errand done. What next? Any other stores worth investigating? I love to window shop and even try on super-expensive clothing just for the fun of it. I love getting those saleswomen's hopes up and then buying a $40 belt." Eve smiled at her new friend and tour guide.

"Well, if you're *really* open to ideas," Megan hesitated. "I would love to look for something new for Thursday night. Would I be horrible if we went looking for a dress for me? I never have any *girls* to give me advice!"

Eve beamed. "That sounds like fun. I'd love to!" She told Megan how Skye, Josie, and she never went shopping without the others in tow. "So, where to, then?"

"One of the best boutiques around is Sublime. It's just up the street a bit. Their line of clothing is geared toward early-evening attire—you know, stuff that's dressier than you'd wear to work but not too dressy."

"Sounds good. Maybe I'll look around too," Eve said. "Let's go!"

The remainder of their afternoon was spent in the small but well-stocked boutique. They both tried on dress after dress, even though Eve already had hers for the gala. Megan found a red number with a plunging back that accentuated her curves. By the time Megan had paid and they left the store—the saleswoman who had been working with Eve looking quite disappointed at her purchase of just sheer black stockings—it was 5:30. They said their goodbyes in the lobby of Eve's hotel, Megan not hesitating to pull her new friend into a quick hug and thanking her again for helping her pick out the dress. Eve waved goodbye to Megan and went up to relax in her room for the night.

Wednesday passed in a blur, and Eve was thankful. After spending most of the morning checking up on her work at the SBMA, she called Josie and Skye. She had to leave voice messages for both of them. She hadn't heard from either of them since the first day of the trip when she talked with Skylar. *What could be keeping them so busy?*

She thought about calling Noelle to tell her about Will, but what could she say? Besides, Eve never knew what Noelle's schedule was. As a pediatric surgical nurse, Noelle worked varying hours, and Eve hated to disturb her at work.

Eventually giving up on talking with any of her friends, Eve decided to spend the afternoon at the Boston Museum of Contemporary Art. As she toured the museum, she kept thinking it was where Julian's work needed to be displayed—so much of the work here seemed to exude the anger, depression, and passion that his work did. Much of it was disturbing, too. Generally, Eve preferred the old stuff to what contemporary artists had to offer. Her trip to that museum confirmed this again.

Thursday morning Eve finally made it to the hotel gym and enjoyed a thorough workout in relative solitude. It felt good to give her body some attention, and she found that by focusing on the exercise, she could keep both Will and the upcoming grant announcement out of her head for much of the time.

After a quick shower and changing into khakis and t-shirt again, Eve finally gave in to the part of her brain that missed Will and walked to Mulligan Stew. She had the chicken sandwich and side of fruit that Will had ordered and enjoyed the atmosphere of the restaurant, which was obviously a local favorite. She wished Will would happen to walk by, but he was likely preparing for tonight's gala with Jeannette. *(Care for another lawyer salad with horse cheese?)* Eve returned to the hotel around four o'clock to get herself ready. Her walk was brisk as anticipation for the night ahead pulsed through her.

Once ready for the gala, and thankful that her bruises had faded enough to allow her dress to work, Eve looked at herself one more time in the mirror. Megan was meeting her in the lobby at 6:45, and they would walk together to the ballroom. And while Eve did like Megan, the thing that she was most looking forward to was actually being in the same room as Will again.

Will stood in the hotel lobby, watching the door, waiting to catch a glimpse of Eve while being interrupted intermittently by various administrative staff members of the BMA and other high-end donors to the museum who tended to flock to events like this. He tried to keep a smile firmly on display, but his heart was pounding. Not seeing her for almost two days was making him a basket case. What was he going to do when she boarded a plane and flew to the other side of the country?

It was Will's responsibility to deliver the speech tonight, and he had worked on it all morning, writing and rewriting until he was exhausted and the words began to run together. In the end, he decided that what was tucked into the inside pocket of his jacket would just have to do. About a hundred people would be in attendance, including possibly the mayor and his wife. This was really just another high-society function where everyone smiles for the cameras and false pleasantries prevail in nearly every conversation.

Jeannette was already trying to steal Will's attention, finding reasons to ask him questions or point out people of importance (to her). She wore a beautiful royal-blue chiffon dress and was noticed by every man in the room, married and single alike. Her eyes and her main focus remained on Will, however. Twice already she had mentioned looking forward to dancing with him later in the evening, giving him flirty sideways glances as she spoke.

Just then, Will saw Megan walk in with Eve by her side, the two of them sharing a laugh. As much as he'd prepared himself to see her again, she still had that amazing ability to take his breath away. The black-lace dress she was wearing, one of his mother's designs as she had told him in the car earlier this week, was stunning. No, *Eve* was stunning. The cut of the dress suited her body perfectly, showing off her lovely shoulders and draping demurely in the front to hint at sexiness without any cleavage being revealed. *Very tasteful.* The waistline accentuated her curves beautifully and the knee length of the dress was just right. Scalloped lace ran along the hem to showcase her legs, but his favorite part was the long sheer scarf that encircled the neckline and hung over her left shoulder and down the back of the dress.

"Will, are you ready?" It was Jeannette again, looping her arm in his and breaking his gaze from Eve. He saw Jeannette look to where his eyes had been, and she squeezed his arm closer to her. *You're trying to claim something that isn't yours, Jeannette.* The two of them *would* be forced to sit together at the head table, though. So for now, Will could only make eye contact with Eve from a distance.

Eve and the other grant applicants were seated at three separate tables among various members of the BMA and local donors, but Megan made sure Eve met a few local dignitaries along the way. Once seated, Will watched as Eve immediately engaged in conversation with those at her table. She glanced up at him once and discretely raised her hand to indicate a hello, then returned to talking. She certainly appeared quite comfortable in this setting. He just wanted to watch her, catch her smiling and laughing. *I hope you'll want to dance with me later.*

As the plates were cleared silently by the hotel staff, Jeannette walked to the podium, ready to begin the awards presentation. Eve couldn't help but be mesmerized by her. She really was beautiful. Eve knew she could never compete with Jeanette. But when she found Will in the crowd, his gaze was locked on her, not Jeanette. That put a smile on Eve's face despite her nerves about the grant.

"Good evening, everyone, and welcome to the fifth annual Boston Museum of Art-Townsend Industries Charitable Foundation awards presentation. This year we received seventeen grant proposals, our largest collection of applications to date. And while it was difficult to narrow down our favorites to only three, we know you'll agree that those three museums—the Salt Lake City Contemporary Art Museum, the Tampa Gallery of Asian Art, and the Santa Barbara Museum of Art—are *all* worthy of applause for the work they are doing and the plans they have for the future. May I please ask that the grant representatives from each of these fine museums stand to be recognized?"

Eve stood up, awkwardly, never liking to have *that* kind of attention brought upon herself—at least not without a blindfold on. Looking around, she saw a stocky woman in her fifties and a thin man who, it seemed, was making eyes at Martin. As the applause died, they all sat back down.

"The Boston Museum of Art has a long history of supporting other museums, but it wasn't until a few years ago that we were able to really provide extensive financial support," Jeannette explained. "Townsend Industries is a young company; it's been barely seven years since they really took off in the business world. But they continue to be a dynamic and innovative force in the medical field and have promised continued support of the arts as a partner in the BMA-Townsend Industries Charitable Foundation. And, so, without further ado, it is my pleasure to introduce the founder and president of Townsend Industries, Mr. William Prentiss."

Eve was surrounded by people applauding as Will stood and walked to the podium, but she remained still. *Founder and president?* Numbly, she began to clap, but her mind was in total confusion. Will had never really clarified his title and had only indicated that the company was named for the founder's mother. *Will's mother is Camille Townsend.*

In that moment, Eve wasn't sure how to feel, other than shocked. Will looked briefly, but intently, into her eyes from his place behind the microphone. Then, turning to Megan, he nodded, and she began the slide presentation.

"Thank you all for being here. Once again, this is a night for celebrating art, and the sharing of art around the country and around the world. My mother, Camille Townsend, was a great woman who taught me from a young age that art is 'life captured for the ages.' It was always her passion to see what others could create from nothing. As a fashion designer, well-established even before she met my father, she could truly appreciate the craft—no, the *magic*—that artists and sculptors created for the rest of us to enjoy and learn from."

As Will spoke, Eve replayed in her mind his words from dinner the other night. It wasn't just Camille Townsend who had a passion for art; she had passed that love on to her son. To Will. Eve wanted to slap her forehead and sink to the floor just then. The man she had been mooning over for almost a week was a gazillionaire who owned the entire company.

"I want to personally thank and congratulate the three finalists sitting before us tonight. Your proposals were outstanding and made our decision difficult."

Another round of applause began at Megan's urging, and the three representatives joined in, the young man from Tampa still looking longingly at Martin.

"This year's winner of the Boston Museum of Art-Townsend Industries Charitable Foundation Award, however, truly captured the essence of what my mother believed in her heart: that it's the children who matter most. She felt it was vital to humanity to be sure that children grow up in an environment where art is not only appreciated but encouraged."

Will hesitated and shot another quick glance at Eve. This was the reason his speech had always gone off track. He knew who the winner was, and every time he tried to describe anything to do with Eve, he would get distracted and start to ramble about her big brown eyes, or the blond hair that curled around her shoulders, or that damn underwear of hers.

"When a museum requests $3 million dollars to build a wing solely dedicated to the education and display of children's artwork, *I take notice*." Again, he let his eyes fall on Eve. "I share my mother's passion for *teaching children* about art because it is in their hands that we lay our past—and our future. If we want the people who will live on after us to continue to appreciate and value what previous generations so graciously left, we have to instill in our children that passion for art."

He took deep breath.

"And so it is with great pleasure that the BMA-Townsend Industries Charitable Foundation presents this year's award to the Santa Barbara Museum of Art. We look forward to working side by side with you to see this dream become a reality." Then Will's eyes stayed on hers, and his face lit up with the most wonderful smile.

Eve sat in shock for a moment, finally nudged back to the present by the man sitting next to her. Rising from her seat as the applause surrounded her, she walked, in a trance, to the front of the room where Jeannette greeted her with a polite embrace and Will shook her hand.

He gazed into her eyes intently with, what was it—love?—*No, Eve!* Perhaps it was more like sincere congratulations. *Yeah, that's it.*

They were immediately engulfed in flashes from cameras. Photos were taken with Eve in the center and Jeannette, Will, and other committee members around her. Photographers also wanted pictures of Eve with the other grant finalists, the mayor, and any person of status in the Boston area. As she smiled repeatedly, there were two things Eve wanted desperately to do: first, call Skye and Josie; second, talk to Will—alone. She realized quickly that her first wish would have to wait until later; she couldn't politely leave the room. Skye and Josie were three hours behind anyway and would surely still be awake later when she did have the chance to call them. And so, Will Prentiss became her priority.

As he watched Eve out of the corner of his eye, Will was suddenly grateful that he had had to be away from her until after this announcement. There was no way he could have kept it from her. While he was happy that a children's art wing would be built with the money, he was personally overjoyed that this decision meant *somebody* would have to make periodic visits to Santa Barbara to check on the museum's progress. But stopping that train of thought immediately, Will reminded himself that Eve had her own life in Santa Barbara. Yes, her relationship with the jerk who tried to kill her was over, but who knew who else was waiting in the wings at the museum, at Stratus, or anywhere else in Santa Barbara. And what was she thinking now—now that she knew who he was? He could explain it all to her, but would she be willing to listen? Would she understand and forgive him? And she still didn't know about his visit to Santa Barbara.

After the photographers were satisfied, Eve excused herself to go to the ladies' room. Will mingled with a few local officials and dignitaries and was glad that Jeannette was nowhere to be seen, either. As the room shifted into dance mode, the last person he wanted to be near was her. The thought came to him that if he could introduce the newest millionaire donor to Jeannette, perhaps he would be free to be with Eve. Keeping one eye on the women's restroom, Will scanned the room for the man he hoped would be Jeannette's new stepping stone.

Eve still wasn't sure what, if anything, to say to Will. All of their conversations played over and over in her head as she tried to make sense of why he'd never revealed his position at Townsend Industries or his influential role in who would win the grant. Had her museum won because she was the most attractive of the three grant representatives? Would Tampa have had a better shot if Martin had noticed the attention *he* was receiving? Eve knew she could never forgive Will if that were the case. Her staff had worked hard, and she knew they *deserved* to win on merit alone.

As Eve sat enclosed in a stall, mulling over all of this, she heard the bathroom door open, briefly allowing in the sounds of the music and crowd. Once the door gently clicked, Eve froze as she recognized Jeannette's nasal voice. She was mid-conversation with someone whose voice Eve didn't recognize.

"Yes, we've been dating now for almost six months. William treats me like gold. And in bed? Mmm...he is incredible."

"Are you two getting serious enough to be considering *ring shopping*?" the other woman inquired.

"Oh, I don't know. For now, just having access to that body is enough for me. I'll be letting him know of the plans I have for him later when I get him on the dance floor."

They both giggled at that as Eve flushed the toilet and emerged from her stall.

"Well, Ms. Carwyn, I didn't know you were in here!" Eve barely caught Jeannette giving a knowing look to the other woman through the mirror's reflection. "Congratulations, my dear! Your proposal was so endearing to Will. He's always a sucker for anything having to do with *children*." Jeannette sneered that last word, but immediately returned to smiling at Eve.

"Thank you, Jeannette—and thanks to everyone on the committee. I haven't called my colleagues yet, but I know they'll be as thrilled as I am when they hear the news." Eve smiled as genuinely as she could. Jeannette *had* been on the committee so Eve was sincere in that aspect of her gratitude. She washed her hands while the other two women touched up their lipstick and exited the restroom together.

Eve stared at her reflection for a few moments after Jeanette left. She was gathering her courage to go out and face Will, now that she had yet one more bit of information about him that might or might not be true. Having just come out of the bad relationship, there was no way that she wanted to be a part of something like that again.

Will had been glancing at the door of the ladies' room for what seemed like hours waiting for Eve to emerge. When the door opened, Will's heart did a strange little skip in his chest, only to almost stop completely when he saw Jeannette, not Eve, walk through it.

"What the hell?" Will spit out under his breath. He quickly scanned the crowds, hoping Eve had come out while he was talking with one of his old professors from Harvard. When he saw her walk out that same door a few moments later, and his heart sank. He didn't like the idea of Jeannette having trapped Eve to tell her Lord knows what.

"Will, honey!" Jeannette approached Will with her arms ready to embrace him. He gave her a polite hug, as usual, and nodded a hello to the woman with her who, in turn, waved and headed to the bar. Eve was still a few steps back, watching their interaction. Her eyes were hard to read, but they didn't look necessarily friendly. Will had to move quickly to resolve this situation.

"Jeannette, there's someone who's been asking me about you all evening," Will said as he walked away from Eve, arm in arm with Jeannette. He looked back quickly to see Eve being approached by one of the BMA's newest patrons—a young, single man who had recently moved to Boston and had reportedly been considered for *The Bachelor* television show. Eve didn't look Will's way at all and instead was instantly immersed in conversation with this man. And she was smiling and laughing. *Damn,* Will thought. *I need to get rid of Jeannette* now.

Lucky for Will, Jeannette found the millionaire intriguing both financially and socially. And from the way she was already pressing up against him, she liked him physically as well. The man's eyes roamed from her face to her cleavage, and Jeannette was definitely enjoying the attention she was getting. Will was pleased with how easily that had gone, but now it was time to find Eve.

She was at the bar with 'Mr. Bachelor,' still laughing and seemingly enthralled by him. Will was seething; he didn't even know this guy and he hated him.

This was a job for indispensable Megan. Will found her and got her up to speed on his desire to get Eve away from the other man. Megan winked at Will, letting him know in an instant that she not only knew why, but she approved. This young woman, Will thought with a smile, will be receiving a big and well-deserved raise on Monday.

Megan and Will approached the bar near Eve and the man, and they each ordered a drink. Then Megan worked her magic. She apologized for interrupting and asked the gentleman to come with her as there were other people she had wanted him to meet that evening.

Before he could refuse, she smiled and hooked her arm in his, pulling him with her to a group of people on the other side of the room who had no idea why they were suddenly being introduced to him.

"*That* was subtle."

Will couldn't tell yet if Eve's sarcasm was biting or coy. Then he saw her face—the confusion in her eyes. It hurt him that he had been the one to put that look there.

"So, let me get this straight," Eve started. Will thought it was a good sign that she was still talking to him. "You're Camille Townsend's *son.* You're the *owner* of Townsend Industries, and you were likely a key decision-maker on the grant committee. Do I have that all right?" She tilted her head as she looked at him, still not even a hint of a smile.

She was angry. Will knew her anger was justified.

"What did you know about me—or even figure out about me *before* I stood up to speak this evening?" Will challenged her. He wanted to make her see that he was still the same Will Prentiss she had laughed and talked with earlier in the week.

"I'm not entirely sure. I didn't *think* you were deceptive or evasive, but now..."

"I thought you had me all figured out the other night at dinner." Eve looked at him, her eyebrows drawn together in confusion. "When I talked about hating the formality of these functions—of being 'Mr. Prentiss' instead of just some guy—I really thought you had me pegged."

"But you *are* 'Mr. Prentiss' in these circles."

"Doesn't make me like it any better. I prefer to get to know people, and have people get to know me, without associating me with money or success or how I look. That's all Jeannette ever saw in me. Look at her over there!" Will gestured to the dance floor where Jeannette was now dancing slowly—and seductively—with the man Will had just introduced her to. He was still finding new ways to look down her dress, and she was letting him.

"She'll act like she's in love with me one minute and then tease some shallow rich guy into her bed the next. You can be sure *that* guy is getting some tonight! That was one thing I was *very* glad never happened between us—not that she didn't scheme to try."

"So you and she haven't been together for six months, and you aren't getting ready to go ring shopping?" Eve finally laughed as she smiled up at him.

Her comments confirmed Will's suspicions about what Jeanette and Even in the ladies' room. "Uh, definitely not."

"Mr. Prentiss?" Eve's smile grew and the sparkle returned to her eyes.

"Yes, Ms. Carwyn?"

"Do you think it would be acceptable for the president of Townsend Industries to dance with the winner of the grant? Strictly business, of course."

"Yes, and no." Will made a point to look into her eyes, wanting her to see how attracted he was to her. "Yes, I think that would be acceptable, but no, I can't guarantee that I will be able to keep things strictly business."

They walked to a darker corner of the dance floor, well away from Jeannette and her stud of the evening. Gently, Will pulled Eve into the embrace he'd been longing for since that night at Stratus. The feel of his arm around her waist and his hand on her back caused his body to hum with pleasure. He had to remind himself that they were still very much in the public eye, and the entire committee was watching.

Eve welcomed the closeness, allowing one hand to lie gently across the back of Will's neck and the other to wrap around his.

Will's hand was warm, and she closed her eyes for a moment to relish the feel of having him hold her in his arms.

Will allowed himself to silently revel in the dance, letting each part of his body appreciate the closeness to hers, but always keeping a modest distance between them. He caressed her fingers as he held her hand in his.

Lost in the moment, Will did the one thing he had told himself over and over again not to do: He moved his lips to her temple and kissed her gently. As soon as he realized what he had done, he froze, expecting Eve to pull away. While she *did* hesitate initially, it was only a moment before she subtly moved her hand more securely around Will's neck.

It took great will power for Will to keep himself from kissing her again. He knew it certainly wasn't appropriate here on the dance floor. And it definitely wasn't appropriate at all while she was in Boston...while she was possibly not even ready to begin a new relationship. Will forced himself to slow down and back up considerably. All the while, his heart was screaming that she was the woman for him.

As the music ended, the DJ began asking line-dancers to gather. Will and Eve remained in their pseudo-embrace for a moment longer, neither wanting to part. Eventually they broke apart and returned to the bar for another drink before going to sit down at Eve's table.

"Am I forgiven for being evasive with you this week?" Will flashed Eve his heart-melting smile accompanied by sad puppy eyes, knowing they would work on her.

"Yes." It was all Eve could think to say out loud. Internally she was asking him up to her room to finish out the evening wrapped around one another.

Eve looked up at the relief that washed over Will's face. Had he actually been *that* worried that she wouldn't forgive him? Really, how could she not? He *had* been truthful all along that he didn't like the attention he got for being wealthy. His evasiveness had nothing to do with Eve.

It was then that Megan joined them. She was astute enough to know it would be best if Will and Eve didn't appear too cozy. The addition of Megan was a welcomed distraction. Will and Eve felt as if they had just crossed into new territory, and neither of them knew quite how to react.

The rest of the evening was full of fun conversation. Megan was quite a storyteller and shared some anecdotes from past awards presentations. She also pointed out how Martin and the Tampa grant rep had been inseparable since dinner.

As midnight approached, Will and Eve finally had to admit that the night was over. As usual, they walked together to the elevator, this time with Eve carrying her shoes to rest her feet. There were still a lot of people in the lobby who had been at the presentation, so they were limited to a formal, business-like goodnight.

The elevator came too quickly, and there were others getting on with her. All Eve could do was gaze at him. As the doors began to close between them, Will gave Eve that smile that melted her and that was enough.

Chapter Ten

"Skylar, could you please come to my office?"

Ugh! Here it comes.

This was what Skye had been trying to avoid. Lucky for her, yesterday she had been out all day meeting with the committee to choose the next artists for the museum's Local Artists Gallery. Maybe she hadn't exactly told Julian the truth, but now it really was too late.

She'd made it almost the whole day today, but now there was no escape. Skylar made her way down the short hallway, dreading the conversation she knew was coming. She dropped into the chair directly across from Josie, but before her colleague could say a word, Skye took evasive action.

"Josie, have you heard from Eve? I mean, I had a few kind of cryptic voice mails, but that's it since Sunday."

"I talked to her on Monday, and all I heard about was that Will guy from Townsend Industries," said Josie. "She did send a quick e-mail after the presentation that said it went well, but nothing else. Should we be worried?"

"No, she's probably just caught up in the city and *Will*. Our little Eve has never been anywhere, so I'm sure she's playing tourist. She can get lost in her own mind sometimes. You know that." Skye knew that if it had been *her* out of town on the museum's dime, she would have been out and about every night.

"Well, she'd better call tonight when she finds out about the grant. I mean, she won't forget to call us, will she?"

"I'm sure that win or lose, we will hear from her sometime tonight," Skye said. *Wow, this is actually working. Josie has completely forgotten why she called me in here.*

"Okay, Skylar Montgomery. I know what you're doing, and it isn't going to work. Now, spill!" Josie seemed to have remembered why she called Skye in. And as kind-hearted and happy as Josie usually was, Skye knew when she meant business.

"What?" Skye tried to look like she had nothing to hide.

"You know exactly what I'm talking about. You were avoiding me yesterday, and you were actually *civil* to people. I saw that little kid drop his lollipop on your Jimmy Choos, and you didn't even try to dismember him. Not like you, Skye."

Skye sighed, trying to figure out how to put into words what had happened with Gage. She wasn't even completely sure herself. But she was already in deeper than with any other guy, and they hadn't even been on a date yet!

"Come on, Skye. I was there at Stratus, and I know nothing happened with Gage, so I can't figure out why you're walking around here like you just found a really good sale at La Perla."

"Honestly, Josie, I don't know what to tell you."

"Well, did you meet someone else on the way home? Call a male escort service? Skye, I have to know. Something is definitely different about you, and I demand that you confide in me."

Only Josie could demand to be confided in and actually mean it. Skye knew she might as well tell her everything.

"Well, as you know, things didn't go quite as I had planned with Gage at the club."

Josie gazed at Skye and actually looked sad for her.

"I realized that as long as he was at work, the things I wanted to do to him were not going to happen. So, I waited and went back to Stratus after they closed." Skye shrugged her shoulders and looked up toward the ceiling innocently.

"You did not, Skylar!" Surprising Josie was not an easy thing to do.

"Yes, I did. And I threw myself at him."

The look on Josie's face was priceless. She didn't approve of most of the things her more experienced friend did when it came to men—few sensible women would. But this time Josie was actually speechless.

"And then he turned me down." Skye threw that in just to watch the expression on Josie's face change again.

"He did what? Never!" Josie leapt out of her chair and clenched her little fists. Gage would have been in a vice hold at this point if he had been in the room with them.

"Settle down, Josie. Let me finish."

Reluctantly, Josie sat back down, but kept her hands tightened into fists. Skye laughed at the image of Josie on Gage's back, choking and pummeling him mercilessly.

"Skye, why on earth are you laughing? You just told me that a man—the man you have been plotting to seduce—turned you down after you threw yourself at him. And you're *laughing*? Now I know something is very wrong."

"Well, I was laughing at you. I love that you're so upset for me. But let me finish before you try to beat Gage to death. He did turn me down...*for now*. Josie, he really wants to have a relationship. Or as he put it, 'dating and flowers and all that crap.'"

"Wow, a romantic, huh?" Josie laughed.

"He mentioned having kids with me, Josie. Kids! I mean I've never thought of having kids with anyone, and now I want that. Someday. And I think I want it with Gage." Skye was sure the look on her own face was a goofy grin; lately every time she thought about Gage, it made her...happy. "Let me ask you a question, Josie. When you're with Beau, do you ever think about the future? I mean, do you think he's *the one*?"

"Oh, Skye. I *know* Beau's the one. I knew when he kissed me at Stratus, and I didn't even know who he was or what he looked like. Every time I kiss him, I can see our future together." Josie drifted into Beau Land, as she often did when she talked about him. They had only been together a short time, but they were as much a part of one another as Noelle and Thomas. And now, Skye realized she wanted that for herself, too.

"So, in the end, while I was able to find out that he is an incredible kisser and has a body that is rock hard *everywhere*, he ended up asking me on a date. And that was it."

"Oh, Skye. I'm so happy for you. I can tell just by the way you talk about him—and the fact that you haven't made anyone cry by yelling at them for two whole days—that this is something that's going to be good!"

Josie flung herself out of the chair and wrapped her tall friend in a hug. Skye hugged her back, thankful for Josie and how happy she was. No matter what, Skye knew that all of them would always be friends.

"Alright, Josie. I have to head home. Gage is picking me up for our official date. And I plan on looking spectacular, because he promised to finish what we started the other night, and I fully plan to hold him to it."

"Do you know where he's taking you? I mean, you should know so you can figure out what to wear."

"No, he never said where we're going." Skye replayed the phone conversations they'd had the past few days in her mind and couldn't come up with a single clue as to where Gage planned to take her tonight. "But, I already know exactly what I'm going to wear. It will be short, low cut, and finished off with my new red stilettos."

"Ah, Skylar Montgomery. That boy doesn't stand a chance against your womanly ways!"

"That's the plan," Skye said with a sly wink.

With that, she strode out of Josie's office to make herself irresistible for Gage.

Gage was once again stuck with one of the "bouncing bimbos" he had to endure to pay his rent. His eyes kept slipping up to look at the clock, and it seemed to be moving backward.

"OK..." Gage stumbled as he tried to remember the name attached to the current pair of silicone boobs he was training. Really, they all seemed the same to him.

The nameless woman glanced up at Gage and batted her eyelashes, thinking she was being alluring. She wasn't. Gage wondered what did she thought he was going to say to her. *I want to do you right now?*

Gage just had to get her on the treadmill, and then he was done. Smiling, he congratulated himself again on thinking up the whole treadmill thing. "Time for some cardio. Fifteen minutes on the treadmill, and you are done for the day. I'll see you next week."

"Gage, you aren't going to leave me here all by myself, are you?" The woman leaned over and ran a finger down his chest, stopping at the waistband of his shorts.

Just the sound of her whiney voice and her touch actually caused a physical reaction. Gage broke out in a cold sweat.

"Sorry..." He still couldn't remember her name. "But you don't need me to watch you on the treadmill. You are a *big* girl and can do it all by yourself." Gage made sure to emphasize the word "big" hoping that she would get the hint. All of them were self conscious enough to think he was commenting on their bodies.

"But, you might *like* watching me on the treadmill." She actually slipped her finger inside Gage's waistband and ran it back and forth.

Gage had to hold back the shiver of disgust. Skye standing fully clothed and in a parka was a bigger turn on than this chick ever would be. But he knew he had to be professional. Gage couldn't afford to lose any of the bouncing bimbos. They paid the bills.

Gently, he removed her hand from his body. If she'd done that in front of Skye, she would no longer have a hand—maybe not even an arm. Once again, thinking of Skye got Gage in trouble as the current bimbo mistook his smile as encouragement. The fact that he had her hand in his didn't help the situation. "Um, I think you are great and all, but you know that the gym has a policy about the personal trainers getting involved with the clients. And I also have a personal issue with dating current or *former* clients." Gage tacked on the last part, knowing where the bimbo's train of thought was headed.

Eventually, he convinced her to get on the treadmill by telling her he thought her glutes needed tightening, and walking was a great way to do that. Of course, what she heard was: "You have a fat, saggy ass, and if you don't start walking, you will never find a man."

Once he had her all set up on the treadmill, Gage was able to sneak out to get ready for his date with Skye. He had been purposefully evasive with Skye over the past couple of days, not wanting to give even a hint of what he had planned. And he definitely had plans for the night.

Gage couldn't help but smile as he drove home. Thinking back on Tuesday night, he wanted to kick himself. *Why the hell did I mention having kids with her?* The only explanation he could find was that he really did love her. He'd been flirting and playing with her for a long time, and having her there in his arms just made him realize she was more than just another girl. She was *the* girl.

As Gage pulled into the parking garage, he had an eerie sense of having done the exact same thing before. He half expected to find the asshole ex in the hall and Skye in the stairwell, but they were both empty. He was pleased with what he saw when he unlocked his front door. Earlier that day, he had taken time to clean up his place. Even though he was going to actually take Skye out, he planned to end things there tonight. Well, tomorrow morning.

It took him only about a half an hour to shower and change before he was out the door. As he drove over to pick Skye up at her apartment, Gage decided to pick up some flowers. Looking around the florist's shop he was at a total loss. He had never actually liked a woman enough—or stayed in a relationship long enough to screw up badly enough—to buy flowers. There were beautiful bouquets of roses, but Gage decided that was too cliché and went with one giant sunflower and a bunch of balloons instead. He was trying to make an impression here, and was sure every guy that had ever given her flowers gave her roses.

As Gage turned onto Skye's street, he was suddenly nervous again. *Come on, Gage, she's just another girl.* He tried to reassure himself, but that was the problem. She was more than just another girl, and if he blew this, he knew she would never give him another chance. That was a lot of pressure on a guy!

SHIT, SHIT, SHIT! He's here!

Skye glanced in the mirror one last time before answering the booming knock. As she opened the door, she froze.

Gage was standing there in jeans which hung low on his hips, exposing a delicious sliver of skin just above his hipbone. Skye had to control the urge to bend down and run her tongue across it. *Wait a minute, no waistband. Is he going commando?* The urge grew even stronger. His t-shirt featured a faded Playboy bunny symbol. If he hadn't been so incredibly sexy, Skye would have closed the door right then. No man took Skylar Montgomery out looking like that.

His casual dress wasn't the biggest surprise, however. In his hand he had a giant sunflower and a huge bouquet of balloons. Skye was about to start into a huge explanation as to why none of this was acceptable, when she looked at his face. He had the biggest smile plastered on it, causing his dimples to deepen, and she simply melted.

"Um, Gage, why do you have a sunflower and balloons?"

He didn't say anything. He just dropped the flower and balloons, grabbed her around the waist, and pressed his lips to hers with an urgency she had never experienced. She opened her mouth and welcomed his tongue into it. Once again, she felt her knees going weak. *Damn! How does he keep doing that?*

She sighed when his lips left hers and moved down, following her jaw line up to her ear.

"Skye, you look...mmm...so beautiful. I want you right now," he whispered in a voice full of lust and want. Her reaction was instant and physical; her beautiful lace panties might just be ruined. "But, you may need to go change for our date," he continued, chuckling as his mouth left her ear and he pulled himself away from her.

"Why, Gage, are you trying to get me naked before we have our date?"

"No, Skye. It's just that for the night I have planned, those clothes may be a problem."

She didn't like how cryptic he was being. She had spent three hours putting all of this together, and there was no way she was going to change.

"I'm not changing, Gage. Maybe we need to do something else if what I'm wearing isn't appropriate."

He stood back and she watched as his eyes took in her entire body, starting with her red stilettos. He lingered there for a moment and then moved up her bare legs to the very short micro-mini and then to the plunging neckline of her blouse, where Skye had made sure her breasts were covered only enough to avoid arrest. His expression never changed. It remained the smile of a little boy on Christmas morning.

"Well, suit yourself, Skye, honey, but I'm not changing our plans. Let's get going."

He grabbed her hand and led her out the door, that smile still plastered on his face.

Dinner was a surprise to Skye. When they pulled up in front of Grizzlies, a hole-in-the-wall pizza joint, her mouth dropped open in disbelief.

Gage had a feeling no one had ever taken her for pizza and beer on a date. But this was his favorite place to eat. They had plasma TVs on every wall with any game you could possibly want to see, and even some you didn't. The pizza was the best in town, and Thursday night was half-price pitcher night!

Skye recovered quickly from her shock as Gage came around the car to help her out. He draped his arm across her shoulders as they walked inside, and Skye actually liked the way it felt.

Inside there was a Dodgers game on, and it was Gage's turn to be surprised when Skye actually knew what was going on in the game. Not only that, but she explained why she thought the Dodgers had no chance at the World Series and her beloved Yankees would be there instead.

Gage added this to the growing list of why he was falling in love with Skye. "So, how do you look like that, and know about the Dodgers' starting rotation?" Gage asked as they sat down in a booth after ordering.

Skylar actually blushed a little, something that she never did. She picked up the glass of beer Gage had just poured her to buy some time and figure out how much she was going to tell him. When she set her glass back on the table, Gage was still looking at her, waiting for her response.

"Well, I grew up with two much-older brothers. Our parents were...preoccupied with life, and so Brant and Blaine ended up kind of raising me," Skylar told him.

"So, are these older brothers something that I have to worry about? Do I have to pass their inspection or something if I want to date their sister?" Gage could tell Skye was a little uncomfortable and wanted to relax her. He knew Skye came from a pretty wealthy family, but apparently that didn't buy anyone an ideal childhood.

"No, they raised me to take care of myself." She laughed. "How about you? Do you have a mom and pop somewhere worrying about you?"

"Actually, yes. Mom, Pop, and baby sister are all home in Cleveland. I call every Sunday night before I go to Stratus. My little sister just started college this past year, and it kills me that I'm not there to scare the piss out of all the boys."

Skye laughed at how much he actually did remind her of her brothers. They had been protective of her for so long, but being twelve and thirteen years older, they had already started their families and had them to worry about now. As she gazed across the table at Gage, she realized that was one of the things that really attracted her to him: He would definitely take care of her.

By the time Gage had stuffed the last piece of pizza in his mouth, both of them were so far gone for each other, it seemed nothing could ruin the night—until the next part of the date that Gage had planned. As the car approached a giant windmill in the distance, Gage could feel Skye's eyes on him.

"Gage, you can't be serious?" There was true panic in her voice.

"What's wrong, Skye? You've never been mini-golfing before?

"Not in four-inch heels and a skirt. I might get arrested if I bend over!"

"Don't worry. I'll bail you out."

"Funny, Gage."

She was pissed, but Gage knew he could convince her to play. The image of her practically crumbling to the floor after a kiss from him spurred him on. Once they were parked, Gage leaned over and brushed his lips against her ear while he slid his hand up her leg toward the hem of her skirt. Skye quivered under his touch, and Gage couldn't help the rush of want that assaulted his body. "Please, Skye," he said.

Gage kissed from Skye's ear down to her neck. She leaned her head back against the seat. He was pretty sure she was going to give in, but just to be sure, he let his hand slip under her skirt and brush again the lace of her panties. "If you do this for me, I will do whatever you want after."

Leaving his hand resting on her panties, Gage kept kissing along her neck. He knew it was driving her crazy. Unexpectedly, Skye opened her legs a little wider, and he had full access to the spot he wanted most. A moan escaped from her lips, and Gage nearly lost it, wanting to turn the car around and take her back to his place right then. He couldn't help himself as he leaned over to Skye, moving his hand to the moist spot under her skirt as he did. The problem was that he also accidentally leaned on the horn. The loud blast broke the mood, and Gage quickly pulled his hand back, but kept his face close to hers. Their eyes locked.

"Fine, Romeo. But if we get thrown out of this place, it will be all your fault." Skye opened the door and got out of the car, pulling her skirt down in the process.

All Gage could think was that chicks had it so easy. Skye could just stop and get out like nothing ever happened. It took him a few extra minutes before he could get out of the car. Skye stood by the door with a smirk on her face.

"Come on, stud. I'm getting cold out here, and that isn't going to help our chances of not getting thrown out of here."

"You know, Skye, I did suggest that you change before we left."

"Yeah, but I didn't think you'd actually be taking me to play mini-golf. I mean really, Gage. No guy has ever taken me mini-golfing before, and definitely not on the first date."

"Well, I'm not any guy. Remember, I'm the father of your children."

Skye looked over at him, and the look in her eyes made him wonder if she was thinking seriously of a future with him, too. He found her hand, pulled her gently to his side, and leaned down to kiss the top of her head. She melted into the side of him. *This is so right.*

When they were set up with their golf clubs and balls, they approached the first hole.

"Here, Skye, hold my balls." Gage started laughing as he held his hand out to her with the two golf balls in it.

"What are you, fourteen?" she scolded him, but he could see a hint of a smile.

Skye had to bend over to place her ball, and when she did Gage was treated to the sight of her red lace panties and just a hint of her ass peeking out.

"Umm… Skye, honey. Maybe you should let me do that for you from now on. I don't want any of the innocent children to see the glorious sight I was just allowed. Besides, you'll ruin every man in the place for any other woman if they see how spectacular your ass is."

"What a gentleman."

For the next few holes, Gage placed Skye's ball at the start, and a few times he caught her checking out *his* ass. He couldn't help but smile, and then on the fifth hole, he felt her delicate hands on each cheek.

"Umm, Gage, how much longer do we have to be on our date?"

Crap! Was she bored out of her mind? He thought she would have fun doing something different. Suddenly he realized he should have just taken her to a nice restaurant like he figured she'd wanted. *Stupid ass!*

"I'm sorry, Skye. I should have changed the plans tonight. I'll take you home."

Gage stood up, but her hands never left his ass. Then she ran her hands up his back, her nails leaving a trail to his neck. He shivered and turned to face her. The look in her eyes was not irritation, but pure sex.

She reached up and wrapped her hands around his neck, pulling him down to her. Her tongue ran along his ear lobe before she put her lips right to his ear. "I didn't say I wanted you to take me home. I just want you to take me."

In a split second, Gage dropped his club, wrapped an arm around Skye's waist, and headed for the exit.

Skye didn't think it would actually be that easy to get Gage to leave, but she wasn't complaining when he practically dragged her to the car, pinning her to the door and assaulting her with a deep, passionate kiss while his hands once again roamed up under her skirt and came to rest on her lace-covered ass.

"I don't think the good patrons of mini-golf land will enjoy the little show we are about to put on for them, so open the door and take me to your place, Gage."

She didn't have to ask twice. Gage quickly opened the door for her and practically stuffed her into the seat, going so far as to buckle the seatbelt for her. Then he ran around the car, flung himself behind the wheel, and was on the highway before Skye could even comprehend what was happening.

When she glanced over at Gage, Skye became a little concerned. He hadn't spoken a single word since she told him that she wanted him to take her.

"Gage? Are you OK?" Skye reached across the console and laid her hand on Gage's arm. The muscles were pulled tight, and she could feel the ropey tendons as they strained beneath her fingers. He seemed so tense.

"I just have to really concentrate, Skye. If I let my mind wander or even look at you, I don't think I'll be able to control myself right now."

Sitting back in the seat, Skye smiled. *Who knew mini-golf could be such a big turn on?* She liked that Gage didn't treat her like a fragile little girl. Most guys assumed that because she was beautiful, she couldn't take care of herself.

Without thinking, Skye laid her hand on Gage's leg. At her touch, Gage stepped on the gas too hard and she was pushed back into her seat as they accelerated down the freeway.

"Skye, honey, while I never thought I would say this, could you please not touch me right now?"

"I'm sorry, Gage, I forgot. Explain to me again what you don't want me to do." She was just teasing him now, and Gage really needed her to stop. She ran her finger up to his ear and traced his earlobe, then down his neck. "Like, is this OK to do?" she cooed.

"Skye. Seriously, it's only a few more blocks, and it would be such a tragedy if we didn't actually make it home." Of course, that didn't do anything to stop Skye's torturous touching. Gage clenched his teeth together and hissed, "Please!"

At Gage's slow hiss, Skye nearly lost consciousness. It was the sexiest thing she had ever heard, and she vowed to make him do it again.

When Gage pulled into the garage of his building, he practically skidded to a stop in a parking space. Jumping out before Skye could get her door open, he leaned down and scooped her right out of the car, finding her lips easily and kissing her with more passion than any man ever had.

He kicked the door closed, and Skye heard the beep of the locks echo in the garage. Once at the elevators, Gage set her down, never breaking the contact their lips still held. "Damn it, this elevator is so slow." Gage added a nice string of swear words as he finally pulled away from Skylar, allowing her to catch a breath.

The elevator finally came and Skye was grateful because she could have sworn Gage had just mumbled something about throwing her over his shoulder and carrying her up the stairs. Gage pulled

Skye into the elevator, pressing his body against hers and pinning her to the back wall. His hands were on her bare thighs, and she immediately responded to him by wrapping one leg around his hip. As Gage slid a hand across Skye's ass, he pressed himself into her. She could feel the urgency in every touch.

The elevator dinged, and the doors opened, startling both of them. They had completely forgotten where they were.

Gage grabbed Skye's hand, pulling her down the hall to his apartment. It seemed to take forever for him to find the key and open the damn door. All the while Skye's hands never stopped roaming over his body. When the door swung open, Gage wrapped one arm around her waist and spun her into his apartment.

A brief—*very brief*—look around his apartment revealed the obvious: a guy lives here. A black leather sofa and giant recliner with a huge coffee table sat in the middle of the room. Of course, a giant plasma TV hung on the wall with a massive theatre system on shelves underneath. The only things on the wall were sports memorabilia. The place was testosterone heaven.

That was the extent of what Skye got to see, though, before Gage was in front of her, looking at her with all that lust and want again. It was at that moment that Skye's phone rang, once again interrupting what she wanted to happen so badly.

"Ignore it," Gage begged her.

This time she listened to him. Skye didn't care who was calling right now; she didn't care about anything at this moment except this beautiful man standing in front of her.

He reached out to her, but instead of pulling her into him, he gently took her hand and brought it to his lips, kissing it lightly.

"Skye, I want you so bad right now. But I want you to understand that I don't just want you tonight. I want you forever."

"Gage, I've never wanted anyone more than I want you. And I don't just mean your body either."

He gave her his goofy grin as he turned around, still holding her hand, and led her to his bedroom.

"But, for tonight I will settle for every inch of your body," he whispered to her as he laid her down on the bed. Every fiber in her body was on fire, and she craved his touch.

"I think I can handle that," Skye managed to say. Her hands went to the bottom of his shirt, pulling it straight over his head to reveal the most orgasm-inducing sight she'd ever seen. To say he had a six-pack would be an understatement; the boy had a case! She ran her hands over his entire body, touching every inch of his bare skin. He let out a low moan and stepped back from her.

A scream of frustration caught in Skye's throat at the loss of Gage's body against hers. She felt suddenly empty without his big body covering her.

Skye pulled herself onto her knees so she was kneeling in the middle of the bed. With his eyes locked on hers, Gage climbed onto the bed. If Skye had been standing, she would have melted at his feet. She had that same look in her eyes as she had the other night at Stratus when he caused her to lose her balance.

He made his way to her and pulled himself up on his knees to match her posture. They were both breathing hard as Gage ran his hands up Skye's body, pulling her shirt over her head as he went. Leaning back, he took in the red lace bra that was barely containing her breasts.

Gage's mouth went to Skye's breast and took the nipple in his mouth through the lace. His tongue gently circled it as it grew harder with every breath. While his mouth worked both of her breasts in equal measure, Skye felt his hands at her back. In one quick motion, he released her from the red-lace torture that was separating them. He gently took her bra down her shoulders, kissing every inch of bare skin along the way. When there was nothing more between their upper bodies, he immediately returned his attention to her exposed, hardened nipples.

"Oh, Gage," Skye moaned, encouraging him. He increased the pressure of his tongue, causing even more wonderful sensations to course through her body.

Skye's hand slid down his beautiful naked chest to find the top of his jeans. She unbuttoned them and slowly slid them down over his hips. To her great pleasure, her earlier assumption that he was running commando was totally correct. When Skye finally got Gage's jeans down to where his knees were on the bed, he carefully stepped back and finished the job.

As Skye drank in the sight of Gage's entire naked body, she stopped breathing. When her head started spinning, she decided she needed to lie down.

"Everything okay, Skye?" Gage had a smile on his face, but it was definitely a naughty smile.

"I'll be fine. Just seeing you like that," she waved her hand toward him, "caught me by surprise."

"Well, let me give you a few more surprises."

In an instant he was hovering over her. He set his knees between Skye's legs causing them to widen. Gage's hands made their way from her knees along the outside of her thighs. Soon, they were under her skirt, running over the small piece of material that now seemed a burden.

Skye felt her skirt slide down her legs, and Gage moved to pull it completely off, flinging it to the ground. Then she saw him looking at her shoes.

"Do you want me to take them off?"

"Not at all."

He was back on the bed and his hands were touching every part of Skye's body. By the little moans and mewls she was making, Gage was pretty sure she was enjoying it. When he finally made his way back to the most aching part of her entire body, he slowly ran a finger over the lace of her still intact panties and Skye moaned.

"Gage... Please...now."

"Patience, darlin', patience."

Skye was sure he was trying to torture her. But, as he moved back up her body to look in her eyes, she could feel his excitement press into her and knew he wanted her as much as she wanted him. His hands were moving again, and they deftly removed the red lace, allowing him full access to her entire body.

As his hands moved to Skye's most heated and sensitive spot, she arched her back to bring her closer to him. A smile bloomed on his face. He began to work his way back down her body, kissing every inch he could get his mouth on, stopping at Skye's breasts to tease them some more with his tongue. She watched Gage duck down between her legs, and let out a small moan, which only encouraged him more.

When he had brought her to the brink of ecstasy without providing the release she ached for, Gage moved back up Skye's body, and slowly, lovingly entered her. They moved together like they had been doing this dance forever. Every move Gage made was countered simply by Skye's instincts. It was the most amazing thing either of them had ever experienced.

Finally, when they were both spent, Gage rolled over and in one motion pulled Skye closer into his body. She was amazed at how well the two of them fit together. Every curve of her body seemed to have been designed to accommodate an outcropping of muscle of in his.

Letting out a sigh of contentment, Skye felt Gage's body shake in laughter underneath her.

"What is so funny?" No man had ever laughed after sex with Skye. Cry, beg, threaten to hurt himself, but not laugh.

"I was just thinking how much better this was than if we had finished the other night at the bar."

"Oh, but that could be fun," she teased as she ran a finger up his chest.

"I love you, Skylar Montgomery."

"I love you too, Gage Vandenberg."

Then Gage kissed Skye's head softly as her eyes closed, and a smile came to her lips. She was safe and happy in Gage's arms.

Chapter Eleven

Everything was packed, but Eve made one last check of the drawers and shower just to be sure. She liked the little body lotion sample the hotel had left on the counter, so she plopped that in her bag as well. The last few minutes in this glorious room, Eve decided, would be spent looking out the window, taking in the view and committing it to memory.

Her flight was leaving at 12:20, and Megan had reminded her last night that Will would pick her up at 10:30. As Eve gazed out over the city, two things became very clear to her: First, she was falling for Will *(Are you sure you haven't already fallen, Eve?)*. And second, she lived three thousand miles from him, far too distant to allow her mind to drift toward thoughts of romance. Not that she could help it.

All she could hold on to at this moment were conversations they'd had, so she let them play over and over in her head, accompanied by the vision of his face and that smile of his, and the kiss that he'd given her last night as he held her *so* close. They didn't discuss that kiss, but it *had* happened, and it didn't feel like the kind of kiss you'd give a friend or colleague, let alone a grant winner. His lips had lingered against her temple, and he'd kept his cheek against her hair from the moment he pulled her to him to dance. And she had embraced him, too. She'd tried to let him know she liked what he'd done. *If only I could have moved my face up toward his and let him kiss me the way I wanted him to.*

The phone by the bed rang, and Eve picked it up before it could ring a second time.

"Hi, it's Will. Are you ready to go to the airport?" His voice was flat. Eve was pleased that he didn't sound enthused.

"I guess. Unless you've got a good reason for me to stay." The words were out before she could stop herself. She wanted to crawl into a hole and hide.

"Well..." Will chuckled. He was at a loss. The words he wanted to say, the ones that would make her stay with him—always—were stuck in his throat. He just couldn't put himself out there yet. There were things that needed to be taken care of with the foundation and his company before he would be able to tell Eve Carwyn that he had indeed fallen in love with her.

"I'll be down in a minute," Eve finally said to fill the silence that hung between them. She wasn't sure what the silence meant, but decided it didn't matter. She was going home today, and Will was staying here.

The ride in the elevator was bittersweet as she realized it would be the last time she had that feeling of anticipation right before the doors opened. When the elevator came to a stop in the lobby and they did, Eve was elated to see Will leaning against that same wall with that same beautiful smile on his face. She committed that picture to memory; it was probably the one she would miss most.

Will immediately jogged the few feet over to Eve to collect her laptop and suitcase. He wasn't about to let her last impression of him be him letting her carry her own things. He offered to take her carry-on bag as well, but Eve shifted it on her shoulder and told him she was fine.

A little disappointed, Will guided her through the lobby to his car. As they walked side by side, Will kept stealing glances at her, wondering if she had meant what she said on the phone. But while her smile was genuine, the sparkle was gone from her eyes, and they seemed to be on a more professional plane again. He knew that it was the damn kiss. Eve had been so polite about it, trying not to embarrass him, but it had definitely crossed the line.

As they drove to the airport the same Lila Marin CD was playing again. Neither Eve nor Will knew quite what to say, so the ride was quiet, and the words of the song filled the space. *"You're mist that surrounds me...You're inside my heart, but I can't hold you...I'm falling apart..."*

"Did you get a chance to call your colleagues last night to tell them the good news?" Will finally broke the silence as he glanced at Eve, making sure to ask something about work.

"Yes. I talked to Josie McInnis, our accountant. I'm surprised you didn't hear her screams of excitement coming from the phone in my room."

Falling apart...lost without you...falling apart... The music kept playing in the background, and both were completely aware of how perfectly the song fit the situation.

"So, what happens now?" Eve asked. When Will didn't answer her, she glanced over to him. He just stared at her. She realized what she had said, and how it must have sounded. Trying to clarify, she quickly added, "I mean, what does the SBMA need to do from here? Is there more paperwork to file? Does someone from our museum need to come back to Boston at some point or will someone from here be coming to Santa Barbara?"

Will relaxed slightly. When he'd heard Eve's question, he'd frozen. He didn't know how to honestly answer. Figuring he was caught, he had been about to confess his feelings for her. But then Eve further explained and returned them to business.

"Megan will be sending information to your museum early next week, including some forms to sign. Martin will get in touch with Josie to go over the spreadsheets we use. You know, money stuff that's best discussed by those who understand it. I believe Megan will also be sending photos from last night to some of your local newspapers, too, for them to have if they want to do a story."

"And, will someone be traveling to actually *see* the museum? Maybe meet with our staff?"

"Oh, yes, of course. I plan to make my first trip out there in about a week and a half."

Eve's heart soared at his words—and this would be his *first* trip? He was planning to visit more than once?

"That will give both sides the opportunity to look over the contracts and address any issues with attorneys or finance people before everybody signs on their respective dotted lines."

"So does that mean you're going to be the person we'll be working with?" Eve asked nonchalantly.

"That's my intent, at least as we get things off the ground. Two of the previous grants are nearly completed, and all but one of the others is going fairly smoothly. A few glitches here and there I can handle by phone or email. With new projects, I like to be pretty hands-on for at least the first six months or so."

Six months of Will being hands-on? Mmmm... While Eve nodded politely to Will's explanation, her mind went wild with excitement.

As they arrived at the airport, Eve stayed quiet as Will steered the car to the parking garage rather than dropping her off at the Departing Flights entrance. He hadn't asked if she minded him staying with her until she boarded the plane; she was just glad he *wanted* to.

He checked Eve's suitcase and tipped the man before she could even get her wallet out. She smiled a "thank you" to him, and he just grinned and nodded his "you're welcome." He then pulled her carry-on from her shoulder, and when Eve went to protest, he gave her a scolding look.

"Do you want my mother rolling over in her grave? She would, you know, if she knew that I let you hold a bag that a gentleman would offer to carry."

That uncontrollable smile once again returned to Eve's face. *Do you have any idea, Will Prentiss, how amazing you are? I bet your mother and father would be* quite *proud of you!*

They'd made good time getting to the airport, and it was still an hour until the first boarding call. Will suggested that Eve have some lunch before leaving since the food on the plane would be, well, airplane food. Before they selected a place to eat, he brought her over to a bench, placed her carry-on on the floor beside her, and asked that she wait for a few minutes. Eve was about to question him when he threw her that amazing smile, making her forget what she was about to say. She simply nodded and sat down, her eyes still on his beautiful face.

"I'll be right back, I promise!" Within ten minutes, he returned, a little winded from apparently jogging but smiling brightly. "Sorry about that."

He immediately picked up her bag again, and they continued on their way. As they approached the security check, Eve's heart dropped. She had a ticket, and Will didn't. He wouldn't be able to go any further with her like she had silently hoped. She wasn't ready to say good-bye to him yet.

As Eve nervously got out her ticket, ready to show the security agent, she wondered if Will could sense her drastic mood change. She turned to him, ready as she could be to say goodbye, and saw that he was holding a plane ticket in his hand.

"What? Where did that come from? Are you flying out today, too? Where's your luggage?" Eve was dumbfounded.

"Umm, I guess I'm going to...let's see, it's either Dallas or San Jose." He glanced quickly at the ticket and then gave Eve a sly smile.

"You're not going anywhere, are you?"

"Sure I am. I'm going with you to have lunch before your flight leaves."

Will Prentiss had just bought a ticket so he could have lunch with her. *Oh. My. Word.*

Will watched as Eve blushed again, that beautiful smile that he loved making an appearance as well. He felt his face break into a returning grin.

Once through security, they settled on the Berghoff Café, both of them much more at ease now that their goodbye had been delayed. The café was crowded, but the line moved quickly. After Will ordered a cup of coffee and Eve decided on a turkey sandwich, the couple found a small table and immediately fell into comfortable conversation.

"Oh!" Eve said, and then finished swallowing the bite she had just taken. "I should give you one of my business cards. I think the phone number we provided you on the grant paperwork had only the main line to the museum, and that sometimes leaves you in a loop listening to our location and hours." Reaching into her purse, she pulled out a card, and handed it to Will.

"Eve Carwyn, Santa Barbara Museum of Art, Curator." Will read out loud as he held the card for what seemed like a long time, studying it. Then, in a very business-like manner, he said, "Do you have a cell phone number I can add?" Eve looked at him with a smile. "You know, in case I need you when you're not in your office?"

"Oh, of course," she laughed as she supplied the number. "So, you'll be coming to visit Santa Barbara in a week or so?"

Remaining casual, Will got out a business card of his own and wrote on the back of it while he spoke. "I'm thinking the week after next, but I'll have Megan check my schedule. I'd like to plan a weekend stay so I can see the museum in action when families are visiting, as well as schools during the week. Probably a Thursday or Friday arrival and staying through the following Tuesday." He handed Eve his card and she immediately put it in her purse.

Eve liked the idea of Will being in town for a weekend. Plans for his visit started to form in her head. "Well, if you'd like, I'll arrange an itinerary for your stay that will include 'seeing the town as only a true Californian can show you.' How does that sound?"

"Do I have any say as to who my tour guide will be?"

"Well, we generally have Helga who is old and yells a lot do the honors, but I don't know, you seem like a very special visitor to our fair city. I may have to take you on myself." Eve beamed at him.

"Good. Then it's settled. I was going to ask for you anyway. No offense to Helga, of course."

They both laughed at that and stood to leave the café. Looking at her watch, Eve realized it was a few minutes until noon. "Oh! I need to hurry!"

When they reached her gate, Eve noticed people were already moving through the doorway to the plane. With a small pain in her chest, she realized her time with Will was almost over. Watching the other passengers board, Eve decided that she didn't care if she was the last person to board the plane, she was going to spend every last second she could with Will.

Will could see the sadness in Eve's eyes. There were tears caught in her lashes, and Will's heart was breaking. He was taken aback when suddenly Eve turned and threw her arms around his neck. Without a second thought, Will wrapped his arms around her and held her to him.

Eve could feel the tears running down her cheeks now, soaking the collar of Will's shirt. There was no way he could not know she was crying. She knew she was being ridiculous, but then Will tightened his hold on her, burying his face in her hair.

The two stayed like that for what seemed like a long time. Will finally broke from the embrace, and Eve tried to compose herself.

"I don't know what's wrong with me. I am *so* sorry! God, this is crazy! Why am I crying?" Will still had his arms around her waist, and Eve kept her head bowed as she wiped her eyes.

"I had a wonderful time this week, too, you know," he said quietly.

"LAST CALL FOR FLIGHT 3819 TO LOS ANGELES."

Leaning back, as he still held Eve, Will tilted his head. He needed to see her face again before she got on that plane. With a nervous giggle, Eve looked up at him, finally allowing her tear-filled eyes to meet his.

"Would it be all right if I called you later so I can be sure you made it home OK?" His voice was full of concern, and Eve was touched—and relieved he hadn't been spooked by her crying fit. She nodded as she wiped her eyes one more time.

"OK. I've got to go or I'll miss my flight," she finally managed with a small smile and a sniffle.

Will walked Eve right to the gate door as it was about to close and then surprised her by pulling her into one more hug. Before releasing her, he leaned down and whispered, "You are *amazing*. Keep yourself safe, OK?"

Just as quickly as he had embraced her, Will let Eve go. Without making eye contact again, Will handed her her bag, then turned on his heel and left without looking back.

The door closed behind Eve, and she walked briskly down the ramp and onto the plane.

Wait a minute... What did he just say?

Before Will was even out of the airport, he was on the phone with Megan. "Hey, I need you to make my Santa Barbara plans for late next week. Same hotel and car company. What's my schedule look like? Can I go Thursday or do I have to wait until Friday? Damn. OK, book the hotel for Friday through Tuesday. Yeah, she just left. I'll be in the office in a little bit. I just want to make a quick stop."

Skylar glanced at the clock on the dashboard in her car. It said 8:57. Silently cursing herself for spending the night at Gage's, she stepped on the gas and prayed she wouldn't get pulled over.

The problem was that every time she got up to leave, those big, strong arms of his would wrap around her, and she would totally forget why she wanted to leave in the first place. This time she cursed Gage for being so damn sexy, because now she was going to be late for work, and Josie was going to kill her. Not because she was late—Josie didn't care about that—but because she would be waiting to hear about the date with Gage.

When she finally made it to the office, only ten minutes late, Skye was surprised to find it empty. She had been sure Josie would be sitting at her desk waiting to pounce. Feeling relieved, she sat down and turned her computer on. When she looked up, she almost jumped out of her skin. That damn little sneak was sitting directly across from Skye, staring with those big green eyes of hers.

"Well, well, well, Ms. Montgomery. You were a little tardy for work this morning, I see. Would there be a reason for that?" There was a smirk plastered on Josie's face.

"As a matter of fact, Ms. McInnis, there are about four, oh no, five reasons I am late this morning."

Skye watched as Josie's eyes grew larger.

"Five?"

"Yes. If you count the last time, which was his attempt to try and keep me in bed with him all day."

"Skye! Don't you know you should never sleep with a guy on the first date?"

"Really. So how many dates did you and Beau have before you slept with him?"

"Okay, well, that's totally different because we're meant to be together," Josie tried to backpedal.

"Uh huh."

Realizing her mistake, Josie went immediately into overdrive trying to make Skye forget that she had slept with Beau only hours after meeting him. Josie knew that Skye would only make it sound cheap, which it wasn't. What she and Beau had was right and perfect and was going to last forever. And considering that Skylar and Gage had known each other for a year, she decided to just let it go. "Tell me about the date. Where did he take you? Was it romantic? Obviously you had fun. But I want details."

Taking her time, knowing she had Josie's full attention, Skye glanced at her computer screen, clicking on her email. There were seven new messages.

"Skye! Tell me about your date with Gage."

"Oh, OK. Well, when he picked me up, I looked hot: short skirt, low cut top with my boobs barely contained, and my red stilettos."

"Ohhh, I can imagine Gage all dressed up. I bet you could barely keep your hands off of him."

"He was wearing jeans and a Playboy bunny t-shirt, and holding a sunflower and a big bouquet of balloons."

Josie started laughing so hard Skye worried that she just might fall out of the chair. Her tinkling laugh was infectious, though, and Skye started laughing too, remembering the sight of Gage in her doorway.

"You have to be kidding me. Where did he take you? Mini-golfing?" Josie laughed even harder and tears streamed down her cheeks.

When Skye didn't answer right away, Josie looked up at her. Her mouth hung open for a second. "Never! He took you mini-golfing?"

"And for pizza and beer," Skye added.

"Then explain to me how you ended up in bed with him and late for work for five reasons. Because I know you, Skye, and I know that if a man showed up like that for a date with *you,* he would have the door slammed in his face."

"I know. But there's something about Gage. I mean, seriously, it was the best date—and sex—I've ever had. I know now what you meant about finding the right fit with Beau. Gage and I fit together perfectly. It doesn't sound like that, I know, but he feels right. Do you know what I mean?"

Josie nodded with a huge smile on her face. There was no need for any further explanation.

As Skye looked back at her waiting email, she noticed a new message from a Megan Stepanski at Townsend Industries.

"Oh! Josie did you hear from Eve? My phone rang at a very inopportune moment, and I didn't answer it. I totally forgot about the grant. Did we get it?"

"Yes, I heard from her. Oh my gosh, I thought you'd heard! Yes, we got the grant!"

The next few moments were spent with the two women jumping up and down like teeny boppers who just saw the heartthrob du jour. When they were finally able to rein themselves in and come back down to earth, Skye returned to her email and opened the message from Townsend Industries.

Josie moved to stand behind Skye so she could read the message also. Together they scanned the text, which was, as expected, congratulations from Eve's Will Prentiss, who apparently was the founder of the company. Skye read that part of the email again. Eve hadn't mentioned that during their phone conversation. The last line of the email read:

Attached please find a photo taken the night of the banquet. I have taken the liberty of forwarding a copy to your local newspaper as well so that they can prepare a story about your lovely museum.

Skye clicked on the attachment. Both women were anxious to see the picture.

When it finally loaded, they were immediately drawn to the incredible blue eyes of the man who must be Will Prentiss. Josie and Skye looked at each other in amazement, and at exactly same time, they both said, "Oh. My. God."

"You are amazing. Keep yourself safe, OK?" Why would he say that—in that way? It was like he was worried something bad might happen to me. Eve's mind was racing as she found her seat.

Thinking back on the week, she was sure she hadn't said anything that would make him think she was in any kind of danger. He definitely didn't know about Julian, and Eve didn't think he ever saw the marks on her neck.

As she contemplated Will's words, Eve remembered that she had heard them somewhere else before. She tried to think, and an audible gasp escaped when Eve realized it had been her fourth fish. *How on earth would Will Prentiss know what a man on the other side of the country had said during a silly bar game?*

As soon as the pilot said it was OK, Eve adjusted her seat, leaning back as much as she could, and put the little pillow between her cheek and the window. She was tired, but still keyed up about all that had happened and what was waiting for her at home.

In the few minutes before they took off, Eve had been able to check her cell phone's voice mail. There was nothing. But she knew she'd find messages on her home answering machine. Eve had changed her cell number after they broke up when Julian wouldn't stop calling. Since she hadn't heard from Gage, she assumed that her apartment was intact.

The idea of Julian following through on his threat to kill her gave her a chill. He was part of her world, and there was no way she could completely avoid him. After all, his art was hanging in her museum. She decided her only option was to come clean with her friends, because she knew they would protect her.

Wanting to rest before having to deal with all of the details of her real life, Eve eventually relaxed enough to close her eyes. Once she was comfortable and able to let her mind wander again over the past week, she relived some of the time she'd spent with Will, but allowed the denouement to be much more satisfying...

Will crouches closely and all but yells in her ear, "Will you trust me about where I'm going to take you?"

"Why?"

"Because I want to take you to my apartment. It's just one block further."

"There's a bathroom just down that hallway. I'm thinking I need to get you some dry clothes. I'm guessing, based on how soaked I am, that your underclothing may also need to go in the dryer?

Would you, um, want to wear a pair of my boxers under the sweat pants I'm going to bring you?"

"Ooh! A pair of boxers would be nice. What have you got?"

Following him to his bedroom, she slithers past him, allowing her soaked and nearly see-through t-shirt to brush up against his chest. His breathing becomes ragged.

She turns, focused on Will's face, and begins to unbutton her khakis. "Well? Have you got some boxers for me?" Will's eyes have glazed over as she unzips her pants and starts to lower them over her hips. Working them down her legs, she slowly steps out of them, standing in front of him in her clinging, wet t-shirt and black satin and lace panties.

He still doesn't speak so she walks toward him. "Do you need help getting your jeans off? Wet clothing can be difficult to remove." She presses her breasts against his stomach and looks up at his face while her hands undo his belt. He finally can't hold back anymore.

Will wraps his arms around her, pulling her into a passionate kiss as his tongue explores. He lifts her and moves them both onto the bed, laying her down gently. Grasping his shirt, she starts to unbutton it. Then he breaks the kiss and yanks the bottom of his shirt from his jeans. Once she finishes unbuttoning his shirt, it easily slides down over his shoulders and arms. Finally free of it, he throws it on top of her pants only to resume kissing her, letting his lips wander down to her neck and collarbone. Stopping for a moment, Will leans on his arm, allowing his fingers to softly run down the front of her t-shirt, at first grazing and then more confidently exploring the hard nipples that are apparent beneath the wet material.

Eventually, she is able to sit up long enough to pull her shirt over her head and toss it to the pile on the floor. Will's hands move over her heated skin and end up resting on her breasts. When he looks at Eve as if asking for permission, her breath catches as she watches him gently pull the lace of her bra down enough to expose her fully. He groans as he takes her into his mouth and flicks his tongue over her nipple.

Her hands are in his hair as she gasps at the pleasure Will is bringing her. She holds him tightly to her, begging him not to stop. As his mouth continues to caress her, his hand begins to move like a whisper down her abdomen to the top of her panties. As she opens her legs to let him know that she wants him to continue to explore her...

"Flight 3819 will be landing in Los Angeles approximately ten minutes ahead of schedule. It's a pleasant seventy-seven degrees with slightly overcast skies. Please return your seats..." the voice droned on as Eve struggled to pull herself back to reality.

All Eve could think about was how much better that dream would have gotten in those ten extra minutes. And if she were ever lucky enough to get Will into that situation, she would need *more* than ten minutes to finish. Hell, she would need a lifetime to ever be fully satisfied with Will.

Once Eve had collected her luggage and found her car in the long-term parking lot, the dread of going home set in. She wondered how many times Julian had called and hoped maybe he had given up after a week.

She decided to take the Pacific Coast Highway home, as it would give her some nice quiet time to think...and hide. As Eve drove, lost in her thoughts and memories, she caught a small record store out of the corner of her eye and made the quick decision to pull in. The song that had been playing in Will's car was still haunting her, and she wanted to see if she could find it for herself.

When she walked in, it occurred to her that she couldn't remember the artist or the name of the song. The thing she remembered was those words that had seemed to have been written just for them:

"...you're mist that surrounds me...you're inside my heart...but I can't hold you...I'm falling apart..."

It was a small, independent store, and the clerk didn't look like she and Eve would have even remotely the same taste in music. The girl had bright blue spiked hair, a piercing in her nose connected by a chain to one in her ear, and was wearing combat boots. Definitely not anything like Eve.

Shoring up her courage, Eve approached the girl and tried to explain what she was looking for. To her surprise, the clerk knew just what she was talking about.

"Could it be Lila Marin's 'Just as I Am'?" she asked. "Here, let me put it in a player for you." She led Eve to a place where headphones and a chair awaited. It only took a moment for Eve to confirm that this was the CD. Skipping through the songs, sure enough, within a few bars of track nine, Eve heard the line about falling apart.

As soon as she started the engine, she immediately loaded the new CD into her player. It was just one more thing that allowed her to hold on to Will, and she relaxed for the remainder of her drive home.

Because Eve had thrown away pretty much everything in her refrigerator before the trip, she decided a stop by the grocery store was also in order before she went home. As she walked each aisle, gathering more than she really needed or usually bought, she knew she was still just putting off the inevitable: going to her apartment.

Three hours after landing, Eve finally felt able to go home.

When she got to her apartment, she dropped her things in front of the door and, before opening it, decided to check in quickly with Gage, just to let him know she was home—not to mention that knowing he was there would definitely make her feel better.

After knocking three times, Eve was about to give up when she heard giggles and commotion coming from behind the door. When he opened it, Gage was dressed only in a pair of gray cotton boxers. Eve couldn't help the journey her eyes made all over the man's body. She quickly tried to divert her attention back to Gage's face.

"Hi, Gage." Eve's embarrassment made her face hot. "I didn't mean to interrupt, um, anything. I just wanted you to know I was home."

From the bedroom behind him came a woman's voice. "*Gage*, get that beautiful ass and everything connected to it back in here right now!"

"Skye?" Eve stared at Gage in disbelief.

"Uh, yeah," he stammered. "While you were in Boston, well, um, Skye and I...uh..."

"Gotcha." She held up her hand to let him know more information on the two of them was definitely *not* needed. "And, way to go! You finally got the girl you wanted!"

Gage just smiled like a big goof. Eve couldn't help but return his smile, as she was genuinely happy for her friends. "Don't keep her waiting!" Eve winked at Gage and returned to her apartment.

Unlocking the door, she entered cautiously. While Gage hadn't mentioned that anything had happened to her place while she was gone, he also hadn't been totally focused. But the apartment seemed to be exactly as Eve had left it. Once she had retrieved everything from the car, Eve closed the door and locked it immediately. She didn't know if Julian knew when she was coming home, so it was best to be safe.

As she began to sort the groceries on the kitchen counter, Eve leaned over to the answering machine. Seventeen messages. Knowing that they were probably all from Julian, she took a deep breath and pressed the play button.

BEEP – *"Eve? Eve! I need to talk to you about last night. Babe, you know how crazy I can get sometimes but I didn't mean to scare you. Come on, Eve, pick up the phone."*

BEEP – *"Eve! Why aren't you calling me back? Are those* friends *of yours telling you not to? I've told you, sweetheart, they don't care about you the way I do."*

BEEP – *"I don't understand why you are doing this to me! What are you doing in Boston, huh? Are you* screwing *someone there? Don't forget, Eve, you're* mine. *Come on baby, we can make this work. Don't do this to me. I love you, Eve. Please call me."*

BEEP – *"Please, Eve, call me. I* need *you, Eve. You* can't *leave me. I won't* allow *it to happen. Do you hear me? I'm sorry. I'm sorry. Please, Eve, I have to talk to you. Don't shut me out. I have to explain. I'll take you back. I don't care about anything that happened in Boston. But you will always be* mine.*"*

Other than a wrong number and a call about a book she had reserved at the library, all the messages were from Julian. With each one, his voice sounded angrier. Eve made a mental note to mention the messages to Gage. The idea to tell Will also flitted through her mind, and she wondered why. The man lived three thousand miles away, but just thinking of him made her feel safer.

At that moment Eve's cell phone buzzed from her purse. She saw a Boston area code. Her heart flew into overdrive.

"Hello?"

"Hey. It's Will. Is it OK that I called? I mentioned at the airport that I would…"

With a heavy sigh, Eve plopped down on the sofa, falling comfortably onto the overstuffed cushions. "Yeah. It's *definitely* OK that you called."

Eve tried to keep things light and could tell he was doing the same—lots of talk about the weather and general work-related stuff. But he *had* called. As their conversation went on, the thoughts of Julian faded like smoke from a candle. Will was the flame that burned brightly.

After about a half-hour, and ten minutes of playing the "you hang up first" game, they finally found a way to say goodnight.

"I've got an idea," Will said. "Both of us should close our eyes. You picture me standing in front of the elevator, waving good night to you, and I'll picture you standing *in* the elevator and waving to me as the doors close. OK? I'll count to five, and we'll both hang up at the same time."

He counted slowly, allowing the images to filter through her mind—his beautiful face and that crooked smile, both attached to his gorgeous body. But there was so much more. The man standing there in her vision was someone Eve was sure she had fallen in love with.

Chapter Twelve

Eve slept fitfully that first night back in her own bed. Being in the same town as Julian once again was a little frightening to her. She realized she needed to let her friends know what happened as soon as she could. Only then would she feel somewhat safe—not as safe as when she was with Will, but safer than she did right now.

After spending the morning doing her laundry, Eve tried to call both Josie and Skye. Neither answered their phones. Ironically, she could actually hear Skye's phone ringing on the other side of the wall when she called. Eve was getting a little tired of being ignored by her friends, but she understood the whirlwind of new relationships and couldn't begrudge them that.

Noelle was working, but promised to call her when her shift ended, adding that she couldn't wait to hear about Eve's trip. Eve missed Will more in that moment than she had thought she ever would. They hardly knew each other, but was a void in her life now that she was away from him that she just couldn't understand.

Figuring she should keep herself busy, Eve went to the library to pick up the book being held for her and ran a few other errands. The whole time she was out, she had the strangest feeling she was being watched, but when she looked around, there was no one even glancing her way.

With her book and a bag of takeout, Eve returned home around six that evening. She checked her messages and was relieved, albeit surprised, to have none from Julian. Curling up on the couch with her book and the Mexican food she had brought home, Eve glanced at the phone, willing it to ring. She wanted to talk to Will—to have him make her feel safe again. She fell asleep on the couch with her book in one hand and the phone in the other. Will never called.

"What the hell?" The bright sun of Sunday morning seemed to be shining right on Skye, and she was not ready to leave Gage's glorious bed.

"Sorry, babe. I was just admiring your hot naked body in the sun."

Gage stood across the room wearing nothing but a big smile, and Skylar suddenly wanted him back in the bed with her very badly. He *very obviously* was thinking the same thing.

"Well, stud boy, come back to bed and you can admire a few more of my outstanding attributes."

Skye didn't have to ask twice. In two huge steps, Gage was back, pulling her into his arms. The two had spent the entire weekend wrapped in each other's arms, and Skye still wanted more. Thinking back on that first night, she remembered her vow to make Gage hiss again, and decided this would be a perfect time to give that a try. Reaching up, she wound her hands around the back of Gage's neck and pulled his mouth to hers.

Gage was a little taken aback as Skye took charge, but he decided he kind of liked it, and just held on for the ride. He eagerly opened his mouth to her and their kisses quickly deepened. Every cell in his body was aching for the beautiful woman seducing him. Skye slowly slid her hands down across his shoulders, tracing every muscle as she went. Gage didn't think it was possible, but his body hardened even more at her touch.

Skye heard a deep intake of air as her hands worked their way down Gage's chest, her tongue following the same path. It wasn't the hiss that she was looking for though, and she was determined. Circling his nipples with her tongue caused a loud exhale. *Close*, Skye smiled, thinking it wouldn't be much longer.

Gage slid his hands up and down Skye's body, leaving a trail of fire over every inch of her skin. She glanced up at him, tossing her hair over her shoulder, and smiled. At the same time, her hands glided down his body again, followed by her tongue. When she lightly brushed Gage's most sensitive area, and her hands came to rest on his thighs, he moaned Skye's name.

Closer...almost there. Then she allowed her tongue to flick across his hardness. *JACKPOT!*

"Pleeease..." The hiss escaped Gage's lips, and with that one plea, Skye couldn't help but give him what he was begging for. Crawling back up, she joined their bodies together, and the way the two moved was the most erotic and loving thing either had ever experienced. Skye initially thought those feelings were because what they had was so new, but after two days and nights in bed, it was still perfect.

When they were both once again satisfied, the sun's rays had moved from the bed, but still lit the entire room. Skye looked at the clock to see how much time she had until she absolutely had to get ready to meet the girls for brunch at Marlowe's. Gage had a client later, so while he really wanted to, he wasn't trying to persuade Skye to stay in bed for one more day.

"What time is your appointment, Gage?"

"Noon. Ugh! After having you in my bed all weekend, I'm definitely not looking forward to staring at Melinda's boobs for an hour."

"Oh, poor baby. Having to look at a perfect set of double Ds for an hour. Rough career choice, huh?"

"Babe, your beautiful, all-natural boobs are all I ever want to look at."

"You really are a charmer, Gage. But, it's nine right now, and I have to meet the girls at 11:30, so we need to get out of bed and get our asses moving."

"No. Come on, at least just stay in bed and read the paper with me. I always see that in the movies, and I know chicks love that. Please?"

Not the same begging as earlier, but he was just too adorable for Skye to say no.

"Okay, cover that fine naked butt of yours and get the paper. You only have thirty minutes, and then I have to get in the shower."

Like a little kid told to pick any candy he wanted, Gage jumped out of the bed, found his sweats and started for the door while trying to dress himself. He almost killed himself when he went head-first into the door frame after tripping on the leg of the sweats, so he tossed them aside and opened the door completely naked. Skye hoped he wouldn't run into Eve in the hallway. She could only imagine how red Eve would be if she got a look at a completely naked Gage.

Within minutes Gage was back in bed opening the paper. He immediately grabbed the sports section. Skye went for the metro section, and there on the front page was the picture of Eve and William Prentiss, accompanied by an article about the SBMA winning the grant from Townsend Industries. She scanned the article to make sure they hadn't screwed up the copy she'd sent them on Friday.

When they had discovered that William Prentiss, founder of Townsend Industries, was Eve's fourth fish, she and Josie didn't know what to do. They were sure he would have recognized her. But had he told her? She never mentioned it to either of them, so they assumed no. The question was...now what? Neither woman had an answer. If he'd wanted to pursue Eve, surely he would have told her, so they thought it better not to mention it.

"Look, Gage. It's the article I wrote about the grant."

Skye shoved the paper in front of him after receiving only a grunt at her declaration. He studied the picture for a minute.

"Hey, that's the guy from Stratus. Wally...or Walter...or Wayne?"

"His name is William Prentiss, and he owns the company providing the grant. Josie and I saw the picture Friday, but we don't think he told her."

"Well, no wonder he never called me. He was keeping an eye on her himself," Gage mumbled, as Skye kept on talking.

"I mean she was with him all week... Hey, wait a minute. How did you know his name?" Skylar's brain finally caught up with what she had just heard Gage say.

"That Will guy, Eve's fourth fish. He came back to the club that night because he forgot his cell phone. We talked, and he asked for my card so he could check up on Eve. I hadn't heard from him, and now I know why."

Skye reached over and slapped Gage on his bare chest.

"Ow! What was that for? And can you do it again? I think I kind of liked it."

"Pig." Skye smiled at him. He was just so hot when he was trying to get some. Again. Skye had to remind herself to focus on what was important: Eve and Will Prentiss. "That was for knowing that Will Prentiss had been asking about Eve and not telling me."

"I kind of forgot about it. My mind's been on other things lately." Gage ran his hands from her knee up to her hip, looking at her with those smoldering eyes.

"Don't even think about it. This changes so much! I have to call the girls." Jumping out of bed, Skye grabbed her phone and flipped it open. She could hear Gage silently cursing, as he decided now was as good a time as any to get in the shower.

"Cold *again*!" he yelled as he made his way to the bathroom. Skye glanced over and was graced with an absolutely wonderful view of his incredible rear end.

"Hello! Skye? Hello!" Josie was yelling through the open phone in Skye's hand.

"Oh, sorry, Josie. I was, uh, distracted by the best ass I have ever had the pleasure to lay my eyes on."

"Thanks, Skye. That is just the way I want to start my day–with Gage's butt in my head."

"If you only knew. Anyway, I just found out something from Gage that may affect how we handle Will Prentiss being the fourth fish. Call Noelle and have her meet us at 11:00 instead of 11:30. We need to talk this out *before* Eve gets there."

"What did Gage tell you?"

"I'll fill you and Noëlle in at Marlowe's. I have to jump in the shower. Bye."

Closing her phone, Skye went to join Gage in the shower. She thought she owed him for the chest slap.

Skye was already sitting at their usual booth when Josie walked in the door, likely her usual fifteen minutes early. Josie made her way over, gave her friend a quick kiss on the cheek, and took her place on the opposite side.

"Where's Noelle?" she asked.

"I don't know. You called her, right?"

"I left a message for her because she didn't answer."

Just then, they saw Noelle come through the door, looking a little out of sorts—very unlike their always together friend.

"Morning, girls," Noelle greeted them in her beautiful sing-song voice. Her chocolate skin and high cheekbones seemed... flushed, was it?

"Noelle, what is wrong with you? You're never late, and I think you have two different shoes on." Skye immediately noticed that little detail.

"Nothing. I was just, uh, busy this morning, and I had to rush to get here."

Both Skye and Josie looked sideways at Noelle. She tried to shift the focus before they could ask any more questions.

"So, why the meeting before Eve shows up?"

"Noelle, you did see the paper this morning, right? The picture of Eve at the ceremony in Boston?" Skye waited a beat before adding, "With the picture of Eve with her fourth fish?"

"What? How...I mean...wait, I'm lost." Noelle looked from Skye to Josie.

"OK, Noelle, what were you doing this morning that kept you from dressing properly and from reading the paper? You read the paper front to back *every day*."

Noelle lowered her eyes and blushed. "Well, Thomas was home this morning. You have *no* idea how long it has been since we were able to stay in bed together. And, that's exactly what we did. We've decided it's time to start a family." She smiled a shy smile. What she didn't tell her friends was that they had been trying for almost a year and a half now, with no luck.

"Oh, Noelle. You're going to be such a great mom!" Josie was so excited for her friend, and she really meant what she had said. Noelle was definitely the most maternal. Of course, she and Beau would be great parents someday, too. And she could see Eve someday, if she could find a decent guy, as a wonderful mother. Skye on the other hand... Because she never had real parents, Josie wondered if she would even want children.

"And, you don't have to hide the fact that you and Thomas are *enjoying* each other. We love you and are happy you're getting some," said Skye, always the sensitive one. "I mean we all are now, except Eve. Which is why we're here."

"Skye, please just tell us what Gage told you," Josie begged, looking at her watch. Eve would be arriving in less than twenty minutes.

"Oh, right. So, Noelle, basically, Eve has spent the last week in Boston with Will Prentiss, owner of Townsend Industries *and* her Fish Number Four."

Noelle's face lit up. "So why all the covert operations?" she asked, leaning forward on her elbows.

"We don't think he told her," Skye continued. "She never said anything to us, so Josie and I decided he didn't. But here's the new bit of information to consider: Gage talked with Will that night at Stratus."

Noelle and Josie looked at one another and said at the same time, "No!"

"Yes. He asked about Eve *and* took Gage's number so he could check on her. Gage thinks Julian did something and that's why Will was worried."

"Ohhh…this changes things!"

Skye smiled. Josie knew Skye well enough to figure she already had a plan. And that, of course, meant work for her, because while Skylar Montgomery was as devious as they come, the execution usually fell to Josie.

"I think we should keep all of this information from Eve." Skye had a mischievous glint in her eyes.

"What? No! We have to tell her," Noelle protested.

"No. Listen. I'm going to call this Megan person who works for Will Prentiss. I'll try to find out what's going on. She's his assistant, and if anyone would know about him, it's her. Once we have some more information, we can decide what we need to do."

Finally, they agreed. None of them wanted Eve to get hurt. After watching her go through so many bad relationships over the years, they didn't want her to get her hopes up. All of this may just have been a coincidence. Kismet. Maybe.

Just then their server came to take their order. She waited on them every Sunday, so all they had to say was "the usual"—and Josie made sure to put in Eve's normal order as well.

When Eve arrived at Marlowe's, metro section of the newspaper tucked under her arm, Noelle, Josie, and Skye were already huddled in deep discussion. Eve thought it was odd that all three were already waiting, especially when Josie hadn't been on time for anything since she was born three days early.

"Hey, guys!" Eve plopped down next to Josie.

Josie gave Eve a big hug and a kiss on the cheek. "Welcome back, Three Million Dollar Grant Winner!"

"I think as soon as I get a cup of coffee in front of me, we need to have a toast to *all* of us and the work we did to earn that money!" Eve waved to the server, and she immediately brought a coffee with hazelnut creamer.

Eve was really trying to be calm and professional about the grant, but it took only a few seconds before she broke. Laying the newspaper in the middle of the table, she pointed to the picture from the night of the gala.

"Oh, and by the way, *that's him*! That's Will!" Eve felt that uncontrollable teenager-with-a-crush grin return to her face. "Gah! I had the most wonderful time. He is as awesome on the inside as he looks on the outside!"

"So, you *did* end up finding a broom closet at the airport before you left, then?" Skye had one eyebrow lifted.

"No! He was just so sweet to me this entire week!"

"So, is he gay, then? I mean, *hello?* You were right there for the taking and he *is* extraordinarily good looking and impeccably dressed."

The whole table laughed at that.

"Believe me, Skye, this man is *not* gay. I can promise you that. No, he was totally focused on business, but at the same time he was definitely flirting with me a *lot*."

"Did you at least make out with him then?" Skye wasn't going to give up.

"No. Not *yet*." Eve paused to let that one sink in for a moment.

"*Not yet*?" Josie squealed. "Spill it, woman. What do you mean 'not yet'?"

"Well," Eve said in her most nonchalant and matter-of-fact way, "Will is coming to Santa Barbara next weekend." She looked at her fingernails as though it wasn't a big deal.

None of her friends bought it for a moment—and Eve couldn't keep from squealing in excitement. But there really wasn't much she could tell them, because Will hadn't given her any details yet. She did know he was planning to arrive prior to the weekend and stay into the following week. Once again, Eve felt like a giddy teen.

She launched into the entire story of her trip to Boston—from Will picking her up at the airport to their "non-date" dinner, and the night at his apartment. There was so much. When she told them about Will's good-bye at the airport, Eve saw them all looking at one another. That look was never good when it came to them.

"Guys! What?!"

"Oh, honey." Noelle reached across the table to hold Eve's hands. "He's got it bad for you."

"I think all of us need to take Eve shopping this week," said Josie. "Who's in?" Even Eve raised her hand to that idea.

"We'll be going to the lingerie store, you know." Skye's stare was intent.

"That's fine. I'd like to get something Will hasn't seen yet." And, of course, that led back to the story about getting stuck in the rain and going to his apartment.

When their food arrived, the conversation turned from Will Prentiss to Skye and Gage. Skye, always the one for providing all of the sordid details, had the other three women blushing and giggling throughout her tale of their first date and things they had done since then.

"In fact, Eve, Gage dropped me here on his way to the gym. I told him you could just take me back to the apartment. He should be home by the time we get back."

Of course Eve didn't mind, but she thought it was funny that Skye never thought to ask, just tell.

Skye took it upon herself to inform Eve about Noelle's morning romp with Thomas, turning Noelle as red as a tomato. With that, Noelle was the one to bring the conversation back to a G rating.

"How about Thomas and I host a dinner party next Saturday night? All of you can bring your men—including you, Eve, your *prospective* man! I've only met Beau a few times and would love to get to know him better, and Thomas has heard of Will's company so I'm sure they'd have lots to talk about! What do you say, ladies? Dinner at our place next weekend?"

They raised their coffee cups and clinked them together three times. First, in celebration of the grant; second, in honor of a fun night together with four *very* handsome men; and, third—as they all looked at Eve—to finding love where they least expected it.

Julian wished he could hear what they were saying as he watched from the sidewalk across from the café. Just seeing Eve had his mind racing with new ideas, and he knew he needed to talk to her. He just didn't know how that was going to happen with all these trying to keep her from him.

He had been waiting for Eve to come home all week, and when she finally showed up late Friday afternoon, his heart jumped. The urge to immediately go to her was strong, but Julian knew the muscle head next door was home. He didn't want to chance running into him. So he waited.

On Saturday Julian's patience paid off when, after several hours of sitting in his car across the street, he watched Eve's car pull out of the parking garage. He had hoped the moron neighbor would leave and he could talk to Eve alone in her apartment, but he would have to make do with just following her. Julian had hoped he could get her alone at some point, but the opportunity never presented itself, and eventually she returned home, where he couldn't take the chance of trying to see her.

Then this morning, there was *his* Eve in the paper with another man. He hadn't liked that at all. While she was, of course, beautiful, the dress she wore was too low cut, making her look like that whore friend of hers. He knew there was no way Eve had chosen something so cheap, and he definitely didn't like the way that the strange man stood so close to her. The smile on her face was angelic, however, and all those familiar feelings stirred deep within him. Julian couldn't wait to be with her again.

The lunch seemed to last forever, but a tiny spark of hope lit in Julian's gut when they all got up to leave. He knew the neighbor was gone, so if Eve were to go back to her apartment, he could finally talk to her without interference. But that hope was dashed when he saw Skye get into Eve's car.

Quickly getting to his car, Julian followed them back to Eve's apartment, where he was again disappointed to see Eve park right next to Gage's car, which had returned to the parking lot. There would be no way for him to talk to her today.

Julian walked into the lobby of the SBMA on Monday morning, confident that he was going to talk to his Eve today. If he just explained that without her there would be no way for him to continue painting, she would come back to him. Eve loved art. So, for the art, she would stay with him. Julian knew it.

Sitting at the main desk just beyond the entrance was an enormous flower arrangement. Julian wondered who would be so garish as to send something that big. *There were masterpieces hanging here for Christ's sake.* He glanced to the hall where his own work hung. Curious, Julian walked to the desk to inspect it. There was a note propped up in front of the huge vase:

Congratulations to the staff at

the Santa Barbara Museum of Art.

We are looking forward to working with you all.

Townsend Industries

Instinctively, Julian's hand went to his pocket, where it wrapped around the article from the previous day's paper. He started back toward Eve's office. This wasn't the ideal place for them to talk, but at least no one would intimidate him. He was Julian Meadows, and they respected him here in his museum.

Having been to Eve's office many times over the past months, nobody made a move to stop him when he pushed his way through the door and into the staff-only part of the building. A few people even said hi to him. They all knew he belonged here, too.

When Julian walked into Eve's office, she was sitting behind her desk turning a small piece of paper over and over in her hand. She hadn't even noticed that he walked in.

"Good morning, Eve."

Eve jumped in her seat when Julian greeted her.

"I'm sorry, I didn't mean to startle you."

"Oh, Julian. I wasn't expecting to see you." Eve could feel her heartbeat accelerate. In all the commotion about the grant and Will, she had forgotten to tell Skye and Josie what happened. While she didn't think he would do anything at the museum, Eve wished there was someone else there with her.

Eve quickly put the card in her desk drawer. That was when Julian noticed a smaller version of the same flower arrangement sitting on her desk. Again, his hand found the article in his pocket. Julian had stared at the picture for so long that he could picture every detail perfectly in his mind. Eve was next to that man with blond hair in a tuxedo, the founder of Townsend Industries, William Prentiss. Julian felt his lip curl at just the thought that he might have touched Eve. On the other side of Eve was a woman with a dress so low cut that Julian worried her breasts might have fallen out. He truly hoped that Eve hadn't become friends with her too.

"So did you get my messages?"

"Um, yeah, kind of hard to miss, like, fifteen messages." Eve was being sarcastic. They had discussed several times how much he despised sarcasm. Julian believed Eve was much too smart to use such a crass form of communication.

When Eve glanced at the flowers *again*, Julian's blood began to boil. They must be from Townsend Industries also, and William Prentiss.

"Did you have to sleep with him to get the grant, Eve?" Julian started around the desk. He wasn't going to let her slip away this time. She needed to answer his questions. She needed to understand that she was *his*.

"Hey, Eve. Did you see that flower..." Skye's voice reached Eve's office first, and then she was frozen in the doorway.

"Um, Skye. Hey. Julian stopped by to talk." Eve was protecting him, Julian noted proudly. *She does still love me*, he thought.

"So I see." Skye looked at Julian with hate in her eyes. The scathing look she gave him didn't bother him in the least. He knew that Eve would be his in the end, and then Skye wouldn't be part of her life anymore.

"Well, that meeting is about to start, and Josie wanted me to come and get you. Are you ready?"

Eve looked at Julian and smiled. His heart swelled. "Yeah. So Julian, thanks for stopping in. I've got to go to this meeting. I'll see you around."

Then she stood up and walked past him as he stepped aside. Julian watched them turn the corner out the door. Before leaving Eve's office he quickly opened the drawer of her desk and took the card she'd placed there, sliding it into his pocket.

Julian walked out the door to find one of the security guards walking toward him. He was sure that Skylar had called them, because *his* Eve never would have.

Chapter Thirteen

It was finally Friday morning. Will would be arriving around two o'clock and Eve couldn't hold back her excitement.

They had talked on the phone every few days, and their conversations had become much more personal in nature—with just a bit of flirtation that let both of them know they were into something more than a business relationship.

Their most recent conversation had been on Wednesday evening.

"So, um, Eve, I was wondering. While I'm in Santa Barbara, what I would like to do most is to take you out to dinner—but this time not as a non-date. I'm sorry, that's coming out funny. What I'm trying to say is, Eve, will you go out to dinner with me while I'm in Santa Barbara?"

He sounded so nervous, and Eve couldn't help the warmth that coursed through her body at his hesitation. She thought by now he would know she would say yes to a real date with him.

"Will, I would very much like to go out to dinner with you while you're in Santa Barbara. Thank you for asking." Eve played the polite young lady to his perfect gentleman. That blasted teen-with-a-crush smile was back in full force on her face, though, and she was thankful he couldn't see it.

"Good." She could hear his sigh of relief over the phone. "Well, then I'll see you Friday afternoon. I'll have a rental car and will come straight to the museum from the airport. My reservations are at the Montenegro Hotel in Santa Barbara until Tuesday. So, you'll find a night that you're free for dinner with me, then?"

"Yes, of course." Eve tried not to giggle at the hesitancy in Will's voice.

The call ended the same way it had since the night Eve had arrived home from Boston: counting down from five while picturing each other at the elevators at The Fairhaven. Eve loved going to bed with that image foremost in her mind.

"Hey, Eve." Skye was standing in Eve's office door. Eve's mind had wandered back to that amazing dream she'd had on the plane, as it often did, and she startled a bit.

"Hi, Skye. What's up?"

"Well..." She had that sly smile that always made Eve nervous. "You, my dear, got a package in the mail today from Townsend Industries. Keep in mind, I said *you*—not the museum."

She handed Eve a box the size of a small microwave oven. It easily weighed eight to ten pounds.

"What's in here—books?" Eve's eyes lit up, wondering what Will—or Townsend Industries—would have sent to her.

"Wait!" Skye held up her hands to Eve. "Let me get Josie before you open it!"

Within seconds, both of them had pulled up chairs in Eve's office and were leaning forward as she began to open the box. Eve tore apart the top flaps and found layers of packing peanuts. "What is in here?"

And then she found the chiseled and cold object that was meant just for her. Tears welled up in Eve's eyes. She pulled the figure out of the box with one hand as the other flew to cover her mouth.

"Oh, my word."

"That is *beautiful*, Eve," Josie said in a whisper.

Eve gazed at her and Skye, tears running down her cheeks, as she sputtered, "It's the sculpture that was at our table at Apex."

"Is there a card?" Skye stood up and began to dig through the peanuts. "Here!" She handed it to Eve urging her to read it out loud.

To Eve

Thank you for the best "non-date business dinner" I have ever had.

Will

"Oh, my word." Eve knew she was repeating herself, but she just couldn't think of anything else to say. Will had thought enough of that night to purchase a one-of-a-kind sculpture as a way for her to remember it. The thought was amazing, but Eve knew she didn't need a memento to help her remember the best "non-date" of *her* life.

"The best *what*?" Skye asked.

"It's how we referred to that night. I told myself over and over that it wasn't a date, and the first thing he had said when I got to the lobby was 'Are you ready for our date?'" Eve laughed while tears continued to stream down her cheeks. "It's become kind of a running joke—how we *weren't* on a date that night, even though everything about it was so date-like."

As Eve held the card and read it again, she remembered she'd wanted to ask Skye and Josie a question. "Hey, did either of you take the card from the flowers Will sent out of my desk?"

They both looked at her. "No, neither of us has even been in your office, Eve."

"That's weird. I thought I put it in my desk, but I can't find it. I'm sure it must be around."

Refocusing her attention, Eve continued to stare at the sculpture, completely overcome.

Josie grabbed the card that had come with the sculpture and read it aloud again. When she was done, she put it in the box and held it up for Eve to put the piece of artwork in. Once the box was closed, Josie sat back down with it on her lap. "Oh, Eve, honey. Noelle was right. This guy has it bad for you!"

Megan had made all of Will's arrangements. He'd be staying at the Montenegro in Santa Barbara again. It offered the amenities he preferred and, if nothing else, Will wanted to thank the concierge who recommended Stratus the last time he'd been in town.

Will had taken care of the most important task he'd wanted to accomplish before his trip to Santa Barbara: calling Gregor Ivanovich to purchase the sculpture of a woman that had graced their table at Apex that night. That sculpture hadn't just been a part of their wonderful dinner. Its design reminded Will of Eve herself: tall, thin, strong, solitary. Alone. Before ending his conversation with Gregor, Will asked whether he could commission the artist to create another sculpture of this woman, but with a man standing lovingly beside her. He said he'd consider it and Will told him he'd let him know if—no, when—he wanted it.

What worried Will the most about traveling to Santa Barbara was the possibility that she was unknowingly leading him on. She *had* accepted his request for a real date, but what if she was simply being polite? No, Will countered, he'd gotten a definite impression that she wasn't seeing anyone. He was thankful that she hadn't mentioned her ex-boyfriend, and Will hoped he was staying away from her. Will made a mental note to contact Gage to make sure Eve was safe.

Will finally allowed himself to assume that there was no one else in Eve's life. That didn't mean she necessarily wanted to start a very long-distance relationship with him, though. Still, he couldn't help hoping she would. He missed her and wanted the chance to see if this could work. More than anything, Will realized, he wanted to kiss her again; no mystery, no anonymity this time. This time she would know it was him.

"Eve! Good God, woman. Will you please calm down?"

Skye had never seen Eve so nervous. She was pacing the entry of the museum. It was like a little dance she was doing: pace, check her watch, look at the doors, pace, check her watch, look at the doors. Just watching her was making Skye anxious too, and she'd never even met the guy!

"Skye, he should be here any minute now. How do I look?"

"For the millionth time today, you look gorgeous. The boy doesn't stand a chance."

Unbeknownst to Eve, since their lunch just after she returned from Boston, Skye and Josie had been getting "Will updates" from his assistant, Megan. Calling Megan had been one of Skye's more brilliant ideas, and that was saying something. They had learned Will Prentiss was definitely as taken with Eve as she was with him. Megan told Josie he hadn't stopped talking about Eve. She also said that when he talked about her, his smile was one she had never seen on him. Josie informed her that they were dealing with the same thing on their end.

After a week of phone calls, Josie and Skye had come to the conclusion that these two had it bad for one another, but were either too scared or too cautious to do anything about it...so far. Of course, the two women had come up with a plan to change that.

Suddenly, Eve stopped pacing, stopped checking her watch, and Skye was worried she had possibly stopped breathing. As she turned to see what had Eve completely mesmerized, a beautiful man walked through the doors. Before Gage, she would totally have jumped on him.

Josie had come into the entry just as Will had come through the door, and both she and Skye watched as he walked past them and pulled Eve into a hug. The only person in the whole museum that Will even saw was Eve.

"Ahem. Hello," Skye tried to get their attention.

"Oh. Sorry. Skye, Josie, this is Will Prentiss of Townsend Industries." Eve blushed slightly at her eager reaction to Will's arrival. They took a step apart from each other to a more business-like distance.

"Skye, Josie. I've heard so much about you both from Eve."

"And we could definitely say the same about you."

Eve shot an "I will kill you" look at Skye, who simply smiled back. If *this* was bothering her, Skye mused, wait until they put their plan into action.

"Eve, I hate to put a damper on this reunion, but I have that meeting with some of the board on Monday, and I need you to look over a few things for me." Josie was playing her part perfectly.

Eve glanced at Will and then at Skye, a nervous look on her face. *Is she kidding?* Skye thought. *Is she actually worried that I would make a move?*

"Don't worry, Eve. I can show Mr. Prentiss around for a few minutes. I have about half an hour before my boyfriend, Gage, will be here to pick me up." Skye hoped the clarification would ease Eve's concern as well as inform Will that she had no interest in him; she needed Eve to go with Josie so she could talk with Will alone.

With a slight hesitation, Eve spoke softly to Will, gave Skye one more warning look, and then departed with Josie.

Skye turned to Will, but he was still watching Eve walk away, a glowing smile on his face. Once Eve turned the corner and disappeared from sight, he finally turned to Skye.

"So, Skylar. You are head of public relations for the SBMA, right?"

"Yeah, yeah. We can talk business later. Right now I need to discuss a few things with you before Eve comes back."

Will immediately backed up a step and glanced back to the hallway where Eve and Josie had gone. Skye was sure he had gotten the wrong impression because he immediately started backing away from her. It made her wonder what Eve had told him.

"Will you please stand still? I don't know what you think I am going to do with you, but I just want to talk about you and Eve."

"Oh, I'm sorry. My natural reaction to beautiful, self-assured women is to run in the other direction. Sorry, force of habit. What about Eve?"

"Josie and I remember you from Stratus. Why didn't you tell Eve you were the fourth fish in our little game?"

Will's eyes grew wide. "Well," he started and then inhaled deeply before continuing. "Given the situation with the grant and the fact that my opinion was the deciding factor in awarding it, I thought it better that no one knew about Eve's and my recent, uh, encounter."

"OK, that explains why you didn't tell the entire selection committee that you 'accidentally' made out with the curator for the museum you wanted to give three million dollars to. But, that doesn't address why you didn't tell Eve."

"You're right. At first I didn't tell her because I didn't want to embarrass her. And then, I didn't know *how* to tell her. Then when she found out that I owned Townsend Industries, she was angry that I had kept that from her. I couldn't tell her after that. I was afraid she'd hate me."

He did have a point, Skye realized, and she appreciated his honesty. He was right; his kissing her was a fluke—he'd had no idea he'd see her again and certainly couldn't reveal that information to her while they were working on business. Skye knew her friend would forgive this little sin of omission.

"Here's the thing. Josie and I are going to give you a great opportunity to let Eve know that you were her fourth fish."

"I'm sorry, but could you not call me that? It just sounds odd." He smiled sheepishly, making Skye laugh.

"Sure. Whatever. Look, she and Josie will be coming back any minute, and I need to fill you in on our plans."

He listened patiently, nodding in all the appropriate places, which gave Skye hope that they were actually going to pull this off.

"I think that sounds like a perfect way to go. Count me in!" he said just as Eve rounded the corner and drew all of his attention.

Eve's eyebrows went up as she approached Skye and Will, wondering why the two of them were still in the same spot.

"Hey, Eve. Will and I were just talking about the Santa Barbara nightlife. I thought maybe he would like to go to Stratus tonight. Gage is working, so the only way I can see my man before two a.m. is by being a patron of the club."

Eve looked panicked; Stratus was not what she'd had in mind for Will's first night in Santa Barbara.

"Oh, well, uh, Will may be too tired from his flight to go to a club tonight?" It was more a question than a statement.

Will cocked his head and smiled lightly. "You know, Eve, actually I think I would like to go to Stratus tonight. Skye mentioned that her boyfriend worked there, and Josie and her boyfriend would be coming, too. I'd like to meet some of the people in your life. And perhaps we can have dinner somewhere beforehand?"

Skye bit the inside of her mouth to keep from smiling too obviously. Will was good; not only was he smooth, but he'd made Eve feel good about going tonight because it would really be about getting to know her better. She rather liked this Will Prentiss.

After meeting the ladies at the museum, Will had gone to check into his hotel before coming to pick Eve up for their first real date. Eve couldn't believe how brazen Skye had been about arranging the night at Stratus. But Eve had to just love her to pieces. She knew shy Eve probably would have chickened out in inviting him there, and Eve was intrigued at how surprisingly keen Will had been about going to a night club. This was a new and pleasing side of William Prentiss that hadn't been revealed to her in Boston.

However, Eve was also a bundle of nerves thinking about going to Stratus with Will. The big question was what to wear. She didn't want to dress too provocatively, but at the same time, she *wanted* Will to see the wilder side of her. At least a little of that, anyway. A few drinks to loosen her up and, well, she'd just see what happened.

The shopping trip had been successful and, despite Eve constantly reminding herself that no one would be seeing her new, all-lace, and very sexy bra and panties, she clipped their tags and put them on anyway. Sometimes having a little secret like this gave her the confidence to be more flirty. And being a little more flirty was *definitely* her plan with Will!

After narrowing her clothing decision down to a few outfits that would be appropriate for dinner *and* Stratus, Eve finally put on a clingy black v-neck dress. It hugged her curves in all the right places, but the lacy material was stretchy enough to make it comfortable—*and inviting*—should there be any dancing later on.

When Will arrived at her apartment right at 6:45 as promised, he gasped as she opened the door. "Wow. You look stunning!"

"Why, thank you!" Eve's shy blush was quickly evident on her cheeks.

"Is that from my mother's company? She used to really focus on using lace in her dress designs because she said it was the best fabric to make a woman beautiful." He looked Eve up and down again. "She was right!"

"Well, thank you again, but no, this was a $45 knock-off I got at an after-Christmas sale. I agree, though, that lace *does* make me feel pretty." *If only he could see the lace I have on* under *this dress,* Eve mused.

Eve had suggested Scales, the restaurant next to the night club, since the food was delicious and the ambiance appropriate for a first date: upscale without being too romantic. The drive was comfortable as Eve and Will talked about the museum and his business. Eve pointed out a few of her favorite places, and Will made mental notes of every café, store, and park they passed as she mentioned it. He was drinking in everything about her.

At the restaurant they were seated immediately, and Eve wondered if Skye had called ahead to make a reservation. After ordering, Eve tilted her head and gazed at Will. "So, mister, how was it that you were able to give me that Ivanovich sculpture? I know you couldn't have just gone to the corner gift store to buy it."

He grinned and sat back in his chair, taking his gin and tonic in his hand. "It took a little bit of work. Luckily, I've become pretty well-connected in the art world."

"Details, Prentiss. I want details."

"I called Ivanovich himself, had him send Apex another sculpture to replace the one I wanted to give you. He was really very amenable to my request."

Will made it seem like no big deal, but as a curator, Eve knew it was. He smiled again and raised his glass. "And so, you have something small—heavy, but small—to help you remember our first dinner."

"I love it, but," Eve leaned forward, looking him directly in the eye, "I didn't need an object to remind me of the wonderful time

I had with you that night, or *any* time that week. Those memories are all up here." She tapped her temple. "They're not going anywhere. I'm just hoping I can add to them over the next few days."

"How about a toast, then? To making new memories." Will raised his drink as he held Eve's gaze. There was something more there than he had ever seen, and it took his breath away.

"And to holding on to the old ones," Eve added, letting her glass touch Will's. She had a feeling the night was only going to get better.

When they had finished their meal, Will helped Eve out of her seat and they left the restaurant to walk around to Stratus. Will kept his hand on the small of Eve's back, which was intoxicating. She allowed herself to just be happy in the moment.

When the couple entered Stratus, Josie, Noelle, and Skye were already standing by their booth. Beau had his arms wrapped around Josie, nuzzling her ear from time to time as they talked. Thomas was just returning from getting drinks. When he handed Noelle hers, the girls heard him quietly whisper, "And your ginger ale, my dear." Josie and Eve both swiveled their heads to look at Noelle, wondering if perhaps there would be some news later on.

Skye, on the other hand, was distracted. She was only partially listening to the rest of the group, while constantly looking across the room at Gage who, once again, was dealing with guys who'd had too much to drink.

"Hey, everybody. This is Will Prentiss," said Eve.

Will extended his hand to Beau.

"Beau Sanderson, nice to meet you, man." Nodding, Will turned to Thomas. After introducing himself, Thomas, immediately engaged Will in conversation about Townsend Industries' work. Beau kissed Josie's neck and turned to join the other men, leaving her to talk with Eve.

"How was dinner?" she whispered, her eyes sparkling with mischief.

"Fantastic. Oh, Josie. Every *second* I find something else amazing about him." Noelle and Skye came in closer and Eve told all of them how Will had obtained the sculpture. After a few minutes, Will broke from the other men to stand beside Eve. His hand returned to the small of her back as he leaned in and asked, "Can I get you a drink?"

"Don't laugh, but I'd really like a Sex On The Beach, please."

Will didn't laugh, but raised an eyebrow at her as he smiled. He wondered where the nearest beach was. "Coming right up."

Skye leaned in toward Eve. "Any tongue wrestling or groping going on yet?" The other women laughed. Only Skye.

"No! We had a wonderful dinner and came right over here."

"All right, I guess I'm going to have to take this situation into my own hands."

Eve really didn't like the sound of that.

"Will!" Skye turned on the charm as soon as he returned. "Did Eve tell you about a little game we like to play at Stratus called Passion Fish?" Eve's eyes went wide. She couldn't believe Skye would do this to her.

"Uh... No." Will smiled at Skye before turning to Eve. "It's got an interesting name, though. Does it involve actual fish?"

It was then that Gage joined the group, pulling Skye into a turn-and-dip kiss before turning his attention to the rest of them. Eve made a quick introduction, and was happy that Will had now met her "family." She thought back to the last man she'd brought into the group—Julian—and again realized what a vast improvement Will was. Eve loved that Will had immediately bonded with her friends, something Julian had never done.

"Well," Skye continued, with Gage's arm around her shoulder. "We girls—except Noelle 'cause she's already married—like to stir things up occasionally."

Will was clearly intrigued. Eve was clearly beet-red. But Will spurred Skye on with a quick nod of his head.

"Depending on the situation, one of us volunteers to be the bait while the rest of us, Noelle included, each find a guy willing—and worthy—to give her one passionate kiss, and that's it. Now, our bait is blindfolded and has her hands restrained, so she has no idea who kisses her. That leaves her and the guys off the hook, so to speak. No option to pursue things any further unless the guy is willing to come find her on a different night."

"And have you had any successful results from this game?"

Josie and Beau said together, "Absolutely!"

Will then turned to Eve. "And have *you* ever played the bait?"

"Um, yes, once." Eve started plotting her revenge on Skye while she stumbled over her words.

"And?"

"And what?" Eve wanted to crawl in a dark corner and die of embarrassment, while everyone else seemed completely amused by the whole thing.

"Any success for you?" Will prompted.

Josie piped in this time. "Well, when we did this a few weeks ago—actually the night before she went to Boston, we found four fish for her. The first two should *never* be allowed to kiss a woman *ever* again." She winked at Eve, who shuddered at the memory, making Will smile even bigger.

"Then, your third fish... Well, Eve? What did you think of him?" Skye asked, her eyes twinkling.

"My third fish was pretty good, I must say..." Eve couldn't hold back a smile, or the blush that went with it.

"And?" Gage urged her on this time. Eve wanted this all to stop, but since this train seemed impossible to derail, perhaps she should have some fun as well.

"And that was that. I don't know who he was, but I wouldn't mind kissing him again at all! He was definitely my type! Josie? Skye? Noelle? Have any of you ever seen this guy again? I mean, if he's single..." Eve knew she was making Will uncomfortable, but turn-about was fair play.

"Umm, about that, Eve..." Gage began to smirk, as did everyone else. "Well, let me just say two things, OK? First, the guys in here that night were either creepy, drunk, or stupid." He hesitated. "And second, thank you for the compliment on my kissing skills."

He suddenly moved to hide behind Skye, as though Eve might attack him. Eve stared, open-mouthed at him. Everyone else—including Will—began to laugh.

"*You* were my third fish?" Eve was stunned as she tried to wrap her mind around why her next door neighbor and friend, who had lusted after Skye since the first day he saw her, would have kissed *her* like that—while Skye stood right there watching!

"But... What? Why? And Skye..." Eve sputtered.

"Yeah, I wasn't quite sure about all that either until the big ape explained it to me." Skye leaned her head back to give Gage a deep kiss of her own.

"Well, Skye. I'm not telling you something you don't already know, but, *man!* Gage knows how to kiss. And, Gage, if I *ever* allow myself to be the bait again, you can be my fish any time!" Eve winked at him. Gage squeezed Skye around the waist and winked back.

"I don't think that's going to happen, Eve," Skye said. She wasn't going to be letting Gage kiss any other woman any time in the near future.

Will wasn't finished with wanting to know more. "And so you had two bad kisses and then Gage? So, no success that night?"

"Oh, no… she had one *more* fish that Noelle found for her," said Skye. "None of us knew him, and *he* had asked *Noelle* if he could kiss Eve. Eve wasn't expecting a fourth fish, but we insisted."

"So how was your fourth fish, Eve?" Will asked.

"Other than the fact that he was a tourist," Eve shot a glance at Noelle, who just shrugged her shoulders, "he was phenomenal. Yeah, that's the word I want. Phenomenal."

Will turned to face Eve, and it occurred to her that she was in the exact position as the night they had been talking about: up against the barrier between two booths. There seemed to be no space between her and Will at that moment.

Capturing Eve's eyes in his, Will made her forget there was anyone else around. "And what was it that made your fourth fish phenomenal?" He moved even closer to Eve. She had to fight to remain standing. "What does a man do to earn such a compliment? Does he do this?" Will placed his hands lightly on Eve's shoulders, slowly gliding his fingers down her arms. He followed his movements with his eyes before returning his gaze to Eve's face.

Uh, yeah, that is exactly what he'd do. Eve's mind was screaming, but she couldn't form any actual words.

"And would a phenomenal passion fish do this?" He brushed his lips against her neck.

Eve closed her eyes, gasping slightly, and brought her hands to rest against his chest.

And then, he whispered in her ear, “If you were with me, I’d be doing *this* to you every chance I had.”

Eve’s mind went on a little vacation as Will’s arms tightened around her and he moved his lips from her ear, kissing repeatedly across her jaw. No longer able to separate the night almost two weeks ago and what was happening at that moment, Eve felt her heart pounding.

“I want to kiss you like I did that night. Let me find out if you still think I’m phenomenal.”

Pulling Eve to him, Will began to kiss her in earnest. Will’s heart leapt when she returned his embrace. The kiss was brief but intense, and Eve knew in an instant.

“You’re my fourth passion fish—the tourist.” She smiled, tears in her eyes at this wonderful, unbelievable discovery.

“Well, sort of. I was a man from out of town who was researching a grant proposal. Hey, are you all right? You’re crying.” Will quickly brushed her cheeks with one hand while keeping an arm around her.

Eve she wrapped her arms around his neck and found his lips again. She was *definitely* all right.

The two were lost in each other until applause from her friends—their friends—brought them back to Stratus.

“Hey, Will.” Skye caught his attention. “I’d say she still finds you pretty phenomenal. Am I right, Eve?”

“I don’t know. I’m going to have to find a better word. ‘Phenomenal’ doesn’t even come close,” Eve said as she returned to Will’s waiting lips.

Chapter Fourteen

Watching Skylar work a situation to get the outcome she wanted was a big turn-on for Gage. But unfortunately, he was still working and had to go back to his post by the door. From there, however, he was able to watch Skye as she shook her incredible ass to the beat of the music. Gage's entire focus was on her butt and the way her jeans hugged it perfectly. However, watching Skye also meant he had to watch guys hit on her all night, and it was taking everything he had to not beat the crap out of each and every one of them.

Skylar knew Gage was watching her, and she took advantage. The idea of even touching another man was already repulsive to her, but Gage didn't know that, and she knew he was about to explode as just about every guy in the place came on to her. Throwing her head back, Skye let out a loud laugh as she held Gage's eyes to hers. The clock was ticking down in her head. She knew there was no way Gage would last much longer.

When yet another guy approached her, Gage decided he'd had enough. Finding Austin, the other bouncer, Gage told him he was taking off. The crowd had been mostly regulars, so Austin would be fine. The only thing Gage could think about was getting Skye out of there. In that instant Gage decided there would need to be new rules about Skye coming to Stratus; as in *never* when he was working and couldn't be with her every minute to keep the idiots away.

Admiring every muscle that rippled under Gage's t-shirt, Skye watched as he strode across the dance floor to the table where everyone was still hanging out. His timing was perfect as he stepped in front of yet another moron about to hit on Skye. Gage glared at the guy and couldn't help letting out a small growl as well. Stopping dead in his tracks, the idiot looked from Gage to Skye and back again. It finally clicked in his tiny brain, and he turned back the way he had come.

"All right, babe. We're out of here!" Gage picked Skye up and threw her over his shoulder.

"Gage! Put me down."

"Sorry, Skye. I've been standing over there all night watching you get hit on, and I'm done."

"Hey, Gage. Could you guys go to Skye's place tonight? Please?" Eve blushed as she made her request.

"Eve! I'm shocked. You barely know the guy." Gage gave Will a nod and raised an eyebrow. Will blushed at the insinuation. Another sign they were made for one another.

"No, no, no!" Eve turned several shades of red. "The walls are thin, and I'm still recovering from 'pirate night' last week. You have totally ruined *Pirates of the Caribbean* for me now, thank you very much."

Skye giggled, and a smile slid onto Gage's lips when he remembered pirate night and Skye in her wench costume. Suddenly it was even more urgent to get Skye out of there. As he turned toward the door, Gage heard Eve call out, "Really, guys, please...Skye's place!"

Gage couldn't see what Skye did, but he imagined she waved to their friends without using *all* of her fingers. Laughter erupted from the table, and Josie called out, "Oh, Gage. Skye is being naughty. I think she needs a spanking!"

Laughing, Gage smacked Skye on the ass as he pushed through the door and out into the night.

He kept her over his shoulder until they reached her car, where he gently set her down on the hood. Her face had turned red from being upside down for so long, and she didn't look happy. *Think, Gage, or you'll be sleeping alone tonight.*

He reached around and grabbed both cheeks of her ass and pulled her into him. His excitement pressed into her, and he was sure she knew how badly he wanted her.

"Man, Skylar. This is what just seeing you in those jeans does to me. I can't wait to see you out of them."

Skye wrapped her hands around his neck and crossed her ankles behind his back, positioning herself perfectly over the tightness in his jeans. Her lips came up to meet his, and he immediately opened his mouth to hers and let his tongue taste her. As he lifted her pulled her closer, Skye's mouth left his, moving up his jaw to his ear. When her tongue darted out and traced his ear, he couldn't help but moan aloud.

Her tongue stopped, and she put her lips to his ear. Then, in the sexiest voice he had ever heard, she whispered, "Gage, after the caveman act in there, do you really think I'm going to *do you* in the parking lot?" And with that she lowered her legs and disentangled herself from him.

"Oh, come on. Don't do this to me." Gage knew how much she liked to hear him beg.

Skye pulled her keys out and with the press of a button unlocked her car, then opened the door.

Gage watched as she lowered herself in and closed the door. When the car started, he nearly cried. He needed to do something fast. There was no way a cold shower and his hand were going to be his fate tonight.

"Skye, baby. I just couldn't stand to be away from you any longer. You know how I can't resist you. I love you."

The window rolled down slowly. Skye's hand shot out and lightly grabbed her man where he so badly wanted her to be touching him right then. *Evil,* Gage thought. *This beautiful woman, who I'm totally in love with, is evil.*

"You heard Eve's request. Are you coming to my place or what?" Then she released him and drove away.

Given the situation she left him in, Gage couldn't exactly run to his car, but he made a damn good effort to get there as fast as he could and sped off towards the hottest woman God ever put on this planet.

Gage and Skye were a sight to behold, that was for sure. Seeing him carry her out the door like that... Again, Will compared Skye to Jeannette and knew immediately Jeannette would never want to be handled that way.

Will hadn't let Eve out of his arms, and he could tell she was quite content. "So, pirate night, eh?" He looked down and saw her blush again, loving how radiant she was.

"Yeah. You're better off not knowing any more than that, I promise."

That didn't keep Will's mind from quickly envisioning Skye and Gage doing their own version of "swashbuckling," so he changed the subject.

"I don't think I've had the chance to tell you how I'd describe *your* kisses."

Eve looked up at him with a sideways smile. "Yes?"

"Irresistible, for starters." He leaned in and stole a quick one before continuing. "I want you to know that it took all I had that night not to just put you over *my* shoulder and take you away."

"Oh, *really*, Mr. Prentiss. You would have done that for me? And why didn't you, hmm?" Eve liked that they were able to tease and be so comfortable with each other already.

"Well, for one, I couldn't reveal who I was that night and..."

"Go on."

"And I *really* didn't want to get on Skye's *or* Gage's bad side," he said with a laugh.

"Wise decision! And don't underestimate Josie. She may not look tough, but I wouldn't cross her either!"

Pulling Eve into another embrace, Will lowered his mouth to hers. It was wonderful after holding back so many times when she was with him in Boston.

"Mmm...this is nice." Eve nuzzled Will's neck and pulled him closer.

A slower song began to play, and Will noticed Josie and Beau had moved to the dance floor. Leaning in, he whispered, "Would you dance with me?"

Eve smiled, allowing Will to take her hand and lead her toward the middle of the floor. The last time they had danced together, he had *accidentally* brushed his lips against her hair. Tonight, they could kiss and touch each other as freely and as often as they wanted. Eve melted into Will's arms while they moved together on the dance floor.

As the evening wound down, Eve and Will remained arm in arm. He was so glad they had shared his car so their evening wouldn't have to end at the club. They gathered with Beau, Josie, Tom, and Noelle one last time to say good night, and Thomas reminded them of their invitation to a dinner party at their home the following evening.

Noelle reached out to Will and pulled him into a hug. "Thank you so much for asking me if you could participate in our silly game. I can tell Eve is a different woman since returning from Boston, and it's because of you, Will."

He kissed her cheek. "Noelle, it's *me* who will be forever grateful to you for giving me the chance to meet her." Then he leaned in. "I love her, you know."

Noelle stood back from him with a look of total joy. Her eyes told him that she was willing to keep this a secret for now. It felt good to confide in someone so close to Eve, but Will was really looking forward telling her himself. *Before I leave Santa Barbara,* he vowed.

Julian watched as the door of the club that he'd followed them to opened. Once again, he was disappointed. It wasn't Eve. He'd never understood how she could want to come to a place like this. He was sure that without Josie and Skylar, she never would have come here. And now she was in there with the man from

Boston, *William Prentiss*. Julian had watched them when they went in. That man had been touching her.

Coming out from the club now were the steroid freak and the whore. It figured that those two would end up together. Julian was disgusted by their blatant sexual behavior, and he knew he was right to try to keep Skylar Montgomery out of Eve's life.

When the ape set her on the car and started to grab at her, Julian tried to control his thoughts. He focused on how it would be when he had Eve back. But that wasn't working—all he could think about was the whore with her legs wrapped around *him*, and it was only making his situation worse.

Julian had to control himself. *I am better than this.* He closed his eyes, but memories of the whores his father had brought him to came flooding back. He'd been forced to touch them, touch himself, or face a beating at the hand of his father. And some of the whores had laughed at him, an inexperienced boy of sixteen. He'd hated the physical reaction he had when the women flaunted themselves in front of him, when they'd put their dirty mouths on him *down there*. Those women didn't love him. They didn't want to know about his art. All they wanted was to provide proof that Julian could "get it up" with women—proof that Julian wasn't gay—so they could get paid and leave. He'd endured nearly a year of that dirty secret, his father watching him, sometimes even participating in the debauchery, only to find out his mother had known all along and hadn't tried to stop it.

Julian came back to the present with a shudder. He had to control himself. Closing his eyes, he tried to get the vision of the whore out of his mind. He lightly touched the bulge that had appeared under the fabric of his pants. *No. Not for the whore. Only for Eve.* Relief flooded Julian when he opened his eyes to discover that Gage and Skylar had untangled themselves, and she was speeding away while the muscle man tried to get to his car.

Rolling his window down, Julian hoped the cool night air would help calm him and focus him on saving his Eve. He leaned over, reached into the glove compartment, and pulled out the two items he had stored there. Unfolding the article from the paper about the museum he saw the beautiful face of his Eve staring back at him. She would always be his Eve. Nothing she or anyone else did would ever change that.

As Julian scanned the entire page, he saw *him*. The man who had touched her. The thought that he was touching her right at that moment entered his mind. It took all his self control not to go in to that place and save her right then. But, growing up with his father, Julian had learned well to control his urges...unlike the whore and her boyfriend who were ready to have sex right in the parking lot. Yes, keeping Eve away from her was definitely what he would have to do.

The second item he pulled from the glove compartment was the small card Eve had been so absorbed in that day Julian was in her office. He had been right. It was from *him*. Julian read it for probably the hundredth time:

Eve, May this be just the start

of a long and lasting relationship. ~Will

Now he had proof that he had also been right when he'd assumed she slept with Will Prentiss in order to win the grant. The proof was that *he* was in there with her right now, touching her. But, Julian would forgive her and take her back when she begged him to. He could understand the things people needed to do for their work...for their passion.

The club doors opened once again, and Julian looked up to see who it was. *Eve*. He slumped down a little further in his seat. His car was well hidden among all the others in the parking lot, and he knew she would never see him, but he wanted to make sure.

Eve wasn't sure why or how she deserved to be with Will Prentiss, but she *was,* and she'd never felt such complete happiness in her life. To stand at his side holding his hand, to be wrapped in his arms as they danced, and to feel the passion in his kisses...Eve knew she was in love. It wasn't the fleeting, giddy feeling that comes with being attracted to someone, although that was part of it. No, she had noticed it in Boston that first night when they'd had dinner together. There was something between her and Will—a love and appreciation for art, sure—but beyond that a *connection* that neither of them could deny. It was electrifying, invigorating, life-altering.

The couple walked arm-in-arm out to Will's car. He was proud to have Eve on his arm, he wanted her to be there for a long time. The evening had been perfect, and now that the last secret he was keeping from her was out, he could relax and just be.

When they reached the passenger side of Will's car, he placed Eve with her back to the door. Cupping her face in his hands, Will gazed into her eyes. Eve held onto his waist loosely as she lifted her mouth to his. He crushed her lips with his and, more than any time this evening, Eve felt his searing passion for her. Moving her arms around his back, Eve pulled Will to her, pressing herself against his chest fully.

Eve sighed when Will's hands left her face. One moved to her back and the other to her neck, his fingers getting lost in her hair. Her pulse began to race as she gave in to desire. Desire to feel his arms around her, his strong chest against her, his mouth exploring hers completely...

When Eve moved her hands up and around *his* neck, Julian watched his hands move down Eve's body onto her back. That was when he decided that he had to leave. He couldn't watch her act like Skylar. Julian knew if he had stayed any longer, his plan would be ruined. And that couldn't happen. There were other ways to release the anger that had built up inside, ready to crash out and destroy all of his plans. Julian started the car and carefully left the parking lot so as not to draw any attention to himself. Eve would need to explain this, but it was forgivable. She would still be his.

Will finally moved his lips to Eve's forehead so they could both catch their breath, but neither wanted to let go of the other even slightly.

"Wow," Eve was eventually able to gasp.

"Yeah. You know you're right, we need a better word than 'phenomenal'." He returned his mouth to Eve's and they let themselves go once more...

After a few more minutes—and Beau calling out, "Get a room!" as he and Josie walked to his car—the two finally stepped back from their embrace. Eve immediately felt an emptiness, even though Will was still right in front of her. Like the gentleman he was,

Will opened the car door and she got in. Leaning in, he kissed Eve again before closing it and going around to the driver's side.

Eve held Will's hand in her lap for the duration of the short drive to her apartment. He stole glances at her when he could, flashing that smile that melted her. At one point, Eve brought his hand to her mouth and kissed his palm gently. When she returned his hand to her lap, still enfolded in both of hers, he just looked at her in wonder, like he wanted to say something. Eve smiled at him and Will, in turn, picked up her hand and kissed the back of it.

When they arrived at her apartment, Will opened Eve's door again and took her hand to help her out of the car.

"Oh, I want to get something out of my car to show you!" Eve said as she walked toward her Honda, Will's hand entwined in hers. She wanted to show him the Lila Marin CD—and tell him she had been listening endlessly to it over the past couple weeks.

As Eve approached her car, though, she gasped in horror. Will had his arms around her immediately and led her to the sidewalk, far enough away for Eve to feel safe as he investigated.

The tires of Eve's car—all four, it turned out—had been punctured with what looked like ice picks, which were still embedded in the rubber. Flush against each tire, stabbed through, were cocktail napkins with the Stratus logo on them.

Eve couldn't help it. She began to shake uncontrollably and thought she might pass out. "Will!" Eve cried, and he came over, crushing her to him. Eve hid her face in his chest.

"Let's get into your apartment and call the police." Will made Eve wait outside the apartment door, but kept hold of her hand while he stepped just inside the threshold. Turning on the lights, Will looked briefly for evidence the place had been broken into.

"It's OK. Let's go inside." He held on to Eve tightly, leading her into the living room and sitting her down on the couch. Eve pointed to the phone on the kitchen counter. Will grabbed it and returned to her side. Pulling her to him, Will called the police while Eve just sat there, holding her hands over her mouth, trying to keep the feeling of sickness from taking over.

"It's Julian. I know it. It's Julian," she mumbled as tears flowed down her cheeks. "He must have been at Stratus... Oh, God, he must have seen me with you." She couldn't stop shaking. "Will, I'm so scared." Clinging to him, she buried her face in his chest.

"I'm not going anywhere." Afraid that Eve might go into shock, Will pulled off the blanket draped over the back of the couch and wrapped it around her. Then he put his hand under her chin. "You know that, right? I'm not going anywhere. I'm not leaving your side for a moment, do you understand? I *will not* let him get near you."

Even with Will's arms wrapped around her, Eve felt so lost. In the safety of Will's arms, Eve remembered her thoughts when she first returned to Santa Barbara—wishing for Will to protect her. That was when she realized Will knew it was Julian that had put those bruises on her neck.

"Let me go—I have to go to the bathroom!" Eve rushed and made it just in time to vomit into the sink. Will was right behind her, one hand around her waist and the other grabbing a towel for her to wipe her face. Eve took the towel, wet it thoroughly, and brought it to her mouth. She hung her head as she began to sob again. Will turned Eve toward him, wrapping her in his arms.

Will held Eve until the police knocked on the door almost an hour later. Between the two of them, they were able to give the officers the information they needed to create a full report. One of the officers pulled Will into the kitchen while Eve signed forms the other held in front of her.

"Here." The officer gave Will his card with a phone number written on the back. "She needs to petition for an order of protection first thing in the morning. Come by the police station and someone there will help her with the paperwork. It's a Saturday, but we can submit this as an emergency order and get it on record right away. We'll go to this guy's place now and have a talk with him, see if he's the one who did this."

After Will shook his hand, he turned to do the same with the other officers before they left. Will had asked that they contact *him* with any news. He didn't want them calling Eve. She was too upset and just needed to rest.

Once the police left, Will made sure to lock the door, as well as check every window and make sure the drapes and shades were drawn. He didn't want Julian—or whoever had done this—to be able to see Eve at all.

Eve stayed curled up under the blanket on her couch, staring at nothing. She was vaguely aware of Will moving about the apartment. He checked on her before returning to the bathroom to clean the sink. As he finished, she came and stood next to him. Looking at their reflection in her mirror, Eve groaned and wiped her tear-stained cheeks with her hands.

"I look like death," she said as she squeezed some toothpaste onto her toothbrush and began to scrub the inside of her mouth.

"You look like someone who has been through a lot tonight."

She rinsed, wiped her mouth, and went back to staring at her own pale face in the mirror, sighing heavily once more. Then he turned her to him. "But you're still stunning, you know. All of that lace..." Will gave her a flirtatious smile and she laughed weakly.

"Beauty is in the eye of the beholder, I guess."

Will pulled Eve to him, and she put her arms around his waist, letting her head lay against his chest. She was finally beginning to relax; the shaking had subsided.

"I know you have a hotel room and all, but Gage's not home and—"

"I told you, I'm not going anywhere." Will kissed the top of her head. "As long as it won't get the neighbors gossiping that you had a man spend the night at your apartment!"

She squeezed him tighter. "I just want you here, if that's OK."

"There is nowhere else I want to be tonight. I'm sorry my staying is due to bad circumstances, but I've got you in my arms, so the evening hasn't turned out *that* bad when you think about it."

"Mmmm..."

"Let's go back out to the living room, eh? Or are you tired enough you want to try to sleep? I'll sack out on the couch so I won't be far from you."

As they walked out of her bathroom, she turned and raised her face to his. She began to kiss him gently but then became more eager and he responded, opening his mouth to her passion.

"Stay with me," she whispered as she guided him to her bed. She lay down and pulled him to be beside her. She continued to brush across his face and neck with her lips, and he held her close. As he rolled onto his back, she nestled into his side, laying her head on his shoulder. She draped her arm across his chest, letting her fingers play with the buttons of his shirt. His lips rested on her forehead as he caressed her shoulder with his hand.

They lay there silently, comfortably, and soon Will realized Eve had fallen asleep in his arms, exhaustion from the shock of the evening finally getting the best of her. He gently slipped away from her, but only to grab the blanket from the living room to place over her. After checking the front door one more time and turning out the lights, he returned to Eve's bed. She had turned to her side and Will lay down behind her. There they remained, with her safely in his arms, until morning.

After the police left, Julian returned to the painting he'd begun this evening. This piece would showcase his passion for one woman and his utter hatred for everyone around her. The ice picks were now black daggers, thrusting outward from his delicate angel, held by the cloaked figure whose only purpose in life was her. She didn't know how to protect herself from the influence of the bitch, from the touch of that man. But Julian did. He would rescue her before she got too far from him. His love for her would be all she ever needed; she'd understand soon. Very soon.

Chapter Fifteen

When Will opened his eyes, it took him a moment to remember where he was. *Eve's bed.* But Eve wasn't there and he immediately became alarmed.

"Eve? Eve! Where are you?"

"I'm right here. I just went to the kitchen to put on some coffee," she said, returning to give him a peaceful smile. Will spread his arms, and she willingly came back to lay beside him. He pulled her close and found her lips. Each kiss they shared became more and more intoxicating, awakening in him a desire to be with her more completely. Will could sense that she felt the same, and his hand wandered down the side of her dress, taking in her curves and feeling her respond to his touch.

Rolling her onto her back, Will moved his hand back up from her waist, across her breast, and up to the back of her neck. He lowered his mouth to hers and kissed her deeply. Her hands explored his chest, and he could feel his own reaction increase. *Time to stop, Prentiss. This is too fast and too soon.*

Will dropped his face to her neck and planted one last light kiss before moving to lie beside her. She turned toward him and nestled back into that perfect spot where they could just hold each other close.

"OK." He took a deep breath and continued. "Today I think I need to make alternate plans." She stiffened for a moment but he continued, sensing her worry. "Instead of spending the morning at the museum like I had intended, I think the two of us have some business to attend to. New tires, filing an order of protection—" He felt her tense and held her closer. "It'll be OK. The police will call me if there's any news."

"I want a new lock on my door," she whispered.

"Yes. I thought of that, too." Will sighed deeply. "So, sounds like we need to get up and face the day, huh?"

"Can we do one other errand?" Eve looked at him with pain in her eyes. "Can we have you check out of your hotel and just stay with me?" Will could tell she had been afraid to ask.

"Oh, Eve, absolutely. I was going to ask you if that would be OK, too, but I'm glad you asked first. I didn't want to assume. You *do* have Gage next door."

"No. I want *you* here...with me."

"Then it's settled. We'll get my things from the hotel this morning—together, if you don't mind. I don't want to leave you alone for even a moment."

Eve finally showed him the beautiful smile that had been absent for the last seven hours.

Will planted a quick kiss on her forehead and they got up from her bed.

"Help yourself to some coffee. There's creamer in the fridge if you want some. I'm going to go take a shower, OK?"

"Not so fast." Will grabbed her hand and pulled her into another embrace, bringing his mouth to hers with deliberateness. Eve immediately let her fingers tangle into his hair. His arms held her to him fully and they soon found themselves breathless.

"Ahh... We are never going to get anything done today if you keep doing *that*, Mr. Prentiss," she whispered against his lips.

"Oh, I think we'd get something done, but it wouldn't be anything on our list." He moved his face to her ear and breathed against her neck. "Perhaps we can put this on tonight's agenda, hmm?"

She gasped slightly. "Um, ahh, yeah. I think that can be arranged. Um, I really need to...take that shower." Will enjoyed the effect he had on her and smiled as he let her go.

The mugs were where he thought they'd be, and he added some creamer to hers before filling two with coffee. After stealing a sip of the rich brew and setting his drink on the counter, Will picked up Eve's mug and walked back to her bedroom.

"Eve, would you like so—" He stopped short.

The bathroom door wasn't completely closed, and he could see Eve's reflection in the mirror. Will knew he should turn and leave, but he just couldn't. As he watched the dress slide down her body to the floor, he was suddenly very uncomfortable, in more ways than one. When she began to lower the straps of her bra from her shoulders, he returned to the living room. It took a few gulps of the hot coffee, as Will let it burn against his tongue, to rid his mind of Eve in all her lace lingerie.

Ten minutes later, when Eve emerged freshly showered, clad in jeans and a t-shirt with her hair pulled up, she found the cup of coffee Will had prepared for her. She topped it off to warm it up before taking a sip, and was surprised to discover he had made it just the way she liked it: lots of cream.

"Thanks!" She swallowed a few sips. "Mmm. Perfect!" Eve's smile touched Will. He loved that the smallest thing could make her happy. "I'm just going to dry my hair enough to put it into a ponytail. I'll be ready to go in about five minutes."

As promised, she returned quickly, looking refreshed and carefree. She came to where he was standing in the kitchen and wrapped her arms around his neck, pulling him down to kiss him. "I'm ready!"

Will looked at his watch. It was just after nine o'clock—plenty of time to take care of the errands on their list. First stop would be his hotel so he could shower quickly, grab his belongings, and check out.

On the way, Will phoned Megan to let her know he would be staying at Eve's instead of the hotel. After a few catcalls from her, which caused Eve to blush profusely, Will was able to explain the reason for the change, and Megan immediately apologized.

Hesitantly, Will looked over to Eve as he informed Megan there was a strong possibility he'd be extending his stay in Santa Barbara beyond Tuesday. Only after receiving an accepting smile and nod from Eve did Will continue to explain that he would keep her apprised of the situation and let her know when he planned to come home. Megan and Martin were a good team and would make sure things ran smoothly in his absence. His priority right then was Eve's safety, and he wasn't going back to Boston until he was sure Julian would leave her alone.

Eve relaxed in a chair by the window in the hotel room while Will showered and changed. He hadn't unpacked much—just toiletries—so they were soon on their way to the tire store. The salesman was able to arrange to have the tires delivered and installed before the day was out. Will could tell Eve was relieved to have this taken care of so quickly. When she'd glanced at her car as they'd left her apartment this morning, it was evident that the memory of last night came flooding back.

The couple stopped for lunch on the way to the police station, and Will could tell something was bothering her as they began to eat.

"Will, I don't want to file that order of protection. It just seems like I'll be adding to his anger if I do. I mean, we don't *know* he was the one to do that to my car, right?"

"Eve, who else could it have been?" Will asked gently. "Is there someone else you haven't mentioned who would have deliberately *stabbed* ice picks into *your* car's tires with the added touch of the Stratus napkins?"

Tears welled up in her eyes and she looked at him pleadingly. "I just want him to get over this—get over *me.*"

Will pushed his plate to the side, his sandwich half-eaten, and folded his hands together on the table.

"And what next?" He was frustrated that she couldn't, or wouldn't, see that ignoring Julian wasn't making him go away. "What if he gets his hands around your throat again? Do you think you'll be able to stop him?"

They'd never talked about the bruises on her neck that first night at Stratus. Will had felt Eve would share with him what happened, if and when she was ready. But now he willed her to open up to him about that night. There was the evidence of his violence on her neck, but had he hurt her more than that?

"Eve, did he...?"

"No! No, he had only gotten rough with me that one time but I was able to knee him before he could do anything else." *Thank God.* Relief washed over Will.

They sat in silence for a few minutes, both of them done with their meals. Will could tell Eve was remembering that night. He reached across the table, and she brought her hands to his.

"So," he said softly, "is there no convincing you to file a report?"

As a single tear fell from each eye, Eve just pursed her lips and shook her head no. "I'm too afraid to, and I want to hold on to the hope that maybe he'll realize I don't want to be with him anymore and just go away," she whispered.

Will caressed her face with his hand, swiping away one of her tears with his thumb. She brought her hand up to his and held it there for a few moments longer.

"Thanks for understanding."

Will decided he couldn't tell her he *didn't* understand why she was willing to continue to risk her life. Right now she needed his unconditional support. And as long as she asked Will to stay by her side, he would, *unconditionally*.

They pulled themselves together after a few minutes, and when Eve was ready, headed out to do their last errand of the day, replacing the lock on her apartment door.

"Have you got any tools at home so I can install this for you?" Will asked as they stood looking at the huge selection of locks at the home improvement store. He hated feeling like a chauvinist, but did need to know if they should wander to the screwdriver section before leaving the store.

"My mom bought me a decent tool kit that I keep in the trunk of my car. It's got two or three different sized Phillips and flatheads in it. Is that all we'd need?"

Will turned the lock package over and scanned the back for directions. “This looks pretty straightforward. We’ll be good with a couple screwdrivers. We should be able to get this done fairly quickly.”

By the time Will and Eve returned to her apartment, the tire store had already been there, and Eve had a new set of tires on her car. She grabbed the tool kit from the trunk, and they were able to change the door lock in less than an hour. It was now a little after two o’clock, and they would leave for Noelle and Thomas’s party no later than six to pick up a bottle of wine on the way.

“Would you mind going to the gym for an hour? I’ve been craving the stair climber since Thursday.” Eve smiled at him as she finished putting the tools away.

“You *crave* a stair climber?” Will laughed at her choice of wording.

“Yeah. I’m a bit masochistic when it comes to exercising. You know, ‘no pain, no gain’?”

“Does the place have a decent treadmill or weight machine?”

Eve lit up. “Yes! Do you want to go, then? And I promise, just for an hour!”

Eve turned from the fridge, chilled water bottles in hand, and froze. Her eyes locked on Will as he emerged from the bedroom, slipping his arms through his t-shirt and pulling it over his head.

To say Eve was stunned was an understatement. She had only seen Will in long-sleeve shirts and pants or jeans. Having explored his chest with her hands that morning in bed, she knew he was hiding a well-sculpted body under those clothes, but she still wasn’t quite prepared for his gorgeously defined chest and arms.

Trying to regain her composure, Eve took a few deep breaths as she rolled the ice cold water bottles across her forehead. Will laughed at her expression as he stepped into her and lightly kissed her forehead.

"You ready?"

"Uh...yeah," Eve answered, still a little dazed by the man in front of her.

When they walked into the gym, it was apparent that Saturday at 2:30 in the afternoon wasn't a big workout time. There were only three other people: a couple preparing to leave and a woman in her mid-twenties wearing the most constricting—and revealing—workout outfit Eve had ever seen. The woman was doing leg lifts on one of the mats, and when she saw Will walk in, she must have swallowed her gum because she sputtered a cough and put her hand to her throat.

Eve headed over to the treadmills, as Will went to find the weight machines. The woman watched him, her eyes never leaving his face as he approached nor his backside as he passed.

Putting her earbuds on and finding a good playlist on her iPod, Eve set the timer on the machine. Before hitting the start button, she glanced over at Will, smiling as she thought about waking up in his arms that morning, and that he would be living with her for the next few days.

Eve was so focused on her own workout that it had been almost half an hour before she looked over to see how Will was doing. The woman from the mat was standing right in front of him, shifting from hip to hip as she talked. For a split second, jealousy shot through her body, but then she realized it was pretty much a one-way conversation. Will was busy with a lot of weights and gritted his teeth with every lift. He was barely looking at her.

Eve did a double take as she noticed the woman adjusting her breasts. She quickly pulled out the earbuds.

"—been to Boston before, is it nice there?"

"It's...pleasant...enough," Will responded through his reps.

"Well, my friends told me, 'Suzanne, you should move to a big city 'cause that's where *all* the hot men are.' They were *right*." She gave Will a lusty look. "Maybe I should come to Boston, huh, Willie? You and me could hook up, you know? I'll bet you know the best night clubs to go to. When are you heading—"

"Excuse me." Will turned toward Eve. "Eve?" Her head shot up and their eyes met. "Honey, we probably need to finish up here if we're going to be ready in time."

Suzanne's chin nearly hit the floor. She had assumed the blonde was his sister or something. She turned toward Eve with eyes full of hate. Eve just shrugged and gave her a smile and a wink.

"You got it, sweetheart. Let me just wipe down my machine and I'll be ready. We can shower at *home*." Eve let that last line sink in with Suzanne.

On the trip back to Eve's apartment, they laughed about Will's admirer. As they pulled into a parking space, Eve leaned over and kissed him fully.

"Wow. What was that for?"

"For not finding her attractive, and calling me 'honey' in front of her."

"You liked that, huh? Hmm...I guess I'll have to call you that more often then."

Will flashed the smile he knew Eve adored and the two joined hands for the walk upstairs to get ready for the party.

"Honey, can you get me a fresh razor?" Noelle called from the shower.

"Absolutely." Thomas handed one to her and he peeked in at the same time. She flicked water at him with her fingertips and giggled at his attentive stare.

"Thomas, what time is it anyway?"

"It's 5:30, dear. We still have some time, don't worry."

"I'll be done in a minute! You finish setting out the utensils and plates and then you can get in here."

Blowing her a kiss, Thomas retreated to the kitchen, listening for the water to turn off between sorting the silverware and serving spoons.

Thomas and Noelle's home was a small bungalow, located just outside Santa Barbara city limits. They'd purchased it three years ago and recently finished adding on two bedrooms for the children they were hoping to have someday. Thomas hoped that would happen soon. He was worried Noelle wouldn't be able to bear trying without success much longer.

Noelle finished ironing her dress while Thomas showered and shaved. She had dried her hair but was still in her robe when Tom emerged from the shower. He caught her unaware, reaching from behind to undo the sash and slip her robe off her shoulders. He brushed his lips against her neck, and she turned around to embrace and kiss him.

"Do we have time to...?" Tom whispered.

"No, dear, we don't. But I'll take you up on that offer later on, if that's OK."

They separated and returned to their task of getting dressed for the party. "Oh, I forgot to tell you, hon," Tom said. "I can't find the paring knife anywhere. Do you know where it is? I need to slice the strawberries."

"I'm sorry, Thomas, I broke it yesterday when I was getting some of the appetizers ready. Are you sure we don't have another?"

"I didn't see any when I was searching a little while ago. Our serrated knives are going to be too rough on the fruits and vegetables."

My husband the perfectionist, Noelle thought with a smile. He was a details person. She knew that if he didn't have the right knife to use on the fruit, he'd be brooding for half the evening.

"Tell you what. I think we could use another bag of ice too. It's only quarter 'til—how about I try to catch Josie or Skylar and ask them to stop by the store on their way here? Surely the grocery store will have a paring knife that will get us through this evening."

Tom smiled at his wife, leaning in to kiss her forehead. "You always know how to make things right! I'll go get the grill started, and you call one of the girls."

"Damn it, Gage! You know how I hate to be late."

Gage and Skye had lost track of time, and she was pissed. Gage was driving as fast as he could through town, and Skye was in the middle of lecturing Gage on how rude and self-centered it was to keep people waiting when her phone began to ring. Gage had never been so relieved to have a conversation interrupted by a cell phone. It wasn't like he had made them late on purpose. How did she expect him to control himself when she was just prancing around in nothing but a bra and panties?

"Hey, Noelle," Skye answered the phone, but was still giving Gage the death stare.

"No. We're on our way right now." Again she glared at him.

"Sure, we can do that... All right, see you soon. Bye."

"What did Noelle want?"

"They need us to stop by the store and pick up some things."

"See, so being late was actually a good thing for Noelle." Gage quickly changed gears, knowing this was a better defense than blaming Skye.

Skye smiled at him, finally, and laughed. Gage was just so adorable, *and sexy*, when he thought he had won an argument. She would let him keep thinking that...this time.

"Well, what is it we need to get? Can we just stop at Carrolton's or do we have to go hoity toity and do Perfect Foods?"

"Carrolton's will be fine. They just need ice and a knife." Skye went quiet as they drove toward Noelle's. She was thinking about Noelle and what a perfect life she had. Before Gage, she would only on very rare occasions envy her and what she had with Thomas. But now, Skye often thought about living with Gage in the suburbs; having the little house and the white picket fence.

When the store came into view, Gage pulled into the parking lot and found a place to park. Looking over at Skye, her bottom lip pinched between her teeth in her thoughtful pose, he wondered what she was thinking about. Gage always worried when Skylar was thinking too hard. He was afraid she would figure out how much better she was than him and leave him.

"A knife? Why the hell do they need a knife? Doesn't Noelle have a kitchen full of knives?"

"She needs a small paring knife. Hers brokc and all they have are steak and butcher knives."

"So, why doesn't she just use one of those to cut stuff?"

"Don't worry about it, honey. I'll get the knife," Skye told him. Clearly he wouldn't know a paring knife from a carving knife. Apparently Skye was going to have to train him.

As they walked into the store, Skye blurted out, "Oh, did you know that Noelle and Thomas are trying to have a baby?"

"Trying to? I've only ever tried *not* to have a baby. How would that work?"

Gage's question made her pull up short. She couldn't imagine *trying* to have a baby.

"Well, I think they just go at it like bunnies until Noelle turns up pregnant. She is going to be a fabulous mother."

The doors of the grocery store slid open as the couple approached. Gage's mind was running at full speed...*going at it like bunnies.* Turning to Skye, Gage had a mix of terror and confusion all over his face. But before she could ask him what was wrong, he was speaking.

"Why don't you go get the knife, babe? I need to pick something up, too, and I'll grab a couple bags of ice."

A few minutes later, Gage found Skye carrying a very small knife in her hand. His hands were full. Along with the bag of ice, Gage had a box of Trojan condoms. Magnums.

When Skye noticed what he was holding, her eyebrows pulled together in confusion. "Gage, what the hell do you have?"

"Well, I was thinking about what you said about Noelle and Thomas trying to have a baby. And it made me realize that *we*, as you so aptly put it, *go at it like bunnies*."

A sudden look of terror washed over Skye's face as she too understood that they had been in a haze of irresponsible sex for the past two weeks. Skye's head was spinning. It wasn't like she had never thought about the fact that they were having unprotected sex. Unfortunately, it was always in the heat of the moment that she thought about it, and when she looked at Gage's incredible naked body, the thought would somehow disappear right out of her head.

With the scary diseases in the world today, Skye had always expected men to use condoms. She wasn't just worried about getting pregnant, she was worried about getting *something*. With that in mind, she had given up using birth control herself long ago. If he wasn't prepared, he wasn't getting anything. But, for some reason, with Gage, she never worried about it.

Skye began counting the days in her head. *Oh God! Please, please, please let it be alright,* she silently begged.

"Shit!" Skye swore loud enough to catch the attention of an old woman walking by. When the woman looked over, she glared back and silently dared her to say something. She didn't.

"Don't worry, it's only been a couple of weeks right? I mean really, what are the chances?" Gage tried to reason with her. It wasn't helping.

"I sure hope you're right about that. Let's pay for this and get to the party." Skye tried to sound casual again, but Gage could tell she was still worried.

Leaning down, Gage brushed his lips against her cheek on the way to her ear. "I love you, Skylar," he whispered as they put their items on the conveyor belt.

While waiting for the cashier to ring up the items, Skye found her datebook in her purse. Pulling it out, she flipped through to find the big red dots. The last day was on the Saturday before she and Gage first went out and, well, that first fantastic night they had spent in his bed.

Skye couldn't remember if it was right before or right after that you were more likely to get pregnant. She made a note to Google that when they got home.

Gage paid the cashier and grabbed the bags. Halfway to the car, in the middle of the parking lot, he suddenly burst out laughing. Skye looked at him like she was about to kill him. The fact that he was laughing when she had just realized that they could beat Noelle and Thomas to the delivery room made Skye's blood boil.

"Gage. Do you really think it's funny that we've been having unprotected sex for two weeks? I mean, I can't be a mom!"

"I'm not laughing at that, baby. I'm laughing because of the cashier."

"What the hell are you talking about? She barely said a word."

"Well, she just rang up ice, condoms, and a knife. And I'm pretty sure she's going to be looking for a headline about us in the newspaper tomorrow."

Gage's little boy grin and boisterous laughter made Skye forget their situation for the moment, and she laughed out loud. There was nothing they could change anyway.

Suddenly, Gage stopped walking and reached over to wrap his arms around Skye, pulling her into a deep kiss. The ice he was holding was pressed into her back and Skye shivered. Gage released her when he realized the goose bumps on her arms were not from his kiss.

He continued to avoid talking about their lack of responsible behavior as he drove the rest of the way to dinner. Instead, they spent the drive trying to imagine what the cashier thought they would do with the bizarre purchases. Skye's theory was a Lorena Bobbit scenario with a reattachment surgery. That suggestion had Gage howling, and she was on the verge of tears from all the laughing.

When the two finally arrived at Noelle and Thomas' it was about twenty minutes after they should have been there, but Skye really didn't care anymore. She was lucky enough to be with the man she loved.

Standing on the porch waiting for the door to open, Skye looked over at Gage, still laughing from their earlier conversation. In that instant, Skye knew everything would be fine. Turning to him, Skye stood on her tiptoes, and softly kissed Gage's perfect lips.

"I love you too, Gage."

Chapter Sixteen

Sitting in a rented car down the street from Thomas and Noelle's house, Julian waited for Eve and *him*, to re-emerge.

The blood in his veins had boiled as he watched Will Prentiss hold Eve's hand as they walked to the door. A vision of *him* with his hands all over Eve began to form in Julian's mind. He shook his head. There was no way he would allow those thoughts to permeate his perfect memories of beautiful Eve.

He settled in to wait, but had been surprised to see *all* of them arrive after Eve went inside. Julian realized he had never been invited to their house, and Noelle was the only one of Eve's friends he liked.

Next to arrive was the other bitch, Josie, and that guy she met playing their whore game at Stratus. Julian had already decided that when he had Eve back, Josie was out. Before she had offered herself up like an animal—blindfolded and bound—to be slobbered on by strange men, Julian had actually considered her an acceptable friend for Eve.

The last to arrive was the whore, Skylar, with the steroid freak neighbor of Eve's. It would figure that she would show up late. Julian was sure she wanted to make an entrance so everyone would pay attention to her. He watched them as they stood waiting for the door, touching and kissing each other. A feeling of total disgust washed over him as he thought how rude it was to show up at someone's house as a guest and act like that. She would definitely not be a part of Eve's life once they were together again.

Hours passed as Julian waited. He thought about getting out to find a place near the house where he could see and hear what was happening, but to get caught now would ruin his plans. So instead he sat in the car with a sketch book, hoping that just seeing Eve would inspire something. Julian hadn't worked in weeks. Not since she left him.

It was amazing—and a comfort—to Eve that Will felt such an instant bond with her friends. Even last night at Stratus they'd had in-depth and ongoing conversations. They were a diverse group of personalities, but they all had true respect for each other. And Will fit right in. It felt like they had always been a group of eight.

"Wine?" Thomas offered after shaking Will's hand and kissing Eve on the cheek.

Will looked at Eve while responding. "Pinot Grigio? If you've got it." Eve smiled and nodded, pleased that Will had remembered her preference from their first dinner in Boston.

They soon had their drinks and stepped out onto the large brick patio off the family room. Noelle had an eye for style and had put her magic touch out here. The eaves of the house and surrounding trees were trimmed with little white fairy lights. Incense candles were placed along the outer wall and atop their large mahogany dining room table, which they had moved outside for tonight's dinner. It was a romantic setting, to say the least. Will must have noticed as well because he came up behind Eve, slipped his arm around her waist, and brushed his lips against her hair.

"You look wonderful tonight, you know, especially in this light," he whispered.

As usual, Eve's heart skipped a beat. "Thank you!" She leaned her head back, pulled his face down, and kissed him just long enough to get Noelle, who was just joining them, to clear her throat. "Sorry...um...still enjoying that whole 'phenomenal Passion Fish' thing," Eve said sheepishly, knowing her cheeks were flushed in embarrassment.

"Hey, everybody!" Josie chirped as she and Beau followed Noelle outside. Soon their larger group became two smaller ones. Will and Beau gravitated toward Tom, who was tending the grill, and Josie, Noelle, and Eve wandered back inside. Just a few minutes passed before Skye and Gage walked through the front door as well, carrying bags of ice and a small package that Skye placed on the kitchen's island countertop. Gage headed outside to join the guys, leaving the women to talk and help Noelle with the last of the dinner preparations.

Tom and Noelle caught each other's eye a few times during the meal, and they smiled at the success of their first dinner party. Conversations ranged from the museum's new grant, to which Beau gave a touching toast, to Will and Eve's interesting afternoon at the gym.

"This woman, I'm sorry, ladies, was literally 'busting' out all over. I can't imagine that she could adequately complete a workout when her internal organs were being constricted so severely," said Will with a laugh.

"Wait, wait—don't tell me," Gage piped in. "Gold top and really short shorts with blue pin striping down the sides? Decent body except for the fact that half of it was *way* too surgically enhanced?"

Will and Eve both nodded as the laughing around the table continued.

"That was Suzanne!" Gage slapped his hand down on the table. "She works out, alright, but I swear she must not have a home because she is there *all* the time, scoping out the men, even the ones there with their wives or," and he waved at Will and Eve, "their girlfriends!"

It was sweet to watch the newest couple turn and lean toward each other at Gage's reference to them. Tom couldn't be sure, but he was guessing that they had been holding hands under the table through the entire meal. *Reminds me of Noelle and myself when we started dating.*

"Did she bounce on her hips when she talked to you so her boobs would jiggle?" Gage was never one to mince words. Again he received two nods.

"God, she is *so*—"

Will joined in as they said together, "—annoying!"

With that, they all broke out in hysterics—at poor Suzanne's expense.

The steaks, salads, and rice pilaf had all been perfect, and when everyone arose from dinner, Tom immediately went over to his bride to capture her in his arms briefly and tell her how thankful he was for the work she did to prepare everything while he'd been out showing properties.

Everyone helped bring dishes to the kitchen, rinsing and piling them for Noelle and Tom to take care of later. Tom made sure drinks were replenished and returned to the patio to sit with the men at the table.

With a fresh beer in his hand, Gage leaned back in the chair and let out a huge breath. Noelle was a great cook, and he had eaten way too much. All through the dinner, he couldn't help picturing Skye and himself hosting a party like this for all their friends. Of course in Gage's version, while getting ready for the party, Skye wore nothing but an apron, pearls, and high heels. More than that, though, he liked the thought of two of them being together in *their* house.

Now with all the women off looking at this house, the conversation quickly turned to more *manly* topics. Gage gave Will a few more digs about his run-in with the "queen of the bouncing bimbos."

"So, Will, let me share my trick for deflecting some of the skank attention. Tell them, in a roundabout way, that they need to work on their ass. The look in their eyes is priceless, and they will immediately get on the treadmill, leaving you alone. Works every time." He raised his beer and took a drink, pondering how he could torture Suzanne with this information at their next session.

As their laughter subsided, Gage looked around at the others, wondering how all of them had ended up friends. And he did consider them all friends—including Will. They all just kind of fit together. It didn't matter that they were all so different; they kept finding new things in common. Tom and Will hit it off talking about business development, while Beau and Gage found common ground in their fascination with Beau's travels around the country and the coins he was currently looking to sell.

Will seemed to feel comfortable with all of the guys too, because once there was a break in their conversation, he leaned in to the table and motioned for the others to do the same.

"I don't want Eve to know I'm telling you this, but something happened last night after we all left Stratus. She doesn't think it's a big deal, but I do. And I think it's only fair that all of you, especially Gage, be aware of what's going on."

Will looked right at Gage, letting him know the next topic of conversation was going to be the asshole ex. Skye had told Gage about Julian showing up in Eve's office, and that, combined with him hanging out at Eve's door, gave Gage a very bad feeling.

"Last night, when we got back to Eve's place, there were four ice picks in her tires. Under each of them was a napkin from Stratus."

Gage jumped out of his chair so fast and with such force that it tipped over, landing hard against the concrete. "What the fu—"

"Gage, settle down a bit. Will said Eve doesn't want us to know, and outbursts like that will bring the girls back pretty quickly." Beau had cut Gage off, but Gage realized his friend made sense. He picked up his chair and sat back down, still pissed as hell.

"Sorry. Sorry, Tom. I hope I didn't damage the chair." He looked for any marks or scuffs and, fortunately, found none. It was taking all his energy not to hit something, though—preferably Julian's face.

"Did you call the police?" Beau asked, again the voice of reason and sanity. Gage could see why he was so good for crazy Josie. He was probably the only one who could rein her in.

"We did, and I checked out of my hotel to stay with Eve. There's no way I'm going to leave her alone. We also changed her lock, just in case Julian still has a key."

Gage was glad Will was staying with Eve. Even though he lived right next door, this was even better. He was also relieved to see he wasn't the only person worked up over this situation. Will's hands kept curling into fists as he talked.

"I've also decided to stay in Santa Barbara for a few extra days. I want to make sure this guy is done bothering Eve before I'll feel OK to leave."

"And she doesn't want help from the police or the court system?" Tom asked.

"No. I've pleaded with her but she won't budge."

"She doesn't need a piece of paper to protect her. If that asshole comes anywhere near her, I'll take care of it. You don't have to worry about that." Gage couldn't help but let that big brother feeling he had for his neighbor bubble to the surface.

"That's why I'm sticking around longer and wanted all of you to be aware of the potential danger." Will gave each of the men a business card with his cell phone number on it. Then he got out his cell and programmed their information in.

Gage was still fuming, and he could tell Tom and Beau were worried he might go looking for the guy. So he took a deep breath and tried to change the subject.

"Hey, Will, you a baseball guy?"

"Why actually, I am. And I believe there's a game on right now that all parties here might want to see, hmm?"

Thomas and Beau both got up, headed to the living room, and soon found the game on television. Will didn't move for a minute, and Gage stayed to calm himself a little more.

"Hey, Gage. It does make me feel better to know that you care about Eve so much. I feel a little better. But just a little."

"No problem. Eve's a good friend, like a sister. If he even sniffs around her, I *will* take care of it."

Will clapped Gage on the shoulder as they stepped back into the house and joined Tom and Beau in the living room. "I trust you will, man. I trust you will."

"Aw, damn! The Angels are already down three runs?" Gage complained loudly after glancing at the score. Will smirked so that Gage could see, but seemed to think twice about praising his Red Sox in a room full of Angels fans. *Smart guy*, Gage thought. *Even if he does root for the wrong team.*

"Noelle, you've decorated everything so beautifully!" Josie said. The women stood around the kitchen, drinks in hand.

"If I give you a key and a few hundred bucks, do you think you could do something with Gage's place?" Skye rolled her eyes. "He is your *classic* bachelor. He even has a Playboy pin-up, *framed* mind you, in his bathroom. He does have a *great* bed,"—both Eve and Noelle blushed at that—"but that and the big-screen TV are about the only redeeming pieces of furniture in the place!"

"Oh, Skye, he just needs *you* to help him make gradual changes—bring him out of the college frat phase and introduce him to a respectable twenty-something's décor," Noelle offered.

"He *is* neat, though. You have to give him that much," Eve piped in. Skye looked at Eve sideways, eyebrows raised. "What? I've been his next-door neighbor for two years. He's one of my best friends. Yes, I've seen the inside of his place—*and* the picture in the bathroom, thank you." They all laughed at that.

"So, I guess the first thing to go would be *that*, hmm?" Noelle asked.

"I've suggested it. And he said the only way it's coming down is if I'm willing to replace it with a similar picture of myself. I told him I'd think about it." Eve's eyes nearly popped. "Kidding, Eve! Kidding!"

Noelle chose to change the subject. "Would you like the grand tour? I know we showed you some photos as the construction was going on, but I'm so excited for you to see how it all turned out."

Placing their glasses on the counter, the women followed Noelle down a hallway that hadn't existed the last time they'd been here. On either side of the hall was a single door, and they progressed through the one on the left. The room they entered was warm and welcoming, with a daybed, an antique armoire, and a plaid stuffed chair. The walls were a deep golden yellow, and the curtains covering the large window were crisp linen with eggplant-colored ties on either side. They continued around to the right and into a Jack-and-Jill bathroom. The room was long, with plenty of cabinets underneath. The gold-and-eggplant color scheme continued, with the addition of sage-green towels and wall sconces that let off soft golden light.

As they progressed through the other doorway, Skye gasped. In the corner was a crib, already decorated with a neutral-toned layette set. A mural of the characters from Winnie the Pooh adorned the walls, and a matching area rug lay diagonally across the floor.

"Noelle? Are you and Thomas...?" Eve asked. Skye continued looking around, mouth agape.

"We're still trying! But we just couldn't see buying adult furniture for both rooms knowing we'd be buying baby things soon enough. So, whenever it happens, we'll be ready—at least with the room!"

Josie looked over at Skye, who hadn't spoken a word. *Are her eyes tearing up?*

"It's just...beautiful, Noelle," Skye finally said in the softest voice.

"Well! That's the whole of it! It may be a small house but it's decorated and designed just the way we wanted it." Noelle was beaming.

Josie reached over and pulled her into a hug. "You've decorated everything so wonderfully! When you're done rescuing Gage's place from Testosterone City, I'll need to have you come over and give me advice on my place!"

"I'd love to!" Noelle smiled.

As they returned to the kitchen, they found the guys watching baseball. The men were so engrossed that the women continued past them and out to the patio, picking up their drinks as they went.

"So, it looks like you and Will are getting on well, hmm?" Josie asked Eve with a wink.

Eve blushed. "He's amazing. He's really amazing."

"Hot damn, Eve Carwyn! You're in love with him, aren't you?" Skye's eyes lit up and the biggest grin came across her face.

As much as she tried to hide it, Eve's smile was a dead giveaway.

"Have you told him?" Noelle asked quietly, taking her hand.

"I want to, before he goes back to Boston. But we're talking about a 3000-mile distance between us! He's got his life back there."

"Do you think he loves you too?" Josie asked. All of their voices had become subdued.

"I don't know. I think he might be heading that way."

Noelle pulled Eve into a hug. "I can see it in his eyes, Eve. The way he looks at you, touches you."

Eve suddenly seemed uncomfortable. At any moment, Skylar was going to start asking her questions of a personal—and sexual—nature. Josie decided to rescue her before Skylar had a chance to start.

"What hotel is he staying at?" Jose asked. She thought she was asking a simple question, but Eve was taken aback. .

"Well...um..."

Skye immediately picked up on Eve's discomfort. "Did he, by chance, *not* go to his hotel last night, hmm? You were pretty insistent that Gage stay with me. Come on, Eve, spill!"

Eve's face was the deepest pink, but it wasn't quite a look of embarrassment on her face.

"Sit down, guys. I need to talk to you." Eve's mood suddenly became serious.

"Honey, what's wrong?" Josie leaned in to place a hand on Eve's.

"I think Julian may have paid me a visit last night." She gazed at her friends one by one as she let that initial news set in. "When Will brought me home, all four tires of my car were punctured with ice picks that had Stratus napkins attached to them."

Eve's eyes began to well with tears, as did Noelle's.

"We called the police but I don't think we can prove he did it." Eve shrugged her shoulders and Noelle moved her chair around to put her arm around her.

"So," she swiped a tear from one eye and gave the other women a half-hearted smile, "yeah, Skye, Will spent the night with me. Just not like you'd think. And he checked out of his hotel. He's going to stay with me until he goes to Boston."

"But that's in just a few days!" Josie's mind began to race. Maybe Eve should move in with Skye or her after Will left. Maybe she could stay in Noelle and Thomas's new spare bedroom.

"Will's going to stay a few days longer. We're just going to wait and see."

"Oh, Eve!" Noelle was distraught over this. But Skye was just plain pissed.

"I *told* you he was a creep, Josie!" She was seething. "Eve, I'm going to make sure Monday morning that we have security guards checking our offices on a regular basis, and *nobody* who doesn't work at the museum will be allowed past the doors that lead toward where you are."

In an earlier life, Skye must have been a lion, Josie mused, the fierce protector of her territory and those in it.

"Look, everybody." Eve was calmer now and attempted to laugh a little. "This is a party, right? I don't want to think about anything but my best friends and that gorgeous man sitting in that chair in there, OK?"

"Good!" Skye's demeanor picked up as well. "So, now that you two are shacking up, any *news* to report?"

Skye always knew how to get Eve to blush, but this time it also helped relax her.

"Tell you what." Eve perked up. "My bedroom backs up to Gage's, and the walls are pretty thin. You two will know pretty definitively if Will and I have anything to report! OK?" She winked at Skye and gave all of them a smile that said she was hoping to have news soon.

And, surprisingly enough, it looked like this time it was *Eve* who made *Skye* blush!

Noelle was the first to stand from the outside table. She raised her glass in a toast. "To those four incredible men inside and to lucky us that they're ours!" The women clinked their glasses gently, and Josie gave Eve an encouraging hug as they moved back toward the house.

"Let's go check on the guys—see which of us can distract our man from the TV the fastest!" Josie said, with every confidence she would win. As soon as she sat on Beau's lap on the sofa, she knew his lips would begin to nibble on her earlobe. *I just love how he does that to me.*

Skye always loved a challenge, so she turned on the charm as soon as she walked through the door. "Oh, Gage!" she began in a sing-song voice. Noelle and Eve followed Skye into the living room where, soon enough, the TV became peripheral to the guys' attention.

It was nearly midnight when everyone said goodnight to Thomas and Noelle and went their separate ways.

Will and Eve walked hand in hand to his car. The night had been a complete success for Thomas and Noelle, and for the two of them as well. Eve realized with a smile that no man had ever gotten along so well with her friends.

She had felt good about herself for the first time in a long time as well. Julian had always been particular about what she wore whenever they went anywhere. He never wanted her to wear anything sleeveless or any skirts above the knee. And he despised high heels—said they made Eve look like a whore. That was why at Stratus the night he had attacked her, Eve was determined to wear everything Julian would have hated: short, skin-tight skirt, stilettos, and a low-cut top.

Tonight Eve felt beautiful, and it was Will who had made that happen. When she'd emerged from the bedroom wearing an A-line dress that buttoned all the way down the front and had an open back, the look on Will's face told her she had picked exactly the right thing. The v-neck revealed a hint of cleavage and the cut and length of the dress, along with a great pair of strappy yellow sandals, showed off her toned legs. Will's appreciative stare had made her heart skip a beat.

And now they were heading "home" to her apartment. As was now their routine, Eve held Will's hand on her lap while he drove. They giggled at their "luck" to hit so many stop lights, since they took the opportunity to kiss while the light was red. Once Eve noticed Will actually slow down as they approached a signal, and he brought the car to a stop while the light was still yellow. She didn't mind.

The porch light came on and drew Julian's attention to the house again. All of them were standing on the front steps—saying good-bye, he assumed. Then each pair moved toward their cars, waving to one another as they closed the doors and drove off.

Carefully Julian pulled out onto the street and followed them, but not too closely. They were all so distracted that he doubted they even knew another car had joined their little caravan.

Skye turned to Gage as they drove home after the party. "Do you know what Eve told us tonight?"

"That Julian stabbed all of her tires with ice picks?" Gage answered immediately.

"Yeah. How did you? Oh...Will."

"He was telling us about it, *and* the fact that Eve doesn't want a restraining order. He's really worried about her."

"So am I."

"Don't worry about Julian. I won't let him get anywhere near Eve."

Skye loved that Gage was so protective of his neighbor. And his response to the Julian situation made her feel better. The creep wasn't getting anywhere near Eve with Will and Gage, not to mention Skye, on duty. Skye sighed and tried to relax.

She was surprised at the way seeing the nursery Noelle had put together had affected her. She knew it was way too soon for Gage and her to be parents, and she was *so* not ready for it, but seeing that room was, well, unsettling. Skye's life suddenly changed gears, and she saw herself standing with Gage, watching a little child with curly hair and dimples just like his father's running through the park. *Snap out of it, Skye, this is not what you want.*

Gage could tell she was still distracted by the baby thing, too. He hadn't stopped touching her all through dinner, and she loved him for it. But now in the car, all of the worry came flooding back. They hadn't had a chance to talk about it yet, and while Skye could guess at Gage's thoughts, she really wasn't sure.

"Babe, are you okay?" Gage reached over and ran his hand along her exposed leg. God, just his touch made her want him!

"I'm fine. Just thinking, you know." Skye tried not to let the tears she could feel welling up escape. She didn't succeed. Leaning her head back against the seat, she closed her eyes, wanting to get all of the emotions she was feeling under control. She detested feeling this vulnerable.

It was after midnight, and there were hardly any other cars on the road, so Skye was shocked when she felt the car slow and come to a stop. When she opened her eyes, they were parked on the side of the dark road, and Gage had turned to look at her. She wasn't sure she could look him in the eye, but shifted in her seat to face him.

"Skye, I know that you're worried about, well, you know...umm." He really was extremely sexy when he was nervous. *Stop it, Skye.*

"It's okay, Gage, you can say it. *Pregnant.*" Skye was thankful for the darkness at that moment.

He picked up both of her hands in his and brought them to his lips, kissing them gently.

"Skye, I love you. You know that."

"But, it's only been a few weeks. What if next week you don't?" She didn't want to hear the answer to her question and really had never meant to ask it.

"I've been in love with you for more than a year now, Skye. I loved you before I even knew how amazing you could make me feel. I loved you before I saw how beautifully your body sparkles in the morning sun. I loved *you*!"

The tears began to stream down Skye's cheeks, and there was nothing she could do to stop them now.

"Oh, Gage. What are we going to do if I'm pregnant?"

"We'll figure that out when we get there. If you're pregnant, then we'll deal with it. *Together.*"

Skye leaned over to Gage and lightly brushed her lips against his. This was the man that she loved. She truly believed that no matter what fate threw at them, it was *their* future. The two—or three—of them.

Gage wrapped his arms around her waist as she leaned over the console, and he pulled her closer to him. Her body immediately responded to his touch as he slowly moved his lips up her jaw line and ended at her ear. In his sexy voice, heavy with desire, he whispered to her, making her heart flutter wildly. "I do love you, Skye. And I want you more right now than I ever have. I want to take care of you." His tongue darted out and traced the shape of her ear. She couldn't help but gasp as she felt her want for him increase.

Are you crazy, Skye? This is why you nearly had a break down tonight. Stop it now!

His hand slid down her back and onto her bare leg, moving up to the hem of her skirt. Skye knew she should stop him, but more than anything she wanted to feel his strong arms around her. She needed to feel safe.

"Oh, Gage..." She never meant for the words to escape, knowing it would only move things along faster. But she couldn't help herself when his hand moved up under her skirt and against the silk of her panties.

"You know, Skye, we have a brand new box of condoms we need to try out." Suddenly, Gage was out of the driver's seat and over at Skye's side of the car. He opened the door and scooped her in his arms, opening the door to the back seat at the same time. He carefully slid her onto the seat, where she moved to the far side, making room for Gage's huge, muscular body.

That wasn't his plan, though, because he grabbed her by the ankles and pulled her back across the seat, the leather upholstery causing her already short skirt to ride up so he could see the red satin of her panties. In the overhead car light, Skye saw the gleam in Gage's eyes. Before getting in the car himself, Gage bent over to kiss the exposed satin just under her skirt. Then she felt his hands under her skirt as they probed for the tiny strings on her panties. He took a step back from the car, gently pulling them down and over her stilettos.

"Damn, I love those shoes on you," he commented as his fingers played with the straps at her ankle.

He finally slid back into the seat, closing the door behind him and pulling Skye to straddle his lap. He unbuttoned her shirt, kissing the exposed skin each new button created. She let her head fall back and a small moan escaped her lips. In this position, she was in full contact with the hardness that strain against his pants, and the sensation was driving her crazy.

With her blouse completely open, he easily unclasped her bra, and she heard his intake of breath at the sight of her exposed breasts. Then his hands moved down to her hips, while he brought his mouth to her breasts.

"Gage, I love you. I want you *now*!" she purred.

As he ran his tongue over her erect nipples, stopping to kiss and nip at her, his hands were slowly grinding her hips into him.

"Where are the condoms? We can't forget them this time."

"Don't worry about them right now." His voice was deep and dripping with his desire for her as he whispered against her breasts, making her body quiver. "Trust me, you can't get pregnant right now."

Skye felt one of his hands slowly move down to the outside of her thigh and continued around and up under her skirt. Then he found the spot she needed him to touch. His fingers moved against her with precision and soon she was writhing in ecstasy, her breaths coming fast and shallow.

"Mmmmm...Gage," was all she could manage.

Both his hands were again firmly on her hips holding her in one spot. The look on his face was one of agony. That was when she realized what her moving was doing to him, still restrained against the fabric of his pants. Skye moved her hands down his chest and found the button and zipper of Gage's pants, easily freeing him from the constraints. Of course, he wore nothing under them. *Perfect! Much easier!*

Once she had his pants undone, she took him in her hand and brought him the same pleasure he had given her. All of her grinding on his lap as he worked her had made her job quite easy, and she leaned in to kiss the man she loved once he had found his release.

"See, there's a lot of stuff we can do that won't get you pregnant," Gage chuckled as he wrapped his arms around her.

They stayed in their loving embrace for a few moments, just enjoying the feel of one another.

When they decided it was time to head home and finish what they had started, Gage looked down and immediately lifted his shirt over his head, handing it to Skye.

"I don't need a souvenir, babe."

"It's for...uh..." He glanced down and she followed his gaze, suddenly realizing what he was referring to.

Cleaned up, zipped up, and buttoned up, the couple climbed out of the back seat and returned to the front. Gage started the car and as they pulled back onto the dark road, Skye looked over at him. She ran her hand down his bare chest, lingering on every muscle. *Ahhhh!*

"Hey, Gage, honey? How long will it take you to get home? I am having a hard time keeping my hands off your body right now."

Skye was thrown back into her seat as Gage immediately accelerated.

Not far down the road, the bitch, Skye, and her muscle-bound boyfriend pulled off to the shoulder. *Good God! They couldn't even wait to get home*, Julian realized. *Whore!*

He drove past them quickly. He needed to keep up with the other cars. Soon, the other car turned off too, and it was only *his* car Julian was following. Holding his breath, hoping Eve wouldn't go back to *his* hotel room, Julian was relieved when the route seemed to be going back to Eve's. Prentiss would drop her off and go back to his hotel. The thought that maybe Eve hadn't slept with him crossed Julian's mind before he remembered how Prentiss had kissed Eve the previous night, and he knew.

As Julian followed Will and Eve through town, he cursed that fact that the car slowed down as it came to each yellow light. Every light they hit was red. It wasn't until the third time this happened that he realized Prentiss leaned over to kiss Eve each time they stopped. This was completely unacceptable.

Will's car turned into the parking garage of Eve's building. Julian stopped and parked across the street where he could see the exit, and he waited.

Although the elevator was only taking them up one level, they spent the ride stealing kisses every chance they could. Once inside the apartment, Will closed and locked the door while Eve leaned on the couch to remove her shoes. As soon as she stood back up, he pulled her into another embrace, and their sweet kisses were quickly replaced by deeper, more passionate ones. Eve could feel her heart pounding in her chest and her breathing becoming erratic. The taste of the wine still lingered on his tongue and she savored it as she explored his mouth with hers. Between kisses, she would gasp for a single breath of air and then immediately return her mouth to his.

When they finally broke their embrace, Eve held both of Will's hands and led him toward her bedroom. If he was going to keep kissing her like *that,* she'd need the safety of being horizontal. *And look, how convenient. My bed is right here.*

They stood face to face, inches apart, and he gazed into her eyes like he was looking into her soul. His fingertips tenderly brushed across her cheek, his thumb tracing the outline of her mouth. He moved both of his hands to her upper arms and then let them glide gently along her skin. When he reached her wrists, he lifted them up to his shoulders and then, once again, began moving downward with his hands, this time along the sides of her body. His thumbs spread out from his fingers as they wandered over the sides of her breasts, and she couldn't hold back any longer, pulling his mouth to hers and letting him know how much she wanted him.

In an instant, Will broke their kiss, brought his arm under the back of her knees and lifted her, carrying her to the side of her bed and then gently laying her down in the center of it, her head on the pillows. He kicked off his shoes and joined her, moving one arm to be under her neck. He lay on his side and placed his other hand on Eve's stomach. She turned so she had one arm around his back and the other by her side, her hand now resting on his.

He kissed her softly, and she opened her mouth to encourage him, teasing his lips with her tongue. Will's hand slipped from under hers and moved up to rest at the top button of her dress. He looked at Eve for permission. Her eyes told him what she wanted, and he unfastened three buttons. Then he moved his hand under the fabric, his fingers tracing the outline of her bra. She brought her hand to caress his upper arm as he spread open the top of her dress. He gazed at the lacy pink bra and Eve's exposed skin, then brought his lips to her collarbone. He placed gentle kisses there but gradually progressed down to the edge of the lace. He cupped her breast in the palm of his hand and used his thumb to draw the material down, brushing over and then releasing her erect nipple.

Will continued kissing her skin but when he reached her breast, he opened his mouth and began to tease with his tongue. Eve's back arched and her hand moved to tangle in his hair. She held him to her as he massaged her with his mouth and she moaned with pleasure. *My God, let this not be a dream!*

Eve brought her leg up to rest on his hip, and his hand slid down her body and to her thigh as he pulled her to him. He straightened, leaving her nipple hard and wet from his tongue, and moved his mouth back to capture her in the deepest kiss they had shared. He pressed against her, and she could feel how hard he was against her stomach. His hand returned to her exposed breast, kneading it with his palm and causing her to gasp and writhe at the exquisite feeling.

"Will." Her breathing was erratic, her heart pounding. "God, Will, we've got to stop." *Even though I don't want to.* "I'm...I just don't think we should. I'm sorry, this is just too fast for me." *Please don't be offended that I'm asking you to stop*, she added silently.

He leaned his head against her neck and brought his hand from her breast to her waist. "You're right. I'm sorry, I just... God, Eve, I..." He fell back against the pillows beside her, his chest heaving. She slipped her bra back in place, but left her dress unbuttoned, then turned to nestle against him.

He wrapped his arm around her back and sighed. "God, you're beautiful. All of you. Your mind, your face and that smile, your body." Then he smirked and kissed her forehead. "You can't blame me for getting caught up in you, you know? I've been wanting to do *that* since that night in the bar after our non-date dinner. Do you remember?"

Oh, yes, Eve thought. She'd wanted to pull him into that elevator and take him to her room that night. She placed her hand on his chest, feeling his heart still racing, "When we asked each other non-business questions? Mm-hmm. I went to bed that night trying to figure out if you were single or not."

He looked down to me. "But I told you that Jeannette and I were over—that we had barely even started!"

"I know, but I didn't know if she had been your most recent girlfriend or just a previous girlfriend. I really didn't ask the question as well as you gave me credit for."

"Hmm." He seemed lost in thought for a moment. Then a smile came over his face. "Care to play that game again?"

"With *that* look on your face? I'm not so sure."

"Come on. Play with me."

"I thought that's what we were just doing."

"Play *this* game with me," he corrected. He was so adorable when she could trip him up like this.

"Still no rules, right? That means I don't have to answer if I don't want to?"

"All right. Still no rules. You can bow out any time."

Eve snuggled in closer and placed a kiss on his neck. "OK. Shoot."

"What's your shoe size?"

"Huh? Eight. Why do you want to know that?"

"I don't know. I just didn't want you to quit right away."

Now it was Eve's turn. "How old were you when you first kissed a woman's breast like that?"

"Oh, is *that* the direction you want our game to go tonight?" he teased. "OK. I was eighteen, a freshman in college."

"Name?" Eve was having fun now.

"Not yet. I get to ask another question first." He brought his free hand to his chin and stroked it as though deep in thought. "Who was the first person to touch *you* like that?"

"Ugh! You're assuming it wasn't *you* just then, hmm?" He gave her a sideways look. "OK. You got me. His name was Shawn. We were both nineteen and pretty inexperienced, but he sure could melt me with his smile back then." Eve let herself remember those days of innocence and exploration.

"Shawn, eh? And what ever happened to this Shawn character?" Will laughed, and she slapped his chest playfully.

"Nope. No info for you yet. It's my turn. What was her name and how old was she?"

He blushed. *Hmm...a skeleton about to come out of the Prentiss closet.* "Her name was Claudia. She was a frat brother's girlfriend." And then his voice dropped to a whisper. "And she was twenty-one."

Eve laughed. "You were mere boy of eighteen and you seduced an older woman, hmm?"

"Not exactly. *She* came on to *me.* I was a pledge and ended up falling asleep in the guy's bed. She wandered in, thinking I was him. Even though she realized pretty quickly that I wasn't her boyfriend, she still just crawled into bed and started kissing me. I thought I was having a *really* vivid dream." He started to laugh. "Nothing happened beyond some making out; she wasn't my type at all. And it turned out he'd been out with someone else behind her back that night. She found out and broke up with him, and he never found out about me. He'd have killed me if he had!"

"Well, I guess I have her to thank for your, um, talents, then, don't I? OK, ask me another question."

Will hesitated, then looked directly at her. "If I promise to behave myself, can I sleep here with you tonight? You feel so good right here with me, and that couch just doesn't look nearly as appealing."

Eve gazed into his eyes and then brought her mouth to his, where he welcomed her into a full kiss. "And what if I can't keep such a promise to you?" she whispered against his lips.

At first he didn't answer, he just pulled Eve to him, and once again they were entwined in passion. Then he moved his mouth to her ear, nibbling the edge of it. "It obviously wouldn't be the first time I was seduced in someone else's bed. But this time, I'd like it so much better."

He had her panting again but she stayed focused. "All right. We have a deal. You can sleep here with me, and any funny business can be initiated only by me. Oh, the power I hold over you!" Eve gave him a flirtatious smile and ran a single finger down the center of his chest, causing him to gasp as she got closer to his waist. *Hmmm...I like his reaction to that!*

Eve turned to get up. "I'm going to go change. I slept in a dress last night and don't intend to repeat that." She started toward her dresser and turned back. "I'm guessing that a t-shirt and shorts would be better for me to wear than a spaghetti-strap silk nightgown, yes?"

"Well, I know which one I'd *prefer* to see you in, so you'd better get into the t-shirt and shorts. Much safer for both of us, I think." Will gave her a defeated smile, then got up to change his clothes as well.

Eve heard him mumble as he headed to the living room for his bag. "Much, much safer. Damn."

The sun shining in his eyes woke him up. It was morning. *Shit!* He had fallen asleep.

It was still early, so Julian got out of the car and crossed the street to the parking garage. He had to know if Prentiss had left.

His car was easy to spot. Very flashy. And there it was parked right next to Eve's car. Julian noticed that her tires were already repaired. *He* had probably paid for them. *Will Prentiss.* I couldn't help but spit his name.

He had stayed all night with Eve.

Of course Julian would forgive Eve. He needed her in his life. But her friends—and him...that would be a different story.

Chapter Seventeen

"Good morning." Will kissed Eve's forehead as she stirred awake.

"Yes, it is *definitely* a good morning." She turned her face upward to nuzzle Will's neck and then rested her head on his shoulder, her fingers tracing circles and figure-eights over his chest. The feeling of Eve's hands roaming across his bare skin made him groan.

"Sleep well?"

"Mm-hmm. You?"

"Wonderfully. I had a beautiful woman by my side. What more could I ask for?"

"Well," she hesitated. "There could have been more last night."

"Last night was perfect, Eve."

"So, you're OK that I stopped us?"

Will pulled Eve into him, caressing her arm as it lay across his chest. "Of course I am! What do you take me for? Don't get me wrong, though, Eve. I *did*—and I *do*—want to. But we'll both know when that time is, and last night, *phenomenal* as it was, was not the right time." He waited a moment and then kissed her hair. "OK?"

"Yeah." Eve breathed a sigh of relief. "Thanks."

"Actually, thank *you.* Like I said, last night was pretty phenomenal." Will paused and looked down at Eve with a smile.

"We've really got to start thinking about a better word for next time, eh?"

"I think that *when,*" Eve looked up at Will seductively, "we get to *that* point, we'll be left speechless." She placed her hand on his jaw as her mouth moved to his.

It was another fifteen minutes—much of it a very nice re-enactment of last night—before the two grudgingly agreed to get up. Eve was meeting the girls for their weekly brunch—no men allowed—and Will already had some plans in mind for the time she'd be gone. After a little more flirting about how he might help her in the shower, she turned toward the bathroom, and he went to the kitchen to make some coffee.

As Eve walked out the door a half-hour later, they agreed to meet back at the apartment around one o'clock. That gave Will two hours to accomplish a few errands. After showering, he got online to search for two different businesses in Santa Barbara: one a place he'd be visiting, the other he would be calling. He found some notepaper in a drawer by the phone and wrote the information he'd need for the day, gulped another cup of coffee, and headed out the door.

Josie had to take Beau to the airport before her standing brunch with the girls, so she was running a little late. She hated this part of her relationship with Beau. He traveled so much. Of course, they talked nightly, but it wasn't the same as falling asleep curled up next to him, or waking up with his arms wrapped around her.

This morning's airport drop off had been harder than the others, and Josie wasn't sure why. As she drove north to Santa Barbara, the scene at the airport played in her head.

Slowing the car to a stop at the departures terminal, Josie looked over at the Beau, thinking—not for the first time—that he really was the most important person on the planet to her. She knew the tears would soon break through. The urge to beg him to stay rose up, but he had to go. This was his job.

Turning away quickly so as not to upset Beau, Josie heard him open the door and get out. After pulling herself together, she followed him to the back of the car where Beau was taking his suitcase out of the trunk. Josie leaned into him, allowing him to wrap her in his arms.

"I'll be home on Wednesday. I'll call you when I get in, and don't be surprised when you get a call from me, like, every hour." He smiled down at her, and immediately the urge to beg him to stay surfaced again. Instead Josie reminded herself that it was only for three days.

Beau held onto her for a few minutes, just enjoying the feeling of her body pressed in close to his, but it didn't last long as he leaned down to kiss her good-bye. Josie clung to him. Eventually, Beau pulled away, giving her one more light kiss before turning into the terminal. When he was right in front of the automatic doors, Beau stopped and turned back to Josie.

"I love you, Josie McInnis," he yelled, causing the crowd of people unloading their loved ones to stop and stare. Then with a blown kiss, Beau turned toward the terminal.

"I love you, too, Beau Sanderson," she called back to him just before he disappeared through the doors.

Wiping her eyes, Josie got back in her car and headed out. In no time, she was pulling up to Marlowe's. Josie looked at her watch and was proud of herself: only ten minutes late. She parked and made her way into the restaurant. Of course Skye was already there sitting at their regular table. She and Eve were laughing about something when Josie slid into the booth.

"Nice of you to join us, Josie." Skye was smiling, so Josie knew she was in a good mood.

"Sorry. I had to take Beau to the airport this morning," Josie said with sadness in her voice.

Eve put her arm around her friend and gave her a little hug just as the waitress came over with coffee and took their orders. Josie mused that the people at Marlowe's should just start cooking their food as soon as they walked in the door. None of them had ever ordered anything different in all the time they'd been meeting there. Then Skye said something that took them by surprise.

"Um, I think I just want some toast, lightly buttered, and some orange juice, please."

Eve and Josie both looked at Skye incredulously. She never deviated from routine; she hated change.

"What? You're not getting the Belgian waffles with strawberries and whipped cream?" Josie asked.

"I'm just not very hungry this morning. Gage likes a big breakfast sometimes, so I already ate something this morning." Her voice was quiet, and Josie looked at her skeptically, but since Skye had let her being late slide, she moved on.

"So, where is Noelle this morning?"

"She and Thomas are, umm, how do I put this?" Eve was blushing.

"Screwing their brains out?" Skye piped in.

"Nice, Skylar. Do you kiss Gage with that mouth?" Since Noelle was otherwise occupied, Josie felt the need to play the mom today.

"All over and every chance I get." Skye smirked.

All three laughed loudly at Skye's too-honest reply, which caused several diners in the restaurant to turn and look at them. Skye wiggled her fingers in a little wave, while Eve hid behind her hair, and Josie just continued to laugh at her best friends and the cavernous difference between their personalities.

"Speaking of screwing your brains out...Eve?" Skye turned to a still-red Eve.

"Skylar!" Josie scolded, knowing if she embarrassed Eve, they would never get the story, but when she glanced over at Eve, there was a small smile playing on her lips.

"Well, did you?" Josie blurted out, unable to corral her curiosity.

Just then the food arrived, and Eve used it as an excuse to avoid the question. The conversation while the three women ate returned to the dinner at Noelle's and how nice it had been to see the men get along so well.

Skye picked at her toast while simply nodding and agreeing with Eve and Josie instead of actually participating in the conversation. Josie knew there was something wrong.

When they had cleaned their plates, except for Skye, Josie turned back to Eve to ask again about her evening.

"OK, Eve. Spill!"

"All right. So, you know that Will is staying at my place?" She finally started after a few moments of silence.

Skye and Josie nodded.

"When he kisses me, my knees go weak. I don't know what it is, but every time his lips touch mine, I suddenly can't even stand up."

"That would be love, my dear," Skye informed her. Eve smiled, and they knew she really was in love with Will. Josie was so happy for her friend, and she wrapped an arm around her shoulder, pulling her into a brief hug. Skye reached out and touched Eve's hands, letting her know that she was happy, too. When Josie looked up, she noticed that Skye also had tears in her eyes.

"Skye, why are you crying?"

"I'm just so happy for Eve. She's found what we all have. I'm just happy," she insisted with a little too much force as she swiped at the tears rolling down her cheeks.

"Go ahead, Eve. We still haven't gotten to the good stuff." Josie urged Eve on, pushing her worry for Skye to the back of her mind.

"Well, we did end up in the bedroom. And let me tell you, being horizontal is much easier when he's kissing me. At least I don't worry about hitting the ground if he lets go of me."

"So, it was a good thing Gage stayed at my place last night then, huh? You can thank me later."

"I'll just say this: You and Gage would have had a peaceful night's sleep."

"What?" Josie was completely confused.

"Shut up! You had him in your bed, and you *didn't* get any?" Leave it to Skye to lay the cards on the table.

"I'm just not ready yet. I mean, he lives in Boston; I live in Santa Barbara. I don't want to sleep with him and then have him go back to Boston and never see him again. I couldn't stand that."

"Eve, honey, I saw the way he looks at you." Josie took Eve's hands and looked right into her eyes. "He is not going anywhere. Trust me, I know about these things."

"Yeah, Eve. You need to just go with it. Whatever the future holds isn't going to be changed now. Just go for it, and then we'll deal with the consequences later."

Skye still looked distracted, like her comments had more to do with something other than the current conversation. Whatever it was, though, she didn't seem to want to talk about it right now. Until she did, they'd just have to act like they didn't know there was anything wrong.

"I'm going shopping," Josie said with a sigh. "I could use the retail therapy, and I saw dress I want to buy for when Beau gets back."

"That sounds like a great idea. I could use some of that therapy myself. Want some company?" Skye asked.

"Oh, Skye, of course," Josie responded enthusiastically. Maybe she could get to the bottom of what was making Skye act so strangely today. "Eve? Are you going to come too? We can make it a whole girls' day."

Eve looked away from Josie, trying to hide. "Umm, I kind of have plans with Will." Her voice was almost a whisper.

"Eve, you don't have to feel bad. We want you to spend time with him."

"Where are you going? Are you at least going to jump him tonight?" Skye and her tact chimed in and Josie turned to glare at her. "What? I just want to know that our sacrificing Eve for the day will result in her getting laid."

Josie just shook her head. "You go with Will." Josie gave Eve's hand a little squeeze to let her know she really meant it.

"Thanks, guys. And I promise to let you know when it does happen. Probably."

They paid their bill and headed out into the beautiful spring day. Josie hugged Eve, and Skye did the same. As Eve turned, Josie linked arms with Skye and began skipping down the street to their first store of the day.

"Josie, ugh. Will you please stop skipping? All the bouncing is giving me motion sickness.

Skye was looking a little green, and Josie was determined to find out what was wrong. She could be very persuasive when she needed to be, and today, Skye would crack.

While Eve was driving back to her apartment, Will called to let her know that he was still running an errand and wouldn't be back until closer to two o'clock. He wouldn't tell her where he was or what he was doing, only saying that she'd find out soon enough.

Once home, all Eve could do was wait around for Will, brooding that her time away from him had been extended.

Eve had given Will a key that morning, but when he returned he thumped on the door instead. When she opened it, he stood there with three bags of groceries in one hand, pulling a rolling cooler with the other.

"What's all this?"

"We're going on a picnic!" He smiled enthusiastically and began to roll the cooler into the apartment. Before he made it to the kitchen, Will stopped to lean down to kiss Eve. He then continued to the kitchen counter where he placed the plastic grocery bags. "Is that OK?"

As Will began to unload the bags of bread, deli meats, a fruit tray, and a package of brownies from the store's bakery, Eve stood in awe.

"Wow! And here I am, supposed to be the host while you're visiting Santa Barbara, and *you're* the one coming up with things for us to do!" Eve was grinning with delight, but Will was suddenly worried.

"Oh, I'm sorry. Had you planned something? It's OK. The bread and meat will keep! And the fruit tray—"

"No, Will. I'm thrilled you did all this. It's wonderful! Thank you!" Throwing her arms around his neck, she kissed his cheek. Will pulled her into on embrace.

"Good. It just seemed to be the perfect day to go to a park or the beach. I looked online but wasn't sure if maybe you had a place to suggest?"

With a small kiss to Eve's forehead, Will released her and together the two sorted the groceries. Eve got out mustard and mayo from the fridge and some plastic zipper-seal bags to put things in. Will opened the cooler to reveal crushed ice, some water and cans of soda, and a bottle of wine. They added the sandwiches and fruit to eat when they got hungry.

Turning to the last bag on the counter, Will pulled out two plastic wine glasses. "The dollar place was right next to the grocery store! And you have a corkscrew—sorry, I rummaged through your kitchen to see what we'd need and what you already had."

"Will..." Eve's voice trailed off, but her mind continued. *I am so in love with you! I wish I could know for sure how you feel about me. About us.*

Will took a deep breath as he cleared off the counter. "So, official Santa Barbara tour guide, now that we have dinner ready for later, what shall we do in the meantime?"

The seductive look that appeared on Eve's face made Will take a quick breath and remind himself that they were taking things slow.

"I meant outdoors. In public."

Eve continued to give him that same look, this time with a raised eyebrow, and he blushed and swallowed hard.

Finally, Eve gave in. "There are lots of parks all around the area. Personally, I like going to Honda Valley. It's about a half-hour's drive but it's got grassy areas for a picnic, walking trails, and beautiful shade trees. I'll sometimes go there to de-stress from a hectic week and just find a patch of grass and fall asleep on it. Would you be up for that?"

He smiled. "Sounds exactly like what I was picturing. Oh. There was one thing I couldn't find at the store. Do you have a picnic blanket?"

Eve snagged the blanket off the back of the couch. "One picnic blanket. Check. I guess we're ready then! Let me just grab a jacket in case it gets chilly."

With the blanket and jacket draped over her arm, Eve held the apartment door open so Will could maneuver the cooler out the door. Locking it behind her, she joined Will as they took the elevator down to his car to start their adventure.

Will and Eve's afternoon had been perfect: just enough cloud cover to keep them from getting sunburned, along with a breeze to keep the temperature hovering in the mid-seventies. They had parked close to where Eve knew a good picnic spot and left the cooler, along with her jacket, in the trunk. As they started down a paved pathway, Will slipped his hand into hers, and she leaned over and kissed his forearm in approval.

Their conversation was varied as usual: favorite movie lines, stupidest joke they'd ever heard, a funny childhood story... They were getting to know more and more about each other and what had made them who they are now. As a boy, Will had dreamed of working for the LEGO company, wanting to build giant structures to display in their stores. Eve's thoughts of growing up changed with each new Barbie doll she had. Will laughed as she recalled trying to bandage her cat's head during her "Veterinarian Barbie" days and how every time she saw a red Corvette driven by a blonde, she was sure the doll had somehow come to life. While Will seemed to have always known he'd create things with his hands, Eve had never expected as a girl to end up a curator in a museum.

Eve occasionally snuck a glance at Will, watching how the sunlight and shadows played against his hair as they walked under trees and through open areas. He caught her more than once, and each time he smiled and either brushed his lips against her forehead or, in the more secluded areas, pulled her into a deep kiss.

Will surprised her when, as they approached a beautiful old tree, he stopped and pulled a digital camera from his pocket. He asked a couple strolling by if they would take a picture of the two of them. Will leaned up against the tree and wrapped his arms around Eve as she stood in front of him. She entwined her fingers in his and leaned back into his chest. He brought his face down to be next to hers, and the warmth and closeness of him gave her a contented smile. *We belong together. I'm sure of it.*

After retrieving the camera and thanking their impromptu photographers, Will asked Eve to pose by the tree alone, saying the way the light shone down made her look radiant. She hated getting her picture taken—absolutely hated it. But the way Will asked, how could she resist a compliment like that? She was actually glad he was capturing their time together. He'd be returning to Boston soon enough, and Eve hoped having her picture meant he wanted to remember her.

Before leaving that area, Eve asked for the camera to take some stills of him as well. Without a doubt, she knew her favorite would be one she took of him leaning against the tree, smiling that beautiful smile. It was the same smile she'd seen every time she got off the elevator at the Fairhaven in Boston.

"Can we download these to my computer when we get home?" He agreed, of course, then pocketed the camera and put his arm around her shoulders to continue their stroll.

By the time they returned to the car to get the cooler, the sun was setting breathtakingly over the trees. Eve pulled her jacket from the trunk and prepared for the wind to turn chilly. After finding a small, private cove along the beach for their picnic and spreading out the blanket, the two nibbled on their sandwiches and fruit and continued to talk about everything that came to mind… and sometimes nothing at all.

As Eve cleaned up the empty plastic bags and other trash, Will opened the bottle of wine.

"What should we toast?" he asked as he passed her a wine-filled plastic glass and raised his own.

"Oh, lots of things. The grant? Being here today? Last night?" she offered.

"I'd like to raise a toast to Passion Fishing and the hope that neither of *us* will *ever* feel the need to play again."

Although the plastic didn't quite make the normal "clink," the feel of the moment was not in any way diminished. With the sultriest look in his eyes, Will gently took Eve's glass and put it with his on top of the closed cooler. Turning back to Eve, he pulled her in to kiss him. She immediately responded, wrapping her arms around his neck and moving her fingers into his hair.

Will lowered Eve to the blanket as he ravished her with his kisses; first at her mouth, but then slowly moving down to her neck and collarbone. As Will's hands began to explore Eve's body, roaming discretely under her open jacket, Eve wondered how much longer she could hold out before she allowed Will to take her completely.

When Will finally stopped himself, realizing they were reaching the unofficially set limit, he fell back onto the blanket and brought Eve's head to rest on his shoulder. Eve loved the way his heart was racing and how staggered his breathing was.

"I've got to say, Ms. Carwyn, this is by far the best business trip I've ever been on! You are truly a wonderful host!" He winked.

"Yeah, that's what *all* the visiting businessmen say when I'm their tour guide. You think *you're* the only one I've taken here or provided sleeping arrangements for?"

With his free hand, Will clutched his chest. "Oh, Eve, you're breaking my heart! You mean there are *others*?"

With that, Eve pulled herself to look directly into his eyes. "Not anymore. I'd like to be exclusively yours." *What did you just say? Are you nuts? How is he going to take* that *statement?* Eve wished she could take the words back.

Will didn't say a word. The look on his face was one of confusion: he wasn't sure whether Eve's comment was part of their joking around or if she was telling him more than that. Up until then, the two had been enjoying each moment as it came. They hadn't talked about what was going to happen when Will went back to Boston. There were questions they needed to ask themselves and each other. And Eve could see in Will's eyes that he was just as curious about the answers as she was.

Chapter Eighteen

Thank God I'm not pregnant.

Skye sat in her office Monday morning and couldn't stop that thought from repeating itself in her mind. After her realization on Saturday night, all she'd been able to think about Sunday was the possibility that she *was* pregnant. She'd even thought about skipping brunch with Josie and Eve, as just the idea of putting food in her mouth made her stomach roll over. But she hadn't wanted them to know something was wrong. She should have just stayed home, she realized too late. That Josie was too intuitive.

During their shopping trip, Josie had kept asking questions about how Skye was feeling. The truth was that her stomach was in knots. She *did* want to have a family with Gage, she knew that, but could they handle it right now? They'd only been together a short time. The whole thing was making her a wreck.

When Skye had drifted over to the baby clothes in one store, Josie's head snapped to attention. Skye hadn't even realized what she was doing. She'd quickly recovered by mumbling something about Noelle having a baby soon. And, while it was obvious Josie still suspected something, she let Skye's excuse pass without a word.

By the end of the day, Skye was so confused and such a total emotional mess, she'd decided to stop at the drug store on the way home and buy a pregnancy test. She had to know.

When she got home, Gage was there waiting. She threw herself into his arms, reveling in his comforting embrace. Her moves must have scared him, though, because he didn't even try to take her to the bedroom.

Shaking the bag from the drug store at him, Skye had watched his confused expression. She took out the little box, and he immediately understood. Gage pulled her into another hug before sending her off toward the bathroom with a swat on the ass. Skye had no doubt that however this test came out, Gage would be supportive and love her.

She peed on the stupid stick and set it on the back of the toilet. It was the longest three minutes she'd ever experienced, and as she waited, she wondered how she'd gotten this far in life and never had this problem. She'd always been so cautious and smart about sex...until Gage swept her away, she realized. *Damn him!*

Gage had been standing just outside the bathroom, and when the timer finally dinged they fought over who was going to have to look. After Skye threatened to withhold sex indefinitely, Gage strode into the bathroom like a warrior preparing to slay the enemy, and he grabbed the stick.

"It just has a blue line. What does that mean?"

"I don't know. Look at the box. I think I bought the 'plus' and 'minus' one." She couldn't make herself actually look at that little stick. While Gage focused on the directions on the back of the box, Skye thought her stomach would explode.

"I think it's a no." His voice sounded a little sad. And although Skye had felt immediate relief at the news, she couldn't help also feeling a twinge of disappointment.

The phone on Skye's desk rang, and she was startled out of her memory. When she answered the phone, she was a little over the top with cheerfulness.

"Hey, gorgeous!" The sound of Gage's voice made her smile even wider. Skye was the happiest she had ever been in her life, and it was all because of the man on the phone.

"Hi, baby. What are you doing?" There was a huge grin on Skye's face, and she hoped Gage could hear how happy she was.

"I wanted to call and tell you I love you. And also there is a Red Sox game on Thursday, and I thought it would be fun for all of us to go have pizza and beer and watch the game somewhere. I know Will likes them. Can't account for taste there."

"Okay, I'll ask when I see them. I love you, too."

"Gotta go. I have a client I need to torture. Talk to you later."

"Bye, Gage."

No longer able to sit at her desk on such a great day, Skye decided to try to find Eve and Will. She knew they would be together somewhere because today was Will's "official" visit as the Townsend Industries grant representative, and Eve had generously volunteered to give him the tour.

Walking into the museum, Julian was careful not to look any of the security guards in the eye. He didn't know if the bitch, Skye, had told them to keep him out. Although he was fairly sure Eve had never told them about the night he almost hurt her, *Will Prentiss* would have told them about her tires. But, since the police had, of course, believed Julian's alibi there was nothing anyone could do.

He was an accomplished artist whose paintings were displayed here. No one was going to stop him from enjoying the people discussing what he had created. No one.

Julian made his way to his usual bench in front of the largest painting in the Local Artists Gallery: his. Remembering the last time he'd sat here, bile rose in the back of his throat. He'd checked into it, and the whore had been right. In three months, someone else's art would be hanging in the spot his currently occupied. But Julian knew when Eve came back to him she could change that. She *would* change that. *Eve.* My *Eve. Only mine.*

Julian thought again about the events of Sunday afternoon. He had followed Eve after she'd left those unacceptable friends of hers. He had always hated that she spent every Sunday with them, excluding him. Julian was sure that that was when they had convinced her to leave him. She really had only done it because of those two bitches. When she was his again, those little weekly meetings would definitely end.

As Eve had pulled into the parking garage, Julian parked his rental car across the street like he'd done the previous night. He couldn't chance going into the garage in the middle of the day to check if *he* was there with her. So he'd sat and waited.

After sitting in his car for about an hour, he was getting anxious. He had been debating checking on Eve when he'd spotted *his* car coming down the street. *Ostentatious.* Prentiss had turned into the parking garage like he lived there. *How dare he.* The more Julian saw of Will Prentiss, the less he trusted him. The thought of that vile man touching Eve flicked through his mind, and he began to shake. He rolled down his window to allow the fresh air in to clear his head.

When Julian saw the black Mercedes coming out of the parking structure a half-hour later, he immediately followed it. They'd driven a good distance, and he was beginning to worry that they knew that he was behind them. When he was nearly convinced they were trying to lose him, they finally stopped at Eve's favorite park. This was a place Julian and Eve had come to talk and stroll. Sharing it with another man—that was a betrayal.

They'd parked the car, and Julian had watched as *he* opened her door and took her hand to help her out. *Stop touching her. Stop touching her. Stop touching her!*

Julian had found a place to park far enough away that they wouldn't notice him, but close enough that he never lost sight of them as they walked off hand in hand. Then he'd followed them along the pathways. He'd watched as that man kissed Eve whenever they stopped. Julian had to make him stop.

When they stood near a huge tree and asked someone to take a picture, Julian had taken his camera out and done the same. He thought it might help to have some evidence to set his plan in motion. They'd taken pictures of each other for several minutes, and Julian was incensed that *he* had been able to get Eve to pose for a picture.

While she was Julian's inspiration, and the reason he was poised to achieve many of his goals in the art world, she had never allowed him to paint her. He had begged her. But now she'd readily posed for a total stranger—someone who could never love her the way Julian loved her, never see her beauty the way he could.

I am an artist!

Eventually the two of them had gone back to the car, and Julian watched as they took a cooler and blanket out of the trunk and walked off through the trees to the water. Trying to keep his distance, he watched as they ate sandwiches and then Prentiss had poured her a glass of wine. As *that monster* laid precious Eve down on the blanket and began putting his hands everywhere on her body—in a public park—Julian knew he had to act. The Eve that Julian knew and loved would never have acted this way. This man—this Will Prentiss—was poison to Eve. Julian had to find a way to be sure she never saw him again, and more of a plan began to formulate in his mind.

Now, as he sat in front of his paintings in the museum, the image of *him* with his hands all over Eve swam through his head again. Then he heard a sound from heaven: Eve's laughter. Julian immediately remembered he had a job to do and a role to play today. He looked up to see Eve walking through the museum with Will Prentiss.

They were not touching, but the memory of the way he had touched her yesterday came flooding back, and Julian had to take a deep breath before he could continue. Once he had calmed himself, he got up from the bench and made his way to Eve, a smile on his face.

Julian saw Eve stiffen, and Will immediately turned and looked in Julian's direction.

"Eve. How are you?" Julian greeted her as casually as he could manage, beginning the game.

"Oh...Julian." He could hear the fear in her voice. *How can she be afraid of me? She knows how much I love her.*

"You must be Mr. Prentiss." Julian turned slightly to address him, noting the questioning look in the man's eyes.

"I saw the article in the paper when the museum was awarded the grant," Julian said quickly. *And I saw you touching and kissing my Eve just hours ago.*

Prentiss' face relaxed infinitesimally. *Keep going, Julian. If you want Eve free to be with you, you have to keep this up.*

"Yes, Julian is one of our local artists whose work is hanging here in the Local Artists Gallery. It's just one of our innovative exhibits, like our children's wing will be."

And I am the man who you really love, Julian thought as he listened to Eve's angelic voice.

Will extended his hand, and though Julian thought it might break his whole façade to touch that man, he took it.

"Julian." It was all that he was going to get, so he needed to push. For his plan to work, Prentiss had to believe Julian had moved on and didn't care about Eve anymore. This would have to be the best performance of his life. *Eve, please understand that what I'm about to say isn't true. I love you. Only you. Forever.*

"So, Mr. Prentiss, have you come to see where all that money is going to?"

"Yes. That is certainly a big part of this trip to Santa Barbara."

"Oh, have you been here before? It is a great city."

"I've only been once before." With this he glanced over at Eve, who tried to stifle a small giggle. Julian made a note to check when Will Prentiss had been previously in Santa Barbara.

"Well, I hope you're getting to see the city, not just spending all your time in the museum, as wonderful as it is."

"I've made some good friends, and they've been showing me the sights." Julian inwardly smirked at the fact that Prentiss thought he was so slick. There was nothing that Julian didn't already know.

"Well, I'm kind of a homebody, but if you like the nightclub thing, I know that Eve and her friends like that one...what is it called, Eve?" Julian turned back toward Eve, looking her in the eyes, lingering long enough to let her think he really had no idea.

"Stratus," Eve almost whispered. She didn't like the way this conversation was going. Julian was acting so strange, and Eve had chills running up her spine.

"Eve, I'm sorry. I didn't mean to bring that up. I mean, the police came to my place the other morning and asked me questions about that place and you."

"Oh, yeah, someone vandalized my car on Friday night."

"I'm so sorry, Eve. They didn't give me the specifics, but they had asked if I'd been at Stratus that night. That's what made me think of it." Out of the corner of his eye, Julian saw Will relax just a bit, and he was certain they were buying his act.

Julian excelled at this game. He had been playing it his entire life. His first real memory was when his father broke his arm after he spilled milk in the kitchen trying to pour a glass by himself. He had been three years old. When they went to the doctor, Julian had played the role of a son who was loved and cared for, telling everyone he had fallen down the stairs on the front porch. Of course they all believed him...just like now.

"Well, we're not sure what happened, but I'm sure it was just a case of mistaken identity." With that response, Julian knew the Eve was playing the game with him.

Click, click, click. The whore. Perfect.

"Eve, I'm glad I found you two." Skye stopped. "Julian," she sneered his name. It took every ounce of self control for her to not knee him in his most precious of places just to watch him writhe on the floor. If she was feeling this way, she could only imagine what Will wanted to do to him.

"Skylar, nice to see you again." Julian flashed a smile. As much as he despised the whore, she was one he needed to win over for his plan to succeed.

"Yeah." She turned away from him back to Will and Eve. Skye smiled thinking that what she was about to do would kill two birds with one stone: let Julian know Eve and Will were more than just business associates, and show him that Will had become part of their group in a way he never had. "Hey, Gage says Will is a big Red Sox fan and thought maybe you guys would like to find a place to watch the game on Thursday. We're going to ask Josie and Beau, too."

Eve's eyes grew wide as Skye spoke. Julian knew she was trying to tell her to shut up. Eve would never want him, or anyone, to know what she had been doing with *him.* Of course, the dumb bitch never got the hint. Julian couldn't help but smile as he thought, *Skye will be the easiest to convince.*

"Um, Skye, maybe we should talk about this later." Eve gave a little nod toward Julian, hoping he wouldn't notice.

"That's alright, Eve, I was just leaving. I have a lunch date." Julian threw that little bit of information out, hoping their guard would drop further.

Skye had to stop herself from laughing when Julian tried to pass that one off.

"You have a date?" She was proud of herself for keeping a straight face.

The implication that Julian couldn't get a date stung only a bit. He had to convince them he had moved on. Not that he ever could or would.

"Well, yes. I do. Her name is Miranda, and I met her at a gallery opening the other night. In fact, the night your car was broken into."

"Lucky Miranda." Skylar again spewed her venom.

Julian stared at her for a moment with his smile firmly in place. It wouldn't do to let her see his hatred. She needed to believe Julian's sincerity and trust him. *This one may be harder than I thought.*

"Mr. Prentiss, it was very nice to meet you. And Eve, I hope the police find whoever damaged your car. Skylar." Julian turned and headed for the doors. He could feel all of them still staring after him.

The warm air hit him, and he was able to breathe again. He found a bench off to the side of the building and sat down to think his plans through. That performance had been step two. He thought he'd at least planted seeds of doubt in Prentiss' head. Eve had to know Julian would always love her.

Step one, of course, had been had been completed last night after Julian could no longer stand to watch that man rolling and writhing with Eve, pawing her like she was raw meat. Even as he'd gone back to his apartment, the scene kept playing over and over in his head. Something had to be done.

The newspaper article had been lying on the desk, right near his computer. He picked it up and re-read the caption under the picture. There was the other woman in the picture, and he decided he needed to find out more. She'd seemed to have something to do with the grant, and Julian had wondered what she would think if she found out the representative for the SBMA and Mr. Prentiss were acting like mating animals all over Santa Barbara?

Julian hated to hurt Eve, but in the end, she wouldn't need the SBMA any longer once he was discovered. Her sole job would be to inspire his great works of art.

As he sifted through the information he found online about Townsend Industries and the Boston Museum of Art, the most interesting article was on a society page. It was a picture of Will Prentiss and the other woman from the picture, Jeannette Sheldon. The caption read: "Last night's mayoral fundraiser attendees included Will Prentiss of Townsend Industries and Jeannette Sheldon, curator of the Boston Museum of Art."

They were close enough together that Julian could tell there was something between them, something he could use to his advantage. *I wonder if Ms. Sheldon would be interested in seeing a few of the photos I took*? Maybe if she were to get a picture of Eve and Will, not only would she have professional issues with the fact that Mr. Prentiss was doing vile things with the SBMA grant winner, she might also have a personal issue with it. *You are a true genius.*

Her contact information had been easy enough to find; he'd simply gone to the Boston Museum of Art's website and looked under "Contact Us." There was a list of museum employees and right near the top was Jeannette Sheldon.

Julian had then hooked up his camera and downloaded the pictures he had taken of them earlier in the day. While the pictures processed, he composed his email, making sure he didn't sound like he was trying to cause any problems, or that he knew about her relationship to Will:

Dear Ms. Sheldon,

I am an artist living in the Santa Barbara area, and I have many of my pieces on display at the Santa Barbara Museum of Art. I really do love our little museum. I have recently learned through the curator here, Ms. Eve Carwyn, that along with the Boston Museum of Art, Townsend Industries has awarded the SBMA a $3 million grant. I cannot tell you how excited I am.

After seeing both your pictures in the paper, imagine my surprise when I recognized Mr. Prentiss and Ms. Carwyn in some very compromising situations. When I returned from an outing in the local park, where I was taking pictures for some studies I am currently working on, I started to look through them, and to my surprise, in the background, there they were. I have attached a few of the pictures for you to see. I can only be sure that it was Ms. Carwyn, as I see her often at the museum. I may be mistaken about Mr. Prentiss, as I have never met him.

The reason I am writing to you is that I am concerned this may have a negative impact on the grant. I would hate for either museum to be scandalized by this. I worry that if the other museums in the running for the grant were to find out about this, the money—and your museum's reputation—would be in jeopardy.

Please advise me as to what I should do about this situation. I really am in a predicament here.

Thank you in advance for any help you are able to give.

Sincerely,

Julian Meadows

By the time he'd finished composing the email, the pictures were done downloading. He'd sorted through them and chosen two that really had the feel that he'd accidentally caught them in a stolen kiss. He'd attached the two pictures to his email, and hit the send button, grinning delightedly at his accomplishment.

The euphoria he felt after sending those pictures last night resurfaced now. He smiled to himself as he sat on the bench in the spring sun, knowing that Ms. Jeannette Sheldon would probably already have opened the email, and hopefully he could count on her to keep his plan going. Just from Ms. Sheldon's picture, Julian could tell she was a prideful woman who loved her position and the power that came with it. If he was any judge of character, she would be plotting something right now.

Will had remained polite, simply watching the awkward exchange between Skye and Julian. There was now no question in his mind that Julian was dangerous, and from the way Skye spoke to him, he was pretty sure she felt the same way.

After they watched Julian leave, Skye continued to share her ideas about everyone going out on Thursday night. The fact that he had been included in the plans was important to Will. He had meant it when he'd told Julian that he had good friends here.

Eve had to see to some things in her office before a scheduled conference with Skye, Josie, the museum's attorney, and a few of the directors. So she quickly squeezed Will's hand and headed upstairs with Skye.

With some time to kill before their meeting, and realizing he was still in the room where Julian's work was displayed, Will thought maybe he could learn more about the man from his paintings. He wanted to understand the man and whether or not he still posed a threat to Eve. Although Will was encouraged by the news that Julian had a lunch date, he was still unsure.

Will perused the eight or so paintings displayed in the room. They were interesting, and he had to admit that Julian *was* talented. His artwork was intense. He was definitely passionate about his work.

The largest piece took up an entire wall of the gallery. Will stepped up to the nameplate below it: Beauty Captured. The work was only a few months old, and Will realized it must have been created while Julian was with Eve.

Studying the canvas more closely, Will was drawn in by the vibrant depth of the colors, which, along with the angle of the strokes, were meant to stir deep emotion in those who looked at it. It really was a magnificent piece. But as Will shifted his focus to the painting's abstract shapes, he began to see what appeared to be a human shape in the center, small and frail, surrounded by strong vertical lines—bars, perhaps? *Is Eve the beauty, and this picture is his way of telling the world he wants to keep her like a caged bird? Psycho.*

Before he would feel comfortable leaving Santa Barbara, Will decided he would need to know a little more about Julian, his intentions with regard to Eve, and the possibility that maybe, *just maybe*, he *did* have someone new in his life—some new obsession that would replace Eve in that cage. Will decided that while Eve worked this week, he would make plans to investigate Julian. Stepping out to the sidewalk in front of the museum, Will opened his cell, and began to make a few calls.

Jeannette Sheldon stood and walked across her corner office, glancing quickly out the floor-to-ceiling windows over the Boston cityscape. She moved the flowers that had been placed on her desk to the table on the other side of the room. Another token of appreciation for a night of bliss from—who was it? Oh, it didn't matter. That one wasn't wealthy or connected enough for her. Still, the expensive arrangement was a nice gesture, and it included some fragrant flowers. Sleeping with him had provided at least one little perk: her office smelled wonderful today.

She checked her voice mail and made notes of calls to return. She had hoped to hear from Will about the Santa Barbara project. As her mind began to ponder why he hadn't checked in with her, an image appeared of him dancing with the Santa Barbara Museum's curator. The woman was cute enough, but certainly not in Jeannette's league, or Will's for that matter. Maybe she'd find an excuse to call him later. He might have decided it was over between them but, really, that was *Jeannette's* decision to make. No man ever left *her*.

As her computer warmed up, she glanced again out the window. Boston's museum was grand, but still only a stepping stone. There were bigger and better museums out there and more prestige to be had. Of course, if she married the right man, she knew she could be equally happy in the role of socialite. Seventeen emails popped up on her screen. As she scanned through them, prioritizing the ones she'd need to respond to this morning, she was intrigued by one with a subject line about the Santa Barbara Museum of Art. While she didn't recognize the name, she figured it had something to do with the grant.

Then she opened it and began to read. Jeannette clicked on the attached photos and let out a low curse. Seeing Will with that bitch from Santa Barbara had her blood boiling. Jeannette's perfectly manicured nails tapped against the hard surface of her desk as she started to formulate a plan. The first thing she had to do was get Will back to Boston, away from *her.* And she needed to make sure *that tramp* understood he was not, and never would be, hers to take.

Secondary to all that ran through Jeannette's head was the possibility of a scandal. That would be her best tool against Will even *thinking* he could, or should, be with *Ms. Carwyn.* Will didn't care what people thought about him personally, but surely he wouldn't jeopardize the BMA or his company's reputation as a respected charitable organization by having a *fling* with the winner of the grant that *he* awarded. Eve Carwyn was just some nobody from Santa Barbara, and Jeannette would make sure she stayed that way!

The bare bones of a plan began to form as Jeannette grabbed her purse and informed her secretary that she was going to Townsend Industries.

"Good morning, Megan!" Jeannette said with a saccharine smile. Will's unusual attachment to the girl was something Jeannette had never understood. She might be efficient, but she would have driven Jeannette insane in minutes.

"Jeannette. Hello. What brings you here? You know that Will's out in Santa Barbara, right?"

"Yes, that's exactly why I'm here, actually." Jeannette continued to be pleasant, certainly not wanting Megan to think she had anything but grant-related business on her mind. "There was a file of mine that Will had accidentally grabbed with his things last week," she lied. "I've got a meeting with the board this afternoon and need it back. Could I just look on his desk real quick?"

Megan stared at Jeannette, scrutinizing every word out of her mouth. While she looked innocent enough, Megan really didn't trust the woman.

Luckily for Jeannette, she and Will had worked together enough over the past five years that coming to grab a file wasn't an unusual request, although most other times he had been in his office.

"I guess." Megan gave in. "I'm heading out on some errands. Do you need Martin's help? He's in his office."

"I'll take a quick look. You go ahead. If I need Martin, I'll ask. Thanks, Megan! You're a doll!" This time Jeannette meant it. She was very glad Megan was willing to let her rifle through Will's desk without watching.

With Megan gone and Martin nowhere in sight, Jeannette began her search. Sure enough, in his top drawer was a spare key to his apartment, clearly marked. *I'll just borrow this for about a half hour,* she thought as she slipped it into a pocket of her jacket.

Smiling at her accomplishment, Jeannette left Townsend Industries for the nearest locksmith. Before Megan had even returned, Will's key was safely back where it belonged in his desk. A copy of it now hung on Jeannette's key ring.

Chapter Nineteen

Will woke on Tuesday morning to find that Eve had already gotten up. Hearing the water running in the shower, he wished he felt comfortable enough to join her, but it was still too soon. Rolling over, Will hugged the pillow she had slept on, closing his eyes again and breathing in the lingering scent of her light perfume.

Within a few minutes, the shower turned off, and Will could hear Eve moving around in the bathroom. He was still dozing until she opened the door, dressed only in a black lace bra and panties. That sight had Will's entire body waking up. Wanting to enjoy the view a little longer, Will remained quiet and just watched her.

Looking at Will's sleeping form, Eve tried to tiptoe stealthily toward her closet to get dressed for work. As she stood with her back to him, perusing her options, Will quietly slipped out of bed and over to her, snaking his arms around her from behind.

"Geez!" Eve jumped in surprise. "Don't scare me like that! I was trying not to wake you, you know."

"And why would I want to be asleep when you're standing here looking like *this*?" Will dropped his face to Eve's neck and nuzzled her ear with his nose. Eve covered his hands with her own and leaned back against his chest.

"Maybe because I figured you'd try to distract me from getting to work on time?"

"What? You don't *like* it when I distract you?" He moved his hands up to gently massage her breasts.

"Uhhh, no. I didn't...exactly...uh...say that. Uh...oh..."

Eve turned in his arms, bringing her mouth to Will's and kissing him deeply as her hands tangled in his hair. Wrapping his arms around Eve's waist, he lifted her, and they tumbled back onto the bed. Eve didn't stop him as Will reached around and unclasped her bra. As the straps fell down her arms, Will followed with light kisses.

"Five minutes," she gasped. "That's all we've got or I'll be late to work."

"Plenty of time," Will whispered as he brought his mouth to one breast and began to knead the other with an open palm.

Completely independent of Eve's own thought, her leg moved to rest across Will's hip. She smiled as she felt his arousal pressing against her. Wanting more, she tightened her leg to pull him closer. Eve's hips moved slightly to create friction between them.

Slowly, Will's mouth moved back to Eve's. Their tongues explored and teased while their bodies continued to move together. Will's hands touched every inch he could of Eve's perfect skin.

"You sure you have to go to work?" Will eventually breathed against her lips before pulling her into another kiss.

"Mm-hmm," she mumbled. Then brought her face to Will's neck. "You do, too, remember?"

Those four little words broke all the momentum of the moment.

"Oh. Yeah." Will sighed. "You keep making me forget I'm *really* here on business."

For Will, work over the next few days would be accomplished in Eve's apartment, using his laptop and cell phone to get caught up on things with Megan and Martin. Without Eve's knowledge, he'd also be conducting some business with a few people in Santa Barbara as well.

Eve breathed softly against his ear before moving her mouth slowly to his chest, leaving light kisses between words. "I'm very...very...sorry. It won't...happen...again."

"Until tonight?" Will begged.

"Until tonight." Eve slid back up to face him again, her breasts pressing deliciously against his body. "Ready to get up?"

"Umm..." Will gave her a sideways smile. "I'm already 'up'—as I'm sure you've noticed—so I'm going for a cool shower while you get dressed. Otherwise, neither of us is going anywhere except under these covers to finish what we've started."

Eve placed her hand on his cheek and kissed him gently. "Gotcha." She rolled out of bed, grabbed her bra, and went back to her closet to pick up where she had been before being so wonderfully interrupted.

Megan picked up on the second ring. "Good morning. Townsend Industries."

"Hey, Meg. It's Jeannette. What time is Will due back today?"

"Oh..." She fumbled, something she rarely did. "He's, um, staying on in Santa Barbara until Saturday." Then, she gathered her composure and spoke in a more business-like tone. "Do you need me to relay a message to him?"

Jeannette tried to hide her surprise. "No. Nothing urgent. Has he encountered any problems with the museum or the grant?" It was a valid question to ask, she rationalized.

"No. I think everything is going well. He just decided to..." she struggled to find the right words, "stay a little longer. You know how he is. Always wanting to be hands-on."

That was exactly what Jeannette worried about—*who* he had his hands on. That Eve Carwyn nobody. She glared at the photos she'd printed out. *That* is a relationship that is *not* going to continue. Will Prentiss was too hot a catch—looks, wealth, status—for Jeannette Sheldon to let him slip away.

Jeannette wondered what could bring him back earlier than Saturday. What would require him to return to Boston as soon as possible? She needed a reason to get Will on a plane quickly. She thought of a few scenarios, but most would take too much planning or involve too many other people. And then, it hit her. *Oh, yes...that should do nicely.* She would need access to Will's data files, but she knew there was no way to get back into Will's office, let alone onto his computer. But now that she had a key to his house... *I'll bet he's got the files I need stored at home, too.*

After clearing her afternoon schedule with her secretary, Jeannette set out for Will's apartment.

The Garden Café was one of Noelle and Tom Stansbury's favorite places to enjoy an elegant lunch together. Today, however, Tom would be dining with Will. Many of Tom's clients were in the medical field; his corporate real estate expertise was in helping professionals—doctors and lawyers mostly—find suitable locations for their offices. If Will's company had other innovations that could possibly impact the medical community even a fraction of the way the Townsend defibrillator did, Tom wanted him to know he would do what he could to help him connect with doctors and businessmen in the Santa Barbara area.

Tom was already seated at the outdoor table when Will approached, his phone pressed to his ear.

"Yes...and the address?" Will quickly pulled out a pen and a business card and scribbled information on the back of it. "Yes, I would greatly appreciate you checking that out for me... It's very important that I hear back from you as soon as you have information. I'll be leaving Santa Barbara on Saturday, and it's urgent that I feel 100-percent assured before leaving. Any photographs you can take would be invaluable to me. My email address is on the business card I provided your assistant... Absolutely... Yes, thank you... I look forward to hearing back from you soon. Goodbye."

Will pocketed his phone and sat down, reaching across the small table to shake Tom's hand. "I'm sorry about that. I'm having to handle everything by phone, including a private investigator who's keeping tabs on Julian's whereabouts. Hopefully, we won't be interrupted during our lunch, but I am expecting a few important calls so please accept my apologies ahead of time." Will smiled, dropping his shoulders to relax.

The server came over and took Will's order for ice water, and the two men began to look over their menus. Both of them decided quickly and were able to let the server know as she brought Will his drink.

"So, Will," Tom began. "How is Santa Barbara treating you?"

"It's treating me so well I keep forgetting I'm here on business." His smile was genuine. Thomas liked this man for Eve.

"And Eve?"

Will turned his eyes away. "Yes," he said, embarrassed. "She's treating me really well, too."

"And?" Tom couldn't help but transform into the big brother. "Are you beginning a relationship with her? You do live 3,000 miles away." He leaned forward on the table. "Understand, Will, I don't mean to pry, but Eve's important to Noelle and me—actually all of us—and we can't help but look out for her."

Will smiled sheepishly. "Noelle didn't share my secret with you, did she?"

"I'm sorry. Secret?"

"The other night at Stratus? When I was saying good night to your wife, I told her I'm already in love with Eve."

"Noelle is not one to break confidences, even to me. But I'm very pleased to hear this directly from you. Eve *is* wonderful—although I'm sure I'm not telling you anything you haven't discovered on your own. Have you and she talked about the distance?"

Will leaned back in his chair before speaking, running his hands through his hair. "Tom, we haven't talked about 'us' yet at all. If we *are* a couple, then this is more complicated than just our living so far apart. I have to figure out whether we can go public—for lack of a better term—because of how our relationship would look to the Boston Museum of Art's directors or to any of the other museums that applied for the grant. We could easily be accused of favoritism, and the whole thing would be a terrible scandal for both museums." He sighed. "All I can tell you is that I'm in love with Eve. I haven't told her, and I don't know for sure, but I think she feels the same about me. If that's the case, I've got to figure out all the implications of that."

"Are you at least going to tell *her* how you feel? I'm fairly sure that she loves you too—that much Noelle *has* told me. She talked with Josie and said Eve pretty much admitted it, or at least didn't deny it, over brunch the other morning. And," Tom added, "Noelle and I both said after our dinner party how much you two reminded us of ourselves just a few years ago. I think you've won her heart, Will, and I think you ought to tell her."

"I plan to—regardless of whether the feelings are mutual—before I head back to Boston. I promise."

Tom extended his hand and Will shook it. "Will, I have a feeling we're going to be seeing a whole lot more of you in Santa Barbara. And although neither of you needs anyone's approval, may I just say that the other six of us are quite excited to consider you a part of our group of friends." Tom raised his glass and Will did the same. "To you and Eve."

Their lunch placed before them, they settled in to discuss Townsend Industries and a different sort of relationship that Tom hoped to cultivate—one that also would result in Will Prentiss spending more and more time in Santa Barbara.

Eve tried to concentrate at work, but once again, Will had her mind flustered. Sleeping in the same bed with him every night had been equal parts bliss and frustration. He had been so patient with her, and it certainly wasn't that Eve didn't want to have sex. God, did she want to! But the fact that in four days he would be going back in Boston...and maybe out of her life, weighed heavily on her mind and heart. Bottom line, the two of them needed to talk about "them."

When Eve got home, Will was waiting with Chinese take-out. Her heart was nearly bursting at his thoughtfulness. She wasn't used to her boyfriends–the word in her head made Eve's breath catch–caring enough to do something for her. The cherry on the sundae? Will actually had *Sleepless in Seattle* ready to go in the DVD player. Eve couldn't help but think about how appropriate the story of a long-distance relationship was to their current predicament. She knew they needed to talk, but still couldn't bring herself to start the conversation.

Later, as they lay together on the couch watching the end of the movie, Eve rested against Will's chest, sighing contentedly each time he kissed the top of her head. Eve eventually fell asleep, waking up only long enough to feel Will carrying her to bed.

The next morning, Will informed Eve that he wanted to do some sightseeing around Santa Barbara. When she offered to switch a meeting to join him, Will said he didn't want her to re-arrange work priorities, but would love to meet for lunch at noon.

Eve was a little hurt, but she hid her feelings. They had been nearly inseparable since Will had arrived five days ago, she told herself. Eve knew smothering him was not the way to foster a relationship. So she kissed him, grabbed her to-go cup of coffee, and went to work.

Time dragged for Eve that day. She looked at the clock every five minutes to see if it was any closer to noon. Eventually, she gave up and left for lunch early, thinking that waiting at the restaurant would be easier than being stuck in her office.

When Will arrived, a smile spread across his face, and Eve's worry subsided. He kissed her lightly on the lips before taking a seat across from her. She relaxed as he told her how he had driven up the coast a bit and ended up in a small tourist village set up like a little Danish town.

Lunch, however, took a bizarre turn and Eve's earlier thoughts resurfaced when they were interrupted twice by calls to Will's cell phone.

"This is Will Prentiss... Have you located what I've asked you to?" He looked at Eve, glanced at his watch, and then raised his index finger to her. "Excuse me a moment," he said into the phone.

"Eve? I'll be right back. Will you ask our server for an ice water for me? I'll be just a few minutes."

Before she could respond, he stood up, grabbed a pen from his jacket pocket, and spoke into his cell. "I'm sorry. All right. Can you repeat the information? And this matches what I told you I was looking for? Good. Here's what I need you to do..." He walked away from the table out to the front of the restaurant.

Five minutes later, Will returned, but as soon as he sat down, his phone buzzed again.

"This is Will Prentiss. Ah! Mr. Lindstrom. Thank you for calling me. I take it you received my email this morning? And are you able to..."

Once again, he looked at Eve and suddenly became selective with his words.

"Are you able to complete the task I've inquired about? And the, uh, number included—does that match with, uh, the range you would set for this task? Excellent. Is there anything further you'd need from me before you proceed? Large enough for, uh, what I described in my email..." He laughed. "Yes, right here." Then he glanced at Eve and back to his plate. "Wonderful. Thank you. Are you sure you can work within the timeframe? Well, then, thank you very much... You have no idea. Yes, sir... Yes... Thank you. Goodbye."

When he clapped his phone shut, Will turned his gaze to Eve, his eyes sparkling. "Sorry about that. Business never ceases, even when I'm 3,000 miles away from it." Will scooted his chair closer to the table and rested his elbows on the edge, folding his fingers together in front of him. "So, how has your day been at the museum?"

The remainder of lunch was spent on enjoyable, yet superficial, conversation, Eve's mind not quite as engaged as it could have been. Whatever he'd been talking about on the phone—twice—he didn't share with her, and Eve wasn't sure why. Neither call had seemed like it had anything to do with Townsend Industries, and that bothered her, but she felt guilty about that. Eve knew she had no right to know who he had been talking to or what he'd been discussing, but she couldn't help feeling like he was hiding something.

After work, Will suggested they visit the gym, so they spent an hour there before dinner, each wearing headphones during their individual workouts. Both dinner and their evening were quieter, their conversations sparse and surface-level. Will asked a few times if anything was wrong, and Eve lied, saying there were some issues at work she was dealing with. He sensed she wasn't going to offer more information, and he let it drop. In bed, they simply held each other, nothing more. Was the romance over before it really had time to grow?

Thursday morning, though, they both woke up renewed, and after feeling Will stroke her hair and kiss her tenderly, Eve reassessed her concerns from the night before. She still wasn't sure where they were relationship-wise, but she recommitted to be brave enough to talk with him before he boarded his plane Saturday morning.

"Tonight we'll be with everybody watching the game," Eve said, "but I'd like to reserve tomorrow night for something special. Would that be OK? I'd like to take *you* out one last time before you head back to Boston. You have to agree, though, that *I* get to pay the bill—the whole bill. I promised I'd play host while you were in Santa Barbara, and I feel like I haven't done that at all."

Will looked down at her as she laid her head against his shoulder. "I must disagree with you, Ms. Carwyn. You have been a most *delightful* host this week." He rolled toward her and swept a few kisses across her neck, making her melt, as usual. She couldn't form coherent thoughts so she didn't even try to tell him her plans for a talk or ask what would happen when he went back to Boston. Instead, Eve simply returned Will's passion.

Later that morning, she sat at her desk at work, allowing her mind to reminisce about the wonder this week had been with Will. As fantastic as Boston had been, their time in Santa Barbara had meant so much more.

Trying to distract herself from the fact that Will would be leaving in just forty-eight hours, Eve got up to wander the halls of the museum. This was something she usually did a few times a day: making sure employees were posted where the more expensive artwork was displayed, and taking time to interact with visitors and answer their questions. As she strolled into the Local Artists' Gallery, she stopped short.

Eve looked from Julian to the attractive, black-haired woman at his side. He slipped his arm around her waist and smiled at Eve, extending his hand to for her to shake.

"Eve, I'm so glad you're here. I wanted to introduce you to Miranda Katz. Miranda, this is the SBMA's curator, Eve Carwyn."

Eve shook Julian's hand and then Miranda's, and realized her look of surprise was probably disconcerting to the woman.

"It's wonderful to meet you! Are you from the area?"

"I'm a recent transplant," Miranda responded, a slight German accent evident in her voice. "Julian and I met about a month ago in San Diego and have been enjoying visits to various art museums all around California. Today is the first time he's felt confident enough to show me his own creations." She looked up at him and smiled. "And they're wonderful!" Turning back to Eve, Miranda added, "Don't you agree? Julian's work is simply spectacular!"

"Yes, that's the reason we've been showcasing his work." Eve gave them a genuine smile, and Julian really looked at ease. For the first time in a long time, he didn't look at Eve like she was his possession.

Eve talked with them for a few more minutes before continuing her tour of the museum. All the tension she'd been feeling since finding her tires punctured just melted away. As she walked away from Julian, she left behind the nightmares and horrors he had inflicted. *It's finally over*, she told herself.

It was Gage's first night off since Sunday, and he was happy. Normally, he hardly worked at Stratus during the week, but he'd had to trade several days with Austin to get the night off for Noelle and Thomas's dinner party, and the little weasel had really screwed him.

Gage knew he must really love Skye, because he had even worked a Tuesday theme night. This time it had been a beach party. The fact that the club was a block from the beach didn't seem to bother the owners when they came up with the brilliant idea. Gage was pretty sure the hope was that a bunch of women would come in their bikinis, and the horny guys would follow. That's not exactly what happened. In the end, it was a bar full of guys in swim trunks standing on the sand-covered dance floor. A total bust as usual.

The memory of how Skye had convinced him to trade away his entire week was still fresh in his mind, though, and Gage felt a smile creep across his face. In her all-white lace bra and panties, she had looked innocent and pure...until his eyes roamed down to her red high heels. Just thinking about Skye like that was making his pants tight again.

The other consequence of Gage's busy week was that he hadn't spent any time alone with Skye since Sunday night. He didn't get home from Stratus until after one in the morning, and since she had to be to work early, Gage had been sleeping alone. That was definitely going to change tonight. And if he had his way, there wouldn't be much sleeping going on.

Suddenly, Gage was rethinking the idea of spending the evening with friends. He just wanted to keep Skye at home with him for the rest of the night...or their lives. But there was no way Skye would let him get away with that. This whole thing had been his idea in the first place. So he headed off for yet another cold shower in preparation for the evening.

When he picked Skye up, she met him at the door, purse in hand and ready to go. Skye was smart enough to know that if Gage came in, they would never leave. As the two walked down the hall of Skye's apartment building, Gage couldn't resist giving her a smack on the ass. Skye yelped and turned to him.

"Gage, I know that look. Don't even think you are going to be getting anything until *after* we've eaten dinner."

"What? I have no idea what you're talking about. I was just admiring that fantastic ass of yours."

Wrapping his arms around her tiny waist, Gage pulled Skye to him, crashing his lips into hers. As her hands moved up and around his neck, he slid his own down to her spectacular rear and gave it a little squeeze. Skye moaned into his mouth, and Gage's body reacted instantly.

Gage pressed her further into his excitement and kissed along her jaw and up to her ear. "Can't we please just go back into your place?" he whispered before letting his tongue trace the shape of her ear. Skye shuddered. It took everything she had not to take him up on the offer.

When he felt Skye's reaction, Gage released her and turned back toward her apartment, but a tug on the back of his waistband stopped him in his tracks.

"Hold up there, lover boy. We are *not* going to blow our friends off to spend the rest of the night in bed."

"Awww, come on, babe. Please. It's been so long." Gage tried to look hurt.

"Gage, I promise that after dinner I will make sure you are more than satisfied. But for now, put this thing away and let's get going." As she said this, her hand slid over the material of Gage's pants.

"Fine, just give me a second here." Gage tried to adjust himself so his "situation" wasn't quite so obvious. Skye just stood back, staring with a smirk on her face.

"Do you want me to help?"

"No! You just stay right where you are and please try not to look so damn sexy."

Skye laughed as he closed his eyes and began doing deep breathing, like he was in labor.

After a few minutes, Gage was able to make his way to the car and opened the door for Skye to get in. He'd never been so thankful that she wasn't wearing a skirt. Seeing her legs would have made him lose it completely.

In spite of their little moment, Gage and Skye were the first to arrive at Grizzlies. Finding the largest booth, they slid in to wait for the others. Thomas and Noelle couldn't make it, so it would just be the six of them tonight. Gage was looking forward to hanging out with Will a little more. After Julian, he had to be sure Will was actually normal.

Beau and Josie came in not long after Skye and Gage, making a scene as they did. Josie was hanging on Beau's back as he galloped in through the door. The entire place looked over when

Josie yelled, "Yippee-ki-yay!" She waved her hands in the air like she was riding a bucking bronco in the rodeo.

Beau smiled as he lowered Josie from his back at the booth. Gage and Skye sat staring and speechless like the rest of the place. Beau was usually pretty reserved and to see him indulging Josie's crazy side was a surprise. In that moment, both of them saw that what Josie and Beau had was real. They complemented each other perfectly.

A few minutes later, Eve and Will showed up, too. They didn't make the grand entrance the other two had, but they definitely looked like a perfect match as well.

Once the group had moved past greetings, Will, Beau, and Gage went to order the food and beer. The trio joked about getting onions and anchovies on the pizza, knowing the girls would kill them. They didn't dare act on that idea—all of them still wanted to get lucky tonight.

After talking the bartender into changing the giant TV to the Sox game, the men made their way back to the table with two pitchers of beer.

"Hey, Gage, if you are going to drink, give me your keys and order me a soda." Gage did what Skye requested and returned a few moments later with a glass of soda.

"So, I actually saw Julian and his new girlfriend today," Eve informed the table as Will and Gage poured everyone's drinks.

"Seriously? She actually exists?" The doubt in Skye's voice was apparent.

"Yes. He was showing her his work at the museum when I saw them. He introduced us, and I have to say, I thought she was very nice. She seemed to know a lot about the art world."

"So, do you think the worst has passed?" Josie asked Eve.

"Yeah, I think so. I think he's moving on, just like I am." Eve looked over at Will, causing the rest of the group to let out a collective "*Awww . . .*"

"Damn! I was looking forward to hurting the guy, really badly!" Gage actually was a little disappointed.

"Well, I still don't trust the slimy prick," Skye said.

Gage found himself looking at Skye with the same starry eyes Eve had just given Will. Reaching over, he laid a hand on her leg, squeezing her thigh lightly. He was rewarded with a smile and a slap of his hand.

Eve was much more at ease than any of them had seen her over the past couple of weeks, which let everyone else relax a little more, and the subject of Julian quickly faded as they moved on to other things until the pizza arrived.

While they ate, Gage revealed how he had tortured Suzanne at her last session. He'd told her about his friend from Boston who'd had some chubby girl hitting on him at the gym, and then asked her if she had been there. Everyone nearly choked on their food as they laughed. The best part of the story? She was now so worried, she booked extra sessions with Gage.

"You may have to share your fee with Will," said Beau with a laugh.

As the night went on, the guys began a great debate about whether any of the teams they followed would make the playoffs this year. Will was adamant that his Red Sox would be there in the end. When they heard a burst of laughter come from where the girls were huddled, the guys all looked over at the same time.

"You have *got* to be kidding me, Will. Boston won't even see the playoffs, let alone the Series," Skye called over to them.

That was it for Gage. A hot, smart, sexy woman who knows sports? *Holy Crap!* He'd hit the jackpot.

"OK, everyone, we're going to call it a night." Gage had done his part and entertained their friends for a few hours, but the fact that Skye was into sports... He had to have her now.

Grabbing Skye's hand, Gage slid her out of the booth. After saying goodnight to everyone, he steered her to the door. Gage knew he needed to get Skye somewhere private before he stopped caring who witnessed the things he was planning on doing to her.

The rest of the group laughed as they watched Skye and Gage leave.

"Good Lord," Josie started, "I wonder if they know anything about each other besides knowing that Gage has a tattoo on his hip, and Skye has a birthmark on her inner thigh?"

"How do you know Gage has a tattoo?" Beau asked, his eyebrows raised.

"Skylar is very detailed oriented, honey. Don't worry, I have no desire to see any other man naked for the rest of my life." Josie leaned in to kiss him.

"Good to know. 'Cause I don't plan on letting you see another naked man for the rest of your life." Beau then took a page from Gage's book and tossed Josie over his shoulder as he headed for the door.

"Bye, guys!" Josie called.

Eve and Will waved as the couple disappeared. They were both a little stunned to be left sitting alone.

"Umm...so, I guess it's time to go home, too?" Will asked with a little chuckle.

"I think that would be a good idea," Eve replied a little apprehensively, as she slid out of the booth. Fortunately, Will slid out right behind her, because the beers she had been drinking hit her, and Eve swayed slightly. Will wrapped her in a hug.

"It's all right, Eve. Just because all the cool kids are doing it doesn't mean we have to succumb to peer pressure."

He was smiling when Eve looked up at him, and her heart skipped a beat. She never thought she would meet a man as perfect as Will Prentiss, or that she would have to say goodbye to him so soon. Determined not to let that thought ruin the rest of their night, Eve gave Will a small kiss before slipping her arm through his. Will made sure he had a firm hold on her as they walked out the door to go home.

Chapter Twenty

The night at Grizzlies had been fun. Will just *fit* with everyone; he'd become an instant part of their group like Beau had. And having Will with her was a wonderful, heady feeling. She loved that although he could be having a great time with the guys, when he was near her, he was holding her hand or had his arm around her shoulder or her waist. His touch was so much more intoxicating than the beer she'd been drinking.

However, probably because of her relief about Julian, she'd celebrated the evening with a little more beer than she should have. Her plan had been to set things in motion for a special night with Will tomorrow night, when she would let him know she loved him and wanted him—all of him.

By the time the two got home, the beer had taken its toll. Will kindly got her a glass of water and an Advil to minimize the headache he knew was coming. And the extra alcohol in her system *did* lessen her inhibitions.

"You treat me soooo good, you know that?" Eve's mouth refused to speak as clearly as her mind wanted it to.

"Thank you, Eve. Do you want to brush your teeth before you pass out?"

He'd surely had as much beer as she had. *Why wasn't he tipsy?*

"I might need you to put the poothtaste...um...the poothtaste... No, that's not right." Eve slowed down and tried to say each word individually. "Will. You. Put. Tooth. Paste. On. My. Brush?"

Will smiled and kissed her forehead. "Yes, Eve."

He led her to the bathroom and sat her down on the toilet lid while he completed her request. Eve stayed seated while she brushed her teeth, and when she got up and moved to the sink to rinse, Will stood behind her, his hands on her hips, to keep her from toppling over.

"I'm *very* kissable now, Will. My breath is minty fresh!" She turned to him and wrapped her arms around his neck.

"While I agree you are very kissable, as usual I might add, you are also very drunk and need to go to bed."

"Aww... Does that mean we're not gonna fool around?" Eve gave a feeble attempt to be suddenly sexy in front of him. At first, she thought he was going to take advantage of her uninhibited state when he gently put her in bed and lay down beside her. Instead, he pulled the covers up to her shoulders, kissed her sweetly, and told her to close her eyes. It wasn't long before she fell asleep in his arms.

Friday morning, sure enough, began with Eve's need for another Advil—well, two this time—but she *was* able to function. Will stepped quickly to the kitchen for a cool glass of water, then sat on the side of the bed as she drank.

"Oh, God, Will. How bad was I last night? Please tell me I didn't do anything embarrassing."

He ran his fingers up and down her forearm seductively. "You were *amazing*...better than phenomenal."

His eyes sparkled at her. Her eyes bugged out at him.

"What? Are you saying–? Did we–?" She covered her eyes, straining to remember. *Of every experience of my life,* please *let me not have missed out on* this *one because I was too drunk!*

"Oh...God..." Eve sat up, pulled her knees to her chin, and buried her face.

Will stroked her hair and rubbed her back. "Was I that bad? Was I that *forgettable*?"

"*Oh, God!*" she yelled into her hands. Eve had never been so mortified. How could she not remember *that?* She lifted her head and faced him. "Oh, Will, I'm so sorry. God, I must have been really drunk. I remember..." She pulled at elusive memories. "You helping me change my clothes. Thank you, by the way. And I remember brushing my teeth...and I...don't remember anything after that. Oh, and I wanted *that* to be special, for *both* of us."

Will put on a sly crooked smile. "And it *will* be *when* we do." He let that sink in for a moment. "Eve. Your memory of last night is perfect. After you brushed your teeth, you fell asleep."

She glared at him. "You let me think— You...you...I can't believe you led me on like that!"

Will continued to smile at her, dipping his head to the side and looking up at her through his eyelashes.

"I know we haven't known each other very long, but do you *really* think I would have taken advantage of you like that? I'm hurt." His smile became a teasing pout, and he playfully clutched his heart.

The look on his face was irresistible. How could she be mad at him for behaving like a perfect gentleman?

"Can I make the hurt go away?" It was Eve's turn to tease.

"Hmm. I don't know, I'm in a lot of pain here."

"Tell me where it hurts, and I'll kiss it and make it better." She began to weave her fingers into his hair and around to the nape of his neck.

Pointing to his cheek, his ear, his neck, and his chest—many places on his chest, Will smiled as Eve sprinkled him with gentle kisses. Finally he placed a finger on his lips, and she raised an eyebrow knowingly. Wrapped in a passionate embrace, the couple allowed their mouths to explore and taste until, once again, Eve had to get ready for work.

She couldn't wait until the next morning, when it was Saturday, and they could just stay in bed and explore and tease one another...maybe even more, depending on how the conversation Eve was planning for later that night went.

After forcing themselves out of bed, Eve headed for the shower while Will went to make coffee. They had come to enjoy the little routine they had fallen into over the past few days, and both wished it could continue.

Before leaving for work, Eve kissed Will fully and told him goodbye. She had already decided to make reservations at Chez Shea for six o'clock so they could enjoy a drink. Eve's head pounded just then, reminding her that maybe she should stick to water. The restaurant's location near the ocean could certainly invite a stroll after dinner as well, unless they just wanted to head back to her place—and her bed.

Eve decided that no matter what happened the next day or the next week or after that, she loved Will and wanted to be with him, to make love to him, at least this one time.

The two had made plans to meet for lunch again, but Will didn't know that Eve would be taking a few hours off afterward with Josie to go pick out some new lingerie.

The goal for tonight was for them both to be left speechless.

Jeannette woke up early, pleased with her accomplishments last night. But to make her plan work, she had to get to Townsend Industries before Megan did. With her all-important jump drive in her purse, she skipped breakfast and headed out the door of her apartment.

Megan hadn't arrived at work yet, but one of the night crew was finishing up in the lobby area and, when he saw Jeannette, he let her into the locked office.

"Thank you, Harold! You're a doll!" Jeannette placed her palm on his cheek and gave him a genuine smile. He must have been nearing eighty years old, but he showed up every night to clean various floors of the building where Townsend Industries had their offices. He always said he was afraid if he stopped moving, people would think he'd died. Will and Jeannette had worked many nights after hours on the grants, so Harold knew her well. Or at least he thought he knew her well.

As Harold meandered down another hallway, Jeannette quickly moved into Martin's office and turned on his computer. It was a fairly new machine, and she was soon able to slip the jump drive into the slot and begin downloading some new files that would replace the ones he already had. A few additional key strokes and she would lead Martin on a wild goose chase with not a trace of who did this or how. Five minutes later, she shut his computer back down and slipped out the door, having been seen by no one but an elderly, near-sighted custodian.

Walking down the sidewalk from the Starbucks she'd stopped at on her way to the museum, Jeannette made a bet with herself: By three o'clock today, Will Prentiss would be back in Boston. When she walked into her office her secretary said, "Wow! Aren't you looking ready to make this a great day!"

"Oh, this is *definitely* going to be a great day, my dear. You can count on it."

When Josie got to her office, she saw Skye across the hall talking to Eve, who was a deep shade of red. Setting her things on her desk, she walked over and joined the two of them.

"Skye, what are you telling Eve that has her so flustered?"

"She asked why Gage felt the need to leave so abruptly last night, and I was explaining it to her."

"In detail." Eve sighed.

"OK, Skye. I think you've tortured poor Eve enough this morning. And I don't want even a single detail of what you and Gage do when you're alone."

"Fine, but I think the two of you could learn a thing or two. I mean, come on. Eve has had that hottie Will sleeping in her bed for almost a week, and they still haven't gone at it yet."

"Oh, don't you worry about Will and me, Skye. Things are going just where and how I want them to. While we might not be up to Pirate Night just yet, things are...progressing."

"Fine. I'll just leave you two with this: Pirate Night was nothing compared to the Slutty Cheerleader/Quarterback Night I have planned for this evening." Skye turned and walked out the door.

"Your place, Skye! Please! Skye!" Eve called after her. "I really do hope they go to her place. I don't think I could handle the 'rah rah rah' coming from Gage's apartment all night."

Josie put an arm around Eve's shoulder as they laughed.

"So, are we still going shopping after lunch?"

"Oh, yes, please! Tonight has to be perfect, Josie."

"Eve, honey, I've seen him with you. He can't stop looking at you or touching you. I don't think you have anything to worry about."

"Thanks, Josie." Eve gave her friend a hug.

"All right, we've got a meeting in a few minutes, so let me go get my things."

Josie went back to her office to find the files she needed for their meeting with the board. They would be discussing the grant and what the money was going to be used for, line by line. Will had wanted to be there, but the board thought it better for just SBMA people to be there for this meeting. In a few more weeks, when Will was back in Santa Barbara, they would sit down with him and his financial people.

This was going to be a long, exhaustive meeting, and Josie wasn't looking forward to it. Before going back to Eve, Josie made sure she had a cold bottle of water and a few candy bars in her bag in case she needed a little pick-me-up.

The women walked together to the meeting, talking about the stores they planned to visit after lunch. Finding seats next to one another at the table, they sat down and took out all their files in preparation for the next few hours.

Almost as soon as the meeting started, Eve's phone vibrated in her pocket, and she covertly slipped it out and opened it. The corners of her mouth immediately turned down, and she thought she might cry.

Josie had been watching when Eve took her phone out, *and* when her friend's expression changed so dramatically. Unfortunately, she wouldn't be able to ask her about it until lunch.

The next time Josie glanced over at Eve, her face was frozen in a look of concentration. One of the board members was still explaining the first item on the long agenda. Something wasn't right and Josie reached over to grab Eve's hand. Eve turned and smiled, but it wasn't Eve's usual smile. Josie was worried for her friend.

The taste of Eve's lips lingered on Will's as he settled into her couch and turned on his computer. He opted to wait on having a second cup of coffee, not wanting to erase that reminder of her. As his computer warmed up, Will turned on his phone. *Hmm... Three messages and a text.* He chose to check the text message first.

Will, Call me ASAP. Martin

Will exited texting and accessed his phone messages to see if his accountant had also called.

He heard Martin's worried voice. *"Will. It's Martin. Something's wrong with the Denver grant. I need to talk to you as soon as you can call me back."*

Erasing that message, Will made a note to call him back as soon as he checked his other messages.

"Hi, Will, it's Jeannette. Martin called me this morning all in a panic. Do you know what that's about? Call me back. And, hey, let's get together for dinner when you get home. I've missed you."

Again he erased the message. There was no way he was going to call Jeannette. Will moved on to the last message.

"Hey, Will. It's Megan. I know Martin's left you a message, but you need to call him right away. He's sweating bullets here and

making me really nervous. He won't tell me what's going on but he's in major panic mode. Call one of us as soon as you can, OK? Bye."

After erasing the message from Megan, Will hit the speed dial to Martin's office. He picked up on the first ring.

"Will! Thank God! What's going on with the Denver grant? *Please* tell me you know!"

Leaning back on Eve's couch as though he could relay calmness to Martin 3,000 miles away, Will took a breath before saying, "Martin. Slow down. What are you talking about? I haven't done anything with the Denver grant in weeks. I thought they were good to go as they start their second year with us."

"Money, Will. Money is missing. Lots of money. Gone." From the sound of it, Martin was close to hyperventilating.

"Martin. First of all, calm down and get your inhaler out, OK? I don't need you passing out on me." Will waited and heard the "shpst-haaah, shpst-haaah" sound over the phone, followed by Martin's deep breath. "Now. You OK there, pal? Talk to me calmly. What do you mean lots of money is gone?"

"I was reviewing the spreadsheets this morning and everything's good—until I look at Denver's numbers. Will, they're reportedly down to $190,000 in their account with us. So, I checked the other database where we keep track of everything. Same thing. Less than $200,000 left in their account. The rest of the grant money, Will. It's gone. From our spreadsheets and from our accounts."

"How much?" Will sat forward again, no longer feeling relaxed.

"We're talking about $1.7 million. Will, I've searched prior databases. Everything matches. I don't know how it happened. I've left messages with my contact in Denver but, shit, Will, *our* account is showing that money is missing. I'm afraid a hacker has accessed our account. This isn't a banking issue, as you well know. This is *me* screwing up somehow, and we're out a whole hell of a lot of money."

There was silence on the line for a few moments. Will was trying to process what Martin had just told him…almost two million dollars missing. There was no need to ask him "are you sure?" Martin was meticulous and would have solved this if a solution was out there. He would have researched and re-researched before contacting Will about any concerns. Hearing from him meant this was real trouble.

"Will, you still there?"

"Yeah, man. Do you have any idea what happened or any speculation as to where that money is?"

"I found evidence that some files were accessed this morning, but I can't trace the source. Whoever did this knew how to do it without leaving a trail. I've changed all the passwords and locked access to the rest of the accounts just in case, but, honestly, if they hacked into the Denver grant money that easily, I can't be sure the other money is safe. Will, you've got over $140 million at risk here. I need you back."

"Absolutely. I'll pack my things and be on the jet within the hour." Will checked his watch. It was a little after eight, Santa Barbara time. "I should be in the office before three o'clock."

"God, Will, I am *so* sorry about this. I know how much you trust me and I can't—"

"Martin, I trust you completely. *You* didn't do anything wrong, of that I'm completely sure. For now, just keep on this and give me any updates you need to. I'll be there in a few hours. Let Megan know, too."

Will snapped the phone shut, then reopened it, dialing a number he had only recently memorized.

"Hello, you've reached Eve Carwyn, curator of the Santa Barbara Museum of Art. I'm away from my desk so please leave a detailed message, and I will return your call as soon as I can."

A hard curse echoed in the empty apartment. Will realized Eve was in that marathon meeting with the directors this morning about the grant. Hanging up, he called the pilot he'd contracted with, arranging to have the jet ready within the hour.

Making a quick sweep of the apartment, Will collected his belongings. The whole time his heart was in his stomach, but not over the money situation. He knew *that* would hit him on the flight to Boston. The immediate ache was that he had to leave Eve without saying goodbye or holding her one more time before they would be separated by thousands of miles. As he looked around, he realized the apartment hadn't been just a place to live for a week, it had been *home*.

Home. Boston had always been that. But now, where Eve was—*that* was home to Will.

As he slipped out the door of her apartment one last time, the spare key in hand, Will locked the door and soberly walked to the elevator. The dream he'd been living for a week was over.

The pilot was waiting for him when he arrived at the small airport. Will left his rental car with their assistant to return for him. As he climbed the steps to the jet, Will felt like his feet were tied to cement blocks. This had not been his plan for the day...for tonight. *Tonight...*

Dialing again, Will got Eve's voice mail a second time. It was killing him not to be able to talk to her, to explain.

She kept her cell with her, even in her meetings, so Will opened his phone again and sent her a text message. The impersonal nature of a text weighed on him, but he had to let her know that he was leaving, and it seemed to be the only way.

Eve

I'm so sorry.

Have to return to Boston ASAP.

Call you later.

Miss you already.

Will.

I love you. That was the part he couldn't put in a text message, and his heart ached once more. As the plane ascended, Will shut his eyes tight. He had promised himself he would tell her before he left Santa Barbara. When he opened his eyes, he glanced out the window to see the Pacific below him disappear. This just wasn't right. Nothing was right.

Chapter Twenty-one

As soon as the jet landed, Will opened his cell to call Martin, hoping the accountant would have better news than their last conversation. The phone immediately indicated a new text message, and Will clicked on it.

Will

Money is fine—bank and Denver confirmed it.

IT is checking security breach.

Martin

Only after feeling his shoulders relax did Will realize how tense he'd been. Within a few seconds, he had Martin on the phone to get the whole story.

"Hey, I just landed... Yes, I got your text—great news. I know, but you've got Robin checking things out? Great. Just what I wanted to hear. I'm heading to the office now. See you in about a half-hour."

Snapping the phone shut, Will slipped it into his pocket before gathering his luggage and laptop. When he found his car in the nearby parking garage, he slid in and sighed at the familiar feeling. He had missed some things about his life here in Boston, but he sighed because as much as he liked these things, he *loved* Eve, and he missed her already.

The drive into the city was mercifully swift, and Will arrived at Townsend Industries a few minutes after three o'clock. When he walked in, Megan greeted him with a warm smile and pointed to Martin's office where he and the IT expert, Robin, were talking.

Extending his hand to both of them, Will took the empty seat across from Martin's desk. "So, what's the latest?"

Robin sank into Martin's leather chair, her yellow-green eyes looking directly at the boss. "As Martin already told you, the money is fine. It wasn't accessed at all, and your accounts are secure. I also took the liberty of checking the computer in your office." She hesitated as if needing forgiveness. Will nodded in approval, and she continued, "Your computer hasn't been touched in over a week. Martin's, however, was accessed just this morning, and it wasn't done remotely. Someone physically came in here, got into the grant-expenditure spreadsheets, and simply changed some numbers."

She stood up and paced the small area between Martin's desk and the large window behind it. "Our issue here, then, is twofold: who got into those files, and why."

Martin and Will looked at each other, and Martin spoke first.

"The building's security cameras—" he began. Robin finished his sentence.

"—are being checked right now. I've got Steve going over the tapes at this floor's elevators as well as those from the cameras in the lobby downstairs. He should have something soon since we've isolated the timeframe based on the timestamp on Martin's computer."

Robin sat again in Martin's chair and leaned forward on her elbows, her fingers laced together in front of her. "From what I can see, this was just someone playing a cruel joke on Martin—or possibly both of you. Hopefully the camera footage will identify who it was. Just to be on the safe side, though, I need both of you, as well as Megan, to change your passwords and make sure they're not written down where someone can find them. You also need to be sure they're not easy to guess." She smirked at Martin. "Please, Martin. Yours was pretty obvious for anyone who knows you—or who looks around your office."

Martin's collection of pictures and figurines of Frodo Baggins from *Lord of the Rings* was obsessive, but he kept it all out of the sight of anyone visiting the office lobby, so Will had never said anything.

"OK, OK. Got it. Changing password immediately. Can I put 'Elijah Wood' instead?"

Will had to swallow his laughter. Martin was an amazing accountant, but one of the quirkiest guys he'd ever met.

Robin rolled her eyes. "Don't tell us what you want your password to be!" She looked over at him and sighed. "How about you pick a favorite line he says in one of the movies?" She knew him too well.

"Ooh! Great idea! I'll put 'Elijah Wood' for today, but I was planning an LoTR marathon weekend anyway. That'll give me something fun to do! Thanks, Robin!"

"OK. We're done for now, then?" Will asked, as he and Robin left Martin's office. "Let me know—"

"—as soon as I hear back from Steve. Gotcha. He's brilliant at enhancing grainy camera footage. He'll be able to give you a clear description of your intruder if not today then by Monday at the latest." Robin shook Will's hand and waved goodbye to Megan on her way out the door.

With things settled for a little while, Will sank into his office chair, allowing the last five hours to finally catch up with him. He couldn't believe it had only been five hours since he was holding Eve.

Checking his watch, it was a little after four, one o'clock her time. Suddenly his cell chimed from his pocket, indicating a new text message.

Marathon meeting just ended. Ugh.

Let me know that you're safely back in Boston.

Eve

Immediately, Will hit the reply button.

Got back an hour ago. Crisis over.

I'll call you tonight if that's OK.

Within a few moments, the phone chimed again.

Yes, please.

Looking forward to hearing from you.

The idea to jump back on the jet to tell her how he felt about her slipped into his mind, but he knew that wasn't going to happen. Real life had reached right out and given him a slap upside his head. While he was sure he would get back to Santa Barbara soon, he *did* have a business to run in Boston.

Snapping his phone shut, Will turned his attention to the computer. Although he'd kept up with email from Eve's, there were some things he needed to take care of in person.

Pulling up his schedule for the next week, Will noticed that—as was the norm whenever he returned from being out of town—Megan had blocked Monday and Tuesday for office time. Wednesday was still open for the most part, and Thursday he'd be flying to Columbus for a medical seminar with some fourth-year residents.

Will liked meeting with residents; they weren't yet so jaded that they just sat and checked their phones during his presentation. They were still eager to learn about new procedures and products.

Then he noticed Tuesday evening marked with an asterisk: Chamber of Commerce Dinner and Silent Auction. Another one of those black-tie affairs where a lot of the guys in black-ties are having affairs.

As a small groan escaped, Will heard a cough and looked up to find Megan leaning against the door jamb, smiling.

"Hey. So, welcome back, huh?" She plopped down into one of the chairs that faced Will's desk. "Your arrival today wasn't exactly as planned, I'm guessing?"

"Not at all."

"How's Eve?" Will cringed, and she hesitated. "I mean, you know, you told me her car was broken into or something. Did they catch whoever did it?"

Will sighed and leaned back in his chair. "No. But we're pretty sure it was her ex-boyfriend. He's a certified psycho, I'm telling you, Megan. But he's kind of under the radar with the police—not doing anything suspicious they can catch. His artwork is hanging in the Santa Barbara Museum, so he just goes there and sits, staring at his work. I swear he does that just to bug Eve and her colleagues."

Megan opened her eyes wide and sat up. "Is he still a threat to her?"

"Hard to say. Her friends are keeping close to her, including her bodybuilding next-door neighbor. And Eve doesn't know it, but I've got a private investigator watching the ex, too. But..." He looked right into Megan's eyes. "*You* know why I stayed longer, don't you?" She had always been able to read him like a book.

A smile appeared on her face, and she clapped her hands excitedly. "You love her! Oh, I just knew it. She's wonderful and *so* perfect for you and, I'm telling you, Will, she loves you, too. I could see it in her eyes at the gala that night."

Will smirked at Megan's enthusiasm. It was a rare day when she didn't have her nose in some romance novel during her lunch. But she was right about him loving Eve. He hoped she was also right about Eve loving him in return. If he'd gotten to stay in Santa Barbara one more night, he might have found out.

"So!" Megan jerked Will back into the conversation. "Tuesday night. Jeannette is, of course, expecting you to be her arm candy at the Chamber function. May I be the one to tell her no?"

"While I know how much that would thrill you, I probably need to tell her myself. We're both expected to be there, whether we arrive together or separately. I'll give her a call in a little while. That will give her time this weekend to find some unfortunate bastard to sink her claws into. Oh, my tux..."

"Still at the dry cleaners—sorry! I'll pick it up for you on my way home tonight." Will started to protest. Her job didn't extend to his dry cleaning! "Don't worry, Will. I've got stuff to drop off anyway, so I'll get your tux and have it in your office on Monday."

Megan stood to walk out, but then turned back toward her boss, smiling. "I'm really happy for you, Will."

"Thanks, Megan."

She returned to her desk, and Will began to attack the dangerously unstable stack of mail on the edge of his desk. He heard another cough and thought Megan had come back. In her place, however, was Robin, one eyebrow raised and a CD in her hand.

"Take a look at this. Steve just downloaded it to a disk for me to bring to you." She came around the side of Will's desk, and he quickly vacated his chair for her. Within a minute, she brought up the video taken from the camera next to the floor's elevator. Clicking the play button and standing back up, she gestured for Will to take a closer look at his computer's monitor.

The motion was choppy, as in any security video, but the person getting off the elevator at 5:30 that morning and leaving ten minutes later was clearly identifiable.

Jeannette.

Skye was leaving for lunch when she saw Josie and Eve sitting across from one another in Eve's office. The look on Eve's face told her something was very wrong, and Josie didn't look much better.

Sure that the prick, Julian, had done something else, Skye burst into the office. "What the hell did the asshole do?"

Both Eve and Josie looked up, their mouths hanging open.

"Skye, I really don't need to hear that right now." Eve was on the verge of tears, and Skye silently vowed to rip Julian's "boys" off and toss them into the Pacific.

Josie gave Skye the death look. It took her by surprise, because Josie didn't look pissed off like Skye thought she should be, but upset instead. Skye knew she was partly to blame for whatever the little weasel had done this time. He was up to something and she had let her guard down, if only a little. She was about to ask again what the creep had done, when Eve started to talk.

"I know that you love me. But please don't be angry with Will. It's not his fault. These things happen."

"Will? Why would I be mad at Will?" Now Skye was totally confused, which seemed to be the norm for her lately. "Didn't Julian do something? I thought that was why the two of you looked so serious."

"Julian? No. Will got called back to Boston on business. I'm just upset because I never got to talk to him, and I really don't know where things stand." A tear ran down Eve's cheek as she took a gulping breath.

Seeing her friend this way was painful for Skye, but this was not where she was any good. Castrating Julian? That she could do. Trying to figure out why Eve and Will, who obviously had strong feelings for each other, never figured it out for themselves? Skye was stumped.

Skye's instincts were good, and there was something tingling in the back of her mind. Although for the moment this wasn't about Julian, she still didn't trust him. There was no way she was going to let Eve spend the night at her apartment all alone.

"OK, right. So, tonight's going to be a girls' night in: classic chick movies, some wine, and lots of bitching." Skye switched gears, trying to find a way to make Eve feel better, and ensure that she and Gage were close by tonight.

"Skye, I'm really not up for that tonight. Will said that he would call, and I'm sure he will, so I wouldn't be any fun to be around." Eve gave a sad smile. "Besides, don't you have a needy quarterback to take care of?"

"Oh, please, Eve. Gage will be fine. You need us tonight. Right, Josie?"

Both Eve and Skye looked over at Josie, who was trying to avoid eye contact.

"Right, Josie?" Skye asked again, this time louder.

"Well, here's the thing. Beau's leaving again tomorrow. I *have* to be with him tonight. But tomorrow night, I am all about you girls. I promise."

"This is totally not necessary. I'll be fine. Skye, you and Gage go and have fun. And Josie, do not feel bad. Give Beau a reason to come home."

"No way, woman. Even if Josie can't make it, you and I are gonna get tipsy on wine while watching *Sixteen Candles* and swooning over that hunky Jake Ryan. And that's the end of it."

Eve let out an exasperated sigh, and Skye knew she was giving in to the slumber party idea. With a small hug, Skye left her friends. There were plans that needed to be rearranged.

"I'll be over around six. Mexican OK for dinner?" Skye called over her shoulder as she headed back to her office. Lunch would have to wait. First she had to let Gage down easy. He was really going to be disappointed.

Skye picked up the receiver and dialed his cell. If she told him in person, he would be able to convince her to stay at his place. That sad little boy look he gave when he didn't get what he wanted always made her cave.

"Hey, sexy lady," Gage growled into the phone. Skye's body instantly reacted to the sex dripping from his voice, and she shifted in her seat.

"Hey, babe."

"You couldn't go the day without me, could you? I know that as you sit in that little office of yours, you think about me."

"Yeah, right. Listen up, Casanova." Skye had to get the phone call under control because he was very close to the truth. "There's been a change in plans for tonight."

"What do you mean? I am *so* ready for slutty cheerleader time."

"Will had to go back to Boston this morning, last minute, and I don't think it's a good idea for Eve to be alone."

"So we just switch stadiums. Let's play at my place. That way everyone wins." The desperation in his voice was clear.

"No, Gage. That isn't how it's going to work. I'm going to spend the night at Eve's, and you're going to be right next door in case the freak shows up."

"I thought Eve said he had a girlfriend now. Why are you still so worried about it?"

"I just don't trust him. He's way too creepy to just give up. So, that's the plan, babe. You in your apartment, and Eve and me at hers. I promise I'll make it up to you."

"Yeah, alright. But I'll be thinking of something really good for you to do. I love you, Skye."

"I love you, too."

Jeannette was putting some papers in the bottom drawer of her filing cabinet, and when she looked up, Will was at the door.

"Oh, my! Will, darling, don't scare me like that!" Walking quickly over to him, she wrapped her arms around him, making sure her breasts rubbed against him as she gave him a quick kiss. Will quickly turned his head, causing Jeannette's lips to land on his cheek instead of his lips where she had intended.

"I need to talk to you."

"Sure. Is this about Martin? I left you a message..." Jeannette was all smiles. This was a game, and she needed to come across as unaware of the computer problems over at Townsend Industries, but she was also really glad to see him. Images of her in Will's bed played in her mind.

"Yes." His tone was serious, and he stood with tense shoulders. "Jeannette. Care to tell me what the hell you were doing at Townsend this morning at 5:30?"

"Oh. Yeah, sure." Thinking fast was something Jeannette excelled at. Making sure to sound flustered, she adopted an innocent tone. "I borrowed a file from your desk on Tuesday and dropped it back off on my way to work this morning. Why? Is there a problem?"

"Yeah, there's a problem. Somebody messed with Martin's computer this morning." His eyes were beginning to bore through her. "And my tech person said it happened when *you* were in the building."

Jeannette sat down in her chair and pushed it back from the desk. As she crossed her legs, making sure Will had the opportunity to sneak a peek up her short skirt, she motioned for Will to sit as well. He remained standing, arms crossed.

"What do you mean 'messed with Martin's computer'? Are you accusing me of something, Will?"

"I'm just putting pieces of a puzzle together, Jeannette, and you seem to fit in there somewhere."

"Well, surely you don't think—"

"I'm not sure what to think right now. All I know is that you were seen on the security cameras entering and leaving the building during the time Martin's computer was compromised."

"I don't care at all for the tone you're using. If your company has had someone vandalize your office, just because I was there doesn't make me the guilty party, Will. Anyone determined to mess with Martin's computer—or yours for that matter—could figure out how to avoid a couple of cameras. I've told you the truth. I went in, dropped off the file on your desk, and left."

"Ten minutes to drop off a file?" There was more than a hint of anger in Will's voice.

"I spoke with Harold for a few minutes. Any crime in that? He was the one to let me in, damn it. Did you bother to talk to *him* before coming over here?" Jeannette's level of indignation rose to match Will's accusing tone.

"No, but I will before I leave work tonight." He paused. "So, you're saying you only went into my office to drop off a file. You didn't see anyone other than Harold?"

"I borrowed the file Tuesday. I returned it this morning. You can check with Megan and Harold. That's it. Are you done?"

"Yes." Jeannette Sheldon was a conniving, power-hungry woman, but Will couldn't figure out how what happened would be something that would help her in any way. He cooled down, slightly.

"Good. Now, about Tuesday night's dinner, I'm planning to wear—"

"You're either going solo or getting someone else to escort you."

Jeannette was speechless. The two of them had always gone together to these functions, and she needed him by her side now more than ever.

"But, Will..."

"I'll see you there, and we can do whatever brown nosing we need to in order to keep donations coming in to the BMA, but *we* are not together. Got it?" He moved toward the door but stopped and glared at her. "And if I do find you had anything to do with Martin's computer files, you can be sure there will be severe consequences, Jeannette. I promise you that."

Before Jeannette could say a word, he turned on his heel and walked out the door.

That evening, Eve couldn't help constantly checking her watch, for the time, and her cell, to be sure it was on. She had changed into the same t-shirt and shorts she'd worn to bed all week. Will's scent still lingered on the material, and she loved that she could feel close to him this way.

Pulling her hair into a ponytail, Eve moved around the apartment, straightening a few things before Skye's arrival. The loneliness was already beginning to consume her, and she felt her eyes tear up. She opened her phone to reread his last text: *I'll call you tonight if that's OK.*

Eve hadn't tried to call him, even though she wanted to, desperately. He was finally back in his office after being away for a week; he didn't need her distracting him. If he'd wanted to talk right then he would have called, right?

A thumping sound on the door indicated Skye's arrival, but Eve peered through the peephole to be sure. After quickly unlocking and opening the door, she reached to take some of the bags from Skye's hands.

"Good heavens, Skye! What did you bring?"

"Well, Mexican as promised." She began unpacking the various paper and plastic bags she had placed on the kitchen counter. "A few movies, all of which have the darling John Cusack in them, a few bottles of wine—if we need more, we'll send Gage out for it—some snacks, and my overnight bag!" It looked like she'd packed for a week rather than one night. Either way, Eve realized she really was glad her friend was there.

Eve went into the bedroom to find some extra blankets for them to snuggle with while they watched Skye's movie lineup. When she came back out, Skye was yelling to Gage through the door. Skye looked over at Eve and winked, not missing a beat in her conversation with Gage.

"Then order a pizza, big guy. But you need to leave us alone!"

"Come on...I can smell Ricardo's," Gage whined. "You know how much I love their food. I'm starving."

"Go home, Gage."

Knowing this was only the beginning of the game that would be played between the two of them all night, Eve got out two plates and placed two tacos and a spoonful of refried beans on hers before putting *Sixteen Candles* in the DVD player.

Skye eventually gave up on her argument with Gage and piled up her own plate, then joined Eve on the couch.

"Sorry," she said with a smile. "He is such a baby."

Eve had her mouth full, so she just nodded at her friend. The movie started at that moment, and the two women turned to lose themselves in a little piece of the 1980s.

Right as the last scene was playing—the kiss over the birthday cake—Eve's cell phone buzzed in her lap. Picking it up, her heart skipped a beat when the screen showed Will's name. Unfolding her feet from under her on the couch, Eve bounded to the bedroom. Just before closing the door, she turned and winked at Skye, who threw a thumbs up in the air as Eve retreated to her room.

"Hi," Eve said, picking up on the second ring as she made herself comfortable on the bed, leaning back against the many pillows that lined the headboard.

"Hey, there. How are you doing?" Will's voice was sultry, making Eve want to climb through the phone to him.

"Well, my roomie moved out this morning without me saying goodbye, so I've been kind of bumming all day."

"Yeah. Me, too. And I'm so sorry about that, Eve. I tried to reach you but you were in that meeting. I did the best I could." Eve took a little comfort in the fact that he sounded as sad as she felt.

"I know you did. What happened?" But then she hesitated. "I mean, if you want to tell me about it..."

Will proceeded to explain Martin's frantic phone and text messages, and when he said that upward of 140 million dollars was possibly in jeopardy, Eve gasped.

"It's OK, though. Our IT person was on it right away and assured us that the money wasn't stolen or even missing—well, other than from Martin's spreadsheets."

"Any idea how or why it happened—or who did it?"

"Well, a lot is still a mystery, but we *did* find Jeannette Sheldon from the BMA on the security videotape from that time frame. Would you believe it?"

"What? What on earth?" Eve hadn't liked the woman from the moment she met her, but never pegged her as a cyber criminal.

"She denies doing anything to Martin's computer. She admitted she'd been in the building—and our office—this morning, but claimed she was returning a file she'd borrowed from me while she was on her way to work. Megan confirmed that Jeannette had been in earlier in the week and taken a file so, I don't know. We don't have any proof yet that she did anything in Martin's office. The cameras only cover the elevators and immediate area around them. Our IT person is trying to see if there's any trace on Martin's computer that could link things to Jeannette. For now, we're all changing our passwords, and I'm having security cameras installed within our offices on Monday."

"I'm sorry you had to leave with such worries on your mind. You must have been going crazy on the flight back. But, I'm glad everything's OK. I'm glad *you're* OK. I'm going to be missing my new favorite pillow tonight, you know."

"Hmm?"

"Your shoulder. I slept pretty soundly when my head was resting there."

"Well, maybe I need to fly back out there before you go to bed tonight, huh?"

"You've got a key. Let yourself in." Eve tried to lighten the mood with her flirting.

"Oh. That. Do you want me to FedEx that to you? I had to keep it—Gage wasn't home, and I didn't have any place to leave it..." Will was flustered.

"Will. You heard me..." Eve let that sink in.

"Mmm...sounds like an invitation to come stay with you again. Do I have that right?"

Eve sensed that their ability to banter comfortably with each other had returned.

"Your room at the Carwyn Hotel is *always* available. No reservation required."

"That's very good to know." The silly flirtations made Eve miss him even more, and she found herself wishing he *would* fly back tonight.

"So, what are you doing tonight, since I so rudely altered our dinner plans?"

The answer came first in the form of a giggle. "I'm having a sleepover. Skye is spending the night and we're going to fall asleep watching movies with John Cusack."

"So...is John Cusack sleeping over, too?"

"Huh?"

"You said you'd be watching movies with John Cusack–I figured he must be there, too. And I must say that I'm a bit hurt that you'd replace me so soon after I left!"

"Will..." Eve knew he could see her smile in his mind, just as she could see his.

"OK. Sounds like a wild and crazy night, but I want to know what we were going to do if I hadn't had to fly back to Boston."

For the next few minutes, Eve described Chez Shea, its beautiful décor, and some of its chef's famous dishes.

"Tell me what you were going to wear." The sultry voice had returned.

"I was thinking about the dress I wore to the gala."

"Mmm. Thank you. I'm picturing you in it now, and you look stunning, just like before. And what was I wearing?"

Eve first imagined him in nothing at all.

"Well, I loved that tie you wore the day that Jeannette ordered the horse-cheese salad—you looked very handsome!"

"You never mentioned it before."

"Couldn't. Felt I would have been crossing that business-personal line."

"Yeah, like me kissing your hair at the gala was perfectly business-like."

"I liked that you did that. You knew that, though, didn't you?"

"Yes. But you didn't know then how much I wanted to kiss you like I had at Stratus only a few nights before."

"I knew how much *I* wanted to kiss you back, though. But if you had, I just might have figured out you were my Passion Fish."

"You think?"

"Will, *no one* has ever kissed me like *that* before."

"Not even Gage?"

That comment earned a loud laugh. "Speaking of which, let me just check on Skye, make sure she hasn't jumped my little boat for the pirate ship next door." Eve peeked out and saw Skye on her cell, twisting her hair in her fingers and smiling, *Better Off Dead* now playing on the TV. "Nope. She's here but I'm guessing she's on the phone with him."

"I'm glad she's staying with you." Will paused and when he spoke again, his voice was subdued. "I know you think you're safe, but I still don't want you being alone too much. I'm not convinced Julian won't try something else when your guard is down."

There was a momentary silence in their conversation, both suddenly reminded of the distance between them.

"So what are you doing tonight?" Eve finally asked.

"Missing my roomie, for one. And I'm picturing you sitting on my sofa in my t-shirt and sweats."

"Walk out to the balcony and tell me about what you see."

Eve heard the click of the door being unlatched, followed by the distant sounds of traffic.

"It's just like the night you were here. The breeze is a little warmer, but I still would have put the blanket over your shoulders."

"I had a nice time in Boston. Would you be my tour guide if I want to visit again?"

"Only if you promise to stay with me and let me be your favorite pillow."

Closing her eyes, Eve wished herself there with him, then stifled a yawn.

"Hey," he said softly. "How about we say goodnight at the elevators again, hmm?"

As he counted down from five, and they each closed their phones, the tears silently rolled down Eve's cheeks.

Chapter Twenty-two

When Skye woke up the next morning on the couch, her whole body hurt. Eve was curled up on the loveseat, and Skye knew she wasn't going to be any better off. The two had fallen asleep in the early hours of the morning while watching *Say Anything*.

Girl's night in had been fun, but Skye really had missed the big goofball next door. She and Eve had laughed all night at the sound of Gage's shower turning on and off several times. It seemed to be driving him crazy knowing she was just a few feet away, and he couldn't do anything about it.

Eve started to stir, and Skye rolled herself off the couch.

"Hey, Eve. I'm going to jump in the shower. Is that OK?"

"Sure," Eve groaned as she stretched, trying to unkink all her muscles. "I'll put the coffee on."

As Skye let the spray of the shower wash over her sore back, she realized she was going to have to do something spectacular to make up for canceling on Gage. Under the warm water, a plan began to formulate.

"Eve, what do you think about heading down to Westwood today? Have lunch, browse some of the boutiques. We can ask Josie and Noelle, too," Skye asked as she came into the kitchen and grabbed the cup of coffee Eve had left on the counter for her.

"Yeah, sure. That would be good. Why don't you call them and see if they are up for it?" The reality of the day—that she was going to be spending it without Will—had hit Eve, and her voice cracked a little when she answered.

While Eve was in the shower, Skye called Josie and Noelle. Noelle, unfortunately, was working, but Josie agreed to meet them after she dropped Beau at the airport.

There was one more call Skye had to make to set her plan for Gage's surprise in motion. Finished with her call, and feeling satisfied that the day was well planned out, Skye decided to run over and see her man for a quick morning kiss before Eve was ready to go.

When she opened Eve's front door, she nearly tripped over the giant bouquet of sunflowers lying just outside it. A huge smile crossed her face. There was no need to look at the card to know they were for her…from Gage. Taking the small note out of the flowers, Skye ripped it open.

Baby –

Love you!

Can't wait till tonight!

Gage

With the flowers in hand, Skye strode over to Gage's apartment and knocked on the door. He didn't answer, and she wondered where he was. Back at Eve's place, Skye dug for her phone and called him. He picked up on the third ring.

"Hey baby. Did you get my present?"

"I did. And I love them and you so much. Thank you."

"Do you remember that I brought you a sunflower on our first date?"

"Of course. I'll never forget that. No one has ever given me anything other than roses. Not to mention it was less than three weeks ago. So, what are you doing?"

"I'm at the gym. I have clients for most of the day, and then I am expecting something special when I get off shift from Stratus tonight."

"Don't worry about that, I've got it under control. The girls and I are going down to Westwood, and I'll see you later. I love you, Gage."

"Love you too, Skye."

Eve laughed at the bouquet of sunflowers when she came back into the room.

"Only Gage would give a girl sunflowers," she commented through her laughter, as she got out a large vase to accommodate them.

"He is an original." Skye laughed with her as they headed out the door to meet Josie.

After the long drive to Westwood, Eve and Skye roamed the streets of the college town, looking in stores and ducking into several galleries until they heard a familiar voice.

"Morning, girls!" Josie's chipper voice reached them from about three stores away.

"Josie, why the hell are you in such a good mood? Didn't you just drop off Beau?" Skye's words had come out much harsher than she had expected, and she immediately felt awful. It seemed like she'd lost her ability to think before she spoke recently. Not good for a person in PR.

Josie's face fell slightly, but she quickly recovered, remembering the reason they were here…to keep Eve's mind off of Will.

"OK, ladies, gather round and let me explain my plan for later, and then we can go hunting for my outfit." Skye smiled warmly at Josie, hoping she understood her silent apology. When she smiled back, Skye knew she had.

Once all the items from Skye's list were purchased, the group decided to find a place for lunch. As they stood arguing over which restaurant, Skye saw *him*.

"Ugh. What is the asshole doing here? And who is that with him?"

Eve and Josie both spun around quickly.

"I told you. Julian is over me. That's Miranda, his girlfriend," Eve informed them. Then she waved shyly, and he started toward them.

"Hi, Julian. Miranda," Eve greeted them. "What are you two doing here?"

"Eve. How are you? Josie, Skylar." No more than a nod for the two of them, and his eyes remained completely focused on Eve.

This guy is not over Eve. He's looking at her like he wants to eat her, thought Skye.

"Well, we have a gallery opening to go to tonight in Beverly Hills, and I needed something for our evening out."

"Yeah, right." Skye couldn't help herself and hoped no one heard her. Unfortunately, by the way everyone was looking at her, she wasn't so lucky. She chose to ignore the glares and try to get the hell out of the situation.

"Come on, girls, I'm starving. Let's go eat." She pulled Eve and Josie by their arms.

"Well, bye, Miranda. Nice to see you again," Eve called over her shoulder.

Skye made the executive decision to eat at the tapas restaurant closest to them. She needed to get them away fast. The hostess found them a table, and as they sat down, she took their drink orders. Eve and Josie both stared at Skye like she was crazy.

"Skylar Montgomery, I can't believe how rude you were," Eve said.

"Look, Eve. I really didn't mean to say that out loud, but I still don't trust him. I mean really, look at that woman. Do you think he could get someone like that?"

"Skye!" Josie yelled, and the other patrons in the restaurant turned to look at them.

"So, she was too good for Julian, but someone like me? I was just plain enough for him?" Eve asked with tears in her eyes.

Shit! I did it again. What the hell is wrong with me? Skye wondered.

"Eve, you know that isn't what I meant. You were way too good for him, and I believe I told you that several times while you were dating him. I still don't get what you ever saw in him. Now Will...that's more along the lines of who you should be with."

Eve wiped a tear from her cheek, and Skye wasn't sure if she'd made things better or worse. Bringing up Will was risky, but she wanted Eve to realize she deserved more than that prick Julian.

"You're just lucky we're such good friends, because I know you mean well. But, please, let's just not talk about Julian anymore. It's over. I've moved on, and he has, too." Eve shot Skye a stern warning look.

"Fine. I won't say anything more about the creep." Skye relented.

Lunch passed quickly, and when Skye glanced at her watch, she realized she had to leave or she'd be late for her "appointment" with Gage.

"Girls, I have to leave and put these new items to use to make Gage smile bigger than he ever has."

"Go get 'em, woman!" Josie yelled as Skye sashayed confidently out the door.

Julian watched, his mouth drawn into a tight line, as that whore Skylar pulled Eve away from him. He could see in Eve's eyes that she didn't want to go. She wanted to stay and talk with him...be with him.

It wasn't until the three disappeared into a restaurant that Julian turned back to Miranda, who just stood staring at him. She looked presentable enough, but she would never be Eve, and the money that he had spent—not only for her time, but for the clothes she wore—was going to become a problem unless he could sell a painting. And in order to paint, he needed Eve back.

Miranda wasn't like the whores his father used to force him to be with. At least she seemed clean and smelled like powder and lilacs. Those...Julian couldn't even think of them as women in his memories...*sluts* he had been with over and over again had always smelled of liquor and cigarettes and filth. And worst of all, his father would provide his mother a full report when they returned home.

His mother's ability to sit by while his father beat and berated him was just as big a mystery as why she'd ever married him in the first place. But Julian knew the story. He'd heard it many times over the years, usually as his father was beating him. Over and over he told Julian he wished he would have let his mother get the abortion. Oddly enough, most of those times Julian was thinking the same thing.

The only reason Julian existed was because his father's mother found out about the pregnancy and talked Arnie into marrying Marjorie. Julian hoped the woman was sitting right next to his dear old dad in hell.

"Julian." The whore touched his arm, bringing him out of his free fall into his past—into Justin Merchant's past. Immediately, Julian yanked his arm away from her touch. When he looked at her, she took a step back.

"What?" Julian hissed through his teeth.

"Are we going to that gallery opening?" Miranda whispered. The look in his eyes was the most frightening thing she had ever seen. The guy had creeped her out from the get go with all his talk about Eve and his insistence that she wouldn't be "performing" any "services" with him because he would never do that to Eve, and certainly not with someone like her. He always seemed right on the edge of crazy, about to tip over into an abyss of madness. But he paid well, bought her new clothes, and she didn't have to sleep with him. She could definitely put up with a touch of crazy.

"No. I'm done with you." Julian dismissed her.

"Umm...I don't have a way to get back to Ventura?" She watched Julian carefully. For some reason he was much more agitated today than he was when they had talked with that Eve woman a few days ago.

Julian pulled several bills out of his pocket, the last of his cash, and practically threw them at her. "Take a cab, or a bus, I don't care. But that is all I'm giving you. Now go away."

Miranda stood completely stunned for a few moments before she bent down and gathered the money scattered at her feet. It was all ones and a few fives, definitely not enough to get her home, but she just wanted to get away from Julian Meadows.

As Julian watched her scramble around, grabbing money off the ground, he was disgusted, but not surprised. In the end, a whore was a whore no matter how much she charged for her time.

When Gage looked at his schedule at the gym, he groaned. They had added a new appointment for him at three. That meant he wouldn't get out of there until around five, and he had to work at Stratus later. That wouldn't give him much time with Skye and her make up surprise.

Gage was pissed. There was a standing rule that on Saturdays they weren't to schedule a first timer that late in the day. A first-time appointment was a lot of paperwork, and then he had to show them each piece of equipment, and not to mention the tour. This was the part of the job he disliked the most. Gage couldn't wait to have his own gym where serious people would be able to use the equipment without him babysitting them.

At a quarter to three, Gage went over to look at the file for his new client. When he saw her name, Gage groaned again. *Cherry Harper? Now if that didn't sound like one of the bouncing bimbos...*

"Are you kidding me, Heather? Why the hell do I always get these?"

"She called this morning and insisted on training with you. She wanted the last slot of your day."

When Gage heard the ding of the doors opening, he really didn't want to look up and see what was coming for him.

"Holy shit! Look at her!" said one of the guys lifting behind him, followed by several low whistles.

When Gage finally glanced up, he smiled and instantly began to get hard. Standing in front of him, in what could barely qualify as workout gear, was Skye. With her hair pulled into a ponytail on top of her head, she looked good enough for Gage to take her into the office *right then.*

"Hi, I'm Cherry Harper." Gage knew every guy in the room had stopped breathing.

Stepping forward, he extended a hand to her.

"Hi, Cherry. I'm Gage. I'll be your new trainer." Not able to stop himself, Gage ogled her from head to toe. "But for the life of me, I can't imagine why that fine body of yours would need to be worked on."

Heather gasped and Gage let out a little laugh. He was about to explain that it wasn't a big deal and this wasn't a new client, when Skye reached over and grabbed his ass.

"Well, the same could be said about your rock-hard body, Gage."

"Why don't we step over into the office and make sure...uh...everything is in order." Gage wrapped an arm around Skye's waist and steered her toward the office.

Skye glanced up at Gage from under her thick lashes, and he picked up the pace. Once in the office, he shut the door and reached out to pull her to him. She danced away and sat in the small plastic chair that clients used.

"So here is the deal, big guy. You are going to give me a good workout—out there." She gestured toward the door and the gym beyond it. "And when that is all done, I am going to give *you* a good workout."

Gage couldn't move a muscle. He was pretty sure this woman was trying to kill him.

"I think you need to get yourself together," she glanced down at his shorts, "before we start my session. You can save that for your session."

"Let me understand this. You actually want to work out with me? And then I get to play with you?"

"That about sums it up. Look, I am going to go check out the women's locker room, while you get things, uh, under control."

She stood up and walked out the door. If Suzanne saw him in this state she was likely to lose it. Some of the pressure subsided, and Gage realized thinking about Suzanne was doing the trick.

After a few minutes of mentally running through the roster of bouncing bimbos, Gage was back to normal and headed out the door. Skye was waiting for him in her barely there spandex, and he nearly lost it once again. Fortunately, Suzanne chose that minute to strut by, and Gage was immediately deflated.

For the next hour and a half, Gage endured the sight of Skye bending over and breathing heavy as she pushed weights off of her incredible chest. Then when she wanted to get on the treadmill and jog, he thought he was going to pass out. Between trying to focus on Skye's workout instead of her body, and concentrating on not beating the crap out of every guy there for the way they were staring at her, Gage was exhausted when he finally looked at the clock and saw it was almost closing time...and his turn.

"Hey, Heather! Why don't you go ahead and take off. I'll lock up. I checked the men's locker room and it's all clear."

"Thanks Gage. I checked the women's, and it's good, too," she called back, eyeing Skye suspiciously.

Gage knew he'd have to explain this whole thing to her later. If she went to the boss, his ass would be fired.

"Alright, I'll see ya then." Heather couldn't leave fast enough for Gage. After locking the doors, he turned to see Skye standing in the middle of the gym. There was a thin sheen of sweat glistening on her body, and it was one of the sexiest things he had ever seen. Every nerve in his body began firing, and all the blood rushed to his lower body so fast he thought he would pass out.

As Gage started toward her, she back-peddled a little, ending up in the free weight room pressed against the mirrored wall. That was fine with him. Seeing her from all angles was an even bigger turn on.

Lifting his shirt over his head, Gage wasn't wasting any time. Skye gasped as he stepped up to her and went right for her top, quickly finding the bottom of the tiny tank top and peeling it off. When it was gone, her beautiful breasts were completely bare. Gage went straight to them, taking her in his mouth. As he bit and sucked on the perfection, he could feel her body moving against his.

"Oh, Gage. That's driving me crazy." Her voice came in a pant, and Gage knew he couldn't hold on much longer without being inside her.

Skye's hand grazed the hardness in his shorts, causing Gage to growl. Her hands moved back up to the waistband and she inched them, along with his boxer briefs, down way too slowly. Once they were on the ground, Gage stepped out of them, then freed her from the remaining clothes she was wearing. His heart nearly stopped beating when he found she wasn't wearing any panties.

Skye's hand felt so good on Gage's skin as she stroked him. Another groan escaped as his head lolled back. When she leaned in and ran her tongue over his nipple, Gage almost exploded. The sensation of heat and electricity ran through every inch of his body.

Wrapping his arms around her waist, cupping her perfect ass in his hands, Gage lifted her. She wrapped her legs around him as he stepped back, knowing exactly where he was going. With little effort, Gage found what he was looking for and sat down.

With one leg on either side of the weight bench, he pulled Skye to straddle him. When she slid down onto him, he nearly exploded.

"Skye, you are the most incredible woman," he whispered into her ear.

Skye rocked against Gage as he sucked and bit at her neck. With his hands planted on her hips, he held her as she found the perfect rhythm. At that moment, they both found release and collapsed against one another.

When Gage looked up into Skye's face, her eyes were shining. Leaning in, he found her lips and kissed her with all he had left.

"What are you smiling about? I mean, I like that I can put a smile on your face, but..."

"Yeah, right, Gage. You *always* put a smile on my face, but that isn't why I am smiling now."

"Then what is so funny?"

"I was just wondering when I could schedule my next session with you."

"Funny, I was just thinking the same thing." Gage smiled as he leaned in to kiss one of her amazing breasts.

"I'm thinking...right about now."

Sitting on the plane Tuesday morning, Beau was eager to get back to Josie. His trip to Boston had been a success on more than one level. He'd been able to find some nice pieces for his store at the coin expo he attended on Saturday and Sunday. The store was doing well, and with the new online feature about to launch, Beau was sure the traveling would slow down. He had also been thinking of hiring another person who could take on the travel so he could be home with Josie—permanently.

Beau and Will had met up on Monday. Since Will had apparently resolved whatever crisis brought him back early, and Beau was free once the expo had ended, they decided to meet for lunch.

When Beau arrived at the little diner, a place called Mulligan Stew, Will was already sitting in a booth.

"Beau. Good to see you again." Will stood to shake his hand.

"Will, sorry if I kept you waiting. I'm not familiar with this part of town."

"That's alright. I've only been here a few minutes."

Sliding into the booth, Beau picked up the menu in front of him. "What do you recommend?"

"Well, I've had about everything on here, and it's all good. So, just go with your gut," Will answered.

Once they had ordered, the two men fell into easy conversation about everything from Beau's coin-collecting business to Will's company and, finally, their relationships.

"I've been doing something I think might make Eve uncomfortable if she knew, and I was wondering if you could give me your opinion on whether or not I should tell her," Will said.

"Sure."

"Well, I hired a private detective to get some information on Julian. I had him followed and a background check done. I think Eve would be upset because she is so trusting and really believes Julian is over her. I don't want her to think that I doubt her in any way."

"Was there anything for Eve to worry about?"

"No. That bothers me a little, but the guy has nothing. No family, no ties to anyone. It's kind of strange, but nothing really wrong with it," Will explained. "And since my private detective has been following him, he hasn't done anything even remotely suspicious. He spends time at the museum and with that woman Miranda."

"It seems to me that Eve isn't in any danger, and for her sake, I would keep the whole private detective thing to yourself," said Beau. "I'm not a fan of hiding things from Josie, don't get me wrong, but I think in this case, Eve doesn't really need to know you hired the detective behind her back."

"Yeah, that's kind of the direction I was leaning. I've already let the guy go. There really wasn't much for him to do."

At that moment, the waitress placed their food on the table and the conversation lightened again, switching to sports. But once they had finished their meals, Beau decided to ask Will for some help.

"Will, do you need to get back to the office, or could I enlist your assistance in an errand I need to run?" Beau asked tentatively.

"Seeing as I own the company, I think I can create some flexibility with my schedule. What do you need?"

"I was thinking that while I was here, I would look for a ring for Josie. I'm going to ask her to marry me soon." Beau couldn't help but smile.

Will didn't answer immediately. He looked like he was trying to figure out what to say.

"Uh...Beau, I'm sorry, and you can tell me to butt out if you want to, but haven't you and Josie only been together for a couple of months?"

"I thought that you might be wondering about that. But, really, Will, I knew when I saw Josie she was what I needed to make myself whole. And I know that she feels the same about me. So, why should we wait?"

"Well, I just thought that maybe the longer you know someone, the better the chance of things working out. For example, you travel a lot, right? What if in a year Josie doesn't like that you are gone so much? It will be much harder to go your separate ways by then."

"If there's ever a problem with something, we'll work it out. When you love someone, and that person is truly a part of you, things always find a way of righting themselves."

Sitting back into the booth, Beau let what he'd said sink in. After a few minutes of comfortable silence, Will made a move to get up.

"So what exactly are you looking for, Beau?" Will waited as Beau got out of the booth as well.

"I was hoping you might know of some nice antique shops that would carry quality merchandise. I'm looking for something unique."

"I think I might have just the place. The owner is an old family friend, and his jewelry is superb."

"Lead the way. For Josie, I need a ring that is beautiful, delicate, and with a sparkle...just like her."

Now as the plane made its descent into Los Angeles, Beau knew Josie was at work, and he wouldn't see her for a few more hours. He felt the weight of the ring he'd found with Will's help in his pocket.

Jeannette decided to go to the Chamber of Commerce dinner alone, a first for her. Although she could have asked any one of a dozen handsome-but-brainless dolts to escort her, she didn't need anyone hanging on her when the goal was to get Will back. Back home and into her bed.

She chose to wear her Roberto Cavalli black stretch-lace dress, as it was perfect for the evening: respectable, classy, yet very sexy—exactly the look she was going for. Will was already there when she arrived; she certainly wasn't going to show up alone *and* early. He was gorgeous, as usual, and absolutely edible in his tux.

Jeannette didn't go over to Will immediately. Her plan was that he to come to her first. Then she'd be able to gloat as other women watched him walk past. But after a half-hour of making herself look irresistible to no avail, she picked up a glass of champagne from one of the servers and strolled casually over.

"Will, darling." Jeannette leaned in to kiss his cheek, making sure to make a show of rubbing the red lipstick mark she left with her thumb. Only after this display did she turn toward the people he'd been talking to and greet them. Remaining by his side, she linked her arm to his. He tried to shift away from her but she held fast, knowing he wouldn't make a scene in public.

The small talk was typical for these functions, and because Jeannette was with Will, she took advantage of looking at him whenever any questions came up about his company's work with the BMA. To everyone around them, the two appeared to be a couple, which was just what Jeannette wanted.

After a while, Will excused himself to use the restroom—the one place she couldn't follow him. He had to get away from her, and he couldn't afford to alienate any of the other people in attendance. When the door closed behind him, he breathed a huge sigh of relief.

Jeannette immediately moved to the bar and mingled with a few women she knew. One of the newspaper photographers, Jorge, asked to take a picture, and all the women leaned in, giving him their best smiles. Jorge took a few candid shots, but when he was done, Jeannette moved closer to him, giving him a decent look at her cleavage.

"Jorge, will you be a *doll* and be sure to get some nice shots of Will Prentiss and me? Nothing posed—he absolutely *hates* to be photographed. We'll be engaged soon, and I'd love to have some pictures of the two of us to send to relatives. If you use your zoom lens you'll be able to capture the two of us lovebirds, right? Feel free, though, to use any good ones for the paper, too! Will will just laugh that you got some good shots without him knowing!" She added a giggle for effect. Jorge agreed, and thanked Jeannette for the tip on how to get camera-shy Will Prentiss' picture for the paper.

When Will emerged from the men's room, he was careful to avoid Jeannette, keeping to the opposite side of the room as much as possible. As he tried to be social and talk to everyone, he was always on the lookout for Jeannette, not wanting to be trapped again. Fortunately, she seemed to be working her side of the room quite efficiently, socializing with the donors and dignitaries.

Jeannette watched Will being approached by various women, many of them fairly attractive, and she noticed that he remained aloof, never engaging in conversation with them for more than a few minutes. He appeared to be disinterested in everyone in attendance tonight—perhaps "distracted" was a better word.

"Hello, Will." Jeannette's voice was harsh in Will's ears as she once again joined him. He stepped back from her this time, but not out of reach. Once again, she was able to link her arm in his and pull him toward her. "Play nicely, Will. The filthy rich like seeing us together since we make them look good in the Boston papers."

Will scoffed but didn't try to detach himself. "We are *not* together, Jeannette. I thought I made myself perfectly clear the other day," he mumbled under his breath.

"Oh, are you still thinking I had something to do with Martin's computer problems?" she asked, pouting at him.

Out of the corner of her eye, Jeannette saw Jorge aiming his camera. She raised her chin and smiled up at Will, placing her palm on his cheek. "How many times do I have to defend myself, hmm?" In the distance, she heard the click and saw the flash. Her plan was working perfectly.

Unlinking her arm from Will's and turning to face him, she took both of his hands in hers. Again, her gaze could definitely be mistaken for love. "Will you look at me, silly?" When he did, another click and flash. "I'm sorry I went into your office when no one was there. I won't do it again. Can you forgive me? Please?" As she pulled his face down to hers for a quick kiss—which Will was obviously appalled by but didn't refuse—Jeannette knew that this would be the best photo Jorge had taken all night.

Mission accomplished.

For two days Will had been thinking about Beau and Josie. The conviction in Beau's voice and eyes when he explained how he felt was inspiring. There were no doubts—only anticipation for a life with her that he was ready to start as soon as possible.

This was exactly what Will had been feeling for Eve. It hit him so immediately that he was glad he was sitting at his desk or he might have stumbled. But could *that* sense of complete confidence really happen after knowing someone for only four weeks? It certainly seemed so. His father told him he'd asked his mother to marry him three days after they'd met. Maybe it was a genetic thing.

If nothing else, Will knew he had to see Eve again. The ache at waking up alone grew worse each day he was away from her. The nights were easier—they'd talk for an hour or more, always finding something new to discover about each other. And when they "said goodnight by the elevators" and counted down, he felt so at peace, falling asleep with her voice and face in his mind.

Taking a deep breath, Will attempted to refocus on work. There were things he needed to do before leaving for Columbus tonight for the med students' seminar tomorrow and Friday. He called out to Megan, who quickly came to his office.

"I've got a few phone calls I need you to make, if you don't mind. Here are the people and their numbers, as well as what I need you to arrange with them. Reaching Brenda is the most vital. She'll know what to do. I just have to be sure everything is coming together as I'd discussed with her and Peter. I'll check in with him today, too since his work for me was more specific. My understanding is that they will have every task complete by noon on Friday."

"You got it, boss." Then she hesitated with a sly smile. "Do you have photos I can see?"

Smiling back, Will waved for her to come around to view the monitor as he opened up the emails, and the attachments, he'd received the other day.

"Wow..." was all Megan could say.

The secrecy of being in Will's apartment was intoxicating. With him out of town for a few days, Jeannette could come and go as she pleased, and he'd be none the wiser. She'd even slept in his bed last night, inhaling his glorious scent from the sheets. Making a copy of his key had been a brilliant idea—one she wished she'd thought of sooner.

The email she'd sent to Santa Barbara had surely been opened by now and, Jeannette smirked, shared with *Ms. Carwyn.* While convincing Will to be with her was a tougher sell, convincing the bitch in Santa Barbara that he already *was* with her could be as easy as a few incriminating photos. Jorge had sent Jeannette the stills Wednesday morning, and they were perfect. The intense look on Will's face could be interpreted as moodiness or restrained passion.

Jeannette had casually asked Megan when Will would be arriving back in Boston and learned he was due back early this evening. Jeannette wasn't quite sure how Will would react to finding her in his apartment, but the absolutely sinful lingerie she'd be wearing would likely make him forget his name, let alone how she'd gotten there. Candles were arranged around his bedroom, and she had a bottle of wine from his kitchen chilling beside the bed, flanked by two glasses. Will was a man with desires. There was no way he could—or would—turn down Jeannette's sultry invitation. She just needed to await his return.

Chapter Twenty-three

For Eve, the week had passed in a blur, and she was thankful. Her days ran together as she spent them daydreaming about the previous night's phone calls with Will. There was so much they'd learned about each other: Both hated beets and loved the Rolling Stones; he admitted he wasn't a very good painter, and she promised to teach him; Eve couldn't drive a stick shift, so Will promised, in exchange for the painting lessons, to teach her how.

Most of all, their conversations were just a way to be together. Eve missed him—and told him so—and she knew he missed her, too. He always tried to keep the conversation going, never wanting to be the one to call it a night.

After making her mid-afternoon rounds of the museum, Eve strolled into Skye's office. She was hovering over her computer screen.

"God, I am amazed at how many emails I get on a daily basis! It's insane how companies always want to ally themselves with the museum so they can advertise themselves as charitable. Can you believe even strip clubs want to use us to drum up more business?"

She flipped quickly through her email, pressing the delete key half the time. "Oh! Something from Boston! Care to take a look?"

Eve walked around to read the email along with her.

Hello, Santa Barbara Museum of Art—

Thought I'd share the latest photos from the Boston Chamber of Commerce Dinner and Silent Auction. These functions have always served the BMA well as excellent fundraisers.

Both BMA and Townsend Industries reps were there. Enjoy!

—Jeannette Sheldon, Curator, Boston Museum Art

"Click on the attachment, click on the attachment!" Eve instructed, unable to hide her excitement.

Sure enough, the first photo showed Will *and Jeannette,* along with four other people from the Chamber of Commerce. Jeannette was grinning from ear to ear, but Will looked downright angry.

"Eww. What's up with Will?" Skye scrunched her nose. "Is that bitchy-looking Jeannette pinching his ass or something?"

Eve cringed. While she didn't know Jeannette well, it wouldn't have surprised her if that was exactly what she was doing.

Skye clicked on the next photo and both women were silent: Eve from shock and Skye from discomfort at having to witness Eve seeing an image of Jeannette and Will kissing.

"Shit." That was all Skye could say. She quickly clicked on the next image to replace the current one, but it was more of the same, this time with Jeannette and Will looking in each other's eyes. The final image wasn't much better, Jeannette's arm linked with Will's and her hand on his cheek.

"What the hell is this?" Skye was furious.

Eve couldn't hold back tears. Running to her office, she slammed the door and fell apart.

A few minutes passed before Skye and Josie tapped lightly on the door and opened it.

"Honey?" Josie whispered. "This *can't* be what it looks like. It just can't be. Will loves you. Everyone in this room knows that."

"Yeah, well, I thought that was where things were heading, but clearly Jeannette isn't as 'out of his life' as he said."

The sobbing was under control, but the tears just wouldn't stop.

"I can't believe he can talk to me every night—even *Tuesday* night after being with *her*—like he cares about me. 'I miss you, Eve!' he says." Turning toward the window, Eve began directing her comments to Will. "Sure you do, pal. You looked like you were *really* missing me while you were kissing *her*!"

Eve rubbed her hands across her cheeks to wipe away the tears.

"Well, there you have it, ladies. Eve has been *screwed* again!"

"No, Eve! I don't believe it." Skye went to the computer and pulled up her email with the photos.

"Look, Eve."

She didn't turn away from the window.

"Damn it, get over here and *look.*"

With an audible huff, Eve did as she was told and went over to see those horrid images.

"What do you see?—and I mean besides what you think is the obvious."

Eve rolled her eyes at her friend. "Get to the point, Skye, and then delete those pictures."

Skye got snippy. "Hmm. Let's see. Photo number one: posed. Jeannette's all smiles. Will looking like he wants to kill someone. Photo number two: not posed, except it's interesting how Jeannette seems to have positioned herself to make the most of the photographer's view. She's *pulling* him down to kiss her. See how her arm is all tensed? She's pulling *hard.* Photos three and four: same thing. These photos may *look* like two people being all lovey toward each other, but I'm telling you, Eve, she's the only one with the lovey look on her face. Will's pissed as hell."

"Whatever." Eve grabbed her purse. "Look, guys, I'm out of here for the day, OK? I just need to go home."

Josie pulled her into a hug while Skye rubbed her back. Then they let her go. Eve needed to be alone to process the information that had been thrown at her.

Wanting to get to the bottom of things as quickly as possible, Eve pulled out her phone and dialed Will's number as she left the museum. It was three o'clock, and she knew he would call in a few hours, but she just didn't want to wait.

When he answered, the sound of his voice almost made Eve forget why she was so upset.

"Eve! Oh, it's good to hear from you. Great timing, too, I was just boarding the jet. I wouldn't have had cell service if you'd called five minutes later. So, to what do I owe the pleasure of a daytime call?"

"I need to talk to you." The anger was re-building inside her, the images from Boston flashing in her head over and over.

"What's wrong? You sound like you're mad at me."

"What's up with you and Jeannette?"

"Wh-what? What do you mean?" That was the last thing that he had expected from Eve. He had thoroughly explained his relationship with Jeannette and couldn't understand why Eve was bringing it up.

"I mean, are you seeing her?" Eve sighed. "Look. We're not dating. I know that, so I realize this is really stupid for me to even be jealous or feel like you're cheating but—"

"Whoa, whoa! Back up. Start over. First of all, I am *not* with Jeannette. I've told you that. Second, you and I may not be dating, but I sure as hell wish we were. Now, what's this all about?"

"Skye received some, let's say, interesting photos of you and Jeannette from the event the two of you went to on Tuesday."

"OK. Photos showing what, may I ask?"

"Well, frankly, the two of you looking pretty much like a couple—including one where you're kissing her. For not being together, you two sure looked cozy."

"*What*?" Will couldn't even pretend to hide his anger over this—just one more sneaky, underhanded attempt by Jeannette to get him in her bed. He knew it.

"Look. We live 3,000 miles apart. Let's just leave it at that," said Eve. "When you're in Santa Barbara, we'll have lunch. But, Will, I don't want to get hurt thinking there's more to us than what there is. Obviously, there's not. My apologies."

"I've got to get on the jet. Can we talk about this when I get home?"

"I don't know."

"I'll be home in just a bit. We'll talk then, OK?"

"Yeah." Eve hung up feeling nothing had been accomplished.

Eve waited until she thought Will would be back in Boston before she tried to call him again. After spending the last few hours alternately biting her nails and wanting to ask Gage if she could use his punching bag, she needed to talk to Will, if only to finish things. She tried his cell. There was no answer.

Remembering that, all those weeks ago, Will had given her his card with his home number on it, Eve got up and searched her purse for it. She tried to figure out how they had gotten to where they were so quickly. Tears began to build behind her eyes, and she took a deep breath to keep them at bay.

Once she found Will's home number, her heart raced as she dialed and waited. The last thing Eve wanted was a confrontation, but she also wanted—no, needed—things to be on the table. If he was with Jeannette, then fine. He needed to be man enough to admit it. After the second ring, the call was answered.

"Hello?" a woman's voice cooed over the line.

"Um, yes, I was trying to reach Will Prentiss?" Eve prayed it was the cleaning woman who had answered the phone, though she already knew it wasn't.

"May I ask who's calling?" The woman's voice was very light—sultry yet pleasant.

"This is Eve Carwyn. I sort of work with him but...um...I'm in Santa Barbara." She stumbled over her words, trying to stay calm.

"Eve! Hello, there! It's me, Jeannette!"

Eve's heart stopped. She was stunned into silence.

"Eve? Are you surprised that I answered the phone, dear?" Jeannette's tone was suddenly condescending.

"Uhhh..." Still nothing but blank space for Eve.

"That's OK, dear. Actually, I'm not surprised at your reaction. All of the women he sees are taken aback when they realize they're not the only one in his life. You see, you're now 'the California one,' and I'm sure after being in Columbus these past few days, he's captured another woman's heart, and she'll call to get the news, too. I'm the only constant one in his life. He may philander around the country, but he always comes home to me. I'm sorry, but that's just Will. He breaks a lot of hearts, and I'm truly sorry yours had to be one of them."

"I just...um..."

A knock at the door interrupted Eve's scattered thoughts. She really didn't want to talk to Gage or Josie or anyone at that moment, so she ignored it. The situation was bad enough without all her friends knowing about this little conversation as well. Skye had a fabulous marketing mind, but as of that moment, there was no salvaging or spinning anything Eve had had with Will.

The knocking continued.

"Eve, understand that Will *does* care for you. He just can't commit to anyone but me. As a matter of fact, he's on his way home right now."

Finally exasperated, Eve pulled the door open, ready to blast the person on the other side with a string of profanities—words she didn't mind Jeannette hearing.

"Hi. I'm home."

Will.

Eve's mind and body were frozen. The phone remained against her ear as she stood there, staring at Will.

"May I come in?"

Still unable speak, Eve backed up, holding the door while Will entered the apartment.

"Eve? Are you still there? I know you're hurt but—"

On autopilot, Eve snapped the phone shut and dropped it to the carpet. The tears were immediate and unstoppable as she threw her arms around Will's neck and buried her face in his shoulder.

Will didn't hesitate to wrap his arms around her sobbing form, holding her tight while placing small kisses on top of her head.

"I take it you're not mad anymore?"

Unable to control the great sobs enough to actually speak, Eve shook her head no against his chest.

After a minute, Will loosened his grip to look her in the face. He gently wiped the tears from her cheeks. He wanted to make the world stop so he could go back and take away whatever had hurt her so badly.

"Now. What happened today?"

With a sniffle, Eve told him about the pictures Skye had received from Jeannette. Then her words became almost incomprehensible as she began to babble…

"...and I know I shouldn't have felt jealous, but I did, and I'm sorry, and I'm just confused because you and I have had...I don't know...*something* going on here, and our phone calls every night were always so wonderful, but then I see the two of you in those pictures and I just don't—"

Will's mouth was suddenly moving against Eve's, stopping her rant and sending waves of passion through her. Her tears and heaving sobs had Will panicked, and he had needed to make sure Eve knew that she was the only one he wanted, ever.

The two stood wrapped together for a long while, neither wanting to give up the security of just touching each other. When they finally released, Will placed one more gentle kiss on Eve's forehead.

"But Jeannette..." Eve started.

Will looked her right in the eye and said, "There is no Jeannette in my life. Only you."

"But I called your apartment, and she was there and—"

"*What?* How the hell did she get into my apartment?" He started to open his phone but stopped, a sly smile on his face as he formulated a plan to take care of Jeannette Sheldon once and for all. If she had somehow wormed her way into his apartment, he certainly was not happy about it, but if it gave him the opportunity to prove to Eve there was absolutely nothing between them, he would do just that.

"Eve. Can you officially be my girlfriend, please?"

"Umm." Eve faltered. She had thought about this conversation a lot over the last weeks, and never did she imagine Will asking like they were in junior high school. "Yes. That's a strange way to ask, but..."

"Good." Will caressed her face as he leaned down to gently kiss her. "I just want the record straight between the two of us, and we have been dancing around it for weeks. I don't want there to be any mistaking of my intentions or misunderstanding what I want from you, Eve."

It seemed like only a minute ago Eve had been ready to say goodbye to Will Prentiss, and now they were apparently "going steady." Eve's head was spinning.

"May I borrow your phone for a moment?" Will leaned down to pick the phone up off the floor. "Will you do me a favor? I'm going to call my apartment, but I want *you* to talk to Jeannette first. But let me listen in, will you?"

Looking at Will wide-eyed, Eve realized his plan was to trap Jeannette not only in his home, but lying about her relationship with him as well. There was a gleam in his eye, like a naughty four-year-old getting ready to build a tower of wobbly furniture to get to the cookies on the top shelf. Eve returned his smile.

With a quick kiss, he entered the phone number.

"Eve! I don't know what happened. We seemed to have gotten cut off." Jeannette's sickening sweet voice came over the line.

Eve gazed at Will as she spoke. "Yes. That was my fault. I dropped the phone, and it closed when it hit the floor." Will moved in closer so he could hear what Jeannette was saying.

"Well, I can't talk for long, dear. Will is going to be here any minute, and I've got a special evening planned for him. You understand, don't you?" Jeannette's condescending tone had returned.

Then Will took the phone, and Eve held his other hand in both of hers.

"No, Jeannette. I *don't* understand." Will's voice was calm but deadly.

"Will?" Jeannette's response was timid, hesitant.

"Yes, Jeannette. It's Will. I don't know how or why you're in my apartment, but you have three minutes to get out because I expect the police will be there in four. Now, they are going to either find my apartment empty, which is in your best interests, or they are going to arrest you for trespassing at the very least, and breaking and entering if I have anything to say about it." Snapping the phone shut, Will opened his own, pressing one number to get Megan on the phone.

"Megan. Hey. I'm sorry to bother you at home, but I need you to call the police and tell them my apartment has been broken into. No, I think everything is fine but when Eve called my apartment, Jeannette answered the phone... I have *no* idea. I never gave her a key... After you do that, call me back. I need you to do two other things as well... Thanks. I'll talk to you in a few minutes."

After ending that call, he began another, leaning toward Eve so she could listen in.

"Jeannette. Good. I'm glad you have your cell phone on. You've vacated my apartment, I assume?"

"Yes. But, Will, you don't understand!" Jeannette was crying.

"I understand that somehow you got into my apartment, made my girlfriend—"

"What? Will, but—"

"Excuse me. I was speaking." He was seething, yet his voice stayed steady. "You made my *girlfriend* think that you and I were together through some photos you sent and by talking to her just now like you're living with me."

"Will, I love you. You know that! I've always loved you. We belong together. Together, we can do great things, unlike that little girl you're wasting your time with."

It was Jeannette's turn to cry. Eve could hear her sobbing and was sure it was the first genuine emotion the woman had ever shown.

"I'm not finished." Will wanted to scream and yell. He wanted to defend Eve, but it wasn't the time for that. For the moment, he would be calm and concise. "Now, listen carefully, Jeannette. I have a little *task* for you to do tonight. I would suggest you get your resume in order. You're going to need it, because you are going to write a letter of resignation to the BMA effective immediately."

"What?" Jeannette screamed into the phone. "You can't fire me, Will! I don't know where you get off thinking—"

"Jeannette, you have two options. Resign and leave Boston or face criminal charges for breaking into my apartment. I believe the first option would be preferable, but the choice is yours. If you choose to call my bluff on this, all I have to do is contact one board member and you'll be fired, your reputation will be ruined, and you *will* be in jail. And right now, Jeannette, that's exactly where you belong as far as I'm concerned."

Jeannette began to sob again. "But, Will..."

Will cut her off. "Furthermore, I still have my IT staff checking Martin's computer. If they find that you were the one to change those spreadsheets, the first option will be off the table."

"Will, don't do this to me! Boston is my *home*! Where would I go?"

"Well, it had better not be Santa Barbara." Will smiled at Eve as she lifted his hand and kissed it.

"Will... Please, let's talk about this..."

"I'll be calling the Boston Museum of Art first thing Monday morning regarding your 'hasty resignation.' If they don't know what I'm talking about, I'll tell them every single detail and then have you arrested. *That* is the extent of any further talking I'm going to do on this subject. Goodbye."

Will tossed his phone on the couch before pulling Eve to him and wrapping his arms around her. He closed his eyes, reveling in knowing she truly was his.

"So, I guess we're dating, huh?" Will's voice was thick with emotion.

"That's the latest rumor. Do you think it's true?" Eve smiled at him, finally easing into his arms and fully processing that he was actually there with her.

"I most certainly hope so," he whispered, and once again brought his mouth to hers, kissing her fully until they were interrupted by his phone.

Will ignored the ringing, instead lingering at Eve's lips. With a sigh, he finally broke the kiss and answered the phone on the third ring.

"Hey, Megan... Oh, good. I was going to ask if you'd go over there for me. I'd really like to be sure she didn't take anything of mine or leave anything of hers... Sure! Take Dan with you, I don't mind! I'll also need you to use your key to lock it back up... Yeah, I'm sure the plants could use watering, too—thanks! Yes, actually, that was going to be my next request... And it's a locksmith you've used before? OK, that sounds good. If you tell them there was a break-in, they should be pretty quick to respond. Make sure you get three keys and keep one yourself, of course..." Then he laughed. "I don't deserve you, Megan. I owe you for this... Absolutely! You and Dan can eat anywhere in Boston on Townsend's dime. Yes, Apex included." He winked at Eve who smiled back at him. "Oh, before you go, did you hear back from Brenda or Pete? Ahh... Just the news I needed to hear, thanks. Yeah, I'm at Eve's... OK. Thanks again, Megan. Bye."

Pocketing the phone, Will turned to Eve, wrapped his arms around her and pulled her into his body.

"Now, Miss Carwyn, since I have intruded on your evening, I guess it's only fair to ask if you already had plans or if the two of us might go for a drive."

"Well, John Cusack wasn't available tonight but I was thinking of watching movies with Johnny Depp."

"Is there any way I can convince you to cancel, or do I have to fight for your attention? Because I'll do it if I need to. I mean, you *are* my girlfriend now, so fighting for you is part of the package."

"Nah. I'll just leave a note on the door for him." Eve smiled, taking in how beautiful he was. "So where do you want to go?"

"It's a surprise."

"Oh, really! You have me intrigued! Let me just change—are jeans OK or do you suggest something else?"

Will thought about suggesting nothing at all, but instead said, "Jeans will be fine."

Now that Eve knew Will wanted more out of their relationship, she had half a mind to go ahead and undress right there in front of him—perhaps even solicit his help—but she knew that *that* would have led to the bedroom rather than the car, and he seemed determined to take her on this mysterious drive. Her bed would be here when they returned, and she wasn't holding back any more.

It only took a few minutes for Eve to change, making sure to put on her new lace bra and panties...*for later*...and the two headed out the door. The same uncontrollable smile that had first appeared on Eve's face in Boston was back in full force—and it felt good.

"Are you going to give me any clues?" Eve asked after they had been driving in silence for several minutes.

"Nope. Not a one."

"Stinker."

Will smirked as he reached over to grab one Eve's hand, pulling it to his lips and kissing the back of it.

Evidently Will knew where he was going, but soon he was driving on roads Eve wasn't completely familiar with. After about fifteen minutes, he turned onto a long and narrow driveway lined with tall trees. The car came to a stop in front of a small home with only a porch light on.

Eve hadn't any idea whose house this was, but it appeared no one was home. Will came around the car and opened Eve's door, taking her hand and helping her out. They stopped in front of the door, bathed in the light from overhead.

"Where are we? Whose house is this?"

"This is my surprise." Will smiled. "Remember last week how I was on the phone a lot and how I wanted to go 'sightseeing' on my own? I know that bothered you, and I hated not telling you, but I didn't want you to know what I was trying to do in case things didn't work out." Her eyes were suddenly sad. "No, no! Not if things didn't work out between *us*, I meant if *my* plans didn't pan out."

"So...?"

"I was house hunting." Will smiled and Eve's eyes lit up.

"You bought a house? You, you bought *this* house?"

"Yeah. I bought this house. Brenda, the real estate agent I've been working with here, has been wonderful. I told her what I was looking for, and she did everything else! Do you want to see?"

Eve nodded her head vigorously, and Will dug in his pocket for the key Brenda had sent to him in Boston, along with the title paperwork.

He unlocked the door and pushed it open, allowing Eve to enter first. *I guess carrying her across the threshold is a bit premature*, he mused. Reaching around just inside the door, he flipped on the light in the small living room.

"It's already furnished?" Eve gasped.

The larger pieces of furniture were still draped in plastic, and boxes were stacked against one wall, as well as some framed pictures that would soon decorate the walls. Over the fireplace that ran along the back wall of the house, a larger piece was draped in dark linen.

"I told you, Brenda did *everything* for me. And received a hefty thank-you check along with her commission."

Eve looked around but didn't move from where she stood near the door.

"How about I give you the grand tour, then?" He took her hand, and they peeked in the rooms, all decorated simply but elegantly. Will noticed Eve's eyes linger over the king-size bed in the master bedroom.

"She even arranged to have linens on the bed and shampoo in the shower?"

"Everything. I think she even stocked my pantry and fridge with a few things. I just told her what I wanted and ordered a lot of things online. She personally came over and got the place ready for me to show you tonight."

"So, this Brenda was in on the whole thing, hmm?"

"She's quite the romantic. When I told her about you, she was thrilled at the opportunity to help me out in any way I needed."

"It's all so beautiful, Will! It...it kind of reminds me—"

"Of Tom and Noelle's?"

"Yeah."

"That was my intent. When we were over there, the warmth of their home was amazing. It filled every room. I wanted that for here, too."

"So, you bought a house. In Santa Barbara." Her eyes narrowed as she looked at him, wanting to understand what that meant for him, for both of them.

Will suddenly became formal, stepping away from her and leaning against the back of the couch. "Well, it makes sense, actually. Investing in real estate is always a good idea, and besides, the SBMA project is much larger than any other I've worked with. Other museums have simply looked to add to their collections or create traveling exhibits. You're creating something literally from the ground up. I'll need to be spending extensive periods of time here to oversee everything."

"And, is that the main reason you chose to buy a house here? I mean, the construction of the children's wing will be done in less than three years."

"Well, truth be told," he said with a smile, "I kind of like Santa Barbara, and I think I've got a good reason to want to spend more time here."

"You do, huh?"

"Come here. I want to show you something." Will reached for her hand and walked her toward the middle of the living area. "It's another surprise." He let go of her hand and walked toward the fireplace. He gently lifted and removed the drape from the picture that rested on the mantle and turned toward Eve, watching for her reaction.

"Oh, Will." Her eyes teared up, single drops falling down each cheek.

Will tossed the drape on the couch and came to stand behind her, placing his hands on her shoulders, kissing the back of her head.

Over the fireplace was a portrait of Eve, created by local artist Pete Norris. It was a painted version of one of the photos Will had taken of her in the park. She hadn't seen this particular picture—Will knew the moment he took the photo what he wanted to do with it and had chosen not to download it with the other shots he put on her computer. In the portrait, which Pete had completed so quickly and perfectly, Eve smiled gently as she looked over at some children playing, a gentle breeze blowing her hair back from her face. She had been leaning against the tree, and the mix of sunlight and shadows made her absolutely radiant.

Will wrapped his arms around Eve's waist and leaned his chin against her shoulder as they both gazed at the portrait.

"It's beautiful."

"It's the woman I've fallen in love with." He turned her toward him and took her face in his hands. "Eve Carwyn, I love you."

"Oh, Will, I love you, too." She immediately threw her arms around his neck and they kissed each other fully but tenderly.

When they parted, she gazed up at him, conveying with her eyes a desire Will had only seen hints of before. "Will you let me show you how much I love you?" she whispered. "I want to make love to you. Will you let me?"

He crushed his mouth to hers, exploring and tasting her, loving her. Sweeping her into his arms, he brought her to the master bedroom and set her down at the foot of the bed. His hand caressed her face as they saw in each other's eyes what they both wanted.

Their moves were slow, both of them savoring each moment, each touch, each tender kiss. He continued to gaze at her as his fingers came together at the top button of her shirt. Eve stood back from him just enough so he could unfasten it. As he moved to the second button, she brought her hands up to caress his arms, willing him to continue. When he had all of them unfastened, he spread open the fabric and moved her shirt down her arms, letting it drop to the floor and leaving her in only her white lace bra. She lifted her face to his and pulled him into another deep but gentle kiss. It felt right to take this slowly, feeling the passion as it continued to build. This was what Eve had been waiting for.

"My turn," she said as she began the same ritual with him. He moved his hands in gentle circles on her back as she unbuttoned his shirt and tugged on it to release it from his pants. As she repeated his motions, pushing the shirt from his shoulders and down his arms, Eve brought her face directly to his chest and laid kiss after kiss on his smooth skin.

She could feel Will's heart racing as her hands and mouth continued to explore him. There was no stopping this time, no holding back for either of them. She moved her hands to his back, bringing them slowly downward until they were on the back of his pants.

"May I?" Will whispered as he placed his hands at the front snap of her jeans. Nodding in silence, Eve then returned to kissing and touching his chest, letting her tongue glide gently across his nipples. *I love how you taste.*

He eased the zipper of her jeans down and caressed her hips as he lowered her clothing to the floor, revealing the lace panties underneath. She stepped out of the jeans and sandals, kicking them aside. Will glanced down at her, a look of pure desire in his eyes, and then pulled her to him, capturing her mouth with his.

They continued to kiss and Eve removed Will's belt. As she moved her hands to lower the zipper, she pressed against him gently, feeling his hardness through the fabric.

Everything about you is perfect. Once his pants and shoes were in a pile next to Eve's, Will lifted her into his arms. He brought her to the side of the bed where she was able to reach down and pull back the covers, revealing beautiful satin sheets underneath.

Will placed Eve gently on the bed and immediately joined her, his hand brushing from her waist, up across her breast, and on to the strap of her bra. He looked at her longingly as he traced the strap around to the back. She leaned toward him as his fingers found and released the clasp. He removed her bra and brought his mouth down to sweetly kiss and tease each breast, flicking his tongue across her sensitive nipples and causing heat to rise in her skin.

Eve tangled her hands in his hair as he continued to caress her. The desire she had for him was increasing rapidly, and she sensed he could bring her more pleasure than she'd ever known. She wanted that. Lord, did she want that.

"Will..." Eve sighed. "God, how I love you."

As he brought his mouth back to hers, she began to move her hands downward on his body, finally touching the part of him she wanted inside of her. *Just touching you is amazing.*

They broke their kiss for a moment and gazed at each other, seeing that they were both ready for more. He brought his hands to her stomach and slipped his fingers beneath the lace. Eve lifted her hips, and Will slowly removed her panties. He placed a warm palm against her leg as he moved back up her body, sending shockwaves through her when he brushed his hand along her inner thigh.

Eve brought her knees up and spread her legs slightly, inviting his fingers to explore further. Her warmth and wetness made him groan with desire, and the slow but deliberate movements of his fingers made her gasp and lift her hips again, begging him to go deeper.

He began to tease her breasts with his tongue again as his fingers continued to move within her, and she felt she was about to reach her peak. Will brought his hand back up, gliding it across her stomach, leaving a trail of moisture. He positioned himself over her, his arms on either side of her shoulders, and leaned in to kiss her mouth gently. Placing her hands on the waistline of his boxers, Eve lowered them to his knees, where he maneuvered them further down and off to the side, buried somewhere under the covers.

"Make love to me, Will." Eve raised her knees again, spreading her legs and moving her hands down his chest and abdomen, then allowing her fingertips to gently caress him. He lowered himself and soon was inside her. They both gasped, taking in the immediate pleasure of the combination of love and desire.

His movements were gentle, meaningful, at first. They gazed at each other, placing sweet kisses on each other's throats and lips. But soon, desire took over and Eve moved with him, increasing the force of him in her. She teased his mouth and chest with her tongue, and he responded until they were both breathless with pleasure. He lowered his chest to hers, their hearts pounding against each other. She wrapped her legs around him, keeping him inside her, feeling his pulse throbbing within her abdomen. He lifted his head to look at her and they both smiled. This had been more than sex. It was perfect.

"Speechless," Eve whispered.

"Yeah, speechless." Will kissed her fully once more as her hands ran over his bare back.

He rolled over and pulled her to him. He moved his lips to Eve's forehead, nuzzling her with his nose. "I love you, Eve."

"I love you, too, Will. Always."

Chapter Twenty-four

Skye saw Julian sitting and staring at his painting again as she came into work Monday morning. If she'd been feeling more herself, she would have gone over and made his life miserable for a few minutes, but with the way things spewed from her mouth without the benefit of censorship of her brain lately, she didn't think that was a very good idea—even for Julian.

Instead, Skye went straight to Eve's office to try to convince her to let her throw him out. But, as she walked down the hall, Skye heard Josie's high-pitched squeal coming from her office and was immediately sidetracked from her original goal. Turning into Josie's office, Skye joined Eve at her desk.

Josie held out her left hand, and there sat one of the most beautiful, flawless diamonds Skye had ever seen.

"Oh, Josie! Beau proposed?" Eve's smile was almost as big as the one Josie was wearing.

Josie couldn't even speak; she just bobbed her head up and down, her eyes welling up. Eve and Skye pulled her into a giant hug. They couldn't have been happier for their friend.

"Josie, how did he do it? We want all the details, woman," Skye demanded.

"Ooh, since I missed brunch yesterday, let's all go to lunch today, and I'll give you the details then," Josie suggested.

"Well, actually we all missed brunch yesterday," Eve chimed in, the smile on her face growing wider as she remembered what she had been doing instead.

Josie looked at her friends with questioning eyes.

"Yeah, Eve was busy doing Will, Noelle was busy doing Thomas, and I was busy...well, you get the picture."

"Wait. Will?" Josie looked at Eve.

"He came back on Friday night, and, Josie, he bought a house here in Santa Barbara!" Eve looked at her watch. I'll tell you all more at lunch. I have a meeting in five minutes, and I need to get my files together. Lunch at Marlowe's at 11:30?"

"Yeah, I'll call Noelle and see if she can make it, too," Skye called after Eve as she trotted down the hall.

"So, Will came back already?" Josie asked, knowing Skye would have the details. But it wasn't her story to share; Eve needed to be the one to tell everyone.

"He came back Friday night, and when I couldn't find Eve all day on Saturday, I panicked. You know I still don't trust Julian."

Josie rolled her eyes at Skye's over-cautiousness.

"So, I was calling her like every two minutes. After about twenty minutes, she finally called me back and told me the whole story. But, you'll have to wait until lunch to hear all the details from Eve herself."

Skye turned back to her office.

"You suck, Skye!" Josie called after her.

Skye just smiled. She was truly happy for her friends, and if she'd felt better, she would have been happy for herself, too. She had everything she needed: Gage. She knew that one day, he would propose and she would accept. Although he was not the most romantic guy—a small twinge of jealousy flashed as she tried to imagine what Beau did for Josie, and buying a house here in Santa Barbara, Will was pretty suave, too—but Skye was sure Gage would always protect her and keep her safe. He had noticed she was feeling a bit off and convinced her to make a doctor's appointment. Skye only did it because she figured it must be bad if even Gage was noticing. Her appointment wasn't until two, so lunch at 11:30 would be perfect.

Julian had once again spent the morning sitting on his bench in the museum. As he watched the people around him stop and comment on his work, he knew today was the day. All his careful planning over the past few weeks was going to pay off.

From where he sat, Julian was able to catch glimpses of Eve as she went about doing her job. He would hear her laughter and look up to see her, a radiant smile dancing on her lips. *She is my Eve and always will be. Today starts our new life together.* The sound of her happiness helped him realize he'd made the right decision to involve that Jeannette woman in his plans.

Unfortunately, the position of the bench also allowed Julian to catch sight of the bitch, Skylar, and that tramp, Josie. Once Eve was away from their influence, she would be the perfect woman he knew she was. As he glanced up, he saw the whore in her high heels standing in the lobby, staring at him. Normally, Julian would have kept up the façade and smiled at her. Today, however, he was finding it very difficult to do.

When he heard Eve's laughter echoing in the marble expanse of the lobby, Julian immediately forced himself to smile at Skylar. He had to do it for Eve. She came into his line of vision, and the smile she had made his heart leap. He was sure it was there for him. *She must know we're going to be together soon.*

Julian knew that Will Prentiss had left over a week ago. On that morning, he'd been parked across the street from Eve's apartment building—again—and when Prentiss left, Julian had followed. If the Jeannette angle didn't work, maybe he could catch *him* doing something that would make Eve unhappy. But instead, Julian followed him to the airport and watched as he left the rental car in favor of a private jet. With Prentiss gone, Julian knew it was time to set things in motion and make Eve his again.

His final stroke of true genius had been hiring the escort. It had cost him a fortune, but it was well worth the money. Having Miranda by his side every time he'd run into Eve had put everyone more at ease. Julian knew Eve didn't really believe he would be with someone else. *That is why she was so sad when I saw her at the mall.* He was sure she had wanted to reach out to him that day.

But, today, seeing him without Miranda, she probably knew it was time for the game to end. The smile he'd seen was the sign he needed. It warmed him and encouraged him to activate the next part of his plan.

Noelle was already at Marlowe's when the others walked in. She smiled at all of them, pulling each into a hug.

It seemed like forever since they'd all been together at the party she and Tom had given, Skye thought. That was the night she'd been convinced she was pregnant. *Had it only been two weeks ago?* A thought suddenly hit her like a blow to the chest: It had been two weeks since she'd taken the pregnancy test, and her last period had been two weeks prior to that. *Oh shit!*

Skye dropped into her side of the booth, and the look on her face must have shown what was going through her mind. All three of her friends were staring at her.

"Okay, Josie. Details. Now." Skye recovered quickly, deflecting the focus from herself.

Everyone turned to Josie, who was beaming from ear to ear. She went through each detail, starting with the way Beau had been acting weird and distant all week and then had asked her to spend Sunday with him.

They were interrupted by the waitress getting their order. Skye tried to remember if they'd ever been to Marlowe's other than for brunch and realized they hadn't. How different all of their lives were from just a few months ago. Once the waitress had taken their orders and left to get their drinks, Josie continued. When she got to the part where she and Beau were having their favorite dinner in a white tent on the beach, with a heartfelt proposal for dessert, the three other women leaned in closer.

"Josephine McInnis," Beau had said. "You are everything I have ever wanted or needed to make my life perfection. There is nothing more I need to make me whole, and when you aren't with me, I feel like a piece of me is missing. I ache when I am away from you. I love you with everything that I am. I don't want to let one more sunset pass without knowing that you will be my wife and spend the rest of eternity with me."

The women sighed in unison.

"Damn, Josie! How did you get so lucky?" Skye asked, still trying to convince herself that what she was thinking couldn't possibly be right.

"I don't know, but I am never letting him go." Glancing at the ring on her finger, Josie sighed. "OK, your turn, Eve."

Skye listened intermittently as Eve explained how Jeannette had answered Will's phone and then Will showed up at her door. She could hear Noelle and Josie gasp and sigh at the appropriate times, but couldn't pull herself together enough to participate. Once again Skye worried about the possibility of being pregnant. And this time she didn't have Gage right next to her to tell her everything would be OK. She really needed that. Panic bubbled up, and Skye did her best to stamp it down.

"So…how was he? You know…in bed?" Noelle asked in a quiet voice.

"No way, Noelle, did you just ask Eve if Will was good in bed?" Skye laughed. About the only thing that would have pulled Skye back to the conversation was Noelle asking Eve about sex.

Turning to Eve, who was bright red, Skye asked, "Well? Was he?"

"Umm…let's just say, phenomenal wouldn't even describe it. I was speechless." Eve quickly moved her hands to cover her face, but the smile never faded.

"And, we were all right, too," Josie added. "He told you he loved you, didn't he?"

"Yes. And, God, do I love him." If it were possible, Eve would have blushed even deeper, but Noelle's question had already pushed her to the limit.

When Skye returned to her office after spending what seemed like *days* in the doctor's office, she was overcome with emotion and went right to her phone to call Gage. He answered immediately.

"Hey, Baby. What did the doctor say?"

"Hi, Gage. Well, let me ask you a question."

"What?"

"Remember a few weeks ago when I thought I was pregnant, and I took the test?" Skye could hear the hitch in his voice as he drew a breath in.

"Uh-huh."

"How well did you read those directions, babe?"

"Skye, are you trying to tell me we are having a baby?" Skye could hear a huge smile in Gage's voice.

"Yes." The word got stuck in her throat. On the verge of tears, Skye wasn't sure if they were tears of joy, anger, or a combination of both.

"Skye, you know I love you, right? I love you, and I love that you are having my baby, and I love that we are going to be a family." His voice was so sincere. Skye knew that although he would never be a big romantic, or a gazillionaire, he was going to be a great daddy.

"I love you, Gage." And with that the tears began to flow. She couldn't stop them, and really didn't try. For the first time in almost two weeks, Skylar Montgomery felt right. Deep in her heart, she knew this was all meant to be.

"Come home to me, baby. Come home and let's celebrate. Wait, did you ask the doctor if it's still OK to have sex?" Gage's voice had been deep and sultry until he thought about the sex part, then he sounded like a little boy. Skye laughed.

"Yes, Gage. He said it was fine, so don't panic."

"Well, then get your beautiful ass home, and I'll be there waiting for you."

"I'm on my way. I just want to check in with Eve and Josie real quick and then I'm headed home." Somehow, they both knew that *home* was his apartment.

"I love you with all my heart, Skylar."

"I know. And I love you."

Skye sat at her desk a few minutes more, thinking about how much her life had changed in the past month. Her hand began to rub circles over her stomach. *Oh, my God. I am going to be a mother.* She smiled to herself at the thought.

The doctor told her that when she took the test before, it could have been too early or they might have read the results wrong. Since Skye didn't check the results herself, she was betting on the latter. Eventually she was able to stand without her knees buckling, and she got up to check in on Eve and Josie before she left. Eve was at her desk, working busily, but as she glanced across the hall, she saw that Josie was already gone for the day.

"Hey, Eve."

"Oh, Skye. I didn't hear you. Are you out of here?" she asked.

"Yeah, Gage's waiting for me. What happened to Josie?"

"She skipped out after lunch. She couldn't sit still so she decided to get started on the wedding plans."

"Oh, geez. She just got engaged yesterday." Skye rolled her eyes.

"I know, but it's so exciting. You can't blame her."

"Do you want me to stay until you're done?" Skye didn't like the idea of Eve leaving by herself, especially as it was starting to get dark.

"No. You go home to Gage." Eve stared at Skye for a minute. "Skye, are you all right? You know that we love you, and you can talk to us."

"I'm perfect, Eve, really." And it was the truth. Everything was perfect.

"OK, see you tomorrow then."

"Are you sure you don't want me to wait for you?"

"No, really. I'll be here, like, five more minutes, and then I'm meeting Will at his house."

"All right. 'Night, Eve."

Skye made her way through the employee door and out into the evening to her car. She was ready to celebrate with the sweetest, sexiest man on the planet.

Julian had been waiting for what seemed like years, watching as museum workers filed out of the building. He'd watched her friend leave hours ago, but still he waited. That wasn't who he was looking for. Then, finally, the door opened and *she* appeared, walking to the parking lot. The sun had just set, which gave him enough darkness to maneuver into position.

She wasn't paying attention to her surroundings and seemed to be living in her own head. Julian couldn't have asked for anything more.

As she walked past, Julian stepped out in front of her and saw fear register in her eyes. She turned to run the other way but wasn't fast enough. Julian closed the distance between them in just one step. Grabbing her from behind, he slipped one hand over her mouth and the other around her waist, pulling her tight to his body. As soon as his arm was around her, her body went limp and she stopped fighting him.

He was able to get her in the car and restrain her with little effort. It was as if she knew this was happening and wanted it. Or maybe she thought he was going to hurt her. Once she was tied and gagged, Julian laid her down on the back seat. The whole thing had only taken a few minutes, and as he glanced around, the parking lot was still totally empty.

The car started easily and Julian pulled out with care. It wouldn't do to get stopped by the police right now. He was good at the game, but with her tied up in the back seat, that one might be hard to get out of.

He glanced back at her and smiled. "This is all for the best. In the end, this will be for the best. Now settle down. I don't want you to hurt yourself."

Chapter Twenty-five

Holy shit! I'm going to be a dad!

Gage closed his eyes and took a deep breath as he ended his call with Skye and shoved his cell in his pocket. *Holy shit! I'm going to be a dad!*

He wasn't sure what he needed to do next, but he had to get his ass home and be there when Skye showed up. *Holy shit! I'm going to be a dad!*

He couldn't tell anyone yet, but that didn't mean he couldn't be happy. *Holy shit! I'm going to be a dad!*

With was a huge grin on his face, he made his way to the front desk of the gym.

"Why are you smiling like that, Gage? Did one of the bouncing bimbos have an implant explode?" Heather asked.

Holy shit! I'm going to be a dad!

When he picked her up and gave her a huge hug, Heather's eyes grew wide. She smacked his shoulder while yelling for him to put her down.

"What the hell, Gage? I mean, I've seen that girlfriend of yours." She glanced at the door, probably afraid that Skye would walk through it. "And I know that I do *not* want her pissed at me for being all over her man."

"Don't worry, I think she would be just fine with it. I am just super psyched right now." *Holy shit! I'm going to be a dad!*

"Why?"

"That part I can't tell. Hey, I'm taking the rest of the day off. I only have one more client; can you call and cancel for me?"

By the look on her face, Heather didn't want to, so he moved into his sad, little boy pout.

"Oh, please. That crap may work on someone who loves you, big guy, but... Oh, what the hell, just go."

"Thank you, Heather. I owe you big time for this." He kissed her on the cheek before heading out the door and home to Skye. *Holy shit! I'm going to be a dad!*

As he drove, Gage thought he needed to do something nice for Skye. He was pretty sure that on an occasion like this, some sort of romantic crap would be a good idea. The problem was, he had no idea what he could do in—how long would it be before Skye got home? He did the math quickly and figured she'd be talking to Eve and Josie for ten more minutes, then it would take her another twenty minutes to get to his place. He had about half an hour.

But what the hell do you buy your pregnant girlfriend to let her know how much you love her and want this...what? What was this? Family.

Gage pulled into the parking lot of the nearest grocery store. He wanted something that would let Skye know how happy he was. Walking up and down each aisle, he knew he had to figure things out quickly. When he rounded the corner onto the baby aisle, his face lit up. Right next to the diapers was a cardboard display with a bunch of books for pregnant women. *What to Expect When You're Expecting*? Perfect. He had no idea what to expect and figured Skye didn't either.

He flipped through the book, hoping it might give him another idea. The word "cravings" jumped off the page at him. Would Skye have those? Well, he was in a grocery store.

Ten minutes later, armed with several bags full of anything chocolate, salty, and tangy the could get his hands on, plus the pregnancy book and a small rattle with a duck on it, Gage pulled into the parking garage at his building. He noticed Eve wasn't home yet and didn't see Skye's car either. Still too early for her to be home.

Gage figured he had less than fifteen minutes, and he went to work setting out all the food he bought. He found an unused Christmas bow in a shoebox in the hall closet, peeled the back off of it, and stuck it on top of the book. Then he headed off to clean up.

Once showered and dressed, he walked back out to the living room, fully expecting to find Skye there. But the room was empty. It had been close to forty-five minutes since they'd talked. She should have been home by now.

Gage dialed Skye, a knot forming in the pit of his stomach. She was *never* late, and if she were stuck in traffic she would have called. The phone rang four times and went to voice mail. He listened to Skye's voice, and after the three little beeps, he left a message.

"Hey, Babe! Where are you? I hope you have at least left the museum. Call me. I love you."

He began to pace. Something didn't feel right. This wasn't like Skye. Another half hour and four more voice messages later, Gage *knew* something was definitely wrong.

Opening the phone again, he dialed a different number this time.

"Hello?" The perky voice came over the phone.

"Hi, Josie. It's Gage."

"Gage? What can I do for you?"

"Are you with Skye?" He tried to keep calm.

"No. I haven't seen her since lunch. Why?"

"She's just late, no big deal. But her phone is off. She said she was going to stop and see you and Eve before she came home."

"Oh, Gage. I left early today. She's probably with Eve." Gage prayed she was right.

"OK, then. I'll try Eve. Thanks, Josie."

"No problem. Tell Skye to call me." And then she was gone.

Immediately, Gage dialed Eve's cell. She answered on the second ring.

"Hey, Gage. What's up?"

"Uhh…Eve, is Skye with you?" Gage's voice wavered, and he tried to get himself under control.

"No. I'm with Will. She said she was on her way home to you when she left my office. What's the matter, Gage?"

"She should have been home over an hour ago, Eve. She isn't answering her phone, and I just have a gut feeling."

"Maybe she went to her place? Did you try her there?"

"No. We didn't say which home we were meeting at though. So, yeah, maybe." It still didn't feel right.

"Give her a call there. We're on our way to my place, I'll check in when I get home."

"All right. Bye, Eve." The pit in Gage's stomach grew wider with each passing minute.

He got no answer at Skye's apartment either, but left a message.

"Damn it, Skye! Where the hell are you?"

"What's wrong?"

Will glanced over to see worry on Eve's face as she put the phone back in her purse.

"That was Gage. He said Skye hasn't shown up at his place yet, and she's not answering her cell."

"Could she have stopped off some place where there's no cell reception?"

Eve thought about that. "I don't know. Maybe. But I can tell he's worried. I told him I'd check back with him when we get to my place."

Will put his hand over hers, squeezing her fingers gently. "I'm sure everything's fine. She's probably there already." But as he turned his eyes back to the road, he seemed tense.

When the pair entered Eve's apartment, she plopped the grocery bags on the kitchen counter. After work, Eve had gone to Will's house, and together they'd gone to the store for things each needed: for her, actual food items and for him, cleaning supplies. The plan was to drop off the groceries, grab a bite to eat, then head back to his place to do some simple sprucing up.

Will excused himself to use the restroom as Eve began to put things away. Seeing the blinking light on the answering machine, she pressed the button to listen, hoping it was a message from Skye. It wasn't.

BEEP – "*Hello, Eve. I've missed you. These past few weeks have been terrible for me, but I had to stay away from you so I could get everything arranged for us. Please don't be mad or jealous about Miranda. I don't love her—I never did. I only love you. You know that, right, Eve? I've got to be away for a few days. There are a few museums interested in my work so I'm traveling to meet with other curators. Plus, I'm taking care of some...issues...that have interfered with our relationship. Very soon we'll have our perfect life, and we can be together forever.*"

Will entered the kitchen as the last few words of Julian's message played, and he saw Eve's face, frozen as she stared at the machine. He immediately pulled her to him and replayed the message.

"Don't panic, Eve. OK? Don't panic."

"He did something. Oh God, he's done something to Skye."

"This isn't happening. This can't be happening." Skye kept repeating the words over and over, trying to calm herself. She closed her eyes as tears began to flow freely. She lay in the back seat of the car, her hands and feet tied and something over her mouth, forcing her to breathe only through her nose. Protecting the baby was the only thought in her head.

When Julian had stepped out of the shadows, she had frozen. Her mind told her to scream—get away from him. But her body didn't obey. She had just stood there. For a quick second, Skye looked right into his eyes, and there was nothing. No humanity. It was the most bone-chilling moment of her life. When Skye's body finally reacted, it was too late. She didn't get far before he grabbed her.

Under different circumstances, Skye would have fought with everything she had. But, in an instant, something told her not to. Right then, Skye knew keeping the baby safe was the most important thing. So going limp, she let Julian take her. As much as she thought the guy was a creep, Skye didn't think he was going to hurt her. That was the hope she was clinging to now.

Her stomach churned as she focused her energy to not getting sick. With her mouth covered, *that* would be a bad idea. All her energy needed to be going toward getting out of this. Getting home to Gage.

Gage would be so worried about her. He knew she would never be late. Her only hope was that he would figure out somehow that it had been Julian. The thought of what Gage would do to Julian filled her with hope, but she couldn't stop the tears. Skye silently prayed for Gage to find her, soon.

Julian was mumbling something from the front seat, but even as she strained to hear him, she couldn't. They seemed to have been driving forever, but Skye was sure it had been less than an hour. If she could figure out where he was taking her, she thought that might calm her. But because it was dark, Skye couldn't see anything as she lay staring out the window. The only hint she had was the brief light as an oncoming car's headlights flashed by.

There had been very few cars on the road with them for a while now, and Skye's heart began to beat harder. The lack of traffic made her realize they had left the main highway, and that wasn't a good thing. Being in the woods with Julian, alone at night, did not seem like a place she wanted to be.

Gage had been pacing the same path for half an hour. He also dialed Skye's cell over and over again. Still nothing. When he heard the knock at the door, Gage stopped in his tracks. The short distance to the door was easily covered in just two steps, and as Gage yanked the door open, he didn't know whether he was going to grab Skye in a hug or scold her for having her phone off. Standing in the door, however, was Eve with Will by her side. Gage cursed under his breath.

"Eve. She isn't at her place, and she still isn't answering her cell. I'm going crazy here."

"Gage..."

"What, Eve? What? Do you know where she is?"

"I think we do. You need to come over to my place, Gage. I have something you need to hear." Eve's voice was even and quiet, as she tried to calm Gage.

"Eve, this isn't helping me. Just tell me!" Before Gage realized what he was doing, he had grabbed Eve's arm.

Will stepped in and peeled the bodybuilder's hand from around Eve's wrist.

"I'm so sorry, Eve. I didn't hurt you, did I? I'm just going crazy." On the verge of losing it, Gage was frantic and hoped they understood that. He would never hurt a woman, and most certainly not Eve.

"Gage. You need to calm down." Will stood directly in front of him. "Eve got a message on her answering machine that we want you to listen to. We don't want to say anything that might cloud how you hear it. Please, come over to Eve's."

Taking a deep breath to clear his head, Gage reminded himself that Skye was a big girl who had lived on her own for years without Gage's help. She was fine. He followed them back to Eve's apartment, his dread deepening with each step.

Eve went over to her answering machine and pressed play. As soon as Gage heard the voice, his blood ran cold.

...plus, I'm taking care of some...issues...that have interfered with our relationship. Very soon we'll have our perfect life, and we can be together forever.

Julian had taken Skye. Gage just knew it. He played the message again.

...plus, I'm taking care of some...issues...that have interfered with our relationship...

"I'll kill him! If he hurts Skye or... God, I'll kill him."

"This is all for the best. Now settle down. I don't want you to hurt yourself."

Keeping the bitch calm was important only until Julian could get her to the house. After that, she could scream and yell all she wanted to and no one would ever hear her. Something Julian knew from experience. No one ever heard.

All the planning and acting like Eve was no longer in his life had gone perfectly. There was only one person among them all who didn't believe, and she wasn't going to be around much longer. Julian knew every time Skye looked at him that she saw through everything, and he couldn't have that.

Flipping on the overhead light, Julian glanced in the rearview mirror. She was crying; an interesting reaction for the whore. He never thought she was capable of any emotion other than lust. As soon as he took the tape from her mouth, she would start with her vulgar language, berating him. But that was OK. She wouldn't be talking for long.

"Only a little while longer, Eve. We will be together again." He hoped the bitch heard every word. He wanted her to know this wasn't about her. It was all for Eve. She was going to die for Eve.

It had taken some time to get the house ready. Just being there for any length of time without hyperventilating had taken a few days. Before he even entered the house, his eyes automatically went to the place where the shed had been all those years ago. Beyond that were two nearly unnoticeable mounds that to anyone else looked like part of the rolling hills of his backyard. Julian knew the truth, though.

The day his parents died, Julian had burned the shed to the ground. He thought that would cleanse him from the memories of the daily beatings he'd received there. In the house, Julian could still hear his father's voice as he yelled at him time and time again. "What are you? A total pansy? Art? What kind of future can you have with that? Be a man." The echoes of his life screamed at him. And his mother hadn't been any better. She never defended Julian against the monster, never tried to help him. Julian hated them both.

The irony of the hell he had grown up in was that he had never been gay—never had one thought about a man. He had fallen in love with Kelly Johnson as a senior in high school, and to his surprise, she had loved him, too.

After having endured all that humiliation, having to prove he wasn't gay, when the definitive proof was presented to them, things only got worse. Kelly had been dragged into his hell, and there was nothing he could do to change that. They had planned to run away together. Julian had wanted to be a good and decent father to his child—nothing like Arnold Merchant. But they had ripped that from him, too.

She's not going to give birth to my *grandchild, Justin. She's a tramp for trying to trap you like this.* His own mother had forced Kelly to have an abortion at some clinic in Oxnard, a place where there were no questions asked, and you paid in cash. *I wasn't going to have our good name stained by that girl, and I certainly wasn't going to bring her to a doctor in Ojai! People would find out!*

When Kelly died a week later from the infection, Justin Merchant died, too. That was the day he became Julian Meadows. He was eighteen—old enough to leave that house and never return. Before he'd left, though, he made sure his parents knew he *was* somebody, and he would be a famous artist some day. They just wouldn't be around to see it.

It had been amazingly freeing, that first punch he threw. As his father hit the floor of the shed, he'd looked up at Julian in stunned silence. Before the man could stand, Julian hit and hit and hit, years of anger pouring through his fists. Then he began to choke his father, knowing the only way to stop the torture was to end his father's life. When his mother had stumbled upon the scene and attempted to intervene, Julian had swung his arm back toward her, hitting her square in the jaw and sending her sprawling to the floor behind him. With his father unconscious and his mother trying to come to his rescue again, Julian had had enough. He turned quickly and got his fingers around her throat, squeezing until he knew she was dead. Minutes later, he finished off his father in the same manner.

Redemption.

The money he got from pawning some of the china and silverware, as well as the trinkets he'd taken from his mother's jewelry box, was enough to get him out of Ojai. A year of working two jobs and selling a painting here and there earned him enough to have his name legally changed.

Julian never thought he would go back to that house. But for some reason, he had never been able to sell the thing. Now he knew why. It was meant to be.

This was the first time in his life he was happy to be returning to his childhood home, and this was also the last time he would come here. Once he was done with Skye, he would sell it. No one would ever know that Justin Merchant had lived through hell here.

Beau and Josie were at Eve's within fifteen minutes. Tom and Noelle arrived shortly after that. Gage kept replaying the answering machine message and calling Skye's cell phone.

Will pulled Beau and Tom aside to let them know he'd left a message with the private investigator, but hadn't yet heard from him.

"Has anyone called the police?" Josie asked from the couch, where she and Eve sat, hands clasped together.

"They won't do a thing for at least twenty-four hours," Will answered.

"But Julian *has* to be involved in this. The message he left proves it. Won't the police even be willing to investigate?"

"I called the detective I'd talked to when Eve's car was vandalized. He said Julian had checked out OK that night. They've got nothing on him." Will paused and sighed. "He said he and his partner will stop by Julian's apartment, but that message *says* he's out of town. The guy has covered his tracks. There's no proof in that message that he's involved in this. And 'taking care of issues' could mean anything, most of it innocent. As much as *we* know he's likely taken her, it's not enough for the police to investigate anything at this point. The detective said if she's still missing by this time tomorrow evening to give him a call."

"It's my fault." Eve whimpered. "I should have filed that order of protection weeks ago. Then at least the police would have *something* on him."

Will sat by Eve as she began to cry, her body going limp against his.

"But that would have protected *you*, not Skye," Tom interrupted. "And even then, that was no guarantee he would leave you alone."

His words were true but not very reassuring. At this point, all of them were convinced: Skye was missing and Julian had something to do with it.

"Let's just stay calm and think about this." Beau began to pace. "I think we need to ask the police to at least come over here so we can tell them what we know and have them listen to the message from Julian. Let them decide what to do next. If they still say we have to wait to file a missing per—"

"Shut up, Beau! Just shut the hell up!" Gage was furious.

"Gage, listen to me–"

"No, Beau. This is bullshit! Calling the police is bullshit. They're not going to do a damned thing at this point. You know it as well as I do. But he's *got her*, and he will *hurt her* if we just sit here and wait around for the police to act on this."

"I don't think Julian is going to hurt her, Gage. We don't even know if he's involved in this. We've just got to slow down and try to—"

"*Slow down*? Are you shitting me, Beau?" Gage's voice was shaking—and then suddenly calm. "OK. Tell me this, then, would *you* be 'slowing down' if it was Josie? 'Cause it sure as hell could have been!"

Josie moved to be behind Beau, clasping his hand, her eyes never leaving Gage's face.

"What if she had been the one to stay late at the museum, huh?" Gage continued. "Who knows? Maybe he'll try to take her, too. Tell me, Beau, how calm would *you* be if it were Josie? And, Will, what if it were Eve?"

"Gage. We're in this together," Will said, calmly. "And I agree with Gage, Beau. The police are going to be no help without evidence of foul play. But I also agree with Beau. We need to think before we do anything rash."

"Right," Beau added. "So let's remain rational, like I said, and think about what to—"

"*She's pregnant!*" Gage bellowed. "She's *pregnant*, Beau! There *is* no 'remaining rational,' OK?"

The group stared at Gage as he dropped his head into his hands. Josie quickly walked over to him, and he gladly accepted her embrace, holding her tightly.

"We've got to find her," he said, softly. "We've got to find her."

Will's mind was racing. Suddenly the urgency in finding Skye increased ten-fold. He looked at Eve. The two seemed to share common thoughts.

"Eve, do you still—"

"—have a key to Julian's apartment? Yes." She ran to her bedroom, rifled through a drawer, and returned moments later, key in hand.

"Gage, you head back to your apartment. Maybe Skye will call there. Eve and I are going to Julian's apartment, see what we can find. Maybe there will be a clue as to where he's taken her—*if* he's taken her. You've got our cell numbers; call if she shows up or you hear anything."

Will then turned his gaze to Josie. "Are you able to get into the museum at night?"

"Yeah, all three of us have keys and know the alarm code. But why? Skye would never have let Julian in there."

"I know, but his work is very personal...dark. He paints with complete and total emotion, and that would be from a past..."

Beau figured out Will's thinking. "We'll go there, see if there's anything in his paintings that gives any clues?" he asked, raising his eyebrows to Will.

"Exactly," Will responded. "Thomas, what kind of connections do you have in the real estate community? Are you able to search property ownership and land deeds? If we find anything, we might need your expertise."

Thomas nodded his head, and he and Noelle followed Gage to his apartment. In that moment, nothing was more important than getting Skye back safely.

Chapter Twenty-six

Skye wasn't sure where they were, but there was no other house anywhere near the one Julian had just brought her into. And it looked like it hadn't been lived in for years. It was filled with old, dust-covered furniture, and there was a musty smell that made Skye's stomach roil. In the dim light from the full moon that spilled through the door, she could see a few small things scurry across the rotted carpet. Being here with Julian was worse than being in the woods. She was trapped.

He dragged her roughly down a small hallway and threw her into a room that had once belonged to a boy. There was a twin bed pushed up against a wall, a dresser with a big mirror over it along another wall, and a small desk and chair facing the third wall. Wild West-themed wallpaper, probably hung in the 1980s, and some cheap art adorned the room. On the desk was a scattering of art supplies and matte paper. *Julian's boyhood bedroom*, she thought.

Skye stumbled as Julian pushed her into the room, hands tied behind her back, but she was quick to recover her footing, keeping herself from landing face-down in the middle of the floor. *The baby*. She made it to the bed, where she immediately rolled over and stared at the ceiling rather than looking at him.

Julian didn't say anything to Skye, but he'd been mumbling under his breath, and she'd picked out "bitch," "whore," and "die"—

several words that had her worried. As much as Skye had always hated the prick, she'd never thought he was capable of killing someone. She now feared that was his plan for her.

After throwing the whore in the room and securing her to the bed, Julian turned and left. He had seen the fear in her eyes. Even if she thought she was acting tough, the fear had been there, and Julian liked it. He remembered the fear in his father's eyes as he stood over him, his hands squeezing the life right out of the monster. Of course, he wouldn't be able to explain away Skye's disappearance with a story about retiring and going to live in the Midwest near family. Eve would be the only one to know the truth, and once they were together again, she would keep his secret.

A few minutes later, Julian came striding back into the room, a smirk on his stupid face. Skye tried to calm herself. If she could appeal to his sense of self importance, she would have a better chance of getting out of this situation. Her life was just starting. She wasn't about to let it go.

"Julian, can you undo the tape around my wrists? Please?" She had to start with pleading to get him to let down his guard a little.

"Um, let me see. No!" He moved his face within inches of Skye's, and his look told her being rational was not going to work.

"Why am I here, Julian?" She kept her voice calm, pleading.

"You're here because I'm going to get Eve back in my life, and I can't do that with *you* always screwing with her head." Skye's stomach lurched, and she vomited on the floor. Julian jumped back, a mix of surprise and disgust on his face.

"Ugh. You really are weak, aren't you? I've never understood why Eve would want a friend like you. She is so much better than you. You don't think I always knew it was *you* who kept her from me?"

Skye watched as he paced the tiny room, like a lion in a cage. "Julian, do you think Eve will like it if you hurt me? I'm one of her best friends. She'd never forgive you. Surely you understand that." She still had to hope there was some way to reason with him.

"Oh, she'll forgive me. Without you, there's no barrier between us—no one there to tell her I'm not good for her. She'll understand that everything was for her, for us."

"Oh, my God. You really believe that, don't you?" The tears started, and no matter how much Skye didn't want to show fear or weakness in front of this psycho, she couldn't stop.

"I know the truth." His eyes bore into hers. "You took Eve away from me! It was you who took all my inspiration. You took my *art*! You took my *life!*"

Skye knew her tears were only spurring him on, and she made a bigger effort to stop them, but to no avail. He was truly crazy. He really believed Eve would be with him—*wanted* to be with him.

"You...don't know then, do you?" she asked through deep breaths, trying to calm herself. All she could think about was keeping the baby safe and healthy.

"What lies are you going to tell me about my Eve? What do you think you could tell me that could possibly change the way we feel about each other?"

"She has a new boyfriend." Skye nearly whispered the words.

"You think I don't know about Will Prentiss? You think I'm that obtuse? Not to have seen the way they were together? But he's gone." Julian laughed maniacally. "He was a passing thing, and I'll forgive her for that."

"No, Julian. Will isn't gone. He's here now. They're together. They love each other."

Skye's only hope at this point was to make him realize Eve was not his. Hurting or...killing her wasn't going to bring Eve back to him. If she could gently convince him of that, she might have a chance of getting out of this alive. *Of getting home to Gage*. As she thought of Gage, she cried harder.

"You lying bitch! Eve loves me and *only* me!"

The last of Skye's resolve was slowly seeping away. With this final outburst, she was out of options. *He is going to kill me. Dear God, he is really going to kill me.*

She lowered her head, not wanting the last thing she saw to be her killer's face. Julian began to pace around again. Skye thought about Gage again and the baby he would never know. She could hear disjointed words coming from Julian, but couldn't bring herself to give him her full attention.

"...will die...never be around Eve...buried in the woods...no one will find you..."

When she could no longer hold everything in, Skye sobbed. "My baby...my baby...my baby..." It was all she could manage anymore.

Julian's feet stopped moving. Skye was sure he was getting ready to do what he had brought her to this house to do. She closed her eyes and waited. *Just let it be fast. Please. I love you, Gage. I love our baby.*

When nothing happened—no words, no movement, nothing—she dared to open her eyes but couldn't bring herself to look up. Julian's feet were still visible and perfectly still. Then, suddenly, he turned and walked out the door, slamming it and locking it from the outside.

"Damn it! Damn it!" Julian swore as he stalked around the house. When he finally stopped walking, he was outside, standing in the exact spot where the shed had been. The ground was no longer charred and black after so many years, but Julian knew precisely where it had once stood.

He had been prepared for the whore to beg and curse at him, even fight him. But he wasn't ready for her to say she was carrying a child. Now he needed to think, needed to figure out what he could do. After what his parents had done to Kelly, after they had taken away his child, there was no way he could harm the innocent child she was carrying. It wasn't the child's fault it was unlucky enough to have a bitch mother.

Skylar had to be lying about this. She had somehow learned of his past and was using that information against him. It was just one more reason she needed to be gone. If she knew his secrets, she would never keep her mouth shut.

Julian stormed back into the house ready to do what needed to be done to protect himself and his future with Eve.

"*You're lying!*" he yelled as he flung the door open and entered the room.

Skye jumped when the door smashed against the wall. She needed to talk fast. "I'm not lying, Julian. I swear." Skye wasn't sure what he was accusing her of. Were they still talking about Eve and Will?

Julian's eyes narrowed. "How would God ever let someone like you become a mother? That is an abomination. You are a lying whore."

Skye wasn't sure why it mattered to Julian that she was pregnant, but this was something that she could use.

"No, it's true. Go look in my purse. I think it's in the car. I just went to the doctor today." Skye sobbed uncontrollably, and her body shook as she began to think she might survive.

Unable to speak to her or even listen to her voice, Julian left the room again. In the car he found her purse and began to look for something that would tell him she was lying. He dug through her things, sinking in his seat when he found what he'd hoped he wouldn't. Holding the doctor's card in his hand, he read it over and over again: first prenatal visit. She really was pregnant.

"What should we be looking for?" Eve asked as she and Will rifled through every drawer in Julian's apartment.

"I don't know, but there's got to be something that will give us clues as to where he's taken Skye."

Eve sighed. "We don't even know he's got her. What if he's got nothing to do with her being gone?"

"It's just a gut reaction. The message he left was too cryptic. He was being too careful with his words, like there was a hidden meaning that couldn't tie him to any wrongdoing, but would convince you—and all of us—that he's up to something."

"He always was cryptic with me; loved confusing me with double meanings."

"Like?"

Eve stopped to think back on conversations she'd had with Julian. "I don't know. It was like he was always showing me puzzle pieces, waiting for me to put them together so I'd understand him better."

"Well, that's exactly what we need to do now. He's left one piece of the puzzle on your answering machine. There have got to be more pieces hidden here somewhere."

Will moved to Julian's bedroom and opened his closet.

"Did he ever write you notes or poetry or anything?"

"No. His messages to me were always in his paintings."

"Like 'Caged Beauty'?" Will asked quietly.

"Yeah. That one creeped me out. I'd been dropping hints that our relationship was too intense, that I wanted to break things off, and he produced that one nearly overnight."

Will pulled a photo album from the shelf. "Hey, ever looked at this?" He met Eve by the bed and they sat down, opening it across their laps. "Who's Justin Merchant?" he asked as he noted the smudged name that someone had tried to erase in a corner of the inside cover.

"I don't know. This album looks old. Maybe he got it second-hand."

On each page were photos of artwork—Julian's art. As Will and Eve perused the album, the quality of the photos improved, indicating they'd been placed in chronological order, the oldest ones toward the front.

The earlier stuff had all been pastoral scenes: trees and mountains. But a sudden change was apparent after only a few pages, as the works turned darker and more twisted. The last few pages were filled with the work on display at the museum. Unfortunately, there were no dates, and Eve knew very little about Julian's early life.

Eve sighed and got up. Then she dropped to her knees and pulled up the bed skirt. "Will! Help me with this." She pulled out a large canvas.

They lifted the unframed piece and placed it on the bed. Eve turned on the overhead light. The painting was filled with dark images and colors, lots of red and long triangles—daggers? Julian had progressed even further into madness. Chills tingled down Eve's spine as she realized he really could hurt Skye.

"He was angry when he did this. *Really* angry."

"How can you tell?" Will asked sarcastically. "It seems most of his work is filled with hate."

"No. Look at the severity of the lines. It's like he was almost digging into the canvas."

Eve leaned sideways to catch the light on the painting differently. "Yeah, come here."

Will followed her lead. "He nearly gouged out this part," he said, pointing to the lower right corner. "The canvas is almost torn through."

Eve furrowed her brow and tilted her head. "This is odd. Most of it is fairly fresh but some parts—" she placed her finger on several portions of the canvas, "some parts, like here and here, are older. Significantly older, I'm betting." She tilted her head a little. "He changed it."

"Huh?"

"You remember that painting in the Boston Museum I pointed out to you? The one that had the soldier with two ears on one side of his head?"

Will nodded and began to grin. "Is there any way to tell what was here originally?"

"Probably," Eve said as she moved quickly to Julian's kitchen. Opening the cabinet below the sink, she searched for what she knew Julian would have somewhere. "I know you've got what I'm looking for, Julian. Where are you hiding it?"

Will stood silently beside Eve as she foraged through the cleaning products and painting supplies that littered the cabinet.

"Yes! Got it! Will, can you bring the painting to the table? I should be able to do a little magic here."

Will complied, and soon the two of them began dabbing the painting gently with cotton strips she'd found under the sink. Eve worked on the gouged lower corner, moving slowly and precisely. Even given her care, a drop of the methylated spirits landed directly on Julian's signature, immediately beginning to melt away the black paint.

Under what should have been an "s" at the end of his name was clearly a "t." Without saying anything to Will, Eve dropped her head closer to Julian's signature. Very slowly and gently, she swiped the chemical-dipped cotton cloth with just the tip of her finger, working backward from the last letter.

It took nearly ten minutes but what Eve revealed was clear. In Julian's precise and practiced handwriting was another name.

"I know who Justin Merchant is," Eve said.

Will looked up from his portion of the painting.

"It's Julian."

Will immediately called the private investigator. "Did you ever come across the name Justin Merchant?"

While he was waiting for a reply, Will explained to Eve that he'd already been looking into Julian's background. Eve nodded and waited to hear what the investigator would say.

Will shook his head as he looked at Eve. She wanted to cry. They kept finding little pieces that seemed to lead nowhere, and the longer Skye was gone... She didn't want to think about that.

"I think that's a name Julian Meadows used to go by." Will continued speaking into the phone. "I need you to trace that name *now*, please. It's vital you get back with me as soon as possible. I need former addresses, anything you can find... Yes, call me as soon as you have information, even if it's the middle of the night."

Before Will pocketed his phone, he took a picture of the painting with the old signature. Eve opened the windows of the apartment for a few minutes to air out the smell from the chemicals. Then they returned the painting to its hiding place under the bed, put everything where they'd found it, and took the used cotton strips with them, placing them in a plastic bag in the trunk of Will's car. If Julian came back to his apartment any time soon, they didn't want him knowing anyone had been there—or discovered his secret.

"Maybe I just don't appreciate art, but this stuff is disturbing, you know?"

Josie nodded as she and Beau looked at each other quickly. "He's talented, though, I'll give him that. But Julian's more modern.

Our museum is just a stepping stone for the local artists, to help them get some exposure in the art world. If he were a big name, we wouldn't be featuring this simply because it's not a style we normally showcase."

The two continued to look closely at each painting—seven in all—scrutinizing the colors and abstract images, as well as reading their descriptions.

"Guy's got a major chip on his shoulder, doesn't he?" Beau mused. "And Eve actually dated him? What the hell did she ever see in him?"

"That was a question Skye and I would ask each other every day," Josie said.

Another fifteen minutes went by as they studied Julian's work, and then Beau began moving between two paintings that hung across from each other. He was a details kind of person—he had to be in the coin business to avoid being conned with fakes. His brow furrowed, then he looked closely at a third painting, and then a fourth.

"Hey, Josie. Take a look at this." He pointed at the painting in front of her. "See this?" He swirled his finger around an area no bigger than three inches across. Then he turned to the next painting. "Here it is again." In similar colors but on a different part of the canvas, the same shape was evident. "And I found it in these two paintings as well."

"It looks like...a house, maybe?" Josie moved back to the paintings she'd been scrutinizing. "God, they're in these paintings as well. Smaller, different colors, but the shape is the same, like a box with a triangle on the top."

"This can't be coincidence. I mean, I know he's abstract and all, but we're both seeing *this* in every painting. It's clear to me he purposefully included it."

"Is there anything else that's consistent?" Josie asked, wanting to be sure they were thorough. After a few more minutes of searching and finding no other patterns, Josie called Eve to fill her in on their discovery.

"We've got info, too. Can you take pictures of the shapes you're seeing in every picture? I'll want to take a look at them," Eve said.

Josie ended the call, captured the images on her phone, then got on her tiptoes to kiss Beau quickly. "You are amazing. Now let's get back over to everyone else."

It was after midnight when everyone gathered again at Eve's apartment. Gage was worried about leaving his place in case Skye showed up, but the others convinced him that if Skye were to come home, she would hear them next door. Eve had a full refrigerator and more furniture.

Will hadn't yet heard back from the private investigator. Gage didn't take that information well, but Will explained that some of the information might not be accessible via computer. It was likely they wouldn't hear back from him until mid-morning at the earliest if he had to contact any county or state offices.

In the meantime, Will and Josie uploaded the images from their phones to Eve's laptop.

"You're right, it looks like a house," Eve commented as she stared at the image, wondering how she had missed that all this time.

"Do you have any guesses as to its significance in every painting?" Noelle asked as she peered over Eve's shoulder.

Eve shrugged. "He never talked about his past or his childhood really. Now we find out there's another name he has gone by—just kind of adds to the mystery. God, you can see in his paintings he's got a lot of anger built up inside."

"Do you know where he was from?" Will asked.

"No. Whenever we talked about our lives growing up, he'd always change the subject. I know his parents are gone, and he was an only child. That's it. He kept so much to himself. That was intriguing to me at first," Eve admitted. "But he hid *so* much of himself from me that it was hard for the relationship to develop." She paused. "Thank God. I just had no idea he was *this* disturbed."

"This touchy feely crap is all great and everything, but it's not doing anything to find Skye," said Gage, breaking into the discussion. "And that's all I care about. So can we do something to find Skye and my baby?"

Eve could see the hard lines of worry in his brow, but the look in his eyes frightened her. As big as Gage was, she had never once been scared of him. But now, she knew someone was going to pay for taking Skye. Eve just hoped he didn't kill Julian when he found him—for Skye's sake.

"Gage, if Julian has her, this is how we are going to find them. He isn't stupid, but he is dangerous, and something made him that way. We need as much information about him as we can get to find Skye. We will get her back. I promise." Will hoped his gut was right about this.

Unable to handle being in the room with everyone any longer, Gage pulled open the door and punched the wall has he headed back to his place. The whole room held a collective breath, but they let him go.

Some time around three in the morning, they decided to try to get some sleep. Thomas and Noelle stayed at Eve's, while Josie and Beau headed over to Gage's for the night, hoping he had calmed a little. Judging by the low growl they got when they knocked, the couple assumed he hadn't.

When he opened the door, Josie immediately wrapped him in a hug while Beau clapped him on the shoulder.

"Gage, you need to try to sleep. Beau and I are going to camp out here on the couch."

Gage didn't say anything. He couldn't. He didn't trust himself after his outburst at Eve's. He simply nodded and went to his room.

As he lay in his empty bed, staring at the ceiling, Gage knew he would never get any sleep. Every time he closed his eyes he thought of Skye and where she might be or what Julian might be doing to her. When he got his hands on the prick, he would make sure Julian Meadows never touched another person, let alone someone he loved and cared about. He was going to kill him.

Chapter Twenty-seven

"Here." Julian's gruff voice startled Skye awake. He threw a grocery bag on the bed before turning to leave. The early morning sun made her squint as she struggled to reach the bag. Skye's stomach was rolling with hunger. She didn't care what he'd brought her, she wanted it.

"Julian?" she called cautiously, stopping him. "Thank you, but...my hands? Can you release my hands so I can eat what you brought me?"

Julian sneered at her as he considered her request. After a few moments hesitation, he moved briskly across the room to her, pulled out a pocketknife, and roughly cut through the tape that bound her wrists. "Eat. I'll be back in ten minutes to retie your hands. And just so you know, that window is nailed shut. The only way out is breaking the glass, and I will hear you. You think you can outrun me?" With that, he closed the door.

As soon as the door locked, Skye reached down into the bag. Inside was a banana, a small bottle of skim milk, and a bagel with a packet of cream cheese. It wasn't gourmet, and she was still his hostage, but she was hungry and quickly devoured as much as she could.

True to his word, Julian soon returned. In the light of day, Skye could see how completely over the edge he was. His eyes kept moving around the tiny room, never focusing on any one thing. Skye was pretty sure he hadn't slept.

"Julian? Can I, um, use a restroom? I promise not to try to escape or anything, but I've really got to go." She gave him a look of submission, which was genuine—she wasn't brave enough to try to escape. At this point all she wanted to do was stay alive.

Thinking it over for a minute, Julian was about to say no, but changed his mind for reasons he didn't understand. "Upstairs. I think that one will work OK."

As she got up, she handed him the bag with her trash in it, adding another "thank you" as she walked past him.

"Do you have any towels I can use to clean up the vomit? The smell is going to get worse as the sunlight warms up the room." It was a small gesture of subservience; hopefully Julian would treat her kindly.

"There's probably something under the sink up there." He pointed to the door, and she walked out and up the stairs.

After she'd returned and scrubbed the wood floor, thankful the house still had running water and that she'd found a bar of soap along with an old hand towel, Skye sat back on the bed. She wanted to make sure Julian could tell she was not going to fight him.

"I want to go home, Julian. Please." Her voice was soft, her eyes pleading, and she made sure her hands rested on her still-flat belly. In Skye's line of work, making people believe what she was saying was a definite asset, but right then, in that small room, she was sincere—and scared.

"I can't do that," he snapped.

Skye took a small amount of comfort in the fact that he wasn't ignoring her, and he hadn't tied her back up.

"I can forget all of this, you know? I can make sure nothing happens to you. I won't press charges if you'll just take me home to Gage."

Julian snorted. "That steroid freak?"

"I love him. We're going to have a baby." She kept her voice gentle, but she had to see where his triggers were. "If you hurt me, Julian, you'll hurt my baby."

Julian rubbed the back of his neck roughly with his hand, looking away from Skye. He shifted on his feet, obviously troubled.

"You don't want to hurt an unborn child, do you?" Skye went straight for the heart of the matter. She now knew why she was still alive, and intended to use it to her advantage.

"Shut up, bitch."

Julian was pacing again, as he had done the night before. Words were tumbling from his mouth. Everything was running together. Skye was only able to understand bits and pieces.

"Why? Kelly was perfect, and they took everything from me. They took our child..."

"Who, Julian? What did they do to Kelly?" Skye watched Julian's face. His eyes were far away.

"I said shut up!"

"What are you going to do with me, Julian? Please don't hurt my baby—"

"Don't! You think you can be a parent? I should kill you. I know not just anyone can be a parent! I know! I know!" His pacing had become more agitated, but he kept talking. "I...I would have been a good parent. But they ruined that, too. Kelly's gone because of them!"

"I don't understand, Julian." All Skye could think to do was keep him talking.

"Just shut the hell up! I punished them for everything. You think I won't do the same for you? I let them take Kelly and my baby away. I won't let you take Eve from me! I won't!" Julian grabbed the rope as he pulled Skye to the headboard, tying her there again.

"You are such a bitch, you know that?"

"Julian—"

"Say another word, and I'll shut that goddamn mouth of yours, too."

Skye knew she'd reached his breaking point. She looked downward, letting him know she was submitting to him again. As soon as he'd finished binding her wrists, he left the room, slamming the door behind him and locking it. She heard him start his car and drive away.

The second pot of coffee was already brewing at Eve's when Gage, Thomas, and Noelle came back over. Between Eve and Will, they'd gotten stacks of pancakes made and had bagels ready for the toaster oven. Three laptops were up and running—Thomas had brought his in from his car—and they were on the hunt again for Skye.

Gage was still a mess. Noelle made it her job to keep an eye on him, making sure he ate even though he'd insisted he couldn't. Thomas quietly checked the California Highway Patrol's website for any accident—or fatality—reports from the previous night, but came up with nothing. As the morning hours passed, they each found ways to busy themselves.

Josie had reluctantly gone to work; the museum was open for business and the directors would not have been happy to find three of their key employees absent. Noelle had switched her hours with a colleague, and Thomas called in to let his office know he'd be available by phone. Eve called the gym on Gage's behalf, simply explaining to Heather that he wasn't feeling well and asking that his appointments for the day be cancelled. Beau's work was mostly handled via the internet or his cell phone, so he was able to postpone tasks until later.

When Will's phone finally buzzed a little after two p.m., everyone froze, and the room was suddenly silent.

As Will spoke to the private investigator, he periodically looked over to catch Eve's eye. At one point, he went to his laptop and opened an email, but most of what he said was simply "Yes... Yes..."

When he hung up, Will turned to the others, all waiting eagerly.

"OK. We're in business, I hope." He carried his laptop over to the corner of Eve's living area where he connected it to the printer she kept on a small table. "I'm printing out the list of addresses my guy found for all the Justin Merchants in California for the past twenty years."

"There could be hundreds of addresses on the list. How the hell are we going to search hundreds of addresses?" Gage asked, his voice full of menace.

"There are twenty-six, but," Will looked over at Thomas, "maybe we can narrow down the list with your help?"

"Will, forward that email to me, please," said Thomas. "I can plug the addresses into a property search. Meanwhile, Eve, will you see if you can find phone numbers for any of them? Maybe we can rule out some of the Justin Merchants that way too."

He handed her the printed list and moved to the kitchen table. For the next hour they researches the list of addresses, crossing out those that were apartments or businesses within the city. Their goal was to find any that might fit with the images Julian had included in his paintings.

Poring over the information Thomas provided—everything from aerial views of the properties to structural descriptions, and, in some cases even photos—the group narrowed their list to seven addresses that needed further investigation.

Everyone agreed that focusing on the four locations within an hour's drive of Santa Barbara was the best way to begin. The other three addresses were several hours north, and Will didn't think Julian would go that far away from Eve.

The women decided to stay at the apartment in case Skye called or showed up, so the men headed out. Thomas and Will led the way in Thomas' car, with Gage and Beau following in Beau's Explorer. Working their way south, they would start with the one property in Carpentaria before checking out two addresses in Ventura. The last was in the mountains of Ojai, but they were hoping to find what they were looking for before they got to that one.

"We'll find her, Gage," Thomas had said before getting into his car. "We'll find her, and she's going to be just fine. I know it."

"She better be," said Gage.

It seemed like they'd been driving forever. As Beau drove the mountain roads toward Ojai, all Gage could think was they were running out of time, and addresses. None of the other houses had even been close to what they were looking for. The two in Ventura had been in quiet residential neighborhoods with nice, normal families living in them. The house in Carpentaria had been renovated to a duplex, and obviously was not a place where Julian could hold Skye. Gage got angrier and angrier as the night went on.

He clenched and unclenched his fists as he leaned forward in the seat, trying to see anything in the darkness. It was now nearly seven o'clock. When he slammed a fist against the dashboard, Beau knew he had to calm him down.

"Hey, Gage." Beau spoke for the first time in half an hour.

"What?" Gage answered through gritted teeth.

"You have to calm down, man. If...er...*when* we find Skye, she's going to need you to be calm for her. I'm sure the stress right now is hard for you, but you need to think about her and the baby."

Gage couldn't argue with him, except he *was* thinking about Skye and the baby—and what his life would be like without them.

Thomas' car turned onto a small dirt road. Thank God for his GPS, Gage thought, or they'd never have found it among the trees and sharp turns. As the two sets of headlights hit the driveway, Gage's heart sank. It was the right kind of house, matching the images in Julian's paintings, but the place looked abandoned. No lights, no vehicles.

Tom and Beau stopped their cars, illuminating the side of the house with the headlights, but no one got out. Gage needed air. Suddenly the SUV felt very small. When he burst out into the night air, all his resolve was gone. He knew they weren't going to find Skye, and by the time the police would do anything, she could be dead, and Julian would be gone.

"GOD DAMMIT!" he screamed in agony.

Then he heard her. She was calling for him. He was sure it was a trick of his mind—the fact that he wanted to find her so badly pushing him over the edge of sanity.

"Skye? Skye? Where are you, baby?" Gage yelled back, still not sure if he was actually hearing her voice or not.

Thomas got out of the car, a look of concern on his face. But just as he reached Gage and was about to grab his arm, Gage heard Skye again. And this time, when he felt Thomas stiffen, he knew he wasn't imagining things. Skye was here!

Before he even had time to think, Gage was sprinting across the driveway to the front porch of the house. He could hear Thomas telling Beau and Will what they'd heard, but Gage didn't wait for them. Skye was inside that house, and he was going in.

The ancient door opened easily as he held the knob and slammed his shoulder into it. He ran to find Skye, calling her name as he looked from room to room. The other three men were soon in the house too, Thomas and Will running upstairs to see if Skye was there.

"Skye! Baby! I'm coming! Keep talking to me!"

"Gage! Oh God! *Gage!*"

When he finally found the door and busted it open, he stopped dead in his tracks. His heart broke as he saw the woman he loved—the mother of his child—bound to an old bed in the dark room. He wanted to hurt someone, something. That scene would never be erased from his memory.

"Oh, Skye." Beau was right behind him, but there was no way anyone but Gage was going to get near Skye.

"Get the hell out! Now!"

Beau froze. The other two hurried back down the stairs when they heard Gage's warning. Thomas silently closed the door, leaving the two alone.

It only took two steps for Gage cross the room to Skye, pulling her to him and wrapping his arms around her. "Oh God, thank you." Then he sat back, seeing her face for the first time in the dim light from the headlights outside. Her makeup was streaked down her cheeks, her hair was a knotted mess, but she was here with him. She was safe now.

Gage untied her and pulled her to him, tears streaming down his cheeks. Having her in his arms was the most perfect thing in the universe.

"Oh, baby. Did he touch you? Did he hurt you?" Gage pushed her back so he could inspect her entire body.

"Oh, Gage... I...I'm...so...sorry," she sobbed.

"God, baby, no. Why would you have anything to be sorry about? It's that prick Julian who will be very sorry."

"I didn't fight him. I just let him take me. I was afraid of hurting the baby."

"Skye," Gage said, holding her face in his hands and kissing her sweetly, "you never have to be sorry for that. I love you. I'm just so relieved we found you. When we got here and there was no car, I was sure Will had been wrong. I thought I'd lost you—both of you—forever." He held her tight again, rubbing her back. "Are you OK? Is...is the baby OK?"

Skye nodded into his shoulder and pulled him even closer to her. "The baby and I are fine, Gage. He didn't hurt me."

Then, Gage's anger was back. "Where is he? When I get my hands around his throat..."

"He left. I don't know where he went. He was going to kill me, Gage. He told me he wanted me dead so Eve would come back to him. Then I started crying, and all I could think about or talk about was the baby. He's crazy, Gage."

"That doesn't mean I'm not going to kill him, Skye." The look on Gage's face was frightening, and Skye had no doubt he was serious.

"No, you don't understand. He was babbling about a girl named Kelly, and his child, and how his parents took them away. Gage, I think he killed his parents. I think whoever this Kelly was, she was the one who saved me."

Skye broke down again at the thought of how close she had come to dying. Her entire body shook as Gage held her.

Gage had to get Skye away from the house before Julian came back. He didn't want her to have to see him again, and he definitely didn't want her to see his rage when it came out full force. Gathering her in his arms, he felt her fear and exhaustion as she wrapped her arms around his neck and pulled her body as close to his as was physically possible. Holding the woman he loved, Gage carefully opened the door and left the house.

Beau, Will, and Thomas were waiting by the cars, each one with a phone to his ear.

"Beau, I want to take her to the emergency room in Ventura, make sure she and the baby are all right."

"Gage, baby," Skye said wearily against his neck, "I just want to go home. Please, honey, take me home."

Thomas interjected on her behalf. "Noelle's still at Eve's. She can look Skye over to make sure she's OK."

Skye nodded meekly and rested her head on Gage's shoulder. "Just get me the hell out of here."

Gage gently put Skye in the back seat of Thomas' car and got in beside her. Will got back in the passenger seat, waving at Beau to meet them back at the apartment. Soon the car was heading back down the driveway toward home.

Driving along the winding backroads that surrounded the house, Julian struggled to formulate a new plan. He was angry for not having something else, but there was no way that he could have planned for this. When she'd said it, she had been reverent, almost as if she was praying, not begging. He'd never imagined she could care about someone other than herself. *Damn it! This is not how things were supposed to happen!*

Skylar still had to go away. The only way Julian could be with Eve again was if that bitch was gone. His only option now was to disappear, go away for a while, maybe create a new identity again. In a few years, he would be able to find Eve. Eve would wait for him. *Or maybe she'd want to leave with me?*

Julian would have to keep Skylar until he could get things worked out and talk with Eve. Since no one knew about the house, it would be easy to keep the bitch there for the few days he would need to make plans. Julian began to envision himself with Eve, living on a small island, smiling and loving each other. This was the perfect way to proceed.

Turning the car around, he headed back to the house. He would have to explain to the whore what was happening. Of course he wasn't going to tell her she wasn't going to die. That scenario was still in her future. Someday someone would find her skeletal remains.

For now, letting her think any breath could be her last would be the way Julian could control her for the next few days.

As he slowed to turn into the driveway, he saw *them*. Standing in a car's headlights were *him*, Noelle's husband, and the man Josie had met at the club.

Quickly, Julian stepped on the gas. *What are they doing here? How the hell did they find me*?

With Skye safely in Thomas' car, Gage holding her protectively against him, Beau waved as they turned back down the driveway. He climbed back into his SUV, but he had something else on his mind.

Just before the others had gotten in the car and left, he'd noticed a car slow to pull in the driveway but then change course and continue down the road. Not wanting to distract Gage from getting Skye home, Beau stayed silent. But he couldn't get past the feeling it had been Julian returning to the house.

As he reached the main road, instead of following behind Thomas, Beau turned in the opposite direction, the same way the car had gone. It had only been a few minutes, and Beau was sure that on these back roads, he could easily catch up to him.

In no time at all Beau could see the tail lights of what he was sure was Julian's car. Staying just close enough to keep track of him, Beau drove with Julian's car as his only focus.

The mountain road north was winding, but offered plenty of shoulder for cars to stop, and Beau eventually saw Julian pull into a turnout along the side of the road. A little further up the road, Beau also found a place to stop. He wanted to surprise the bastard.

By the time Beau made his way back to Julian, he had gotten out of the car and was gazing out over the edge of the cliff. Beau was able to get within a few feet of him before he turned around.

The moon was full and without the lights of the city dulling its glow, it lit up the night. Beau could see every detail before him.

He watched as Julian's eyes narrowed and his lips curled up into a truly evil smile. Beau thought Julian would be afraid or worried about what would happen next, but he saw neither of those things.

"So, you saw me?" Julian asked with total calm. An eerie chill ran up Beau's spine. This guy wasn't done.

"Yeah." Beau slipped his hand in his pocket for his cell, wondering if he could even get service in such a remote area.

"Well, go ahead." Julian nodded at Beau's hand gripping his cell phone. "Call the police. What exactly do you think they're going to do to me?"

The utter calm and menace in his voice was terrifying, and Beau let the phone slip back into his pocket. Julian was absolutely right. Even if they arrested him, he would get out someday, and people Beau loved and cared about would still be in danger. As long as Julian was still drawing breath, he would come after them.

"You think you can watch them forever? Eve is always going to be mine, and none of you will keep her from me." Julian's laugh was the most chilling thing Beau had ever heard. Julian was crazy, and he wouldn't stop until Eve was with him or dead.

Without thinking, instinct took over and Beau lunged at him. This psycho was not going to hurt anyone else. To avoid colliding with the giant body coming at him, Julian took a step back with a smug smile on his face...until his foot landed on nothing.

Beau watched in what seemed like slow motion as the man in front of him tried to correct himself, but it was too late. Momentum and gravity worked together, pulling him over the side of the mountain ledge. Beau heard bone-crushing thuds as Julian fell what must have been about seventy-five feet to the ground below.

When he looked over the edge and saw the crumpled body lying there, Beau knew it was over. Julian's body was lying face up—his arms and legs splayed at odd angles and his head turned too far to the side for his neck not to have been broken. Beau felt nothing for him. His only emotion was relief.

Leaving the crumpled and broken body, Beau walked back to his car. Once inside, he pulled his cell phone out and called the police. He told the operator there was a car parked along the side of the road and gave her the location, emphasizing that since it was night, he was concerned that someone may have gotten lost on a hike. She said she would send someone out to look.

Beau didn't care about Julian. He could have left him there for the animals to devour, but the others needed to know he wasn't a threat any longer. Only that would make them feel safe again, but Beau didn't want them to know he had been the cause, even though his hands had never touched the man.

As he drove south again, Beau felt another wave of relief wash over him. It was finally over.

Chapter Twenty-eight

Body of Local Artist Found

The body of local artist Julian Meadows was recovered early this morning from the floor of the canyon along the Maricopa Highway north of Wheeler Springs, where he appears to have fallen last night. Meadows was a renowned local artist whose work is currently on display at the Santa Barbara Museum of Art. He was known for his thought-provoking interpretations of everyday life and was well on his way to being known on a national, if not worldwide, level.

Meadows' death, according to the police report, was an accident. "It appears that Mr. Meadows was enjoying the scenic vistas and miscalculated the cliff's edge. There is no evidence of foul play. It was just a tragic accident," said police spokeswoman Campbell O'Hara.

> At press time, no relatives have been found for Mr. Meadows, and funeral arrangements have not yet been made. Public relations representative for the SBMA, Skylar Montgomery, was unavailable for comment, but an unnamed source at the museum confirmed that Mr. Meadows' work will remain on display for the next two weeks and will include a placard noting his untimely death.

The art community in Santa Barbara was shocked at Julian's death, as were seven of the friends who read the article the next day. Beau didn't tell anyone what had happened. The other men had their suspicions, but they kept them to themselves.

Because there was no family, and Julian hadn't left any type of will, once everything cleared probate, his paintings would become property of the museum. There were already several collectors interested in purchasing the pieces. The money would be used to create a small meditation garden behind the museum. Eve decided that although the money would be gained from Julian's work, given what they knew about him, there would be no plaque or permanent memorial to him. They all needed to move past what Julian Meadows had done to their lives.

"Thomas, put me to work." Will watched as his friend slaved over the hot coals of his patio grill, flipping barbecued chicken breasts and beef kabobs.

"Could you let Noelle know that I need the second baster and more sauce for the chicken? Then, if you want, you can check on the roasted corn. Thanks, Will!"

The ladies had put together an impromptu wedding reception in Noelle and Thomas' backyard for Gage and Skylar, who had gotten married that afternoon, nearly two weeks after her kidnapping.

They had decided that night to make arrangements at the courthouse and would have tied the knot even sooner if Josie hadn't insisted on making the occasion special for them. Tonight, they were told to stay seated while their friends prepared the dinner.

As Will looked around at the group, he thought about his life in Boston before Eve had changed everything. In his old life, he didn't have friends, he had work. Now, he was part of a group of people that meant more to him than anyone since he'd lost his mother.

The past two weeks had gone by in a flash. But everything was right now, and everyone could feel it. Julian's artwork had even been removed from the museum at the end of the previous day. Eve and Skye wouldn't have to live with the daily reminders of him anymore. The rope burns on Skye's wrists would take some time to heal, but the doctors had assured her that there would be no scars.

Eve and Will had grown closer, spending as much time together as they could manage. Will hadn't been back to Boston since the night he'd surprised Eve at her doorstep, and although the two had no plans to live together, they did spend most nights in each other's arms. Their relationship, and their love, grew daily. They were meant to be.

By promoting Megan Stepanski to Vice President of Townsend Industries and, in effect, giving her full reign of the Boston office, Will found he was quite able to run his business from the house in Santa Barbara, where he planned to live permanently. There would still be plenty of traveling—presentations at medical conventions, checking up on the various grants, visiting the manufacturing facility—but having Eve to come home to made his life complete. Well, *almost.* Now he just wanted to make her his wife.

As the eight settled down for their meal, starting with an alcohol-free toast to the newlyweds out of respect for Skye's condition, they fell into easy conversation, just as they always did. They talked about a little bit of everything—sports, the stock market, movies they'd seen. Laughter was easy and constant. Either Gage or Skye always had a hand on Skye's belly, a reminder that the baby was healthy and already loved tremendously.

"Are you sure you don't mind helping me design a baby's room, Noelle?" Skye was cautious, knowing that as happy as Noelle was about her pregnancy, it was surely also a bit difficult for her.

Noelle raised her chin high, though, and gave Skye a genuine smile. "Skye, I would be delighted to help you. Thank you for asking!"

Gage and Skye had found a home at a decent price not too far from Will's and would be moving in by the end of the month. Gage had already vacated his apartment next to Eve's and was living with Skye. They were more than ready to begin their lives as a family.

"Hey, Will," Beau asked during a lull in the laughter. "What happened to that curator from the Boston museum that was causing you trouble?"

"Would you believe she moved to Helsinki? She sent me an email just the other day, gloating about having found true love with some guy who supposedly owns half of Finland. It's the perfect place for someone with an ice cold heart," said Will. "And the guy's kids are grown, so she's happy since she never wanted children anyway."

Everyone's eyebrows were raised, but had one other piece of information to add. "I did a little investigating on him, just out of curiosity, and he's evidently been married—and mysteriously widowed—a number of times. But, if she's happy and out of *my* life, then I wish her well."

Will raised his glass and the others followed suit. Eve squeezed his hand in hers, and he leaned over for a quick kiss.

"It all gets better from here," he whispered.

"Absolutely." She flashed him the smile that always took his breath away.

As Noelle finished wiping down the kitchen counter, Tom noticed for the third time that she moved her hand to her eyes. He could tell she didn't want him to see her tears, but he'd been expecting her to eventually react to Skye's pregnancy. It pained Tom to see his wife like this, and he wished they also had baby news to share with their friends.

"*We* are going to have a baby, too, Noelle." Tom came up behind her, wrapping his arms around her waist. "I have no doubt it'll happen for us soon."

She turned around and buried her face in his chest. "I'm trying not to be jealous, Tom, I really am." Her emotions were finally free, and she sobbed openly.

He simply continued to hold her, caressing her hair. "I'm enjoying how much we're trying, you know," he said seductively. "And I wouldn't mind spending the rest of tonight trying some more." Tom's voice trailed off as he leaned down to lay kisses on Noelle's forehead, nose, and finally her soft lips.

She allowed only sweet kisses at first as she reigned in her sadness, but Tom continued to embrace her, moving his mouth to her neck and letting his breath tickle her ear. Before long, Noelle brought her arms around his neck, pulling him to her and letting him know that being "successful" tonight was secondary to her desire to show him how much she loved him. And Tom was more than willing to do the same.

Skye was certain that the smile she wore now was the same one that had been on her face all day. *My wedding day.*

Never in a million years did she think she would get married at a courthouse in a simple, white Camille Townsend dress, holding three sunflowers, with only her closest friends as guests. But now, she couldn't imagine anything more perfect. She was now Mrs. Gage Vandenburg.

When she'd heard Gage's voice on that horrible night, she vowed that if she got out of that house alive with the baby healthy, she wasn't going to waste any of the time she had with Gage. Skye knew in that instant that he and their baby were the only things that mattered. Her closet full of designer clothes and shoes and all of her possessions meant nothing without Gage; he was the only thing she needed to be happy.

Once she back at his apartment, Gage wouldn't leave her alone for a minute. He even scared her half to death when she'd stepped out of the shower. There he stood, taking up half of the tiny bathroom, ready to pull her into one of his bone-crushing bear hugs.

"Skye, I was so scared of losing you and the baby tonight, and it made me realize that I want us to be a real family. I want us to get hitched, babe, and soon. I don't want to wait."

Once he released his grip on her, she'd kissed him softly and agreed to be his wife. Her one stipulation had been that they do it fast. She wasn't going to waste precious moments of her life on planning. Of course, after they'd told their friends, the women had insisted they wait a few days so they could plan something special.

Tonight had been just that: special. To be surrounded by all the people they loved as they declared their love for each other was the best way they could have started their life as a family. And a casual dinner full of laughter and great conversation afterward was the perfect conclusion.

Now, as Gage carried her over the threshold of her—or their—apartment, Skye could feel that smile on her face and knew it had been the best day of her life. Things were moving fast, but they seemed right. As Skye looked into Gage's eyes, she felt safe. Even after everything that had happened, Gage made her feel safe.

Gage strode through the apartment right into the bedroom where he set Skye back on her feet. Unable to stop herself, Skye's hands moved over her husband's body. Finding the hem of his shirt, she lifted it over his head.

"Are you sure about this, baby? I don't want to hurt the little guy." Gage had been worried about sex for the past two weeks.

"Gage, you were right there with me when I asked the doctor. He said it was perfectly safe. You can't hurt *her*." She emphasized the last word to counter his assumption that they were having a son. "Now, are you going to make love to your wife or what? This *is* our wedding night, after all."

Skye felt the zipper of her dress slide down as she moved her hand to the front of Gage's pants. He loved the feel of her hands on him, and had been thinking about this moment all night. Skye's hand rested against his arousal as Gage slowly inched her dress down, gasping when it finally pooled at her feet. His wife was completely breathtaking.

"Holy hell, Skye. Are you trying to kill me?"

"I thought you might like this. And enjoy it, because all too soon, I'm going to be gigantic, and you won't want to look at me anymore." Skye stepped away so he could get a better view of the fabulous white corset that pushed her breasts together and created a spectacular silhouette.

"Baby, I will always want to look at you," he said, pulling her back to his body.

Skye's fingers unbuttoned and unzipped Gage's pants. "Gage, you went commando to our wedding?"

"It was either this or my Superman underwear," he replied sheepishly, causing a very feminine giggle to bubble out of Skye.

"You know, usually I don't really like a woman to giggle when I'm standing bare ass in front of her, but that sound from you gets me going even more."

With this declaration, Gage scooped up his wife and stalked across the room to set her on the bed. His huge body loomed over her much smaller form, and Skye had never wanted him more. When he moved himself to kneel between her legs, Skye felt her body ready itself for the man she loved—her husband!

Running his hand up her leg, Gage wanted her badly. As his journey up her body came to a halt, his hand resting on the satin of the corset, where he wanted, needed to touch her, he groaned. "Good Lord, Skye. How the hell do I get you out of this thing?" His eyebrows knit together. He was desperate to find a solution.

Skye sat forward and untied the white lacing on the back, pulling the satin until it hung loosely off her body, allowing Gage to peel it off.

"That's what I'm talking about." Gage exhaled and leaned in to kiss her glorious breasts, lightly running his tongue over a nipple before taking it between his teeth. As fire shot through Skylar's body, she moaned incoherently, which only urged Gage on.

He ran his tongue the length of her body, finally finding the spot that would bring her the most pleasure. Skye gasped as he took her into his mouth, his tongue teasing the sensitive skin.

Reaching her limit quickly, Skye's body arched into him as he took her over the edge. Gage's lips never left her skin as he kissed his way back up her body, lingering at her belly. Skye heard him whisper loving words, and she wasn't sure if he was talking to her or the baby. When she heard him whisper the promise to always make them both happy and protect them, Skye's heart nearly stopped.

By the time Gage made it up to pull Skye's lips to his, tears rolled down her cheeks. Immediately Gage panicked. He had made this beautiful woman cry on her wedding day. What kind of man did something like that?

"Are you OK? What's the matter? Did I hurt you? Did I hurt the baby?"

"No." Skye cupped her hand to his cheek. "I am just so happy. I love you so much."

Gage relaxed and smiled. Stretching up to kiss him with all that she had, Skye wanted him to know just how content she was, how much she loved him, and how badly she wanted him.

"Make love to me, Mr. Vandenberg," Skye pled breathlessly.

"With pleasure, Mrs. Vandenberg," he replied as he moved himself to be fully merged with the woman he loved.

Eve and Will's ride back to his house was spent laughing and talking, but once they were inside, Will's mood changed immediately. Upon closing the front door, he pulled Eve to him and pinned her against the wall, a passionate hunger in his eyes.

"God, Eve, I've been wanting to do this all night." He ravaged her neck with wet kisses and ran his hands across her body.

"Well, Mr. Prentiss! What brought this on?" she teased, weaving her hands into his hair and pressing her breasts against his chest.

"Do you really want to know?"

His hesitation made her curious. "Mmm hmm," she hummed as she nuzzled his neck and nibbled on his earlobe.

Will brought his head up to face her, gazing deeply into her eyes. "Seeing all of them tonight, two married couples and the third engaged... It just got me thinking. It got me thinking a lot."

He cupped her face. She placed her hands gently on his chest. Eve could tell he really wanted her to hear him—not just his words but his heart.

"I don't want to rush you, Eve, but I *do* want to marry you. If you were ready, I'd marry you tomorrow. I'm so in love with you." Will's eyes brimmed with tears. "I love you, Eve. I want you to be my wife. I want to spend the rest of my life with you. If you think you could love me enough to someday say—"

"Yes."

"Wha—?" His eyes flew open, and he moved his hands to her shoulders.

"If you're asking me to marry you, Will, the answer is most definitely yes." Eve smiled brightly, taking in every detail of this moment: Will's beautiful eyes as they gazed at her in amazement, the grin that slowly formed as he understood she wanted to marry him, too.

He crushed his mouth to hers and lifted her in his arms. Their kisses were full and passionate as he moved them from the front entry to his bedroom. Over the many nights they'd spent together, they'd become less bashful with each other. Eve was able to let him know what she wanted, and he knew where to touch her to bring her the most pleasure. It was the same for Will: Eve had learned what made him moan and was more than willing to please him.

Their lovemaking was intense because of the teasing and foreplay. Tonight, the talk of marriage was neither, yet as they stood by his bed their desire for each other skyrocketed. Eve had imagined what passionate lovemaking was supposed to be like, having read her share of romance novels in college, but Will surpassed everything any writer had ever put into words. They truly belonged together.

Will pulled the sheet up to cover them and snuggled her, kissing her hair. "You are amazing, Eve Carwyn."

"Yeah, all the guys tell me that."

He stiffened a little and Eve knew it had been the wrong thing to say. They'd never really discussed their past sexual encounters.

"So...how many guys, if you don't mind my asking."

Will had basically proposed marriage to Eve tonight; she wanted him to know the truth.

"Only one other."

He jerked his head back, clearly surprised by her response. But then she felt his shoulders drop as he sighed. She knew what he was thinking: Julian.

"I never slept with him, you know." Eve gazed at Will. "I didn't love him."

He pulled her closer.

"Call me old fashioned, I guess, but it never felt like the right decision with him or any of the other guys I dated. My first love was Shawn, and he and I had one fantastic weekend in college, but we both soon realized that 'first love' and 'forever love' were two different things." Eve snuggled closer to Will, whispering now. "I decided the next time would be someone I wanted to spend forever with."

"So you haven't...?"

"Not in ten years."

"I feel like I've stolen your virginity," he said.

"No, Will, I *gave* it to you because I could see us together. I *want* us to be together. Like I said, I was waiting for 'forever love' to come along."

"I can promise I'll give you *my* love forever. I mean it that I want to marry you." He gazed down at her, lifting her chin with his finger. "Will you marry me?"

"Yes, Will. Yes."

Eve looked in Will's eyes and saw his soul: his honesty, his love, his compassion, his intelligence, his strength, his beauty.

This man was all she could ever want. She buried her face in his shoulder, wrapped in his loving and protective arms. She fell asleep, blissfully happy at what the future would bring them together, forever.

Epilogue

There had been something between the two of them from the beginning. And while Will insisted his late mother had a hand in getting the two of them together, Eve only knew that whether it was kismet or divine intervention or just great timing, after the night of the "non-date" at Apex, they were meant to spend the rest of their lives together.

The night Will asked Eve to marry him—the same night Skye and Gage got married—was the beginning of a new life for her. The next morning, they called Eve's mother, Gretchen, in Taos. She was surprised, but trusted Eve and welcomed Will with open arms.

Monday morning, they flew to Boston where they stayed in Will's apartment for the week. Eve loved that apartment, and made him promise to keep it for when they were in the city for his work. During their stay in Boston, Will "officially" asked for Eve's hand in marriage—even got down on one knee—and placed his mother's three-diamond platinum ring on her finger. It was beautiful.

Will also met with the Boston Museum of Art Board of Directors to inform them of his relationship with Eve. It was important to the reputation of the museum, the foundation, and Will himself that they understood the relationship began *after* the grant committee had selected the SBMA to receive the $3 million. Fortunately, because Will had never given anyone reason to question his ethics, and he had worked with the board for many years, the directors accepted the truth for what it was, and did nothing but congratulate the couple on their engagement and issue a press release to quell any questions of impropriety.

One night during their stay, they were requested to attend an engagement dinner at Apex. Arlene brought first Eve and then Will into full bear-hugs as soon as she saw them exit the elevator. She beamed at Eve, while throwing a sideways glance at Will.

"He told me you were the one."

When Eve looked at both Arlene and Will quizzically, she continued. "He had Megan make the reservations, but later that afternoon he called me himself to make sure that night would be very special. 'Arlene, I'm bringing the most amazing woman to dinner,' he told me. I've known Will since he was a boy and never, never did I see him like he was with you." She switched her gaze to Will. "We both knew you'd be back to tell me you were going to marry this woman, didn't we?"

Will smiled and bowed his head in embarrassment. "And you always told me, Arlene, that you'd know the right woman for me when you saw her. That's why I wanted you to meet Eve."

"Your parents would be proud, Will," she said softly as she pulled him into another embrace.

After dinner, Arlene stopped them again before they could leave. "Now I expect an invitation to your wedding, young man!"

"Absolutely, Arlene. You're family to me."

"To us," Eve corrected and received a teary-eyed smile from the woman as she hugged them both one last time.

At the end of the week, as they returned to California, Will surprised Eve with a quick side trip to New Mexico so he could meet her mother and her new partner, Sam. Gretchen could tell just by the way Will looked at Eve that he was the right man for her. And she didn't even give them a hard time about *actually* getting married. Thoughts of being the mother of the bride and a future grandmother had her beaming.

When they arrived home—Will's house—at the end of the week, Eve noticed he had been a little quieter than usual since leaving New Mexico. They were putting groceries away in the kitchen when she decided to ask what was wrong. After all that had happened because of Jeannette and her lies, they had learned that talking things out, even if the topic was uncomfortable, was better than shutting down.

Will hesitated, but Eve moved to him, wrapping her arms around his waist. Looking up at him as she placed a soft kiss on his neck, Eve said, "Talk to me."

"We've never discussed this, but...do you want to have children?"

Thinking for a few minutes on how best to say what she wanted, Eve took a deep breath. She knew she needed to be truthful, and trust him to understand.

"Yes, but, I think we'd benefit from waiting a little while. How about you? I mean, I'm OK if you're not sure or already have your mind made up and—"

"No, no! I *do* want to have children. God, Eve, I would love to know that we'll raise a family together!" The relief he felt was clear in his voice as he quickly wrapped his arms around Eve and held her to him. "My only concern is the timing. I...I'm happy for Skye and Gage, but I'm not sure I'm ready that soon."

Eve finally realized that her mother's babbling on about grandchildren, coupled with their friends' impending new addition had kind of spooked Will. She wanted to laugh, but the look on his face was still a bit fragile, so instead she reached up to caress his stubble-roughened jaw.

"No worries, Will. I have things under *control.*" She looked up at him with a hint of playfulness. "I am a modern woman, after all."

"So, that means we can..." and he winked at her, "...*any* time we want to, hmm?"

"That's my plan!" Eve purred back. With that bit of encouragement, Will picked her up and headed to the bedroom. The canned goods on the kitchen counter would just have to wait.

As the girls got ready that morning, Eve kept humming a song that was stuck in her head. Before long, Josie, Skye, and Gretchen were all singing the bouncy oldie too. They danced around Eve's apartment singing about chapels and getting married, knowing the men were at Will's house, probably playing video games or some nonsense as they all got ready, too. Eve had never been happier and couldn't wait to start the rest of her life with Will.

Noelle had opted not to be in the wedding party since she knew she'd be in no condition to stand up for long periods of time. She and Thomas would meet everyone at the church instead—unlike Josie's wedding, when Skye was forced to stand up in front of literally hundreds of people in a maternity version of Eve and Noelle's bridesmaids' dresses. Skye enjoyed people looking at her...usually. But at seven and a half months pregnant, she was extremely uncomfortable and unhappy that day. Eve had learned from Josie's mistake. Noelle would be there, and that would be enough.

Once ensconced in the limo with her mother on the way to the church, Eve couldn't help the hint of sadness that crept up on her. Gretchen turned to her daughter because she knew immediately why.

"Eve, honey. You know your father would have loved Will. All we ever wanted for you was to be happy." She wrapped an arm around her daughter, careful not to disturb the perfectly placed veil that rested at her shoulders.

"I know, Mom. It's just that for the first time since he proposed, I thought about Dad, and how much I wish he were here to give me away." A small tear formed in the corner of her eye that Eve wiped away with one finger.

"Oh, Eve. Don't cry. Skylar will kill you if you ruin your makeup," Gretchen tried to joke. Seeing her daughter upset was heartbreaking for her. "You know, Sam would have given you away..."

Eve loved Sam because he made her mother happy. But their relationship began after Eve was away at college, and she really didn't know him. He wasn't her dad.

"No, I want you to give me away, Mom. I'm glad you're doing it."

Gretchen gave her daughter a peck on the cheek. She had only been half joking about Skylar and Eve's makeup. "I love you, baby. And Will does too. Otherwise I wouldn't be giving you to him. Although it is kind of an archaic tradition when you think—"

"Mom! Please, not today." Eve laughed as they pulled up to the church.

When they arrived, all the men were already inside. Josie had insisted they stick to tradition, just like she and Beau had five months earlier, so Will and Eve would not see each other until the doors opened at the end of the aisle. Standing to the side, Eve watched as each of her friends headed down the aisle to stand across from their love. She knew Will would be waiting for her, that heart-stopping smile on his face, and she couldn't wait.

The doors opened as the beginning strains of Mendelssohn's "Wedding March" began to play, and butterflies began fluttering in Eve's stomach. Standing there, her arm linked with her mother's, Eve could see Josie and Skye already waiting at the altar, Gage and Beau looking incredibly handsome on the other side.

Finally, Eve let herself look at Will. He was the most incredible man she had ever seen. He was amazingly handsome in his dark-gray pinstriped tuxedo, his sandy-brown hair perfectly styled, and his attention focused completely on the woman walking toward him.

A feeling of pride and joy bubbled up in Will at just the sight of Eve coming down the aisle. He had always heard people talk about their breath catching at the sight of something amazing, but this was the first time it had happened to him. Will Prentiss was breathless as the woman he loved got closer.

For a moment, Will looked out at the crowded church. Sitting in the front row were Thomas and a very pregnant Noelle. She looked tired and uncomfortable, but also at peace as she held a sleeping baby girl on her lap. Noelle had volunteered to keep Gage and Skye's daughter with her during the ceremony. Chandler was a beautiful baby who seemed to have gotten her mother's looks and her father's demeanor. Will only hoped that when he and Eve were lucky enough to have children...years down the road...they would have a baby as good as Chandler.

Will smiled as he remembered Gage and Skye's argument over the baby's name. Gage had opinions on what he wanted his child to be named. When the baby was born, and a girl, things got ugly. There was no way Skylar was going to allow him to name her daughter Charger, Seau, or Fouts. The others were pretty sure she wouldn't have allowed it even if the baby had been a boy. Instead, they compromised, and Gage convinced Skye to name their daughter Chandler, after a former San Diego Chargers wide receiver. He was pretty proud of himself for winning that argument.

Eve and Gretchen reached the front of the church, and Will's attention focused on the beautiful woman he was lucky enough to be marrying. He watched Gretchen lean in to kiss her daughter, then squeeze Eve's hand as she placed it into Will's. He wished again that *his* mother and father be there to see this.

As Will and Eve turned to face the minister, Eve was nervous, ever fearful that she'd do something horrid—trip, faint, fall into a fit of hysterical laughter—that would, of course, be caught on film and used to embarrass her for years to come. Will held steady, until it was time for him to put the ring on Eve's finger. In that moment, tears brimmed in his eyes.

As the minister pronounced them husband and wife, Will leaned down and kissed Eve heartily, and their friends and relatives clapped and cheered. Beaming as they headed back down the aisle, they made it to the entryway at the back of the church before stopping for another kiss. As Will wrapped his arms around his new wife's waist, he lifted her up, twirled her around and kissed her long and deep.

"I *love* you, Eve Prentiss!" he said as he nuzzled her neck.

"I hope so, 'cause I am *never* going to let you go!" Eve smiled and returned to his lips for a few more kisses.

As people began to file out of the church, Will put her down and clasped her hand in his, pulling Eve behind him as they escaped through a side aisle.

Will Prentiss was the man of her dreams...and he was hers.

As the happy couple exited the church, Gage watched Skye across the aisle from him. These days, he was always watching Skye, so that wasn't really a big deal. They'd been married for a year now, and every day with her just got better and better. The surprise was that he caught her trying to wipe away a tear.

When she glanced up and met his gaze, he couldn't help but smile at her. She smiled back.

"I love you," he silently mouthed to her.

"I know, me too." They both looked over at Noelle sitting in the front of the church, looking like she could give birth at any minute, holding the most perfect and adorable creature ever born. Gage had never loved anyone as much as he loved his baby daughter, and seeing her sleeping peacefully made his heart swell.

A year earlier, just before that freak had taken Skye, Gage had only seen her cry once—when she'd thought she was pregnant. But being so close to losing everything had changed her in more ways than anyone else was able to see. That's why Gage couldn't help but watch her all the time. Granted, she wasn't hard on the eyes. But she was beautiful from the inside out. She didn't like most of the world to see her vulnerable side, but she shared it with him.

For months, Gage had watched as Skye glowed with the happiness that was their child growing inside her. As her belly grew more and more round, Gage's love for her grew too. During those last months of her pregnancy, poor Skye was miserable, though. Gage had spent a lot of time trying to reassure her that no matter how big she got, she was still the sexiest woman on the planet. His methods of convincing her were mutually beneficial, because they always ended up in bed, completely satisfied.

Good thing I have this tux on. Gage pulled the coat closed a little more as the image of a naked Skye danced across his mind and immediately had his body wanting her. *Nothing new there.* He thought back to the last wedding, when Skye was just about to pop. She'd been royally pissed that Josie wouldn't postpone until after the baby was born. Gage had spent most of the reception in the coat room "convincing" her how much he was still attracted to her.

He shifted a little to relieve the strain *that* memory was causing in his fitted tuxedo pants. *Dammit! Will I ever be able to control myself when it comes to Skye?* Gage looked around to see if anyone had noticed his dance of relief and was happy to see all eyes on Eve and Will. *Thank God for that.*

It was only a month later that their wonderful gift came into the world. They'd been getting ready to meet everyone for dinner when he'd heard Skye curse from the bathroom.

"What? What's wrong?" Gage had run into the small room, a look of pure terror on his face. Then he slipped and fell flat on his ass in the middle of the bathroom. When he looked up at Skye, her nose was wrinkled, and Gage could tell she was fighting laughter.

"Ew! Gage, get off the floor. My water just broke, and you're now sitting in it!"

Gage tried to jump up, but when he planted his hand on the floor, the thought of what he had his hand in made his stomach flip-flop, and he quickly snatched it back. It took him a few more tries before he was able to get his ass off the floor without touching anymore of the stuff that had pooled there. When he finally made it to his feet again, no thanks to Skye, Gage's mind went into full panic mode.

"Are you OK? What do we need to do? Where's your bag? You have a bag, right? Holy shit, I'm going to be dad!"

"Honey, you need to calm down. Please, I need you to be sane here. First we need to change your clothes." She put her hands on either side of his face and held his gaze. He melted when he saw the fear in her eyes. She was trying to calm him with her words, but it was the look in her eyes that made Gage get himself together and get going.

"OK, babe. I'm good. You sit down on the bed, and I'll get everything together. Do you want to call the doctor while I put your bag in the car?"

On the way to the hospital, he called their friends to tell them what was happening. They all wanted to meet us there, but Gage wasn't ready to share that moment yet, so he told them he'd call when Skye was closer to giving birth.

"Breathe, baby! Remember? Heee heee haaa. Heee heee haaa." The couple had taken a class, and that was about all Gage could recall.

"Oh, for God's sake, Gage! Shut the hell up! That crap isn't going to make the pain stop!"

Gage had kept his mouth shut for the rest of the drive and chose instead to hold his wife's hand, letting her squeeze when she was in pain. When they arrived, he considered having his hand checked for broken bones.

Nine hours—and a whole lot of swearing—after arriving at the hospital, Chandler Grace made her grand entrance. With her first breath, she had her daddy wrapped around her little finger. Gage couldn't understand how something so tiny could command so much awe and love from him. Skye never looked more beautiful than when exhaustion from the delivery overtook her and she fell asleep feeding their daughter for the first time. Chandler's fingers had wrapped around Skye's. Gage had never cried over something so sappy, but he did then. There in that room was his whole world…

As Skye came to Gage's side for their walk back down the aisle, he leaned in and kissed her on the cheek. "So, do you need me to show you how sexy you are later? I hear they have a coat room at the reception hall."

Skye's face blossomed into a big smile, and Gage hoped all their friends were as happy as they were.

As he looked around the reception hall, Will was happy to find so many people important to him: Megan and her boyfriend, Dan, Martin, Arlene and her husband had all flown in from Boston on the Townsend Industries jet. He had seen Megan taking mental notes of the ceremony, somewhat to Dan's dismay. Soon she'd be looking for a ring and a date as well.

As Will sat beside Eve, their hands clasped under the table, he just couldn't keep his eyes off her. "You look amazing. That dress, Eve... That dress...wow. I knew you'd be beautiful today—I mean, you are every day! But, Eve." Will sighed as she brought her forehead to his. "You take my breath away."

She gave him a quick kiss. "Thank you for making my dreams come true, Will. I don't know if I'll ever be able to show you how completely in love I am with you."

Will cupped Eve's face in his free hand and kissed her deeply, almost too eagerly given they were in the middle of a room filled with people. He didn't care, though. He wanted and needed to kiss this woman—*my wife.*

Once dinner was cleared, Eve and Will were called to the floor for their first dance, soon to be joined by the rest of the wedding party. Gage wasn't the smoothest dancer ever, and Skye's feet were aching by the time the song ended. She walked over to Tom and Noelle. As she looked at Noelle holding Chandler, Skye recognized her look of utter exhaustion. Her friend's giant belly made a place to prop the baby up, and it looked like her ankles were swollen.

"Good Lord, Noelle, how much longer until Robert Charles makes his entrance into our lives? You look miserable," Skye asked, taking Chandler from her. She remembered the last few weeks of pregnancy as some of the worst—and the best—of her life.

"Any day now, so the doctor says." Noelle rubbed her stomach with both hands.

"So, I take it dancing is out of the question?" Gage slid in behind his wife.

"No, I don't think that would be a good idea. But thanks for the offer." Noelle smiled weakly.

"Well, I guess I'll take my best girl out on the floor then."

"Honey, there is no way—" Skye started to protest, then realized that it wasn't her he was talking to, but Chandler.

The final event of the evening was the throwing of the bouquet, and as all the single girls flooded the dance floor, Josie, Noelle, and Skye sat back and watched. Josie held Chandler, who was wide awake, giggling and smiling for everyone she met.

"You need to be out there, little one," Josie cooed to her.

"Yeah, maybe she can catch the bouquet, and she and RC here will get married someday," Noelle joked as she patted her belly.

"No way!" Gage's big voice boomed from behind them. "There is no way my little girl is getting married yet. In fact, I think I need to get a gun."

"Gage, what the hell are you talking about?" Skye tried to figure out where her husband's crazy mind had gone now.

"For when she starts dating. You know—I'll be cleaning it when the guy comes to pick her up. See, that's why we can't set up RC and Chandler; he'll know I wouldn't hurt him. I need the boys to fear me," Gage explained.

They all began to laugh.

"What's so funny over here?" asked Eve, arriving with Will in tow.

"Gage is coming up with dating rules for Chandler," Skye said. Gage huffed at the group, picked up Chandler, and headed back to the dance floor with her.

"He really is just a big pile of goo when it comes to her, isn't he?" Eve asked with a laugh.

"Yeah, he—"

"Ohhhh!" Noelle gasped and took a deep breath as she clutched her belly.

Tom was immediately at her side, and she leaned toward him, whispering in his ear.

"I think we need to get to the hospital, honey."

Tom was the total opposite of Gage: pure calm. He gathered Noelle and they headed for the door, his arm tightly around her waist as he spoke softly to her. Skye was pretty sure he wasn't telling her some crap about how to breathe.

"See, Chandler, your new best friend is about to get here," he told the baby. "One of mommy's best friends is having a baby, and you'll be forced to spend many, many play dates with him.."

"Gage, stop it. Ass," Skye said with a smile on her face.

"Did you hear Mommy call Daddy an ass? That wasn't very nice." He looked at Skye with nothing but love in his eyes. "And do you see all your aunts and uncles here? One day they'll have babies, and they'll be your best friends, too."

"What about brothers and sisters, Gage?" Beau had to throw *that* out there.

Gage looked over at his wife and before he could utter a word, she cut him off. "That won't be for a few years. I have enough to handle with you and Chandler without adding a *third* child."

Stepping up behind Skye, Gage wrapped his free arm around her waist. "But if it were up to me, I'd keep you barefoot and pregnant for the next ten years," he said, just loudly enough for her to hear as he let the hand holding her waist make its way around to her ass and give it a nice squeeze.

"Pregnant for ten years? Don't know about that. And there is no way you are getting my Jimmy Choos away from me." Skye laughed, turning to take Chandler from him and kissing him with all that she had as an indication of what he could expect later.

"Ah, Skye. I am the happiest guy on earth right now."

"Sorry, my friend, but I beg to differ," Will said, winking as he gathered Eve in his arms and carried her out the door.

The End

ACKNOWLEDGEMENTS

To my many, many friends I've met through writing. Your encouragement has been amazing and inspirational. Jami, you're my best friend who recognizes all the God things that brought us together, even though we live three thousand miles apart. To my family, I thank you sincerely for allowing me to pursue this strange obsession of mine. Most of all, though, this is for Diane, the most gifted writer I know.

~Alison

To my husband and my kids, Q and J, who on a daily (and sometimes hourly) basis have me laughing, crying, seething…but I always thank God that I have them in my life. And to my mom, who has always encouraged me to chase my dreams. Finally to my friends and family who support me every day. Thank you all for your love and encouragement.

~Jessica

ABOUT THE AUTHORS

Alison Oburia has always had novel plots moving around in her head but has only recently begun to delve into getting those ideas down on paper. She's fortunate to have a husband and two sons who support her in her endeavors and constant possession of the family's computer as she writes late into the night.

A former teacher, Alison now works as a consultant for two companies, which allows her to have a flexible schedule to write when the inspiration hits. *Passion Fish*, borne out of a very strange dream, is her first published novel.

Jessica McQuinn is a mom of two very active kids. They keep her busy running from activity to activity, but it is in those moments that she finds inspiration and has no problem pulling out a notebook to write down a few lines for her next book.

Married for 20 years to her high school crush, Jessica lives in Utah with her family. As a family they enjoy taking advantage of the extremes that can be found there. From skiing in the winter to hiking the mountain trails in the spring and summer, the whole family loves to be together.

Jessica has been writing all her life, but it wasn't until her kids started school that she decided to think that she could do it and actually share it with others. Now she hopes that you will enjoy the result of the process that has helped her find herself again.